Thermal Image

The window darkened. Two floors below, on the rain-washed pavement in front of the shops, I heard myself bark a warning and before anyone could move there was the tortured splintering of glass as a man burst through the window and tried to run through the air, his body wreathed in flame.

Helplessly, I watched the descent of the human flare as he seemed to gasp in disbelief at the impossibility of what was happening to him, before thudding into the ground a few feet to my left.

I ran a glance over him. He had at least sixty per cent burns and I knew he would die.

About the author

Pat O'Keeffe, an Operational Station Officer in the London Fire Brigade, is also the holder of a 5th degree black belt in Karate and fought twenty-eight times as a kick-boxer. His opponents included three world champions and Nigel Benn, who later went on to become the world middleweight boxing champion. He is a kick-boxing commentator on the Sky Sports television channel and has written a book on the subject, *Kick-Boxing: A Framework for Success*. This is his first novel.

Pat O'Keeffe

Thermal Image

nel

NEW ENGLISH LIBRARY

Hodder & Stoughton

First published in Great Britain in 2002 by Hodder and Stoughton
First published in paperback in Great Britain in 2002
by Hodder and Stoughton
A division of Hodder Headline
A New English Library paperback

A CIP catalogue record for this title
is available from the British Library

ISBN 0 340 82016 0

Typeset in Linotype Sabon by
Hewer Text Ltd, Edinburgh
Printed and bound in Great Britain by
Mackays of Chatham plc, Chatham, Kent

Hodder & Stoughton
A division of Hodder Headline
338 Euston Road
London NW1 3BH

This book is dedicated to my father John O'Keeffe
and the memory of my mother, Marie O'Keeffe

My grateful thanks to my family for giving me the space to write and genuine joy on my success; the Dunford Novelists aka the Dunford Mafia for their kindness, support and solid advice; novelist Julia O'Sullivan for her support, sponsorship and being a pal. Special thanks to my editor Carolyn Caughey for her unerring guidance and warmth and Vanessa Holt, my agent, for her professionalism and continuing efforts on my behalf.

Chapter One

Thursday, 16 April, 8.50 p.m.

When Jenny reinvaded my life it was like having a freshly healed scab ripped from the wound. From the day she'd left I'd lost myself in a black rage that had stayed with me for months, tearing me from sleep, my fists clenched and adrenaline screaming through my system. Now she was back and I was numb.

I still didn't know why she'd returned. She'd just shown up one night two weeks ago, wet eyed and pale, her face a silent demand for entry. Just when I thought I was getting over it, when I could bear to be alone without feeling abandoned.

It had taken months to panel-beat my pride back to respectability, but slowly I'd stopped hoping when the phone rang, stopped listening for the door, and stopped reaching for her in that half-sleep which was all that stress had allowed me. Not that anything had been resolved, but at least the blind anger and destructiveness had been contained. I'd pushed them into a dark corner and had had every intention of keeping them there. The problem was that one look from her had been enough for self-doubt to reach up and swallow me whole.

'Guv.'

I heard the voice and ignored it.

'Guv'nor.'

This time it was more insistent, and to one side I could see the crew hovering.

I closed my eyes and sighed, pushing the demons away for a brief moment. Then slowly looked around.

We were on the very edge of our ground, a strip of wasteland covered by thin scrub and the accumulated rubbish of a thousand environmentally hostile neighbours – a desolate patch split by a metallic stream that traced an irregular line through its middle. A local developer had described it as an 'urban opportunity'; the locals called it 'the tip'. Either way it was a running sore that had festered through years of neglect.

It was not alone; the whole area was pockmarked with similar sites, a political legacy to which no one wanted to hold up his hands.

For the first time I noticed the raw wind that was driving rain into my face. Mechanically, I pulled down my helmet visor and tightened the throat strap of my tunic. The crew watched me, sensing the disinterest.

We'd been here countless times, always to abandoned burnt-out cars. This one was lying upside down on a steep-sided bank, just clear of the swollen stream, completely gutted by fire; steam issuing from its baked shell and small, stubborn flames clinging to the remains of its tyres.

Two policemen stood near by, unsure whether they were needed. I stared at them for a moment before returning my gaze to the car.

'Go on, then.'

Sandy Richards nodded and scrambled down the bank, torch in hand. He was my temporary Leading Fireman, keen as they come and the youngest on the watch. We were all very protective of him.

The policemen moved alongside me and waited as Sandy flattened himself along the edge of the water.

'Can I have your name, guv?' asked one of them.

'Station Officer Jay – Steven Jay,' I said quietly.

He turned away from the rain and scratched at a notepad.

Below us, Sandy was crawling forward on his belly, the beam from his torch searching the car's interior. Minutes passed. I thought about going down to help him, but weariness and overfamiliarity rooted me. My thoughts drifted back to Jenny. I would phone her when we returned to the station.

Sandy's legs projected from the rear doorway of the car as he edged himself out and crawled forward, his body turning and twisting as he entered the front. Finally he came out and stood up.

'Well?'

'You'd better take a look, guv.'

I walked forward and lowered myself down the

greasy bank, clutching at a stunted bush for balance. Sandy handed me his torch as I reached him.

'There seems to be something in the driver's side, guv.'

I bent down and pushed my head into the vehicle. The torchlight was barely adequate.

'Something' just about described it. It was hard to see at first, but as I ran the torch beam around the interior I started to make sense of what I was looking at.

You would think that in such a confined space it would be easy to spot a human corpse, but fire, particularly an intense, confined fire, can consume flesh quite efficiently.

All that was left of this individual was a sticky residue clinging to charred bone. Having identified the right femur, I followed it back to the smashed pelvis and the blackened basketwork of the ribcage.

Turned upside down and slumped by gravity, the carbonised body had merged with the steel framework of the seat and only careful study revealed it. The size suggested it was someone young, a teenager. It was such a waste.

I withdrew my head and stood up. A line of pinched, cold faces looked down from the top of the bank.

'One for you, I think,' I shouted up to the policemen.

They slid down, looking from the car to me and back again. They seemed reluctant at first until Sandy stood to one side and said, 'It's in the front, mate.'

The first one accepted my offer of a torch and bent over to inspect the car interior. The other one peered up and down the stream, as though he knew what he was looking for.

I wasn't totally surprised by what Sandy had found. We'd always said that sooner or later we'd find a joyrider in one of these cars, but the sight of a human being destroyed like that disturbs you, no matter how experienced you are . . . or what in life is distracting you.

It's unnerving to imagine that such a thing was once alive. A part of me always wants the dead to look peaceful, pain-free, perhaps existing in some other place, not like this, a blackened stump.

Like anybody else, I try to console myself with stock phrases like 'they probably wouldn't have known about it' or 'they were probably unconscious at the time'. What I – we all for that matter – turn away from is what we don't want to face, the notion of someone trapped, writhing in agony as the flames creep nearer. None of us wants the truth when it's this stark.

'What do you want sent, guv?'

I thought for a moment, trying to get my head around the series of procedures and messages that would tie this incident into the neat sterile bundle so beloved by the Brigade.

'Ask for the Fire Investigation Unit, Sandy . . . and a Brigade photographer. No! Send me a stop message first . . . "Motor car damaged by fire, nothing. One person found in passenger compartment apparently dead." Then send, "Further traffic, FIU and Brigade photographer required."'

I climbed back up the bank and scanned the distant flats that ringed the wasteland, wondering aloud what family was going to get a knock on the door. Someone out there was going to have to identify the body . . . or try. It made me realise how shallow my own worries were.

Sandy seemed to read my thoughts.

'A local, guv?'

'Probably.'

Joyriders plagued the estate – bored kids looking for a buzz, many of them from single-parent families, where the sheer grind of producing enough money to exist meant that the kids were all too often left to their own devices. Well, someone would now have to take time out for one of their own, if only to bury them.

'It's taken a whack on the side there, guv.'

'Pardon, Sandy?'

He pointed. 'There, on the side, the doorpost's crumpled.'

We'd waited over an hour for a Fire Investigation Unit. The nearest Eastern Command unit was out on another job, so the next one down the line had been called. The rain had eased off, but the biting wind was still whipping the tops of the exhausted vegetation.

The gutted vehicle and a wide section of the stream bank were illuminated by our lighting unit, a set of lights elevated on a telescopic pole at the rear of the appliance. The wreck was just short of the stream. I studied it carefully, then saw the battered doorpost.

'Probably dented as it rolled down the bank,' I breathed.

He didn't let it go.

'The panels might push in, guv, but not the doorpost. Something's hit that hard.' He squatted on the top of the bank, his face fixed in a frown.

We'd spent most of the waiting time sitting in the appliance, keeping out of the weather. Sandy, unable to keep still, had walked about outside, talking to the police, who themselves had been waiting for a Scene of Crimes Officer and the CID.

Everyone was taking their time arriving. No one was going to hurry for something so straightforward, not in this weather.

'Look how it's come across the ground. It was twisting and turning, like it was trying to avoid something.'

I turned and saw the double tyre tracks snaking away from the cinder track that provided access to the site.

'Going too fast.'

'I think it was hit by another . . .'

'Leave it, Sandy.' My voice was more tired than angry. 'We're firemen, not the police. The FIU will be here soon and then we can go.'

He wanted to say more, but thought better of it. Instead, he sat, took out his notebook and began sketching the car. One of the crew caught my eye and gave a chuckle. I shrugged.

'Mind if we get out of this wind, guv?' asked Harry Wildsmith, my driver.

'Why not.'

Harry and the others climbed back into the warmth of the appliance. I didn't join them. Despite myself, I was beginning to find Sandy's persistence catching. Maybe he was right about the doorpost. I hesitated, curiosity vying with fatigue for my attention. Then I followed the tyre marks back to the track.

From there the stream was invisible. Even with the headlights on full beam the broken ground and low bushes hid the sunken stream perfectly.

It was possible that the driver was just haring up and down the track and then decided to go 'cross-country'. If so, it had been a fatal error. The car would have plunged down head first, perhaps rolling on the way because both wings and all four doors were caved in. It was easy to imagine the petrol tank rupturing and catching fire.

There had been confusion in calling us. People had rung in giving several locations for the fire, some up to half a mile away on the other side of the wasteland. By the time we arrived it was all over. The fire had burned itself out, the rain hissing as it dappled the steelwork.

There was little for us to do. Back at the station I would write the Fire Report and send an Area Commander's message about the body we'd found. The rest was down to the Fire Investigation Team – they would tie up the paperwork for the coroner's court. Nowadays they tended to do the lot. I couldn't remember the last time I gave evidence at an inquest. Even their input was limited. With a body involved, the police would assume responsibility. That meant the FIT could neither take samples nor examine the car too closely. They would observe and record, then back off.

I shone my torch along the cinder track. It stretched back to the road, two hundred yards away. The track veered sharply to the left at the point where the car had left it. I came to the conclusion that it had been speeding and had seen the bend at the last moment, the driver having no choice but to go across the broken ground and down the unseen embankment.

I should have had my camera with me. I normally carried it on the appliance – not for anything official, just to take snaps of anything interesting. Occasionally I used the prints for lecture periods. Tonight of all nights I had left it in my car at the station.

'Guv, the Fire Investigation Team's here.'

I gave Harry a nod and saw the blue flashing lights coming down the cinder track.

We pulled into the station yard just after half ten and John Blane, my Sub Officer, came out to meet us in the appliance bay. As Harry brought the appliance to a halt I climbed out and began taking off my fire gear, shaking the water from it. I felt cold and tired.

'We heard the stop message on the radio. Anything good, guv?'

'Gutted car and an ex-joyrider. We left it with the FIT and the Plod.' I pulled my boots off and stood them on the floor, next to the cab door. 'Any phone calls for me?'

'Only Staff, guv, to remind you to send an ACO's message . . .'

I closed my eyes.

He gave a low chuckle. 'Not their fault, it came from higher up. There's a new divisional officer on tonight, a DO Charnley, bit keen. What's the story on the joyrider?'

Sandy stuck his head out of the rear cab window. 'Having a tear-up, Hoss.'

'We don't know that, Sandy.' I must have sounded irritated because John gave an embarrassed smile. Sandy's use of his nickname annoyed me more than it did him. I tried to take the edge off my voice and explain further. 'The car was well battered. It went down the stream bank . . . petrol tank split and fried the driver.'

He nodded slowly. He'd been my Sub Officer for three years and had learned to read me. God knows what vibes he was picking up just then because I felt like crap and must have looked worse, but all he said was, 'You look soaked through, guv. There's a fresh pot of tea made. Get yourself cleaned up and I'll bring you one through.'

'Thanks, but I'll rough out the Fire Report first. Perhaps you can complete it while I have a shower and eat.'

'No problem.'

By the time I'd showered, the rest of the crew had eaten and were sitting around the mess table bantering with the pump's crew. Apart from some initial enquiries, they quickly picked up my mood and left me alone.

I ate, then tried to phone Jenny from my office. The line was busy. I tried again ten minutes later, but there was no reply.

Since she'd returned we had circled each other warily. For my part I didn't want to ask questions when I might not be able to handle the answers. She, on the other hand, had been subdued, which I wanted to believe was contrition. The past few days, however, I thought I had detected a mood change. The old Jenny, angry, bristling, looking to push the blame elsewhere, was re-emerging.

She'd slept on the divan since returning and I had lain in bed feeling her seethe on the other side of the wall, daring me to invite her into the bedroom. But I couldn't ask because I wasn't in shape for a refusal.

She had to come to me; it wasn't pride, it was survival.

Once, at the very depths of my crisis, a friend quoted Nietzsche at me: 'That which does not destroy me makes me stronger.' Well, Nietzsche had never cycled past Jenny.

I rubbed my face in my hands and drew my mind back to the task in hand, then walked through to the station office, where John was working. Halfway there the bells went down and the dutyman's voice came over the Tannoy. 'Fire, Ilford Broadway . . . multiple calls being received.'

Chapter Two

The window darkened. Two floors below, on the rain-washed pavement in front of the shops, I heard myself bark a warning, and before anyone could move there was the tortured splintering of glass as a man burst through the window and tried to run through the air, his body wreathed in flame.

Helplessly, I watched the descent of the human flare as he seemed to gasp in disbelief at the impossibility of what was happening to him, before thudding into the ground a few feet to my left, writhing in agony, a magnet for the gaze of the crowd.

I ran a glance over him; he had at least sixty per cent burns and I knew he would die.

John Blane went past, helping one of his crew drag a bight of hose. I cupped my hands around my mouth. 'John! Check the back.'

He spun, saw me and nodded.

A roaring sound came from above, and I switched my attention back to where the fire was snaking out of the first floor. The flames had shattered the window of the floor above and were devouring everything inside. A shrill, piercing scream issued from the glowing interior, and a woman's ravaged face appeared at the second-floor window.

A tongue of bright orange flame grew from the side of the window and enveloped her for an instant. Then she was gone.

Raising an arm across my face to shield it from the intense heat, I scanned the building. Glass and debris showered down as the fire struggled to take hold and break the building in its grasp.

All around, without having to be told, crews were working rapidly to carry out rescues and get water on to the fire, ignoring the wind-driven rain that pounded them.

I moved back and to the side to allow a crew to pitch a ladder. I wasn't sure if they'd seen the woman, so I grabbed one of them by the shoulder. 'On the second . . . there's a woman up there!'

He looked up at the window. 'We'll try, guv.'

I turned back to look at the street and saw the man I was looking for. 'Harry!'

Harry Wildsmith dropped the hose he was carrying and ran towards me. I scribbled an assistance message on a pad and thrust it into his hand.

'From me. "Make pumps six . . . persons reported."'

He glanced down, checked the written note, then nodded and turned away.

'And when you've sent that,' I called after him, 'send the informative . . . "A block of shops and dwellings of three floors, forty by fifteen metres, fifty per cent of ground and first floors, twenty-five per cent of second floor, alight . . ." It's written on the other side.'

He turned the pad over and held his hand up to indicate that he'd understood. For the briefest moment he held my gaze, absorbing the uncertainty he found there, and then a smile spread across his face.

As Harry disappeared I took a moment to survey the entire scene. My eye fell on Wayne Bennett and Mike Scott, off to my left. They were rigging in breathing apparatus with the intent efficiency of men only too aware of the danger awaiting them. With them was Dave Chase, who took their name tallies to enter them on the BA control board.

People, neighbours and strangers, were milling around uneasily, sensing the increasing urgency of our efforts. Their faces painted hostile beneath the harsh sodium lighting of the streetlamps. One of them, a thin man with a shock of dark hair and the glazed look of a drunk, shouted for us to hurry.

I glared at him, bit back my anger and ran over to make sure that Dave and Mike knew about the woman on the second floor. I watched as they climbed the ladder towards the inferno above them. It was then that realisation flooded the drunk's face, and his hand came up slowly to his mouth as his head shook from side to side.

John came running up to me, his long face calm, but tension edging his voice.

'What have you made them, guv?'

'Six for the moment, but I'm considering eight. What's the back like?'

'It's going like a bomb. If those extra appliances are going to be any use they'd better put their foot down.'

'Best get back round there, John. Keep me posted.'

'Will do, guv.'

He loped off, zigzagging between the men laying out hose. I glanced at my watch. It was 11.55 p.m. We'd been in attendance just two minutes, but time was meaningless.

At fires like this the situation is punctuated by incidents – water on, breathing apparatus crews entering, people rescued, bodies recovered. You send messages which the driver tells you have been sent, quoting a time that has lost the power of reference. Time has shifted. It has lost hours and minutes and gained instead intervals of action. It has shortened, contracting to rob you of what you need, conspiring with the fire to set you an impossible task.

I ran to the side of the building, from where I knew I would be able to see the front and rear at once. The back of the building was shrouded in thick black smoke, contrasting the sheets of flame erupting from the front.

We were losing it. Everybody was doing three jobs at once, but the fire was getting away from us. Time!

At the front the men were performing miracles; ladders now reached up to both the first and second floors and crews climbed them, dragging charged lengths of hose, their shadows thrown against the brick exterior by the lighting units.

I ran back and stood at the centre of the building from where I could see and direct things more easily, and grabbed a fireman who was laying out hose for one of the ladder crews.

'When you've connected up, stay at the foot of the ladder and feed it up to them,' I shouted.

I was telling him the obvious, things he would have done automatically, but he replied with a simple 'Yes, guv' and returned to his task.

The fire was moving rapidly upwards, seemingly away from the men climbing towards it. Then another window burst and a swirl of red and orange lunged at the men on the ladders before being replaced by a dense cloud of smoke.

A lone fireman dropped the hose he was carrying and picked up a covering jet laid out at the base of the ladder. He opened the jet up and subdued the flames threatening the men on the ladder.

'Guv'nor!'

John was running towards me, his face taut and his normally deep voice tinny, strained from taking smoke.

'Have you got enough men round there?'

He shook his head. 'We could use another crew.' He wiped his face, leaving a greasy smear down one cheek. 'If we don't get hold of this quick it's all going to turn to rat shit.'

'I'm going to make pumps eight . . . do what you can.'

John disappeared and I went in search of Harry. I found him at the back of our pump ladder.

'Eight it is, guv . . . how're we doing?'

'Marvellous.'

'I'll pass it on.'

'Do that.'

A voice from behind alerted me to the arrival of two reinforcing machines; Ilford's pair. Control had sent them on receiving multiple calls. I spoke hurriedly to Stuart Docherty, Ilford's Station Officer.

'I need a BA crew to make an entry up the main staircase, Stuart. The stairwell's smoke-logged and there's flats above this lot. We've already had one jumper.'

He nodded. 'Anything else, Steve?'

'John's at the back and he's struggling.'

'I'll take a crew around there myself and leave the other here for BA.'

With Ilford I had a chance to swing the fire back to our advantage. As the designated crew collected their BA sets and returned to me, I gave them a briefing. Quickly, I outlined the task and what we knew of the building. They absorbed the disjointed pieces of information and asked the minimum of questions. They knew there wasn't time for more.

I struggled to hold a mental picture of the whole fire. As more elements were added to the equation, I was getting more and more drawn in. It wasn't a question of not knowing what to do, but rather of wanting to be actively involved with every action, to influence each task.

The jobs to be done poured out like a stream of consciousness, experience, learning, intuition all playing a part. To read a fire you must anticipate its options; allow for the shape of the building, the extent of it, its fire loading. Each in turn will contribute to your decisions, yet barely any of it is seen in isolation. You don't think it, you feel it, and all the time a little voice is telling you to remain detached; see it all without seeing one part too intensely.

A flash of white in the corner of my eye alerted me to the arrival of an ambulance. The crew were two women whose faces I knew from previous jobs. They were both good paramedics, and more than once I had seen them pull someone back from the brink.

There was a half-smile of recognition in the driver's face. 'Casualties?'

'There.' I pointed out the burnt man lying on the pavement, being attended to by Sandy Richards with a resuscitator.

'Anyone else?'

'We're searching for at least one woman . . . could be more.'

They took over from Sandy and quickly intubated the man, leaving Sandy to continue the resuscitation.

It was finely balanced now, that 'dead time' when you know what you've got, have all your people committed; yet are still waiting for the arrival of enough resources to contain it. The trick was to keep your nerve.

In the distance, above the noise of the fire and the shouts of the men fighting it, I could hear the faint wailing of approaching appliances. For the hundredth time I scanned the building; had I missed anything?

My thoughts were interrupted as a white Rover came through the slanting rain, forcing the crowd, who were pushing forward, to ripple from its path. The car pulled in behind the ambulance and from it climbed a heavy-set man, his tunic collar turned up and his helmet angled across his face: Bob Grant, the Station Commander from our neighbouring station.

He retrieved a radio and lamp from the back of the car, then walked slowly towards me.

'What have you got, Steve?'

'I've just made them eight, Bob . . . one jumped virtually as we arrived and there's a woman up on the second.'

He peered at the paramedics and Sandy working on the horrifically injured man. 'That the jumper?'

'That's him.'

'Will he make it?'

I shook my head. 'Don't think so. He's well burnt.'

Bob turned and surveyed the building, pausing momentarily at each area of interest, each micro-incident within the whole, nodding slowly as his appreciation of the situation grew.

'Anything else I should know?'

'You can see what we're doing at the front and I've got John Blane and Stuart Docherty around the back.'

He stared at the shopfront. Dummies lay scattered among the shattered glass in a way that seemed to mock the dead. Normally jokes would flow out of such a situation, but not tonight.

He nodded slowly as he looked from one end of the building to the other, 'What were you intending to do next?' he asked.

'Commit the additional crews in BA as soon as they get here. The whole block will need to be searched from end to end.'

'Fair enough.' He didn't add to his words, just stood with his hands behind his back, his heavy body still, but his eyes darting from side to side. If you didn't know him you could have mistaken the look on his face as amusement.

Somewhere a burglar alarm screamed its indignation against the night and the scenes of chaos that held us. The voices of the crowd rose up behind us as a large sheet of flame surged from the second floor. They were caught by the drama now, unable to leave.

In the aftermath, the media would deplore them, calling them ghouls and thrill-seekers, but they were neither, just human beings awed by the horror before them. Despite the wind and rain, they would stay till the end.

'Are you going to take over straight away?'

Bob shook his head. 'Five minutes . . . just to weigh it.'

A few moments later a second car weaved between the appliances and came to a halt at the kerbside behind us. Bob turned and peered through the rain.

'God help us . . . it's Charnley.' He sighed.

I looked at Bob.

'Divisional Officer Maurice Charnley, fresh from eighteen months in Fire Safety, two years at Fire Service College before that.' His voice trailed away.

'You know what they say at the College, Bob . . . experience isn't everything.'

'Do they, by Christ.' His mouth turned down at the edges. 'Find out where the control unit is parked. They were just behind me. I'll brief Mr Charnley.'

We both looked in Charnley's direction and saw his pale, boyish face set in a frown of uncertainty; a child who had enthusiastically bought a ticket to the zoo only to find that the cages didn't have bars.

An hour and a half later, after the last pockets of fire had been extinguished, we had completed the search of the building. Steam now seeped from the gutted shop and flats, and the whole operation had wound down.

As the crowd reduced to a straggle of drunks and a few of the more curious neighbours, the adrenaline ebbed from me and I began, for the second time that evening, to feel cold and tired.

With the major drama over, Charnley had disappeared, leaving Bob Grant in charge. He'd given orders for the hoses to be withdrawn and substituted with the smaller hose-reels, to minimise water damage.

Apart from Bob, only my two appliances remained at the incident, awaiting the relief crews. In twos and threes the lads sought out 'bulleyes', hot spots in the building timbers, as I walked about the fire-black-ened interior of the shop, trying to piece together the way the fire had spread and, most importantly, its point of origin.

The bitter aroma of charred timber was every-where. The fire spread had been fast. Plaster had spalled away in great chunks, and the brickwork beneath was smoke-damaged. This and the fact that the glass that remained was marked by gently curving cracks pointed to rapid temperature rise.

I made notes on where the fire had burned the most intensely, how it had moved through the ground floor and spread vertically. Automatically, I allotted per-centages to the heat, smoke and water damage.

The area around the staircase was virtually de-stroyed, whereas the lower portions of the walls and timber flooring were only superficially damaged, and everywhere the metal skeletons of dress racks lay twisted and scorched in tangled heaps.

A triple extension ladder had been laid across the charred timbers of the open-plan staircase to the first floor. I was about to climb it when Mike Scott shouted down the ladder.

'Guv, can you come up here a minute?'

'On my way, Mike.'

My eyes felt red raw and I rubbed them, only to see the image of a man coming through the second-floor window and hitting the ground. I sighed.

The anticlimax of the aftermath of fire-fighting always strikes me the same way. Some men joke too readily, some want to relive their every action, others go quiet. I rerun it all in my mind, like a slow-motion video, wincing when I detect a mistake or think of something extra we might have done.

When I first joined the job there existed among some of the older firemen a mythology that fire was a woman, that it behaved like a woman. As a young fireman I found that too fanciful; now I'm not so sure. If it is a woman, then it's a particular type – a bitch, a siren that lures . . . and kills. Either way it's hard to deny that fire does appear to have life, for it needs oxygen to breathe, it deceives and stalks you, and is never the same twice.

I took off my helmet and glanced into a cracked and smoke-stained mirror hanging lopsidedly on the rear wall. My face was smudged and blackened and my blond hair lank and sweat-soaked. When you added that to the unease and insecurity that had taken up residence in my face since Jenny's return, the result wasn't attractive.

I replaced my helmet and adjusted the chinstrap, then climbed the ladder to the first floor. Mike Scott and Wayne Bunnett stopped working as I appeared and pointed to a doorway.

'There's a staircase behind it, guv,' said Mike. 'It leads to a flat on the second floor.'

I quickly looked about the first-floor workshop. It was gutted. Heaps of dresses and coats lay burnt where they had been turned over and dampened down by the crews. A steel-framed chair lay on its side in the middle of the room, at the centre of most of the damage.

'Show me the flat, Mike.'

The door to the staircase was badly charred on the workshop side, but its inner face was relatively untouched.

'Fire-stop door to protect the flat,' said Mike.

I nodded.

We climbed the single flight of stairs, its walls bearing random sticky patches of black. Thin, wispy smoke hung at the head of the stairs and it snaked and coiled as Mike swung the door open.

The top of the staircase opened out into a large living-room area, across which an erratic trail of burnt debris led to a smashed picture window. None of us spoke.

I studied the room. Even with the damage, it was possible to see that whoever lived here had expensive taste. The furniture was modern and stylish, the choice of which strongly suggested a man.

The window drew me.

I looked down at the wet street below and saw Bob Grant at the front of the building. This was without doubt the window the human torch had jumped through.

'He was trying to put the fire door between him and the fire.'

Even as I said it I conjured up a vision of the desperate man; burning, blind, his melting skin sticking to the staircase walls as he stumbled upwards, probably from sheer instinct.

It would explain why there was only slight smoke and fire damage this side of the door. In agony and dying, he would not have been aware of having left the fire behind; for by then his clothes would have been alight and everywhere would have been pain. Jumping through the window had been a last desperate act to flee.

'Was this where you thought you saw the woman, guv?' said Mike.

'Yes.'

'We couldn't find anything . . .'

'I saw her, Mike.'

He shrugged. 'Probably managed to get out herself. It was pandemonium at the time.'

I didn't reply. I had had the crews search every inch of the building, but the woman had disappeared. No one other than me had seen her at the window.

Wayne broke the awkward silence. 'Can't you smell it, guv?'

I looked up. 'Smell it?'

'Petrol,' said Wayne quietly. 'The workshop stinks of it.'

He led me back down the stairs to the workshop. I

blew my nose and sniffed hard, just catching the petrol through my cold.

'It started here, then?' I offered.

'Looks favourite, guv,' said Wayne.

Looking from the metal frame of the chair to the head of the extension ladder as it poked up from the ground floor, I had to agree.

The fact that the lower levels of the ground-floor shop were not as badly damaged as the top suggested strongly that the fire had spread from above. Falling debris and sparks would initially have caught the racks of dresses alight.

'Guv?' John Blane's head popped up from the stairwell. 'The Fire Investigation Team's here . . . Jesus! Can you smell it?'

'Smell what?' said Wayne.

'The petr . . .' He stopped and gave his face a small slap. Mike and Wayne grinned like a pair of kids. 'Best leave it all to the FIT, guv.'

John was right. I had been on an emotional rollercoaster, and whether I realised it or not, any judgements made would be influenced and my senses dulled.

The whole point in having Fire Investigating Teams was to place objective brains at the scene of the fire. They were able to interview the crews and witnesses as well as collate evidence before deciding on a cause; although in theory the officer whose fire ground it was had the responsibility for deciding the cause of fire.

'Which FIT is it?'

'George Harris and Jack Grocott.'

I left Mike and Wayne on the first floor and climbed down to the shop with John. As we emerged out on to the street, Sandy Richards came up to us.

'Guv, the plod are here and they want a word.'

I yawned. The fatigue was like a lead overcoat. 'The law can wait a bit until I've spoken to the FIT.' I turned to John. 'Make sure we leave a hose-reel in there for the moment, John.'

As long as we were still technically fighting the fire, the police couldn't take over and our FIT would get a chance to look for a cause.

Sandy looked behind him at a group of uniformed and plainclothes police gathered about a patrol car.

'Something else, Sandy?'

Keeping his body between the police and us, he reached into his tunic and produced a six-inch tangle of plastic binding, about half an inch wide. When he spoke again his voice was low.

'That bloke, guv . . . the one that crashed through the window just after we arrived . . .'

'Spit it out, Sandy.'

He leaned forward. 'This was wound around one of his wrists and the other wrist had a loop of it melted into his skin.'

I suppressed a yawn and Sandy nearly danced in front of me.

'He stank of petrol, guv.' His voice was rising. 'I think he was tied up . . . and torched!'

Chapter Three

I was dozing in an armchair when the phone rang. Jenny picked it up quickly and I could tell by the look on her face that it was Alex McGregor. As our eyes met she tried and failed to mask her hostility. She placed the phone on the table and walked away.

I gave her a guileless smile and caught the tail-end of some physically impossible advice as she disappeared into the kitchen.

'It's me – Alex . . . is there anybody there?' His broad Glaswegian accent boomed down the line.

'Yes, Alex,' I replied, 'there is now.'

'Are you alone, Stevie? Is anything wrong?'

I glared in the direction of the kitchen. 'Nothing new.'

There was a pause. Alex and I had not seen each other for a few weeks. He didn't know Jenny was back, no one did, but he was always quick on the uptake.

He had been the one person I'd confided in about my domestic crisis. Like the shrewd judge that he was, he'd resisted the urge to pass comment or offer advice.

We went back many years, Alex and I. We'd served at several stations together, and he'd been my Sub Officer, before John Blane. Three years ago he'd been pensioned off with an injury to his back, sustained while attempting to rescue a man from a collapsed trench. Since then he'd worked for his cousin Andrew, a loss adjuster.

Alex was a lean, hard Scotsman with a biting humour and a tendency towards loyalty that would have done a sheepdog proud. Our friendship had always irked Jenny, and she took the trouble to make sure he knew.

'Stevie, did you attend a fatal fire last night?'

I yawned. 'I had two fatal fires last night, Alex. Which one did you have in mind?'

'Ilford Broadway . . . where was the other one?'

'Chadwell Heath. Joyrider crashed a car and got cooked in the process. How did you know about the Ilford job?'

'Where the hell've you been this morning? It's all over the news.'

'I've been asleep, Alex. I was up all night and I've got a second dose of it to come tonight.'

He chuckled at the irritation in my voice. 'Can you meet me for a lunch-time drink?'

Something in his voice said it wasn't social. Despite myself I snatched a look at the kitchen doorway. 'Where?'

'D'you know the Lifeboat in the Mile End Road?'

I knew the Lifeboat, but only by reputation. It was

once a villains' pub, made famous when Jack Vinnicombe literally nailed a rival gang leader to the floor of the saloon bar. That was years ago. Nowadays it was full of office types who came only at lunch-time, to experience the 'lap dancers' and to congratulate each other on how daring they were to enter such a dodgy dive.

At night the danger groupies stayed well clear, for then it was reclaimed by the locals; shifty, sour-faced young men in their teens and twenties, pushing E, a little 'speed' and maybe a line of coke. Heroin chic was five miles west, on a totally different planet.

'What time's lunch-time, Alex?'

'Twelve.'

I looked at my watch. It was twenty past eleven. 'There's no way I . . .'

'Half past, then? You'll manage that, nae bother.'

It was his perverse Scottish sense of humour. I was meant to bite. 'Half past it is, then.' I paused before adding, 'Don't worry if I'm twenty minutes late,' and put the phone down.

Jenny's face appeared around the side of the kitchen door.

'I'm meeting Alex lunch-time.' My tone was neutral. Experience had taught me to construct conversations without handles.

'I heard. He asked if I was here, didn't he?'

I shook my head.

'I don't believe you.'

'Fine.'

She folded her arms. 'Tell him nothing, Steve.'

'He won't ask, Jen.'

'He judges me . . . always has done.'

'I doubt that.'

Her voice was a hiss. 'He has no right to interfere!'

'He won't interfere, but he has a right to an opinion.'

A strand of blond hair fell across her face. She pushed it back angrily and her brown eyes took on a look of sullen belligerence.

'He's always tried to get between us.'

'Well, someone did,' I breathed.

I regretted the words the minute I'd said them. Sadness flickered across her face and her lip quivered, like a child's. I felt myself go cold and whispered, 'Do you still miss him?'

Her mouth opened, but nothing came out.

I don't know who was more shocked; her by my question or me by the eloquence of her silence. I felt foolish.

I pushed past her into the passageway, snatching up my barn jacket as I went. She was six feet behind and gaining fast. I could feel her mind working furiously to regain the situation, but whatever it was she wanted to say I didn't have the strength to hear it.

I slammed the door shut behind me and bounded down the stairs and out into the street.

Outside, the grimy thoroughfare of Exchange Street, Romford was choked with traffic as I retrieved my Laguna from the carpark at the back of the Ford and Firkin pub and slipped into the stream of slowly moving cars.

The crowds in South Street were negotiating the pavements with all the haste of people with money in their pockets and a place to spend it. Brassy women with Tenerife tans and bob-cut hair, middle-aged men in the garish clothes of youth distended by beer guts, and see-it-want-it kids screaming at the top of their voices with every second word an obscenity.

The caring, sharing nineties, the ad-men had wanted to call it, but the truth was everyone was growing more selfish and insular by the day. I don't suppose the people around here were any more hard faced than elsewhere, but me first had become the rule and everybody seemed to be obeying it.

A driver of a Ford Mondeo made a liar of me by flashing his lights and letting me through. By the time I had turned left out of North Street and on to the A12, I had slid an Aretha Franklin tape into the cassette player and was letting the haunting intensity of her voice distract me.

I submerged myself in track after track, playing it at full volume and drifting away from Jenny and the dark thoughts that swam around the edges of my reason like sharks.

I had hated Kris Mayle long before Jenny had moved in with him. He was a user, a street-sharp wheeler-dealer who made money out of other people's misfortune.

We'd met him at a shop launch, where he and I had taken an instant dislike to each other. Alex had come as a guest and had shared my opinion.

Jenny owned a shop selling good-quality womenswear and accessories. Mayle had offered to supply her with stock. Against my wishes she had done business with him.

At first it seemed I was wrong, then things started to go bad. The tail-end of the recession was still hitting the high street and Jenny had a cash flow problem. Mayle extended her credit. On the occasions that he and I met he put himself out to needle me, particularly where Jenny was concerned, and when the business started to flounder it was to him that she went for help.

I was slow to catch on at first and when, after an affair lasting several months, she moved in with him, it seemed like a double betrayal. Every part of me screamed for revenge.

Now she had reappeared.

I thought I was strong enough not to take her back, but spite is a luxury you can't afford when you love a woman, and I love Jenny. Every blond hair, every inch of skin, every soft curve, is burned into my soul, so that without her I'm bereft, an addict without a fix.

She's as complex as a cat. On the one hand a self-serving bitch, who ultimately does what she wants and justifies it with your faults, and on the other a soft, sensual and deeply knowing lover, capable of touching you more deeply than any sane person should allow.

This combination of extremes made her a threat to any form of emotional security, and to make life bearable I found myself handling her, steering her moods, her tantrums, until the softer side of her slipped back into view. The irony was that for this she accused me of being manipulative.

Like all people trapped in a relationship with a disruptive lover, I frequently asked myself, why didn't I just let her go? Or, more to the point, why did I take her back?

The answer is perhaps more revealing about myself than anybody should admit; she had become part of me, had burrowed so deeply into my psyche, my thoughts, my feelings, that I could no longer function without the dramas, the sexual provocations, the yin and bloody yang of our relationship.

I always felt that one day we'd part for good. I imagined that it would happen when she decided that she wanted something more than she wanted me and I was shoved aside in her rush to get it, or maybe when I was forced away because her destructive side had taken over and I had to run for safety, for sanity.

I really thought Mayle was the end. Six months without a word, a call; now she was back and I didn't know why.

I was making good time along the A12 and sped through the once Jewish neighbourhoods of Newbury Park and Gants Hill; enclaves of neat detached and semi-detached housing built in the thirties and now surrendered to newer immigrants from Asia, who would doubtless give them up to some future influx, perhaps Slavs from eastern Europe.

Beyond was Wanstead, along what used to be the southern border of Epping Forest and was now just a fragmented patchwork of fume-choked woods and sterile flat grass holding out against the concrete, traffic and creeping pollution.

As a child I came here at weekends, to catch tadpoles and sticklebacks and generally run wild. It was a magical place, alive with all the romance that childhood fantasy can embroider. I still smile when I remember faces and incidents amidst summers that are forever locked safe in my memory, untouched and untarnished by the corrosiveness of adulthood.

I glanced at the speedometer. Normally the journey would take the best part of an hour, but I raced on through Ruckholt Road and down the A102 dual carriageway before turning off into Tredegar Road with the traffic seeming to part before me.

Here the nostalgia of Wanstead was abruptly pushed away by the grim encampments of inner-city estates, defended by their rearing tower blocks and pervasive air of sadness and menace.

I was raised in similar surroundings to this, but became an outsider, seduced by the dubious status of a matchbox house, a postage-stamp garden and a newish saloon car.

When, on fire calls, I entered these estates, I was

struck not so much by the squalor and aggressiveness, as by the signs of hope and struggle to make them liveable. A window box tended with all the care of a real garden, a front door freshly painted red, and brass letterboxes polished to mirror brightness.

These were the true clues to what was hiding behind the blank windows. Yet always I felt part of an army of occupation, a faceless representative of the very thing that ground these people down. I was near enough to them to identify, but too distant to be able to cross the divide.

I swung into Coborn Road and then finally emerged on to the Mile End Road, not far from the Underground station. I was less than five minutes from the Lifeboat and, because of my premature departure, ahead of Alex.

My own dream of security had crashed along with Jenny's business. Extending the mortgage was always chancy, but the shop was her cherished ambition and despite my reservations I borrowed twenty-five thousand against the value of the house.

Her reign as an entrepreneur had been brief – just over a year. Having tried to borrow a way out of her problems, I had to sit back as Kris Mayle took the lion's share of the twenty-five thousand against stock taken on credit. The remainder of the money went on the shop lease renewal, phone and electric bills.

The classic sting was when he pitched in to help her out as the business went into a tailspin. First he bought back the stock he'd sold to her, for a lot less money. I believe he called it 'a favour'. Then he bought the lease from her, again for less than she paid, but the *pièce de résistance* was letting her stay on as the manageress. She had been grateful to the point of blindness.

I had no choice but to watch as he took the shop, Jenny and my pride, knowing that I had paid him to do it.

Without money coming in from the shop I ran into trouble and was forced to sell the house. The problem was that the value of it had shrunk to less than the mortgage. Result – a small flat in Romford town centre and crippling debts that threatened to submerge me any day. Jenny lasted for one week in the flat then left without a word of goodbye.

The humiliation was complete.

Turning off the Mile End Road, I parked at the rear of the Lifeboat and bought a midday paper from the news-stand outside. Splashed across the front page was a report on the Ilford fire. The headline read 'Human torch in death dive'.

I sighed heavily and folded the paper as I pushed the door of the pub open.

Just inside the door stood two minders, who glanced at each other, presumably to see if I was on the banned list, then parted to let me through.

The place was packed with pin-stripes. The only women appeared to be the barmaids and one vacant-eyed nymphet gyrating topless at the far end of the bar. No one seemed to be watching her directly, but peripheral vision had been honed to an art form.

I bought a drink and noticed a display of postcards pinned above the optics. One depicted the crucifixion of Christ with the legend 'St Peter's Rome' crossed out and substituted in felt tip by 'Another satisfied customer of Jack Vinnicombe'.

The humour around here was as uncomplicated as the clientèle.

The only table free was at the far end of the bar, next to a crowd of semi-pissed blokes in their early twenties. I sat and buried my nose in the newspaper. Inevitably the lap-dancer sought me out and the cheers went up. I looked at the girl, shook my head and willed Alex to get a move on.

Bypassing the news section of the paper, my eye fell on a piece about Mark Nichols, an up-and-coming welterweight who had just turned pro. Alex and I had been to see him box at the London ABA Championships a couple of years ago. Nichols was a sharp technician who could go a long way. I noted the date of his first pro outing and decided to mention it to Alex in case he fancied it.

Turning back to the front-page story of the fire, I searched it for details, only to grind my teeth when the report began to speculate wildly about the cause. From fire-bombers to a bolt of lightning, it spared their readers nothing. The absence of hard fact was doubtless viewed as an opportunity rather than a hindrance.

Suddenly I was aware of somebody standing next to me and an unmistakably Scottish voice growled, 'Why on earth did you suggest this place?'

I looked up sharply into a leather mask of a face crowned by tightly cropped steel-grey hair. The hard blue eyes penetrated me and, as I've had to on more than one occasion, I reminded myself that this broad-shouldered, thuggish-looking character was my best friend.

'I didn't pick it, Alex, you did.'

His expression didn't change. 'Are you sure?'

'Positive. You must've had a reason . . . no one's this unlucky.'

He retrieved a chair from another table and sat down with his back to the heavy-breasted lap-dancer who had replaced the nymphet.

'They'll put me off my stroke,' he explained with a chuckle.

I bought him a beer and placed it down in front of him. He took a sip, looking around the pub as he did so. Eyes turned away from him. Even the minders at the door became more absorbed in their conversation. Alex had that kind of effect on people; you could believe him capable of anything.

'So, Stevie, how goes it?'

I shrugged.

He nodded and the blue gaze softened. His suspicions were confirmed without him needing to ask.

For a time we talked old ships and old fires; the

fire-ground humour black and the judgements of ourselves and others harsh, if only by their accuracy.

Gradually the subject came around to the fire of the previous night. Alex said it was being covered in depth by the radio and TV. I told him how touch and go it had all been.

'Cause?'

'Arson,' I said simply. 'Someone had sprayed petrol everywhere. Looks like the poor bastard that jumped through the window had been tied up and torched along with it.'

He nodded, took a sip of his beer and, switching the subject to money, tactfully brought up my debt problem.

'If I don't find a solution soon I'm in dead lumber.'

'What happens if you don't sort it out?'

'Bankruptcy.'

'That bad?'

'In a word . . .'

'Can't you get the debt rescheduled?'

'I've tried that, mate. I was laughed at. Do bank managers have the power of execution?'

'Only in Scotland.'

Pausing for a moment, as though giving something final consideration, he reached beneath the table and brought up his briefcase. He snapped it open, took out a file and placed it on the table between us.

'Take a look, Stevie.'

He watched me as I flipped it open. Inside was a

bound set of A4 pages with a stiff plastic cover and the word 'Current' in black across the front.

The contents were a business profile of a couple called Eileen and Robin Sheldon.

'Why am I reading this, Alex?'

He sat back, his arms folded and his face creased into an enigmatic smile. 'I need some help, Stevie.'

'With what?' I asked suspiciously.

Taking out a packet of thin cigars, he selected one and lit it, blowing blue-grey smoke out of the corner of his mouth.

'Andrew, my cousin, represents their insurers.'

'Go on.'

'The Sheldons have had a bad time of it, what with the recession and everything. So much so that their solicitors are currently dissolving their partnership, marital as well as financial. Rumour has it that insurance money would be the fastest way to realise capital.'

'I must be slow. Where's this leading?'

'That fire last night . . . the shop's owned by the Sheldons.'

'So what d'you want from me?'

Again that smile crept across his face. 'I, or rather Andrew and I, want you to make some enquiries for us.'

I shook my head. 'I still don't follow. You must realise that last night is now a murder inquiry. You must be talking to the police and the Brigade will answer most of your questions if you write to Legal Section at Lambeth.'

He puffed at the cigar and examined the end of it. 'This is not the first time the Sheldons have had a fire. A number of years ago they failed to claim on a policy. Then six months ago they had a fire in a warehouse they part owned . . . by all accounts an accident. They lost goods to the value of over two hundred thousand pounds . . . given that they also own five shops, not including last night's one, and you can see why their insurers are as nervous as hell.'

'You think there'll be more fires?'

'Don't know.'

'This warehouse fire . . . were they paid out?'

'Aye. As I said, by all accounts, fire, police and independent insurance investigation, it was a pure accident.'

'And now they've had this fire. That's a lot of bad luck, Alex.'

'Exactly. The police have been sniffing around them for months. They, and we for that matter, have been watching Robin Sheldon very closely.'

'So why don't the police just drag him in and apply a bit of pressure?'

'Oh, that was tried after the warehouse fire. They got nothing out of him.'

'But last night must have changed the picture, surely. He must be worth a further tug?'

Alex rocked back in his chair, his mouth a tight smile.

'Proof, hard proof, is a rare commodity in insurance fraud, Stevie. Often you're suspicious, but are working blind. The initiative always lies with the criminal. They can plan something over many months.'

'But you've got this Robin Sheldon in the frame for it?'

He gave a mirthless chuckle. 'My gut feeling was that he was as guilty as hell.'

'Was?'

His eyes narrowed, like a cat cheated of its prey. 'The man that crashed through that window last night, Stevie, was Robin Sheldon.'

Chapter Four

Alex fetched us each another beer while I sat and wondered what was going through that Chinese puzzle of a mind of his. I didn't have to wait long.

'How would you like to earn some serious money, Stevie?'

'The idea appals me. What do I have to do?'

He hunched forward and took a sip of his beer. 'We want to know everything on the fire investigation side, preferably before the police.'

'Sounds too easy to me.'

'And . . .' He paused, watching me carefully. '. . . we want you to do a little off-duty detective work. Talk to the original Fire Investigation Team that attended that warehouse fire. Sheldon's son Michael is involved in the running of the business. Find out how much. Perhaps even interview a few of Sheldon's business associates.' He tapped the plastic file on the table. 'Build that into something substantial, something useful to us. We'll pay good money, Stevie.'

'How much?'

'Two hundred a day, plus expenses . . . and a big fat bonus if what you dig up directly leads to a conviction.'

I was finding it hard to keep still. 'Bonus?'

He held his cigar in front of him, vertically, letting the smoke spiral upward. 'A percentage. Last night's escapade has yet to be priced, but I'll bet we're talking fifty grand's worth of stock alone. If you can dig deep enough and find a reason to refuse payment and demand back the warehouse money as well . . . you'd be on five per cent of the gross.'

'Five per cent?'

'Aye. The insurance company will pay out fifteen, maybe twenty per cent to us and then we'll pay you. We've done a lot of work on this already.'

'Unsuccessfully,' I pointed out.

'D'you want the job or not?'

The lure of the money was tempting, but I was a fireman, not a copper, and I couldn't see why he hadn't gone to a proper inquiry agent.

'Why me, Alex?'

'Why you? You're on the inside, Stevie, with access to the FITs and their files. Digging up info should be easy for you.'

'That's not what I meant and you know it. Why do you want me to snoop around off duty?'

He took a moment and then grinned. 'Because you're an analytical bastard. Methodical, tenacious to the point of insanity, suspicious minded, halfway intelligent . . . and financially up shit creek without a paddle.'

I didn't know whether to wince or smile. 'Know me inside out, don't you?'

'Well enough to know we can both benefit from you accepting the job.'

The money was tempting . . . no, it was irresistible. I felt like a starving man who'd stumbled through the back door of a bistro.

Although Alex knew I was in trouble, up until now he had been unaware of how bad it had become. Yet I had serious doubts about playing detective.

'Can I think about it? You have to admit it's a bit "left field" of what I'm used to.'

His hands came together, as though he were praying. 'How long d'you need?'

'I don't know . . . a day, maybe a couple.'

He shook his head. 'I've gone out on a limb here, Stevie. We need this information fast. And you need the money.'

I studied his face and reminded myself that I'd never known this man be reckless.

'What is it you're not telling me, Alex?'

He drew slowly on the cigar. Try as I might, I could read nothing into his expression. Then, from under the table, he produced another file. Slim, it contained just one large photograph. He handed it across the table.

It was of two men.

'The one on the left is Robin Sheldon,' he said. 'The other . . .'

I stared at the face of the other man, not accepting the evidence of my eyes. Yet there could be no denying it was Kris Mayle. Now I understood.

'You think. . . ?'

'I don't know,' he said, and ground his cigar out in the ashtray.

This was clever of Alex, clever and typical. He knew that I needed money and he knew that no matter how I'd tried to push my feelings aside I would want revenge on this man. If Mayle was connected to this then who better to pursue him. He was a shrewd bastard, Alex McGregor, the shrewdest.

Having made his play, Alex kept quiet and let me think.

Finally, I said quietly, 'Can you give me till tonight? This isn't as easy as it might seem.'

He reached into his briefcase, took out a fat file and handed it to me. 'This is everything we have on the warehouse fire.'

'If I take . . .' I began.

'The Sheldons part owned it with a firm called Ladyfair, owned by a James Chasteau. We're interested in Chasteau. He's proved to be a hard man to get to talk with.'

'Alex, I appreciate what you're trying to do, but . . .'

He ignored me again. 'Just read it. I'll phone you at the station tonight. If you can't decide quickly I'll have to put it elsewhere.'

I left Alex at about half one and started the drive back to Romford, but the thought of Jenny's remorse, which now had surely turned to anger, made me turn south and head for Limehouse instead.

As a kid I had been brought up in dockland by Aunt Doreen and Uncle Cliff – not real relatives, foster parents, people who had taken me out of a home when I was six and raised me as one of their own.

Before then life had been a bit careless with me, giving me a dad who'd packed up and left and a mum who'd drunk herself into a hospital, never to return.

At six years of age I was sullen, spiteful and very mistrustful of adults; particularly those who baled out when life took a swing at them.

Doreen and Cliff took me in, fed and loved me and, most importantly, stayed around. They're both dead now, but they had left their mark on me to the extent that I no longer felt the world to be a cold place. Cliff taught me to be honest with myself and, if life cut up rough, then look inside for the reasons, not outside for the blame.

Doreen taught me the value of tolerance and the necessity of love, more by example than anything said.

They're both buried in a neat double plot on the Isle of Dogs, down the southern end of the island, well away from the soulless concrete and glass of the Docklands development.

By the time I reached the graveyard the sky had clouded over and rain was in the air. I turned up the collar of my barn jacket and stood with my back to the rising wind.

Whether it was tiredness from fire-fighting the night before or just an attack of frustration I couldn't be sure, but I felt restless. Jenny, Mayle, the rising debt – it was all blurring into one and, try as I might, I couldn't shake free from any of it.

I had run up so many blind alleys in my life, and never more so than lately, that I seemed to question everything, particularly where the Brigade was concerned. If I was honest, then I was never going to be more than a Station Officer – I was too outspoken, too disenchanted and at odds with a system that spoke at you rather than listening to its own heartbeat.

Symptomatic of this was the ad-speak that had crept into memos and instructions; victims of fire were now 'customers' to be serviced and firemen had, by some bizarre convolution of semantics, become 'resource pools'. Image had replaced substance in the order of priorities.

My private life was no better. Debt had strangled any chance of starting anew. No matter how many times I did the sums, my Brigade salary would be insufficient to dig me out of the hole I was in. I felt as helpless, as marooned, as any of those families incarcerated on an inner-city estate.

I needed something, anything, to grasp and make my own. A new direction, not a way back. Something worthy that would dissolve some of the bitterness and give me back a little self-respect, or at least some money.

Did Alex's offer amount to that? Or was it one more blind alley? Perhaps Alex offered an answer of sorts. Here was money to be made, doing something I knew about – fire investigation. Not forgetting the chance to even the score with Mayle.

Wouldn't that be sweet, to know he was banged up. What was the going rate for murder and arson nowadays – fifteen, twenty years? Why the hesitation? Too soon? Too easy? Yes, that was it, too easy. I'd been battered for so long I had lost confidence.

On the surface there were few arguments against it, and as I felt the first drops of rain on my face I thought wryly that the one plus about despair is that you haven't the energy to argue with yourself. My genius for grasping the obvious was surfacing.

Somehow it felt right to make the decision here, near Cliff and Doreen. They were still my emotional bedrock; immutable, safe, pre-Jenny.

I climbed back into the car, took out the file marked 'Warehouse fire, Marshgate Lane, Stratford E15' and began to read.

Half an hour later I'd barely gotten through half of it. The thing that struck me most was the fact that although nearly two hundred and fifty thousand pounds' worth of stock had been damaged, by far the greater part of this was by smoke or water rather than direct burning.

The warehouse itself had measured forty by twenty-five metres and was of brick construction up to the level of ten feet; the remaining section of wall and roof being formed by light cladding over a metal framework. Inside, a steel-mesh mezzanine floor had been constructed in order to provide additional storage space and a platform for offices. A staff of fifteen worked on the premises.

Because of the extensive hanging garments, Carter and Woodley, the insurers, had insisted on smoke detectors linked to a high-rated sprinkler system for a fast reaction to fire. They had also laid down a requirement for back-up pumps and emergency water supplies in the event of a mains failure.

They could be forgiven for thinking the risk was covered.

The Eastern Command's FIT report made fascinating reading; the fire had broken out at twenty past one in the morning of Saturday, 22 November. The last people reported on the premises were the partner, James Chasteau, and Stephanie Sheldon, the daughter of Robin and Eileen Sheldon. They had locked up at eight-thirty, Friday evening, after working late in the office.

The point of origin of the fire was apparently in the electrical intake box, which was partly sheltered from the sprinklers by boxes and packaging on the mezzanine floor.

A number of captioned photographs were attached to the report, and as I studied them I could make out the pattern of the fire, a fanlike shape growing upwards and outwards towards the mezzanine. Around it the walls were bare brick.

The intake box was fixed closely to the lowest point of the fire, and I could see no other point that suggested the origin of the blaze so strongly. Here and there it was possible to see other points of burning, but these were undoubtedly caused by hot debris falling and igniting the surrounding area.

The photographs were very detailed; all the right angles, close-ups and long shots, to show the fire's development, had been taken. It was a complete pictorial history of the job. Someone had been very thorough.

The amount of information was daunting. There was no way I could absorb it all in one go.

The last photograph I looked at was a detail of the inside of the intake box itself. It consisted of a metal flap bolted over a cast-iron box, from the base of which the supply cable exited towards the floor. On the back of the photograph was the caption 'Most of the insulation burnt away and the copper wiring has heated to a black and brittle copper oxide. What remains of the insulation has melted and is sticking to the wire.' The caption was signed Sub Officer Harris, G. Eastern Command FIT.

I smiled. I knew George Harris very well. He was a crafty old bastard who had been on the FIT for years. He had carefully worded the caption to show his suspicions that the fire hadn't started in the intake box; if it had, then the remaining insulation would have bubbled away from the source of the heat, not stuck to it.

So why had the cause gone down as electrical?

Turning to the very end of the report, I saw why. The signature was that of a fire safety officer who had been moved when it became apparent that he was out of his depth on the FIT.

I vaguely remember meeting him once. He'd been genial, but a bit overwhelmed by his job – not a crime, but then again the Brigade is hardly a forgiving environment.

George had obviously taken umbrage with the man's findings and had sneaked in his objections with the captions, guessing correctly that the man wouldn't twig it.

Whatever the cause, though, the effect wasn't in doubt. When the smoke detectors initiated the sprinkler system, the material stored in the boxes on the mezzanine had cast, in effect, a rain-shadow over the electrical intake box area and the surrounding garments. The fire had raced along the racks of dresses and coats creating thick smoke, which together with the sprinklers caused the damage.

When the Brigade arrived, the crews had experienced problems getting in due to the heavy metal security doors and the barred windows, with the result that on gaining entry they found the entire premises smoke-logged.

They had had to search every inch of the warehouse in breathing apparatus before finding and extinguishing the fire.

The scale of the loss to Carter and Woodley meant that a great deal of investigation had taken place, but, finally and unhappily, they had paid out two months ago. Before they did, however, they passed the file on to Alex's cousin Andrew with instructions to keep a watching brief on the Sheldons and James Chasteau.

The words on the page started to dance as a wave of tiredness swept over me. I closed the file, pulled the seat reclining lever and closed my eyes, letting my mind go blank.

I knew it wasn't just tiredness – At that moment, if I could have, I would have walked away from the Brigade, Jenny and just about everything in my life.

I wasn't sure how long I was out, but I came to with a jolt and sat up.

On an impulse I opened the glove compartment. Inside lay my camera. I checked – there were still a dozen frames remaining. That decided me.

I drove off the island, heading north. The rain came down harder, bouncing off the tarmac and turning it slick black. It seemed the sky had been the same gunmetal grey for a month. We were more than halfway into April and every day it had poured. Winter was hanging on by its fingertips.

Chapter Five

The clock on the dashboard read half past two as I swung into the fast lane and put my foot down. The traffic slowed and compacted, slowed and stopped, before edging forward sluggishly. I didn't reach Marshgate Lane, Stratford until just after three.

The warehouse was on an industrial estate just off the lane. A grey, almost featureless block standing among row after row of identical buildings, each with a number painted in white across the lower sections of their walls. I stopped the car and parked outside the next warehouse up, number twelve, alongside a big Scammel artic.

I could see the sign for Ladyfair Garments, its paint peeling and one end fire-blackened. There were no lorries being loaded, no shutters open, just a white Luton van with a blue flash down the side parked nearby.

By contrast, the other warehouses had lorries and vans drawn up, with forklifts buzzing around and drivers sheeting and roping loads. I watched for fifteen, maybe twenty minutes, but nothing stirred from the Ladyfair place.

At the far end of the building an iron staircase led

to a wire-glazed door with the word 'Drivers' marked in red across the top pane. I got out and walked towards it.

The handrail was rusty where the paint had been burned off, and the whole place had a stillness, like it had been abandoned. At the top of the stairs I tried the handle. The door seemed stiff rather than locked. I gave it a tug. Inside, immediately to my left, was a glass sliding hatch. I tapped hard and listened. Nothing.

I pulled at the hatch, but it wouldn't move. Ahead of me was another doorway, I went through and found myself inside the warehouse. There were no sounds, no movement, just a faint background smell of stale smoke, the kind of smell that never quite leaves a property after a serious fire.

My footsteps echoed as I walked through the centre of the building. Everywhere were clothes racks, mostly empty, but some intermittently hung with old coats and dresses.

I tried to match what I was seeing with the photographs in the file, but the shape of the interior seemed wrong. From the outside the building had looked larger; then I realised that a partition had been erected, just short of the length of the warehouse. At its centre was a large steel-shutter door, padlocked shut. The lock was new, of the hardened security type; bolt-croppers wouldn't have touched it.

The silence, together with the smells of dust and stale smoke, lent a dead air to the place, added to by the fact that the only illumination came from the skylights far above me. The gloom and the stillness seemed to cloak the interior, making my presence an intrusion.

If found, I told myself, I was guilty of no more than trespass, yet it felt more than that. I was walking around blind, not knowing what I was looking for and perhaps disturbing something better left buried. Whatever Robin Sheldon had been involved in had led to his death and the warehouse had something to do with it. At least, that was what Alex felt.

There was no denying the place had resonance. Part of the puzzle was entwined with the fabric of the building, and as I absorbed the surroundings a process somewhere between instinct and logic warned me that the answers would have a price.

My eyes returned to the padlocked shutter.

Suddenly, a smacking sound broke the silence. I looked up, and above my head a bird flapped through the forest of roof trusses.

Back and forth it flew within the maze of steelwork, its flight erratic and uncertain.

It appeared distressed; mesmerised perhaps by the combination of bad light and unfamiliar surroundings. Then it struck a truss and feathers spiralled downward. I watched it circle and hit another truss, then another, until finally it turned and hit the central spar full on.

It seemed suspended in the air for a split second before tumbling to the concrete floor and lying still a few feet from me, its eyes open, but unmoving.

A few errant feathers fell softly, one touching my face. Then, slowly, the creature's eyes closed. I stared at the small lifeless body and in my mind's eye saw Sheldon falling from the window.

I don't know how long I stood there or why the irrational connection of Sheldon and the bird wouldn't leave me; I knew only that I felt cold and disoriented, as though something threatening had been revealed to me and I was unable to answer it.

My legs felt weak and my breathing changed. It was like waking from a bad dream where your mind knows the fear is unreal but your body can't deny the effects.

Irritated and shaken, I finally forced myself to move away and continue the search of the building.

It was then that I first felt I wasn't alone.

I tried not to react. What had alerted me? The building was still.

The feeling of being watched was strong, but no matter in what direction I looked all I could see were barriers of clothes racks and their abandoned occupants.

Slowly, I retraced my steps towards the warehouse entrance, listening hard. As I moved, I took in as much as I could about the building. I was trying hard to be casual, but no one watching would have been fooled.

I re-entered the reception area and stopped. Still the silence loomed from the maw of the warehouse. Tugging at the stiff door handle, I emerged on to the iron staircase outside and shut the door firmly behind me.

'Can I help you?' A shaven-headed man in his middle thirties blocked the bottom of the stairs. His voice bordered on hostile. I walked down to him, stopping a few stairs from the bottom.

He had a dark, almost swarthy complexion accentuated by the stubble along the line of the jaw. Above and below both eyes were the faint but unmistakable thin white lines of scar tissue. His nose was broad and flat, a boxer's nose.

He was a little taller than me, just over six feet, but twice as broad, though he carried his weight well, with only a slight thickening at the waist. The scowl on his face looked resident.

Dressed in a black bomber jacket and jeans, his clothes were neutral enough for him not necessarily to be a warehouse worker, but his tone was more than a touch possessive. He looked and sounded like help wasn't on his mind.

'Is Mr Chasteau about?' I smiled.

'Who wants to know?' He stood with his feet a shoulder's width apart, his hands partially clenched; violence seeping from him. When I held out my hand he ignored it.

'I said, who wants to know?' A subtle shift of his feet and now the left shoulder was turned towards me.

'He won't know me . . .'

'What do you want with Mr Chasteau?'

I didn't think he was interested in the answer, so I said nothing, but watched him carefully. Both hands were bunched now, and I could see his weight was on the balls of his feet, like he was expecting to have to move fast any moment.

He leaned forward and I caught the rank smell of his breath.

'You're making me repeat myself,' he hissed. 'I asked you why you want to see Mr Chasteau.'

'That's between him and me,' I found myself saying. 'I take it that you're not . . .'

'He's not here.'

'Missed him, have I? Perhaps you can give me his phone number, only I . . .'

'No.'

That was the third time he'd interrupted me. 'I didn't catch your name,' I said lightly.

The door at the top of the stairs swung open behind me and two men stepped out on to the landing. One was as big as the pug, the other small, but with a sharp, vicious look to him.

The smaller, weasel-like character spoke. 'Problem, Len?'

The pug's expression changed, as though the idea that I might be a problem was an offence in itself.

'No . . . least, there better not be.'

I looked from Len to the other two. 'All I want is to talk to Mr Chasteau. If you can't help me, then I'll find someone who can.'

With that, I turned to walk back up the stairs, but

the weasel shook his head. 'Don't push your luck, mate.' The voice was bleak.

Beside him, the other character stepped towards the edge of the landing and pulled something that gleamed from his jacket pocket.

Common sense screamed at me to back off, but a more basic emotion was measuring distances and wondering whether to start before they did.

I was at a distinct disadvantage on the stairs with them at back and front of me, and either way it went I was going to get hurt somewhere. The thought went through my mind that it would have been nice to have found out what they were so sensitive about before I was beaten to a pulp.

Behind me, 'Len' moved up the stairs. I spun round quickly. His face came close to mine; he was itching for me to start.

'You're a nause . . . people who stick their nose in where it's not wanted end up getting slapped.'

He grabbed my right arm and I felt each one of the fingers in his grip. The weasel and his mate started to move. My breathing changed and a slight tremble through the body told me the adrenaline was starting to flow. I'd already made up my mind to belt the pug between the eyes as hard as I could. I wanted at least one of them to remember me.

'Len!' the weasel shouted.

We all looked up and saw a white Mercedes Sports coming towards us. They froze as the car swung in and came to a halt alongside the staircase.

A smooth-looking guy in his twenties with swept-back blond hair and designer tanned skin climbed from the car and stared at us.

If he was surprised by the scene in front of him, he failed to show it. Gradually his stare turned to a look of impatience and he tossed the car keys in his hand as though expecting an explanation.

They all seemed genuinely worried by the young guy's sudden appearance, and whatever it was had gleamed in the weasel's mate's hand disappeared back into his pocket quickly.

At that moment I took the opportunity to break Len's grip and push past him.

The newcomer wore a scarlet wool jacket, black collarless shirt with black trousers and a thick gold chain around his neck. He reeked with the arrogance of young money.

'What going on?' The accent was Home Counties, polished, but nothing to get excited about.

It was Len who answered him, and there was a clear edge of defensiveness to his words.

'We caught him nosing around . . . he says he wants Mr Chasteau.'

A look passed between them.

'I just want a few . . .'

He ignored me. I began to think it was a local custom. As I folded my arms and waited, he opened the car door and took a briefcase from it. When he turned around again he sighed, as though irritated that I was still there.

'Leave your phone number,' he said quietly. And with that the audience was over.

I shook my head and walked back to the car. I could feel their eyes on me all the way. They were a pack of dogs seeing someone off their territory and looking for an excuse to tear the interloper apart.

At the car I opened the door and paused to look back at them. It was then that I had my second bad idea of the day.

I started up the car and left it idling. Then flipped opened the glove compartment and took the camera from it. The light indicator lit up when I switched it on so I popped up the flash. Then I got out of the car again and started walking back towards them.

The effect surpassed my expectations. The four of them looked stunned as I brought the camera up and depressed the button.

The pug reacted first, but then checked himself and looked at the young guy, who nodded. That was all it took, and they charged down the stairs towards me. They were thirty to forty yards away when I clicked the first frame, but they moved fast and the gap closed rapidly as I fired off several more.

In the viewfinder the pug's face was twisted in fury. Pushing my luck to the limit, I took one last picture, then sprinted back to the car, jumped in and slammed it into gear.

They caught up with me just as the car surged forward, and I ducked as a massive fist smashed through the window, showering me with glass.

I hit the brakes hard and heard a satisfying thud as one of them hit the car rear. A hand clawed at my jacket as I put the gear lever back into first and then second, pushing the accelerator to the floor.

The front wheels spun as they tried to gain purchase, then swung as I turned the wheel hard. The hand disappeared.

In the rear-view mirror I saw the pug and the weasel bent over the writhing figure of the other thug, his screams drowned out by the squealing of the tyres.

I drove clear of Stratford, along the Romford Road, wondering what the hell I'd stumbled into. What should have been a brief survey of the warehouse and a few polite enquiries had exploded in my face and nearly got the shit kicked out of me.

The incident with the bird was nagging at me, though common sense had by then entered a plea of tiredness and disorientation.

Either way it seemed as though Alex's mystery had reached out and claimed me, or at least the prospect of money had.

At Forest Gate I stopped the car and cleared the glass out as best I could, but in that peculiar way of car glass, it had spread into every seat fold and corner.

It was then that I noticed in the rear-view mirror that my face had been cut; a slit just on the cheekbone that was deep. A tiny piece of glass from the side window had embedded itself in the wound, leaving dried blood caked to the side of my face. I dug it out with a fingernail and applied a handkerchief.

I wanted to ring Alex, but there was no way I could drive around with the window smashed and a sliced face. First things first. There was a place at Seven Kings I knew of that repaired car glass while you waited. I gave them a bell and they agreed to do the job on the spot.

It took twenty minutes to get there, but half an hour before they would even look at the car. The two clowns allocated the job seemed more interested in the cut. I said it was a sabre scar, but I think it was lost on them. On the spot looked like turning into a saga, so I left them to it and decided to get a coffee and a packet of plasters.

In the Seven Kings Road, next to the station, I bought a late afternoon edition of the evening rag and stopped dead. Splashed across the front page, in big black letters, was the headline 'Daughter arrested for arson and murder'.

I cancelled the coffee and went in search of a phone.

Chapter Six

I tried Alex's mobile first, but it was switched off. An answering service transferred me, gave me his office number and suggested the alternative of leaving a message, which I did, telling him to ring me at the station at six.

Next I tried his office number and got another answering service, which gave me his mobile number and asked if I wanted to leave a message.

It was perfect, circular non-communication; very Alex, a surreal technological cul-de-trap. I left the same message as before and finished by musing on the benefits of semaphore.

I went back to the garage and waited. It was gone five by the time the car glass was fixed, and by then there wasn't time to go back to the flat.

The flat. I still couldn't bring myself to call it home. Home was a place that had roots and memories; the flat was a hole into which I had crawled after losing my previous life, the place from which Jenny had fled.

And the place to which she had apparently returned.

Since then, we had slept in separate rooms. It

hadn't been discussed. We both knew I needed her to ask.

That brief interval of pain that I had so clumsily evoked before storming out the flat was my finest screw-up to date; 'Do you still miss him?' Jesus, I was subtle. Why fuck about with flesh wounds when you can drive a stake through the heart?

Yet I knew why I had asked. Her silences since returning, her failure to tell me what I needed to hear, frightened me. Maybe she was back because she needed me; needed me, but wanted him.

Whatever had happened between them had left her hurt, the pain subcutaneous, waiting to erupt, and it had shaken me to see it. I wanted answers, but the right kind, for however much I wanted her I had no intention of being her refuge on the way to somewhere else.

No matter what it cost I had to protect myself.

For a moment I considered ringing her, but couldn't imagine what it was I wanted to say or hear, so I drove straight to the fire station.

As I turned out of Chadwell Heath High Street and into Wells Lane, I could see that both machines were out on a call.

I managed to slip in, grab a shower and clean the cut properly before anyone saw me. It took two paper sutures to seal the wound and a clumsy looking plaster to hide the result. By the time I'd finished playing nurse it was nearly six. John stuck his head into my room.

'D'you want them on roll-call, guv . . .' He stopped. 'What happened to your face?'

'Stone hit the window of the car and a piece of glass caught me. Don't bother with roll-call, a head count will do.'

'Righto. The FIT rang this morning about the Ilford job, just after we went off duty. They're coming down straight away. Should be here about seven.'

'Talking of FITs, we've got to sort out the details of that joyrider with Clerkenwell.'

John smiled. 'I'll ring them,' pausing, he added, 'You look tired.'

'Didn't get much sleep today. Let's hope tonight's quieter.'

'Let's.'

The machines returned with the other watch just after six. Danny Grimshaw, their governor, said that the press had been ringing all day. Staff's instructions were to refer any calls to PR Section at Lambeth.

I collected my fire gear from the drying room, but it was still damp and reeked of smoke; a series of yellow/orange burn marks, like rust spots, trailed down the back of the tunic. I threw the lot back into the drying room and transferred my notebook, whistle and everything else to a fresh tunic.

Next I checked my BA set and had trouble focusing on the gauge. I closed my eyes and breathed deeply, then rubbed my face hard.

I felt drained. Everyone around me seemed full of the excitement of the night before, the appliance bay echoing to their shouts and laughter, but I felt detached and moved like a drunken man.

Dave Chase, a thick set fireman with a cheerfully insolent grin nailed permanently to his face, jumped into the driver's seat alongside me.

'You looked shagged, guv.'

'Cheers, Dave.'

He looked at me hard. 'Seriously, guv, you look like you could do with a good night's sleep.'

'Yeah, well, after writing out the Fire Report, talking to our Fire Investigation Team, Clerkenwell, Staff and Christ knows who else, I will.'

'Barring fire calls.' He grinned.

'Barring fire calls,' I agreed.

I left Dave to his vehicle checks and went to the station office to access my e-mail. A duplicate of the message that John had given me about the FIT was the first to come up. Next was one from Bob Grant, saying that he was on a twenty-four shift and would catch up with me some time during the evening. He ended it with a warning that the press were being a serious pain in the arse and that I should be on my toes.

I made a note to ring Photographic Section in the morning. I wanted a copy of everything they'd taken at the scene. I intended to photocopy their shots and start my own file. The more I thought about it, the more Alex was right – I had access to a lot of information. I was going to have to take an angle on everything that came my way.

John, reading me well, organised the men and left me alone. I was grateful and took the opportunity to close my eyes in an armchair.

Sleep hit me like a brick and I fell quick and deep, my body slumping into the hollow shape of the chair. I would have stayed there for a week, so badly did I need the rest, but in the event, an hour later, Mike Scott's voice over the Tannoy ripped me from the warm darkness.

The FIT had arrived.

George Harris, the FIT Sub Officer, was an old hand who had ridden the 'Unit' for about five years, and the man who had captioned the Stratford warehouse photographs. He was in every respect an old-style fireman; short on words, independent of thought, and the possessor of a tongue that could flay varnish from woodwork.

Since reading the warehouse fire file I'd realised that George was an important source of information, perhaps the most important available to me. He would be the first to bring onside.

The other half of the team, the station officer, was Jack Grocott.

Jack was a tall Geordie with dark features and a bony, hard-looking face that masked a genuinely gentle character. We had met a few months ago when he'd first joined the FIT, shortly after he had transferred to London from Tyne and Wear.

John had suggested that, with Jack's unintelligible

Northern dialect and George's estuary patois, I should try using sign language. In the event it wasn't far off being good advice.

I had always got on well with George, and had taken an instant liking to Jack, but however friendly we were I knew I would have to watch what I told them about my involvement with Alex.

After greeting them in the appliance bay I led them through to my office and sat them down. John joined us, bringing a pot of tea with him.

The shock of waking from such a deep and needed sleep had left me feeling nauseous. Knowing I didn't have the stamina for small talk, I poured the tea and passed it around, steering the conversation quickly towards the Ilford fire.

'So what did you make of it last night, Jack?'

He smiled and shook his head. 'Strange, very strange . . . what's that expression you're always using, George?'

'Moody, Jack.'

'Aye, moody.' He turned back to me. 'What did you see when you first arrived, Steve?'

'Ground and first floors were well alight and the second was building nicely . . . we had our hands full from the off.'

' 'Ow long d'you reckon it was going before yer arrived, guv?' asked George.

I looked at John. 'With petrol involved it would be fast. The spread would argue for ten, fifteen minutes at most. John?'

He nodded. 'That's about where I'd put it, although the open-plan staircase from the ground to the first floor and early failure of the glazing could have distorted the timeframe.'

'Good point,' agreed Jack. 'Did you see anything out of the ordinary?'

John shook his head. 'The guv'nor thought he saw a woman on the second.'

'Steve?'

My eyes must have closed for a moment as he was speaking; the sleep in the chair hadn't helped; if anything it had left my body screaming for rest and having sat down again, it was desperately trying to resume where it had left off. The weariness was suffocating me.

Jack leaned forward. 'Are you all right, Steve?'

'Fine. Tired, but it's passing. Go on.'

'This woman?'

'I was mistaken.'

'Tell us what you saw.'

'It was at the front . . . a couple of minutes after we arrived. I heard a scream . . . least, it sounded like a scream, from the second-floor window that the guy jumped through. It was for just an instant, no more. I thought then it was a woman, but I was wrong.'

'How d'you know?'

'How do I know I was wrong? I don't for certain, but I had the place searched from top to bottom. There were no women casualties and I was the only person who saw her.'

'No way she could have escaped?'

'When I saw her she was surrounded by flame. She wouldn't have stood a chance.'

'So you did see something?'

Pressed to answer, I hesitated, trying to recapture the image again and fighting the tiredness that was eroding my concentration. Then my mind seemed to go completely blank and I lost the thread of the conversation.

Jack was staring at me, waiting for an answer.

'You did see something?' he repeated.

'Sorry, Jack . . . something, yes . . . a reflection of flame on the broken glass, smoke . . . I don't know. Last night I would have said it was a woman. Tonight . . .' I shrugged.

He put down the mug of tea and crossed his fingers in his lap, the softness of his voice alerting me to the terseness of my own.

'It's okay. It was a canny ol' fire, man; lots of odd bits and pieces don't tie in.'

His tone was conciliatory, placating, but I felt as though he was making allowances for me.

'Bits that don't tie in. What does that mean?'

Jack and George exchanged looks and I read their silent agreement to change tack. It was George who spoke next.

'Have yer 'eard the news today, guv?'

I shook my head.

'The geezer that jumped through the window was the owner, Robin Sheldon, a name I've come across before. They've arrested his daughter.'

'Daughter? Why?' asked John.

George's grey eyes crinkled at the corners, holding a look somewhere between humour and cynicism. Slowly, he dug into his anorak pocket, took out a pipe and filled it with tobacco from a worn leather pouch. There was the brief rasp of a match and a cloud of faintly aromatic smoke jetted from the corner of his mouth.

'Apparently the rear entrance is partially covered by CCTV cameras that are positioned to monitor the carpark and the service road. The rumour's that the daughter can be seen arriving at the place not long before the fire was first seen.'

'You're asking me if this could have been the woman I saw?'

He nodded. 'It's a possibility, guv.'

'Who called the Fire Brigade?'

'The call was made from a public phone box in Ilford rail station. A woman's voice.'

'Could the daughter have started the fire and then phoned it in after she left?'

'Possible.'

'How do you know all this, George?' I asked.

'When the police Fire Investigation Unit turned up they spotted the cameras straight away and made a beeline for them.'

'That was sharp of them,' said John.

George looked rueful. 'Maybe.'

'We think that they were tipped off,' put in Jack.

George folded his arms and gave a snort. 'They

buggered us off out of it well quick; too quick for smart guessing. They knew what they were after. I know one of them fairly well and 'e gave me a bell just after we came on duty tonight. Told me not to bother too much with our investigation as they had it wrapped up tight and suggested I study the evening paper.'

This was important to Alex, and with an act of will I forced myself to listen.

'You don't sound convinced, George,' I said.

He looked at the glowing bowl of his pipe and frowned. 'A man is tied up, doused in petrol and set alight by 'is daughter . . . do you believe it?'

For a moment I thought he was going to say more, but Jack spoke instead.

'Whatever happened it's well out of our league now.'

'Did you . . . did you speak to my Leading Fireman last night?'

Jack smiled. 'Can't really avoid him, can you. We checked with the hospital. Just as he said, Sheldon had plastic tape wound around both wrists. That's a sharp young lad you've got there, Steve.'

I stared back, but couldn't think what to say. My mind had frozen again. There was a brief awkward moment with everyone staring at me. Then John came to the rescue.

'For Christ sake don't tell Sandy!' he laughed, but the laugh was forced; an attempt to lighten the atmosphere.

I smiled and made an attempt to recover the situation, to act and sound normal, but it was transparent. In fairness to them, they realised what I was doing and just went along with it.

'What . . . what's the plan from here, Jack?'

'I think we should let you get some rest, Steve . . . I'll take statements from your lads, put together what we know and await the coroner's court. George can take your statement now or the next tour of duty . . . whatever's best for you.'

'I'd rather do it now, get it over with. Look, I'm sorry if I seem out of it tonight, but I feel exhausted. Maybe I'm coming down with something.' I turned to John. 'Give Jack a list of all the lads on duty last night and use the lecture room to take the statements in.'

They rose to their feet and Jack gave a smile that was meant to reassure me, but the fact that he had to do that told me he – they thought I'd been acting strangely and were convinced that more than lack of sleep was causing it. They were wrong.

Chapter Seven

As soon as they left to take the statements I went into the bathroom that connected the office to my locker room. Taking off my shirt and tie, I splashed my face with cold water, leaving the door half open so that I could continue to talk to George.

'Overdone it, guv?'

'No, I just feel lousy. I didn't get much sleep today and last night is catching up fast.'

'Only lack of sleep?'

I peered around the door.

'Sorry, guv, I don't mean to pry, but yer lost the plot there a few times.'

'That's it, George, cheer me up.' I dried my face on a roller towel and looked into the mirror. Dark rings had formed under my eyes and the whites were bloodshot. I looked totally wasted, but at least I was finally waking up. I put my shirt back on and threw the tie on to the bed through the other door-way behind me.

'You're not ill or anything?' There was genuine concern in his voice.

'Just bone tired. Tell me, George, what do you make of Charnley?'

His eyes twinkled. 'Bloody barking, seeing as yer ask. Why?'

'He's our new group DO.'

'Lucky you . . . watch yer back.'

'A bit like that, is it?'

'A lot like that. I knew 'im when 'e came to Bethnal Green as a recruit . . . a real charmer, all the necessary qualities to become a senior officer.'

'Ouch.'

He laughed. 'Still, perhaps 'e's changed.'

I stepped back into my office. 'D'you reckon?'

'Nope.'

I felt the teapot; it was still warm. I poured us a cup each and leaned back on the radiator, not trusting myself to sit down.

'George, when you spoke of Sheldon being tied up and torched I got the impression that you wanted to say something more.'

He sucked on the pipe and a small debate chased across his face. Self-absorbed for the moment, he stared at the floor. Then he grinned as he realised I was studying him. 'Jack thinks I'm trying to prove a point.'

'About the daughter?'

'Sheldon and the daughter.'

'Are you?'

He folded his arms, the pipe cupped in one hand. 'I don't think Sheldon was killed by his daughter.'

'It's a pretty bold statement from this distance.'

'I've met 'er, guv. She's strange. There's something

going on behind the eyes, like she's not connecting with what's around 'er.'

'Disturbed?'

He shook his head. 'Disturbing.'

'When did you meet her?'

'Last November, when the warehouse owned by 'er father had a fire; a ten-pumper, on Stratford's ground.'

'Go on.'

He paused, managing this time to keep the debate from his face, but it was there, hidden from view and chained by caution. Smoke trickled from the edge of his mouth; like a diver trailing bubbles behind him as he swam for the surface.

Then, almost reluctantly, he said, 'It was arson.'

'I've seem the file, George, fairly recently. It went down as electrical.'

'Oh?'

'I'll tell you about it in a minute. Go on with what you were saying.'

When he spoke the words came out flat, stark, neither emotion nor embellishment colouring their delivery. They were long-considered words, the words of a witness waiting to be called.

'That warehouse fire was moody; moody and very clever. It was the work of a torch, a pro, someone who knew what they were doing.'

'How d'you know?'

'Because whoever set the fire knew enough to throw us off the scent.'

'Too much for this daughter?'

'Exactly.' He paused and puffed thoughtfully at the pipe. 'She's . . . beautiful.'

It seemed an unusual word for George. He said it as though it added to her strangeness.

'So she couldn't start a fire?'

'Didn't say that, did I. Maybe she could, but not the Stratford fire, nor last night's little effort.'

'But last night wasn't subtle, George. Anyone can splash petrol around.'

The look on his face set. I had blundered into the ranks of the unbelievers; I tried to recover.

'I do believe you, George, and I can see you're peed off with trying to make people listen, but the police aren't mugs.'

'Aren't they?'

'We're back to the Stratford fire?'

'In a way.'

He was fighting himself, wanting to tell me and wanting to keep it locked inside. It was a wariness not uncommon in firemen who had fought the system and come off second best. I waited, knowing that to force it was to lose him.

'Suppose it was arson last night, but not murder?'

'Sorry?'

'Sheldon. Suppose 'e was behind the Stratford fire and last night's fire.'

'But he's dead, George . . . you're saying he killed himself? Suicide?'

He peered from under his eyebrows, controlling

the release of the information, checking me to see if I was accepting his logic.

'Maybe, or maybe 'e got careless, burnt 'imself along with the shop.'

'Is that what you believe?'

'I don't know, but I don't think the daughter's the answer.'

'What is it that you're keeping back, George?'

His mouth smiled, but it didn't reach his eyes. It was acknowledgment, not humour.

'A couple of years ago I started to put together a database, all doubtful fires on our patch.'

'Doesn't the Brigade do that anyway?'

'Yes and no. The Brigade 'as a database, but it isn't . . . doing anything.'

'It isn't proactive.'

'I 'ate that word.'

'Me too, George, but it fits, doesn't it?'

This time the grin was guileless. 'It fits.'

'But you now have your own database?'

He nodded. 'From time to time I've asked the Brigade database for information and gradually loaded it on to my own notebook computer. I can now cross-reference and run any amount of searches, by owner, firm, trade name, type of business, method of ignition . . . anything.'

'You're giving me the big build-up, George. Where's it all leading?'

'At the moment, nowhere.'

'So?'

'So I think that if there's a professional "torch" running around we should at least be logging what we know, not waiting to mop up afterwards.'

'Why not let the police handle it? Whether it's murder, suicide or misadventure, it's a crime and the police won't let you near it.'

'That's Jack's view.'

'But not yours?'

'What if there are other fires, guv?'

'Look, George, I'm interested, but you're not making sense. First you say that Sheldon's behind the fires; "moody and clever" were your words. Then you say that he might have topped himself or at least scored an own goal, and then you say that a professional fire-raiser is behind it all.'

He ripped the pipe from his mouth and stabbed the air with it. 'Why doesn't it make sense? I never said that Sheldon was the "torch," did I?'

'No, you didn't.'

I let the thought surf. Alex wasn't going to like much of this. A can of worms barely described it.

'Look, guv, I'm not saying I 'ave the whole picture, only that the daughter strikes me as being an unlikely candidate.'

'If what you've told me is correct, she was seen leaving the Ilford place just before the fire, and the Stratford report states that she was the last one to leave there too.'

'And Sheldon's partner Chasteau.'

'Okay, and Chasteau. Tell me about him.'

'Can't. I didn't interview him. Worthington did.'

Brian Worthington was the station officer who had ridden the Fire Investigation Unit at the time of the Stratford fire.

'You think this Chasteau is involved?'

'Don't know.' He picked up his cup and sipped before placing it down again. 'That is a nasty drop of tea. Now, I've told yer what I think. Tell me why yer were reading the Stratford file, guv.'

I trusted George, but the job that Alex had offered me wasn't without its dangers.

No fireman was allowed to do part-time work without written permission, and there was no way I could apply to do a job that might compromise the Brigade.

Release of information on fires to outside bodies had to be cleared by Brigade Legal Section. Alex knew this when he asked me, and he knew that I would weigh the risks; he also knew that I needed the money.

I would have been uncomfortable lying to George, but telling him what I was doing might have scared him off. The truth, partial truth, seemed the best way.

'Do you remember Alex McGregor, George?'

'Your ex-sub?'

'That's the one. He works for a firm of loss adjusters nowadays. He's got a problem.'

'Oh?'

'He's asked me to look at some back files on the Stratford fire. He thinks Sheldon was involved and he wants a second opinion on the evidence.'

His grey-green eyes bored into me. Slowly, he crossed his arms, then his legs – a behavioural psychologist wasn't required.

'You're going to ask me a favour, aren't yer, guv.'

'No.'

'No?'

'I'm going to help you solve your riddle.'

'Oh, yeah. Why?'

'Because there might be other fires.'

We stared at each other, both knowing, yet neither wanting to put it into words. If we did then there would be nothing for either man.

The silence hung between us.

'I've got less than four years to go, guv . . .'

'I won't tell a soul, George. My word on it.'

His face was pale, intense. 'What d'yer want?'

'Not sure for the moment, but I can tell you there are other shops owned by the Sheldon family in the area. I'll collate the info that Alex has and give it to you. Hopefully when you cross-reference something might be thrown up.'

'Have you thought through all the implications?'

'Yes,' I lied.

'Sure about that?'

I nodded. 'Is now a good time to take my statement for last night?'

The legs and arms uncrossed, 'Yeah.'

By ten, Jack and George had finished taking the statements and had left the station. I wandered into the Mess to eat what was by then a well-spoilt supper. I had just taken my first mouthful when the bells crashed down.

Mike Scott announced the call over the Tannoy. 'RTA A12 Eastbound, junction of Whalebone Lane, two cars involved, persons believe trapped.'

The road traffic accident was the start of a brutal night that saw us dragged out every hour or so, dealing with nothing fires in rubbish skips, malicious false alarms and drunks shut in lifts.

Time and again we drove like scarlet ghosts through concrete landscapes, oblivious and indifferent to us; the blue flashing beacons coming back at us off a thousand windowpanes, like a visual echo.

The rain-swept streets and precincts filled and emptied with faceless figures that tumbled from the clubs and bars, until at three in the morning the world finally went to bed and the calls stopped.

The watch, now beyond sleep, sat in a daze around the Mess table drinking coffee and wishing the night away; their voices low and the wit veering from the juvenile to the subversive.

'How're you feeling, guv?'

I turned to the speaker, Wayne Bennett, one of the four anglers on the watch, whom Harry Wildsmith had surreally dubbed Hook, Line and Sinker.

'Numb, Wayne.'

'Going away this year?' asked Simon Jones, another of the anglers.

No one on the watch knew the financial straits I was in, though John Blane suspected.

'I've nothing planned, Simon.'

'You're off to Austria soon, aren't you, Hoss?' said Simon.

John nodded. 'Looking forward to getting away from you lot.'

'Gonna look in on the Spanish Riding School?' chipped in Dave Chase.

John's eyes narrowed over the rim of his coffee cup.

'Ignore him, Sub,' said Simon. 'How many weeks before you go?'

Before John could answer, Dave Chase stamped his foot three times and Wayne Bennett fell sideways laughing. John, in acknowledgment of the joke, nodded slowly, and that set everybody off.

The watch contained a number of strong personalities, and it was due in part to John's steady good humour that major in-fighting never took place. He seemed to sense the areas of potential trouble and steered the watch clear. He should have been a Station Officer years ago.

None of this, of course, spared him from Dave Chase's wit, or Harry's acerbic observations.

His own retaliatory humour was slower, but cultivated and beautifully plotted, as the watch had discovered over the years. Dave called it 'death by gardening'.

The banter continued for another hour and

eventually swung around to fishing. My eyes gritty, I left them to it and turned in.

Fatigued to the point of standstill, immediate sleep somehow eluded me, and I lay in bed turning over the events of the past twenty-four hours.

It had felt as though I were being sucked into a whirlpool. Alex's solution to my troubles was far from being a mundane series of enquiries. It felt deep – deep and treacherous. Either I went after this mystery or it would turn and savage me. George thought so too; it was etched into every sceptical line on his face.

A trapdoor marked 'doubt' slid open, but tired though I was, I was sharp enough not to peer down it, for I had been this route before, with Jenny.

I had spent countless nights screaming and arguing inside my head, denying myself rest, only to rise on to a new day with neither a solution nor peace of mind.

I had learned about myself during those dark nights and refused to allow 'maybe' to torment me. The money was needed and I had no other options.

At some point I must have slept, for the call bells of the seven o'clock wake-up knifed through my brain, causing me to sit up sharply, my hands clasped over my ears and my eyes shut fast against the glare of the accompanying call lights.

When the bells had finished their cycle I fell back and lay unmoving, neither asleep nor awake. Eventually I turned to look at the clock. It was twenty past seven. Dragging myself from bed, I shaved and showered, switching to cold for the last two minutes in an attempt to shock myself into life.

Breakfast was like a funeral, with lines of wan faces down both sides of the Mess table; talk was minimal and the appetites automatic. All I could think about in that last hour of the shift was getting home and getting my head down.

Then, just before nine o'clock, the phone rang. Alex.

'Stevie, I'm returning your call.'

'We need to talk, Alex, but not till this evening. First I need to go home and catch up on my sleep.'

'Anything important?'

'You tell me. You must know that the Plod arrested the daughter, Stephanie Sheldon. I did wonder whether that means I'm not needed now.'

'No. If anything you've become even more important to me.'

'Good. After I left you I visited the warehouse at Stratford.'

'Good man, Stevie. I knew you couldn't resist a challenge.'

'Challenge nothing. I need the bread. Look, I think I've found Chasteau . . .'

'Save it for tonight. Come to my place at seven and wear something smart.'

'Smart? Why? Where are we go . . .' He hung up.

Chapter Eight

Saturday, 18 April, 9 a.m.

I slumped into the car, knowing I was going to collapse unless I got several hours of uninterrupted sleep. As I pulled out of the station yard I wound the window down and gulped at the air like a beached fish.

It took an act of will to concentrate on the road.

The Saturday morning shopping traffic was already choking Romford, and with each successive stop and start I felt more nauseous. After what seemed an age I finally arrived home and turned off the engine, sitting there for a few minutes while I summoned up the energy to climb the stairs.

It was then that the realisation that Jenny might not be there made a grab for me. I'd like to think that I was in control, but the truth was I didn't have the strength to panic. I turned the key in the lock and pushed open the door.

Jenny appeared from the bathroom, wearing a white towelling robe, her damp hair brushed back behind her ears and the soft brown eyes weighing me.

'I need to sleep.'

She took my arm and steered me towards the bedroom.

Not a word passed between us as she undressed me and helped me into bed. Through half-open eyes I watched her as she threw off the robe and climbed naked in next to me. As I turned on to my side I felt her breasts against my back and her arms fold around me. I was asleep instantly.

I woke late afternoon, the numbing fatigue of recent weeks missing. Feeling warm and cocooned from the outside world, I lay with my hands behind my head and conjured up the delicious sensation of Jenny pressed against me.

There had been times when I had missed that so much that the pain had been physical. Equally, there had been times when the thought of her lying with Mayle had reduced me to helpless fury.

That one act, that crawling into bed beside me, had disconnected the pain.

Nothing else could have, for so tangled were the emotions between us, so fucked-up was my head, that I could place no trust in words; they had been the poison that had deceived me.

Bodies were different, weren't they?

The flat was quiet, with only the muted noises of traffic filtering through the walls. I listened for a while, then wrapped myself in the duvet and patrolled the flat.

A note was tacked to the kitchen door: 'Shopping – back around five'.

I was almost grateful that she had gone out.

I showered, scrubbing my skin hard before switching to cold and letting the icy water hit me for as long as I could stand it. Finally I climbed from the shower gasping and towelled myself dry.

I wanted her then. I felt sure, equal.

Since her reappearance I had resolved that she had to be the one to ask. The act of returning wasn't enough. There had to be contrition, regret.

She knew this. She knew it because she knew me.

For that reason her timing had been perfect. Clever bitch that she was, she had negotiated the barrier by pretending it wasn't there. It was Jenny under Jenny's terms.

The irony made me smile. Funny how we never feel turned over when we see the art for what it is.

Had she been there then, had she walked through the door, the chances are the past would have been wiped away.

But she was shopping.

I made coffee and sat in the lounge reading a day-old newspaper and flicking idly through the television channels. I caught the local news bulletin and sat upright as the announcer mentioned the name Sheldon.

The brief clip of film showed a dark blue BMW pulling up outside a very expensive-looking apartment block in Docklands, and a cluster of photographers descending on it. The announcer said that Stephanie Sheldon had been remanded in custody and would appear in court on Monday.

As the car door opened, cameras flashed and scuffles broke out on the pavement. In the mêlée it was impossible to see anyone clearly. The police were taken by surprise and pushed to one side.

A television reporter reached forward and jammed a microphone towards the car, only to be shoved back violently by a large, dark-suited arm. Then a hand went over the camera lens and the screen went blank.

The announcer apologised for the loss of vision.

When it came on again the story had changed and pictures of the Millennium Dome were being shown. I switched off the set and sat back in the chair. It seemed a good time to organise my thoughts.

First I poured myself more coffee and retrieved the Stratford warehouse file from my grip bag. Then dug out a pad and pen before rereading the file in its entirety.

After my visit to the warehouse, George's photo captions took on a different perspective. What he had noted was thin in terms of proving deliberate ignition. His main area of concern, the insulation bubbled into the wire, not away from it, as in the case of electrical overload, was not enough to prove anything one way or another.

It didn't make him wrong, just a little short of the finishing line.

I drew a mind-map. The words Insulation, Rain-Shadow and Padlock attracted an individual bubble, as did Professional Torch, Divorce and Money Crisis.

In the last bubble I wrote, Stratford-clever, Ilford-blatant.

On another page I listed the names and faces connected with the case – each of the Sheldons, Chasteau, 'Len', the 'Weasel' and 'Walks with a limp'.

I resisted the urge to link the information bubbles of the mind-map to the names on the list. There had to be links, but sitting there I made myself a promise that only when logic, evidence and instinct all coincided would I draw a connecting line.

I sat back, reading and rereading my notes, checking to see if I'd left anything out. That was when the image of the woman at the window jumped into my head.

Instantly I was back on the street with the rain hammering down and the noise of the fire roaring in my ears. It was so sharp, so unmistakable, that I thought I could see her mouth moving as the orange-red flame swirled about her. Yet the moment I tried to concentrate, the image lost focus.

Then, just as suddenly, it was gone, and I was back in the living-room armchair, aware only of the fading light from the window and the dampness of the bath-towels making me cold.

Automatically I started to sketch the image.

I was no artist, but as a kid I used to amuse myself by drawing people, then slowly transforming their portraits into caricatures. It didn't matter for now that the sketch was rough; rather it helped – it would provide a focus for my thoughts. I would work on it, refine it, until it was accurate.

I had been tired to the point of disorientation when Jack and George had interviewed me at the station. I hadn't been able to explain to them why I had seen the woman when there had been no trace of her at the fire, but the more I stared at that sketch, the more difficult it became to dismiss it.

That fire-ravaged face really put the hook in me.

Mayle, the money and now the image – the reasons for becoming involved in the Sheldon investigation were piling up. Sitting there, in the half-light, mulling over the events that were taking me down a path I couldn't control, I realised that it wasn't a question of what I wanted, but what I needed to do.

When I eventually glanced at the clock it had gone five.

I threw everything back into the grip bag and quickly changed into jeans and a sweatshirt. No sooner had I emerged from the bedroom than I heard her key in the lock.

She paused on seeing me. 'I thought you'd still be in bed.'

I looked down at the shopping bags.

She smiled. 'Pasta . . . and wine. Is that . . .'

'I have to go out tonight, Jen.'

'Oh.'

'It's important.'

'When are you going out?'

'I have to be at Alex's by seven.'

'Alex again?' She picked up the bags and took them into the kitchen.

I followed her. 'Perhaps we can have the wine later.'

She stopped unpacking, but didn't look at me. 'If you want.'

I took her shoulders from behind and gently turned her around. She looked directly into my eyes, softness and vulnerability radiating from her. I leaned forward to kiss her, but at the last instant my lips found her forehead.

She shook her head, took my face in her hands and guided my lips down to hers. 'I'm here,' she said softly.

'Are you?'

'Yes.'

I searched her face. There was nothing I could detect; nothing to warn me.

'Yes,' she repeated.

Gently, awkwardly, we kissed.

'I've missed you . . .' She started.

I placed a finger on her lips and pulled her closer to me. Christ, I needed her then, yet I knew if we made love I would never get to Alex. She must have read it in my face.

'If you're going out I'll need to cook this straight away.'

I left her to it and went to sort out something suitable to wear.

Smart, Alex had said – not smart casual, not smart lounge suit, just smart. Well, smart wasn't so easy when you hadn't bought anything decent in months.

Eventually I settled for slacks and a cashmere jacket; a remnant of a once proud wardrobe. I laid them out on the bed, together with a collarless white shirt.

Over wine-less pasta we had an artificial conversation punctuated by long silences. It seemed that with the physical touch gone a gulf opened out alarmingly quickly. We were both conscious of it. At one point I reached out to touch her hand, but it felt clumsy and just underlined the tension.

We finished eating and stared at each other. I glanced at the clock.

'Go!'

'I'm sorry about this, Jen.'

'Go, for Christ's sake . . . just don't leave it too late,' she added quietly.

I changed and left around half-six.

Alex lived alone in a large detached house in Upminster. His wife, Hannah, had died three years previously, after a long illness during which Alex had nursed her. I used to think of them as the original devoted couple, having married in Edinburgh in their late teens and moving south after Alex left the navy.

Their son Iain was at London University, reading

for a doctorate in maths, and was the one area of boasting that Alex permitted himself.

Whereas Alex had always been solid and dependable, Hannah had been as bright as sixpence, holding down a successful private accountancy business, hence the house and the smart neighbourhood.

I arrived at seven dead. Alex opened the door with a Scotch in his hand and a smile that said it wasn't his first.

He ran a critical eye over me.

'You said smart. You didn't specify, Alex!'

'Nice jacket. Come in, Stevie, come in.'

He took me through the spacious hallway with its scroll plasterwork and into the lounge where Hannah's touch was still very much in evidence in the décor and the furniture. A large framed oil portrait of her hung above the fireplace; the room just stopped short of being a shrine.

Alex paused before sitting. 'You look better than yesterday.'

'Not difficult. I caught up a little today.'

'Good. D'you want one of these?' He held up his glass.

'Not for the moment.' I sat down on the sofa. 'I've found out a number of things that I . . .'

'Later, Stevie, later. I've something to show you.'

He bent over in front of the television and loaded a video, then sat next to me and pressed the remote control.

Up came a film of the fight between Roberto

Duran and Iran Barkley back in 1989, an absolute war in which Duran outfought the bigger Barkley with a combination of technical skill and sheer toughness that at times was heartachingly brilliant.

I'd seen highlights of it before, but as Alex explained, he'd sent away to a private fight archive and had the whole fight put together on one tape.

It was brutal fight, the kind that fight fans love and the kind that had bleeding-heart politicians climbing the walls. It showed Duran at his best; an old lion with still enough fire and savvy to outgun the formidable Barkley.

'He's a giant of a fighter, Stevie. Never have I seen a man with so much guts . . . no, no, that's wrong, it's not guts, it's abandonment. He doesn't give a flying fuck for anybody. D'you know, he was broke when he took this fight, flat broke. Thirty-nine years of age and he summons up the wit and sinew to produce that fight from God knows where.'

'It's one hell of a performance.'

'Just look at the bastard, Stevie.'

Alex freeze-framed the film. Duran stood with his legs astride, pointing to his own chest in a show of real machismo. There were many negative things you could say about Duran – out of the ring his life left a lot to be desired – but seeing him stand there with such utter belief in himself made you realise what a powerful thing the human will can be. It made me embarrassed for the times when I'd almost buckled, and for the level of self-pity I had once sunk to.

Alex switched off the video and regarded me carefully, holding up a finger, as though in accusation. 'You were quite good once.'

'A long time ago.'

'There was talk that you might turn pro.'

'Not from me there wasn't.'

'Ah, come on, Stevie . . .'

'It wasn't possible. Too many things against it.' He shrugged. 'D'you still work out?'

'Sparring? Christ, no!'

'Bag work?'

'Where the hell can I hang a bag in that flat?'

The bitterness of my own words took me as much by surprise as it did Alex. We both knew its roots had nothing to do with boxing. For a moment neither of us spoke.

'You should come down to the club,' he said softly. 'A couple of nights each week we have special sessions; over-thirties night. We've a mix of ex-pros and amateurs, good lads that do it just for the craic. What do you weigh nowadays – twelve, twelve and a half?'

'Twelve and a lot.'

'Even more reason to start training again. Do you run?'

'Alex! There's more to life than bloody boxing.'

The leather mask became serious, and those hard blue eyes bored right through me. 'Yes,' he said quietly, 'there is, but there's little more important than self-respect.'

'Crafty bastard, aren't you?'

'Just concerned.' He swilled the Scotch in the glass and emptied it in one go. 'She's back, isn't she?'

'Two weeks ago.'

'For good?'

'Don't know.'

He nodded and stood up. 'Follow me.'

Chapter Nine

He snatched up the decanter and took me through to the study at the back of the house. It was large enough to hold a big leather-topped desk as well as a computer station and fax machine. On the walls were a series of prints depicting bare-knuckle pugilists.

Alex sat himself in a leather swivel chair behind the desk and placed his feet on one corner. I made myself comfortable in an easy chair on the other side.

'So, what is it you've found out, Stevie?'

I told him about the warehouse and my conversation with George Harris and Jack Grocott. He didn't interrupt, just sat and sipped at the Scotch. When I got to the part about being chased by the three thugs he gave a wolfish smile.

'You're going to have to tread more softly, Stevie.'

'Just beating the bushes a little.'

He opened a drawer in the desk and took out a mobile phone. 'Here, you can use this to keep in touch. Don't go beating any more bushes without letting me know.'

'I'll try.'

Alex topped up his glass and held up the decanter

to me. I shook my head.

'So come on then, Stevie, tell me what you make of the Stratford warehouse fire.'

'What I think or what I feel?'

He shrugged. 'Both.'

I took a minute. 'I think George Harris is right – only a professional torch could have set that fire in the way it was done. Equally, I think proving it will be nigh on impossible.'

'And what do you feel?'

'I feel that now that Robin Sheldon's dead the pressure on everyone will be intense. The police are going to climb all over this. Our best bet is someone losing their nerve and talking.'

'It's not only the police putting on the pressure, Stevie. The press are gathering, hordes of them.'

'So beating the bushes is not such a bad idea?'

He laughed. 'It's why I persuaded Andrew to take you on.'

'Oh?'

'For as long as I've known you, Stevie, you've always thought logically but acted impulsively. This investigation has been dead in the water for six months. Six wasted months. The money's been paid out and we've had to sit back and watch. Andrew and I realised that we needed a catalyst.'

'Me?'

'Don't look so surprised. Life doesn't pass you by . . . most of the time you seem to be on a collision course with it.'

I smiled. 'Have you considered the possibility that the Stratford and Ilford fires aren't linked?'

'Aren't the Sheldons the link?'

'A link, but perhaps not the cause. Just suppose different persons and different reasons; what then?'

'Is that what you think?'

'Don't know. What I do know is that both fires were entirely different. One was subtle, the product of a crafty mind, and the other was blatant, almost like revenge. And why go to the trouble of concealing one fire only to advertise another?'

'So, the fires are not connected?'

I sighed. 'I'm going to argue against myself here . . . they have to be.'

He brought his fingers together to form a steeple. His brow was creased in concentration. 'Explain.'

'To solve the first fire we have to go through the second.'

'I was right to bring you in on this, Stevie.' He opened another desk drawer and took out a wad of money. 'I thought it best if we paid you in cash – no records that way. I'm going to give you two days' wages and pay for that car window.' He grinned. 'It'll save you putting it through your insurance.'

I took the money. 'I'm concerned about the Brigade finding out.'

'As I said, everything in cash. Neither Andrew nor I will tell them anything.' He suddenly sat up straight. 'If we're going to be there by eight-thirty we'd best get a move on. I'll change.'

'Where are we going?'

Again the wolfish grin. 'To see the widow Sheldon.' He looked at the empty whisky glass. 'And you're driving.'

In the car Alex asked, 'Do you know Virginia Quay?'

I knew it well enough. It was one of the many new developments that were springing up all over the old dockland of East London, near where the first settlers set off for America in the early seventeenth century.

Under a swollen and threatening sky, I headed for the A13 while Alex took the opportunity to fill me in on some more of the Sheldons' background.

'Nearly five years ago, Stevie, they were riding the crest of the wave. Robin and Eileen Sheldon were being credited as the couple that brought haute couture to the high street, or, as the tabloids put it, 'Selling Class for Brass'. They set up a chain of shops, originally all to the east of London – Romford, Ilford, Hornchurch, as far out as Chelmsford and Colchester.'

'How many shops?'

'At the height of their success . . . about twenty.'

'That's a lot of money.'

'They couldn't put a foot wrong.'

'So what happened?'

'The recession. They made their money by selling their own-labelled goods to the high-street department stores. Good stuff, by all accounts. They used the profits to expand, but it was all a bit too rapid.

When the recession saw the department stores cut back on buying, it hit them hard.'

'I know a little of what that feels like.'

'Five years ago they had a fire. Or rather a series of fires.'

'Serious?'

'Extinguisher jobs in the main.'

'Arson, obviously?'

'For sure, but they were small and no claims were made. Then they had something bigger. It destroyed a fair amount of stock and the manageress of the shop called the police.'

'Go on.'

'It turned out that all the fires were started by the same person . . . Stephanie Sheldon, the daughter. By all accounts the archetypal disturbed adolescent.'

'Charges?'

'No. As the Sheldons didn't claim and had no wish to see their daughter prosecuted, the whole matter was resolved by having young Stephanie treated by a psychiatrist.'

'How old was she when this happened, Alex?'

'Fifteen.'

We had just reached Canning Town flyover when a bolt of lightning arced across the sky and a tremendous crack of thunder shook the car.

'Sweet Jesus!' swore Alex.

Within seconds the rain was hammering on the windscreen and the wipers were fighting to sweep it aside. I slowed the car to thirty as the violent downpour rapidly transformed the roadway into a shallow lake.

As we neared Virginia Quay the visibility was down to fifty yards and I slowed the car to barely twenty. Alex spotted something and pointed up ahead.

'Take the next left.'

I recognised the building he indicated as the one that had been on the news bulletin earlier. The rain had thinned out the press, but a few die-hards lurked under umbrellas, trying to keep their lenses dry.

I drove past them and turned out of the rain into a carpark beneath the building, only to be stopped immediately by a barrier and an alert carpark attendant. Alex wound the window down.

'Mr McGregor to see Mrs Sheldon.'

The attendant went back into a control room. We watched him speak into a phone. He emerged again.

'Park it over there and leave the keys in it. You want the top floor – penthouse suite.'

From the carpark we went through a double doorway into a large foyer of stainless-steel panels with holographic images and marble geometric shapes. Next to the lift was a coded panel. Alex tapped in a number. The lift doors opened and we got in.

'Why are we here, Alex?'

'To speak to Eileen Sheldon . . . at her request.'

The lift went upward at a speed that made you want to hold on to something solid. When the doors opened we stepped out into a spacious lobby with another panel controlling access. Again Alex entered a code.

'She left me the details on the answerphone,' he replied to my unasked question.

We went through toughened glass doors to a plain oak door on the other side. A dark-haired woman in her late twenties was waiting.

'Follow me, please,' she said.

She led the way up a winding cast-iron staircase. At the top it opened out on to a huge room with a hardwood floor and minimalist décor so stark that it was almost abstract. *Gemütlich* it wasn't, but there was no denying the confidence of style.

We sat on a sofa of white leather and steel as the woman brought us drinks.

'These people are in financial trouble?' I hissed.

He nodded. 'Rule number one in business, Stevie, always keep your personal wealth separate from the company's. That way if everything goes down the plughole you can keep a clean pair of Guccis on your feet.'

Ambiguity was never one of Alex's faults. The embarrassment kept me quiet for all of thirty seconds.

'Is this a good idea?'

'Patience.'

'You said a little snooping around. I have a job I want to keep.'

'Relax, Stevie. No one except Eileen Sheldon and me knows that you're here.'

'Trust her, do we?'

A white sliding door, not unlike a Japanese shoji, slid back to reveal Eileen Sheldon.

To call her good looking was an understatement, and to describe her as elegant was merely stating the obvious. She was stunning; all five feet of her.

Her black hair fell to the shoulders and her pale skin had an almost doll-like quality, but it was the electric blue of her eyes that drew you. Here was a creature of such beauty, such poise, it was unnerving. A woman to die for.

She wore a black dress, but hardly widow's black. The thinnest of straps held it in place, and the hemline would have attracted the wrong kind of attention in a chapel of rest.

A gold chain holding a single large sapphire hung from her neck, and on her right hand was a ring with a white diamond cluster. The file had given her age as forty-five, but on sight you'd probably knock ten years off that.

I could see the strain of the past forty-eight hours in faint lines at the corners of her eyes, and although her make-up was perfect, I gained the impression she had been crying and had been forced to remake her face before we came in.

Alex and I got to our feet as she approached us, and part of me felt instinctively irritated for doing so.

She smiled and said hello to Alex. Then the blue eyes swung towards me, where they rested for the briefest of moments.

'Mr Jay?'

'Yes,' I managed.

'Please sit down.'

Without taking her eyes from us, she said, 'You can leave us now, Suzanne.'

The woman went out noiselessly while Alex and I sat like dogs.

She looked at our glasses. 'I think I'll join you.'

Drink in hand, she returned and sat down opposite us on another sofa. Reaching for a cigarette case on a wedge-shaped coffee table, she took a luxury-length filter tip and offered the case. We shook our heads in unison. She lit the cigarette and leaned back into the sofa, blowing smoke delicately from the corner of her mouth.

When she spoke she looked directly at me. 'Mr McGregor tells me that you are the principal investigator, Mr Jay.'

I looked at Alex.

'I did explain to you, Mrs Sheldon . . .' he began.

'It's been an horrific two days, Mr McGregor. Please tell me again.'

Alex smiled politely. 'Mr Jay has only just taken over the case.'

'Just?'

'Yesterday,' I broke in.

'But he has read and been briefed on the files,' added Alex.

'Files . . . yes, I'm afraid we have a history,' she said without irony.

'Your family attracts too many fires, Mrs Sheldon. Most people consider themselves unlucky if they experience one,' I said.

Alex spun, immediately uncomfortable, but she was unfazed.

'Attracts fires?'

'Yes.'

'I suppose we do, or at least someone seems determined that we do. Hopefully you're going to help stop them.'

'We are not the police, Mrs Sheldon. Mr Jay and I can only deal with the investigation of insurance matters,' said Alex.

She drew on the cigarette and blew the smoke slowly. For the first time she looked vulnerable.

'Why have the police arrested your daughter, Mrs Sheldon?' I asked.

'They're saying that she was seen entering the premises shortly before the fire broke out and that she has a history of starting fires.'

'You've seen your daughter since she was arrested?'

'Yes.'

'What does she say?'

'That she visited her father and that when she left he was working on some new lines in the design room between his flat and the shop on the ground floor.'

'Your husband had moved out?'

'Some months ago. As I'm sure you know, Mr Jay, we are . . . were going through a divorce.'

'Do you believe your daughter?'

'Stephanie loved her father, Mr Jay. She could no more kill him than I could.'

'You were in the throes of divorce,' I said neutrally.

She took a sip of her drink, her hand trembling as she did so. 'He was divorcing me.'

'Did you hate him for it?'

Alex practically did a back-flip. 'Stevie!'

'It's all right, Mr McGregor.' She turned to me again. 'Yes, I hated him. He was leaving me. I also loved him very much. Perhaps that's hard for you to understand?'

It wasn't. 'Make me understand,' I said.

She looked calm, unemotional, practised perhaps. 'Our business was in trouble. It was his life, his passion. He had been under tremendous stress. It's no secret that we argued. Eventually it all proved too much. I believe the Stratford fire was the final straw.'

'You seem to be blaming your business worries for your marriage breakdown. Do you believe that he still loved you?'

'Of course.'

'Of course?'

'Divorce doesn't mean the death of love, Mr Jay. Sometimes . . . sometimes people just can't live together any more, despite their love for each other.'

'So your daughter Stephanie didn't kill her father and you and he were madly in love?'

She drew on the cigarette. 'Madly, no. In love, yes.'

'Why are we here, Mrs Sheldon? You must know that we are investigating the possibility of your family's involvement in an insurance fraud. Why entertain us?'

She downed the remainder of her drink, got up and walked over to the minibar and topped up her glass. She brought the decanter back and placed it on the coffee table.

'Do help yourselves,' she said.

Alex topped up his drink. I shook my head and waited for her to reply. She took her time. When the answer eventually came it hit me straight between the eyes.

'My husband is dead, Mr Jay, my business is crumbling around me, and my daughter is being held by the police. I can do nothing about the first, little apparently about the second, but my daughter is precious to me. I won't give her up. I want to hire you, Mr Jay.'

'Me?'

'Yes, to prove my daughter's innocence.'

'That's not possible.'

'I'll pay double your present rate of pay.'

'It's still not possible . . .'

'And if you are successful I'll give you ten thousand pounds.'

Chapter Ten

Every insolvent has his price.

So numerous were the reasons for refusing to take the offer I didn't even try. Eileen Sheldon had offered me a 'get out of jail free' card and I wasn't going to let a little thing like zero experience get in the way of that.

Throughout this surreal exchange Alex had sat very still. He watched her, but I knew his senses were tuned to me.

I heard myself say, 'What happened to your cash flow crisis, Mrs Sheldon?'

She looked at the diamond cluster on her hand and without theatre slipped it from her finger. 'This is worth twice that. If all my shops burn to the ground tomorrow I'm still good for the money.'

'And if what I dig up proves she's guilty?'

'It won't.'

'Humour me.'

There was the suggestion of a shrug. 'Then you'll tell me first and you'll get half.'

I nodded. 'I have another condition.'

I could feel Alex's agitation like a sonic wave, but still he said nothing.

'Name it,' she said.

'This will be a one-off payment. You don't hire me as such, just pay the lump sum when I turn my findings over to you.'

I caught Alex's eye, and I swear I saw some admiration there, but then again it could have been the Scotch.

She took her time answering, and I could read nothing in her face. That worried me. There should have been something, anything, but the voice, the body language, the gestures even, were all neutral.

We were negotiating proving the innocence of her daughter, but the tone was of cutting a business deal. I felt that there were so many layers to Eileen Sheldon that you could dig for years and never get close to the bedrock.

What had she read in me? A knight or a pawn?

She pushed the ring back on her finger and sat down, her body straighter than before, like she was preparing for a confessional. 'Agreed,' she said finally, and extended her hand towards Alex.

He looked a little bemused, but took it all the same. Then it was my turn. She lifted her head a little and then hit me with a smile. It didn't seem like she was trying to flirt, but it was impossible not to be aware of her beauty. I knew another woman who did that and the thought made me wary.

'If I am to prove your daughter's innocence you're going to have to be very open with me, Mrs Sheldon. I'd like you to start by telling me about the fires Stephanie started five years ago.'

'A number of years ago, before the first of the small fires,' she began, 'my husband and I had been going through a sticky patch. Put simply, I found out he was having an affair.'

The word 'affair' was forced out, and as she said it she wrapped an arm around her waist protectively.

'We argued quite badly,' she continued. 'It hurt. I felt . . . humiliated, more so because he refused to give her up.'

'Did you know who it was?'

'Yes.'

'Who?'

'That's not really our business, Stevie,' put in Alex.

She shrugged, as if it no longer mattered, but I thought for the first time that the casualness was forced.

'A young woman I knew, not much more than a girl.'

'Name?'

She crossed her legs. 'Rachel.'

'Surname?'

'I . . . I didn't know her that well. She worked part time in one of our shops. My husband hired her. Evidently there was a price.'

'What happened to her?'

'Pardon?'

'You said your husband wouldn't give her up. What happened to her? Did you fire her?'

'I . . . we paid her off.'

'Paid her off? What does that mean?'

She wasn't enjoying the questions, but she'd brought up the affair and for all her outward calm I felt I'd hit a nerve.

'We gave her a sum of money to go away.'

'Why would you do that? You could have sacked her.'

She ground her cigarette out in the ashtray and immediately lit another from the case. I saw her glance at Alex, as though to draw him into the exchange. He ignored her and sat tight.

'The girl made it clear she wanted money, Mr Jay.'

'So it wasn't your idea?'

'Does it matter?'

I hesitated. As deftly as a boxer trapped in a corner, she'd swung me round and had me defending.

'We're supposed to be examining the motives of people who could be targeting you, Mrs Sheldon. First you said your husband wouldn't give this woman up and then you said she wanted money to go away. Perhaps she felt she had reason to get back at you or your husband.'

She shook her head. 'The money we gave her was generous. She took it and left. There was no reason to get back at us.'

'So she's not contacted you or your husband since?'

There was the briefest suggestion of a pause. 'No.'

'And your husband just accepted that?'

'When he saw what it was doing to Stephanie he let go.'

'So Stephanie knew about all this affair?'

She gave a short nod. 'I think at first she suspected; later, she knew. The rows between my husband and myself had got worse. I believe Stephanie may have started the fires as a sort of protest. It just got out of hand, that's all.' Her eyes hardened. 'She's not deranged, if that's what you're thinking.'

'At the moment I'm just listening. Go on.'

'The last of the fires was quite serious, and when a member of our staff caught her, something urgent had to be done.'

'Who was this member of staff?'

'The manageress of the shop where the fire was, I believe.'

'Her name?'

She shook her head.

'Could you find out for me? You must keep employment records. Does she still work for you?'

'I've already told you, my husband dealt with hiring staff. Most of the staff records were kept at the Ilford shop and were, I imagine, destroyed.'

'So you don't know if she still works for you?'

'We may have paid her off.'

'Another person paid off?'

She looked at Alex again. 'Look, none of this was very pleasant for me. The truth is I made my husband get rid of the manageress. It was bad enough being held up to ridicule by my husband's affair, but there was no way I was going to see my daughter suffer by having her name linked to arson. He'd made the mistake. I thought it only right that he should pay for the deceit.'

The heavy rain was beating noiselessly against the window and vivid forks of purple-white light split the night sky, throwing up brief silhouettes of the South London shoreline across the water.

Eileen Sheldon's ultra-modern penthouse, with its stark interior and monochrome tones, was an artificial sanctuary, a void, but one that promised only temporary respite. The police, the press, and her sins were threatening to break through and engulf her.

'You were saying that you felt your husband should pay for his mistakes. What happened next?'

'We all received counselling.'

'All of you?'

'Stephanie, my husband and myself. The psychologist thought that it was a family issue and could only be dealt with if we all faced up to what had happened and dealt with it.'

'And?'

'Sorry?'

'What was the outcome? Did Stephanie ever repeat this business of starting fires?'

'No.'

'So the fires stopped immediately after the counselling?'

'Yes.'

'This Rachel and the manageress were paid off, and you all went back to being a happy family?'

'Not at first, but we coped. Eventually things got better.'

'So the past was the past? No hangovers . . . except of course your husband decided to divorce you some five years later.'

'I have explained that.'

'If Stephanie was upset by your husband's affair, how did she feel about him divorcing you?'

'Hurt and angry.'

'As angry as five years ago?'

'Not angry enough to kill, Mr Jay.'

'What about your son?'

'Michael? Why do you . . .'

She was interrupted by the shoji-like door behind her sliding back, to reveal Suzanne, the woman who had shown us in earlier.

'Excuse me a moment, please.'

Eileen Sheldon stood up and went over to her and they spoke quietly. Suzanne kept looking over at us with a worried expression. I saw Eileen Sheldon shake her head once, and it looked for a moment like she was going to protest, but then stepped back and slid the door shut again.

Alex leaned across and whispered, 'You're pushing a bit hard, Stevie.'

'She's brighter than the pair of us and I have no intention of getting drawn into any word games. Better to keep her off balance, for now anyway.'

He grinned maliciously. 'Well, it's your ten thousand you're playing with.'

Eileen Sheldon returned and said, 'I'm sorry about that.'

'Something important?' I asked.

She waved her hand dismissively and sat down, curling her legs up on to the sofa. She gave a tired smile and said, 'What were you saying?'

'I was asking about your son, Michael.'

'What about him?'

'Did he share Stephanie's feelings over the affair?'

'Yes, as you might expect with twins.'

'Twins?' I looked at Alex.

His face darkened, and he mumbled that it wasn't on the file.

'It's hardly a secret, Mr McGregor,' she said quickly.

Uncomfortable and clearly angry, he shook his head slowly. 'I can't explain that.'

There was a strained silence. With the backside hanging out of our credibility, the only thing to do was press on and hope nothing else too embarrassing broke the surface, but hope was about to disappear over the horizon with its arse on fire.

'Your son was involved in the business?' I asked.

'Of course. Stephanie worked on design as an assistant to me, and Michael helped his father run the business.'

'How does James Chasteau fit into the picture?'

'Chasteau? Oh, you mean Ladyfair.'

'Yes.'

'Ladyfair was our partner in the warehouse.'

'The one at Stratford?'

'Yes. Robin and I had our own label which we called Robes, as in Rob and E for Eileen and S for Sheldon. Our label formed the backbone of our business, although we supplied other lines as well.'

'Why Ladyfair?'

'They supplied us with some of those other lines and we went into partnership to franchise certain shops, to sell the Robes label. That meant we needed more warehouse space, and Ladyfair owned the Stratford warehouse. Later we bought a share in the warehouse.'

'What was Stephanie doing at the warehouse on the night of the fire?'

'She had stayed behind to work on some new lines.'

'Our file shows her as having left the building at eight-thirty with James Chasteau.'

She frowned. 'James Chasteau?'

'You said that he was the partner in the warehouse.'

'No I didn't. You did. I said we went into partnership with Ladyfair.'

'But wasn't Ladyfair owned by Chasteau?'

'No. In fact until you mentioned the name just now I hadn't heard it since we first entered into negotiation with Ladyfair.'

I gave Alex a hard stare. 'Who owns Ladyfair?'

She looked from Alex to me, her expression somewhere between amusement and disbelief. 'Stephanie's fiancée, Kris Mayle.'

Chapter Eleven

There had been no point in continuing the interview following Eileen Sheldon's revelations. Alex had looked embarrassed, but not entirely surprised, which meant explanations were due.

Going down in the lift, neither of us spoke. It was only when we drove out of the underground carpark that Alex attempted an apology.

'I know what you're thinking, but I'm as sick as you are, Stevie.'

I snatched a sideways look and then spoke at the windscreen. 'We must have looked total prats.'

'Aye.'

'How could you investigate this case for six months and not know that Mayle was the owner of Ladyfair? Or, for that matter, that Michael and Stephanie Sheldon are twins?'

There was a heavy silence. Alex stared ahead through the rain, the frustration evident in every line of his body.

'It's complex, Stevie.'

'Try me.'

He drummed his fingers on the dashboard, having

a private argument with himself. When he spoke his voice was thick.

'In the Lifeboat you asked why we hadn't gone to a proper inquiry agent . . .'

'Yes, I did.'

'Well, the reason was we already had one.'

'You've lost me.'

'We had a man, on retainer, an ex-detective sergeant with the Met, Roley Benson.'

'So why use me?'

Alex rarely lost his temper, but when he did it was volcanic. These eruptions were always preceded by a period of quiet. I didn't think the anger was coming in my direction, but it was apparent that someone was due an earful. Then, instead of the expected explosion, he closed his eyes and let out a long sigh.

'Andrew knows one or two people in the Met,' he said quietly. 'Six months ago one of these people approached him and said that they had a chap retiring, a Detective Sergeant Roland Benson. Andrew was told that this chap was a hero. He'd been decorated for bravery.'

'Decorated for what exactly?'

He loosened his tie and ran a finger around inside his collar.

'Benson and another copper had been involved in the arrest of a drugs dealer. During the arrest the other copper was savagely stabbed, lost an eye and a lung. Benson was also stabbed, but managed to overpower the man and arrest him.'

'Sounds heroic enough for me.'

'Problem was that the other copper died a few weeks after the stabbing. Benson had a breakdown and was pensioned off. What Andrew wasn't told was that Roley Benson had a drink problem as a result of his experience.'

'Andrew retained a drunk as any inquiry agent?'

'Aye.'

'When did you find out about the drink problem?'

'Two weeks ago.'

'How?'

'Roley had been handling the Stratford warehouse investigation for us. He was supposed to be working on it full time. At first he seemed okay – he had connections in the Met and seemed to be putting them to good use. Within a short while, though, he became unreliable.'

'How does that work?'

'We couldn't get him on the phone and he never seemed to be at home. The only way we kept track of him was through his expense claims. Then he had a car accident.'

'Drunk?'

'Rotten! So smashed he'd piled into several parked cars – lucky to get away with a broken arm. Tried to say he'd been run off the road.'

'You didn't believe him?'

'No. Neither did the police.' Alex half turned towards me. 'He was pissed as a handcart, Stevie, and conveniently there were no witnesses.'

'So you sacked him?'

'Andrew did. I went to see Benson to retrieve some of the so-called evidence that he'd collated in the time we were paying him. Most of it was nonsense, irrelevant. Basically an excuse to hit us with expense claims. There were, however, one or two bits of interest. One of which was the photograph of Robin Sheldon and Mayle.'

'And you thought of me?'

He nodded. 'When the Ilford fire occurred I rang Andrew and suggested you. With the investigation bordering on farce, he was happy to step back and let me decide.'

'So why didn't you take it to a proper inquiry agent?'

Alex took his time answering, and when he did it was like he was reasoning aloud. I realised that he must have been under some pressure himself.

'No one likes cleaning up after somebody else's mistakes, Stevie. What we had was a case six months old that had been screwed up by a drunken ex-copper. Look, I meant what I said in the Lifeboat. You were made for this, plus you have access to Brigade files and the Fire Investigation Teams. We needed to get someone on the case fast.'

'Why is it that I finally believe you?'

He gripped my arm. 'I'm truly sorry, Stevie. I should have told you at the beginning.'

'Yes, you should have, but then I'd never have been offered ten grand.'

'Now that I had no prior knowledge of.'

The rain was easing off and I picked up speed. I was rapidly running through all the implications of what I heard, both from Alex and Eileen Sheldon, none of which put me off. In fact my curiosity had never been more aroused. Ten grand will do that to you.

'You'd met Eileen Sheldon before?'

'Once, shortly after the warehouse fire. I interviewed her and Robin Sheldon together. It was obvious we needed an inquiry agent to get anywhere.'

'You said in the Lifeboat that Robin Sheldon was a smoothie.'

Alex let out a bitter chuckle.

'Slippery. I don't think any of the questions I asked dented him. He was clever and devious. The police didn't appear to like him much either. Andrew figured Roley Benson was a good way of finding out what they knew. And in fairness to Andrew, at the time it seemed a good move.'

'And?'

'Roley found out that the Sheldons were in deep financial shit. They were closing premises by the week and losing the business of the franchised shops. The fire at Stratford was just too convenient.'

'But Benson found no evidence of fraud?'

'No.'

'Can I have everything you got from him?'

'Of course.'

'What reason did Eileen Sheldon give you for wanting to speak to us tonight?'

'To discuss Stephanie.'

'Not to take a look at the new investigator, then?'

He frowned. 'I'd not even considered it. Why would she want to do that?'

'I don't know, but just let's suppose for a moment that Roley Benson was proving to be a pain. Someone takes the decision to take him out of the game . . . run him off the road. A new man is appointed and you want to see the measure of the opposition. Just a thought.'

Alex chewed on that for a moment and then shook his head.

'Roley Benson crashed his car while blind drunk. Apart from the background material on how the Sheldons' businesses were going, I don't believe he found out anything useful.'

I listened carefully to the irritation in Alex's voice. It was as though he was only just weighing up the extent of the damage that employing Roley Benson had wrought.

A change of subject seemed in order.

'What do you make of Eileen Sheldon?'

He didn't answer automatically, so I repeated the question.

'Enigmatic . . . and sad.'

'Enigmatic? Yes. Sad I'm not so sure about. My instinct tells me she's hiding something.'

He cranked his head to one side. 'Tell me why.'

'Don't know.'

He nodded. 'So, Eileen Sheldon's got something to hide?'

'No. At least, not in the sense that she's deliberately keeping stuff from us, although that's more than possible. No, what I mean is that she's frightened, so frightened she's in denial over it. I wouldn't have thought she could tell us even if she wanted to.'

'How d'you arrive at that?'

'Gut feeling.'

He pulled a face. 'Nothing so ordinary as fact, then?'

'In the absence of fact gut feeling is better than diddly squat.'

He took out a cigar and twirled it in his fingers, debating whether to light it. He settled on sticking it in the corner of his mouth, unlit.

'You're definitely going to take up her offer, Stevie?'

I smiled. 'Why not? It gives me direct access to her and through her to everybody else.'

'That's very useful, but it places you in a potentially awkward spot. Dual loyalties.'

'Not exactly. What I am worried about, though, is Mayle being so close to the Sheldons. He knows I'm in the Fire Brigade.'

'Tread very softly, then. Don't go near him directly. Anything you find out you let me deal with.'

'Christ, how I'd like that bastard to be in this up to his neck.'

'Now that, Stevie, would be righteous.'

We arrived back at Alex's around half-ten and spent more than an hour going over everything again. At my insistence, Alex dug out a folder with the sheaf of papers that comprised Roley Benson's report.

One glance and I saw why Alex hadn't been impressed. It was no more than a series of rough notes of conversations with shop girls and cab drivers, for the main part interviewed in pubs. There were no times and few dates or addresses, though every last drink or meal was carefully itemised or backed up by a receipt.

Knowing that we couldn't take a chance on being professionally embarrassed again, we agreed to keep each other informed of all developments.

It was then, having talked the Sheldon case into the deck, that Alex made his second attempt of the evening to drag me back into boxing training. I talked him out of replaying the video of the Duran fight, but he'd decided his mission was to rescue me from sloth and he wouldn't be deterred.

'Why not?'

'That's not the question, Alex, is it?'

'Oh?' He was leaning back in his easy chair in the den, and saw no irony in lecturing me on physical fitness while consuming a huge glass of malt.

'Come on, Alex, my life's complex enough at the

moment, some of which is your doing, and the last thing I need is to get bashed by some ex-bruiser.'

'It's exactly what you need.' He said it with a straight face.

I stared up at the ceiling, trying to avoid the hex he was putting on me. Boxing had been very important to me at one time, as had fitness in general, but that part of me had been pushed on to the back burner. Reviving it could be painful in more ways than one.

'Spare me the "life is a question of balance" speech. My life's been in a tailspin for so long I've grown to like the g-force distorting my features.'

He scoffed. 'You? Giving in? I doubt it.'

'Look, even if the idea appealed, which it doesn't, I would need to get fit before I showed my face at a gym. Boxing clubs aren't as user friendly as fitness centres.'

He put his feet up on the desk. 'Run, then.'

'Just like that?'

'Aye.'

'I'm thirty-three years of age, Alex.'

'Fitness. That's all we're talking here.'

'No we're not.'

'Just try it, that's all I'm saying.'

Finally, to shut him up, I agreed to look in at his boxing club Tuesday evening.

'Good man.'

'I'm not sparring. I'll come and watch.'

'Good man.'

'If I do anything it'll be bag work.'

'Aye.'

'And stop bloody agreeing with me.'

I left him an hour later, after having my earlier decision reversed and being browbeaten into watching the Duran fight again. Despite my protests I enjoyed it, as of course the old bastard knew I would; Alex used a caveman's club with a surgeon's skill.

The flat was quiet when I entered.

The promise that I'd made Jenny, about not being late, had been forgotten almost before I'd reached Alex's.

I found her asleep on the sofa with a glass in her hand and a half-empty wine bottle on the floor beside her. A table lamp gave a soft light to the room, and in its mute glow she looked incredibly beautiful.

Quietly, I sat down in an armchair and studied her.

How had I let her escape? What in my life had distracted me enough not to give her what she needed? How would I make it right this time?

Could I forget the past and let her back? Really let her back? Or were we destined to circle each other, warily, defensively, until my nerve broke or she gave up?

Once, when we were tearing pieces from each other, she had accused me of not allowing her to get close. She'd said that it was a legacy of my childhood. I had been abandoned and could not, would not, give myself to love. I held back, afraid, needing love, but unable to surrender to it.

I didn't accept it then. I felt she was justifying her

own behaviour, her betrayal, with Mayle, but was there truth among the lies? Had I grasped at anger as a defence?

Sitting there, in the flat that had once been my prison, I realised that whatever the rights and wrongs I had been given a second chance. She was here, with me, had earlier that day crawled naked into my bed and embraced me.

There could be no looking back. If I wanted her then I had to be strong enough to let the past go.

I stood up, walked through to the bedroom and turned back the duvet. Then returned to the living room and gently picked her up.

Instinctively, still wrapped in sleep, her arms came up and closed around my neck as her face burrowed into the fold between my neck and my shoulder.

'Kris,' she whispered.

Chapter Twelve

Sunday, 19 April

The early morning mist clung to the trees like bunches of chiffon and lay as tattered ribbons across the still, damp, glistening hillside. The sky held the promise that later the sun would strengthen and burn off the mist, for already there were rents in its fabric, enabling me to look down from the heights of Orange Tree Hill towards the concrete rim of Romford.

Beyond, across an enormous patchwork of roofs, lay the town centre; proud of its status as the owner of new precinct developments and oblivious to the fact that, like so many others of its kind, it was squandering its character, its past, its soul in the rush to build and consume people's money.

Here, upon the hill that dominated the skyline, the countryside could still display tall trees amidst fields and the feral beauty of horses running free.

I had paused on the crest to take in the view, hands on hips, breathing deeply and feeling my heart pound. The run up from Lower Bedfords had mocked any pretensions I might have had about retaining fitness from fighting days. Over the last quarter of a mile of steep roadside my breath had come in gasps and my legs had been unwilling to respond.

Alex knew what he was doing when he stirred up the past. During the months that Jenny had lived with Mayle, I had taken out all my aggression on a heavy bag suspended in the bedroom doorway of the flat.

I had beat it each and every day, pounding it furiously until my arms ached, my lungs burned and the crushing futility of it had finally percolated the self-obsessed wall I had built around me.

Angrily I had cut down the bag and thrown it away, along with bag-gloves and skipping rope; another grand gesture that amounted to little more than personal improvised nasal surgery.

From the summit of Orange Tree Hill, however, life held the prospect of something very different. Alex had sparked a feeling of guilt that I had taken an easy option. With the intriguing prospect of the Sheldon case, the lure of ten grand and the knowledge that Jenny was back, I had a future.

Her unconscious use of Mayle's first name when I'd lifted her the previous night could have destroyed me, but I'd refused to let it. It had been a small thing, a product of instinct, of sleep and a residue of the past.

So I had set out on a run to blow away old cobwebs: exercise to exorcise.

Alex had been right; part of the cure could be had by getting down to his boxing club and putting the gloves on again. If I was honest I missed the burst of adrenaline that came from the pressure of sparring and the grudging acceptance of boxers that was extended to anyone prepared to climb into the ring.

It didn't end with getting Jenny back; I had to get myself back as well.

I waited until my breathing steadied, then set off along the loop of Broxhill, down to Lower Bedfords, where I'd parked my car, my mind more focused than it had been in months.

Downhill was easier.

Back at the flat, Jenny had risen and read my note. Breakfast was being cooked and the aromas of the food and coffee made my stomach growl.

'How was it?' She cocked her head to one side and smiled.

'Hard.' I took off my wool cap and wiped the film of sweat from my face. A dark semicircle extended down the front of my sweatshirt. I hoped the tremor in my shocked leg muscles didn't show.

Her face was full of mischief. 'The ambitions of the mind . . .'

'. . . And the limitations of the body. Tell me about it.'

'How long will you be?'

'Give me ten minutes.'

I showered and changed into jeans and a heavy cotton shirt. Through the half-open doorway I could hear her singing softly. It felt strange; the energy between us was as if the episode with Mayle had never happened.

As I entered the kitchen, Jenny had her back to me. Absorbed in the cooking, she didn't hear me. Instinctively my arms went around her waist. She spun and kissed me.

There was no awkwardness this time. We acted on pure reflex, our bodies needing neither permission nor signals. Close in, we thought and acted as one.

Her head rolled back and she whispered, 'It'll burn.'

I kissed her softly and let her go. She turned back to the cooking.

Unable to take my eyes from her, I stood and watched, fascinated by the reality that she was back.

Everything about her was feminine, sensual, and it had always been that sensuality that had drawn me. The feel of her was incredible. Especially after love-making, when we had lain together, skin on skin, her back towards me, foetal, my arms around, hands on her breasts; the deepest needs within me satisfied.

The sex between us had been darker.

Then we were different people. Predatory, possessive, each claiming the other. The heat of wanting needing its own satisfaction, the control vanishing as nihilistic hunger engulfed us, wilful, reckless, until sated.

Now she was back, the light and the dark.

There was something in her movement. She was

wearing nothing beneath the angora jumper. I took hold of her waist and then slipped my hands under the soft woollen fabric. She gasped and bowed her head, her eyes closing as I kissed the back of her neck and took her breasts in my hands.

She turned off the cooker and her hands came up and took mine.

Without looking back, she led the way into the bedroom. There she stopped and stood, allowing me to stroke, hold and kiss her, but she didn't face me.

Instead, still with her back to me, she pulled the jumper over her head.

I kissed her shoulders and neck and slowly she turned her cheek towards me, her eyes closed fast. Wrapping one arm around her waist, I undid the top button of her slacks and with the other hand slowly slid down to her sex.

Still she kept her back to me.

As I touched her, her head rolled from side to side, her eyes closed and her mouth half open. I knelt, kissing the length of her back and pulling the slacks to her feet. She stepped out of them, still turned away, still waiting.

I ran my hands into each and every fold, tracing her outline with my fingertips, caressing the warm silk of her body. She moved in response to my touch and a small shudder coursed her body, but still she wouldn't turn; still she waited.

'I love you,' I whispered.

Now she turned. Now she kissed me.

Fierce tears ran down her face as her tongue found mine and she clawed at my shirt, pulling it from my shoulders and throwing it aside. I reached for her, but she shook her head and pulled away from me.

Kneeling, she pulled my jeans to the floor, making me stand there as she touched, kissed and probed; making me wait, making me want.

Her tongue licked. I thought I would explode.

When I couldn't stand it any more I reached down and lifted her up. She buried her head in my chest, but I took her face in my hands and licked away the tears. Then I kissed her eyes, her lips, her throat, before lifting her and placing her on the bed.

We made love, slowly.

I awoke half an hour later, with Jenny cuddled into me, the warmth of her body protection against previous and regressive wisdoms.

Jenny's body and, of course, Eileen Sheldon's words, for my anger with Alex during the drive from her penthouse wasn't born of embarrassment; it was shock mixed with disbelief.

Kris Mayle was Stephanie Sheldon's fiancé back in November, at the time of the Stratford warehouse fire. That was the same time that Jenny had left me for him. So if Mayle was still Stephanie Sheldon's fiancé, then what the hell had being going on during Jenny's absence from me?

I knew then why she had come back. I knew then that she must have found out about Stephanie and had run, hurt and panicked, back to the only place she had to go. It wasn't flattering, it wasn't romance, and it wasn't what I'd have chosen, but ironically it was about the only thing that could have laid the ghosts in my head.

That was why Jenny mentioning his name while asleep the previous evening didn't matter, because she had no way back to him. Stephanie Sheldon had money, lots of it, and Jenny, for all her charms, couldn't match that, not where Mayle was concerned.

I could just imagine her finding out; sweet Jesus, the fireworks must have been impressive. Jen never took defeat lightly. She would have been a howling banshee; vengeful, shrill, wanting blood under her nails. I'd take any bet that she'd left her mark on him.

So I knew why she was back.

I hadn't any doubt that she could twist the logic in her head so that it came out as her choice; but my cynicism was small challenge to my need. As long as I knew what the game was I could cope. It was the uncertainty that had always consumed me, that and the betrayal.

By default she was mine again, and this time I would not lose her.

There could be no more slip-ups or reckless fishing expeditions. And any mention of knowing about Mayle and Stephanie Sheldon would be fatal. Pragmatism might shape my own choices, but with Jenny it would be pride.

So I lay next to her, enjoying the sensation of her

nakedness against me, and made a promise to myself never to use what I knew in anger. She'd been hurt, and I cared for her. I knew whatever face she put on it she must have been beaten up inside.

After a while I slipped from her arms and out of the bed. Quietly I got dressed, retrieved my grip bag from under the bed and went through to the living room.

Alex had given me the last of the Sheldon files the night before. Most of it consisted of an untidy bundle of notes and receipts from Roley Benson, and it was easy to see why Alex had been so dismissive. The handwriting was a scrawl and, as he'd said, more often than not dates and times were missing.

I tried to get them into some kind of order.

The only pattern, if you could call it that, was a batch of three scribbled notes and receipts stapled together with the letter 'M' in the top right-hand corner of each piece of paper. Was that Mayle or Michael?

Each receipt was for the same place; the bar of a hotel called the Amery Lodge. There was no address. The drinks bought were always the same, a bottle of high-alcohol Pils, a Scotch and glass of white wine. Knowing Roley Benson's history, it was a fair bet that both the Pils and Scotch were for him. Did the white wine suggest a woman?

The only other item of interest was a sheet from a spiral notepad with the names 'Ruth Heller/Sheldon – connection?' Again there was an 'M' in the corner.

I would have to meet up with Roley Benson and ask a few questions. Alex had said that he'd been paid off, so there shouldn't be a problem with him parting with any information he might have, and if there was ... well, I had half an idea what his weakness might be.

Maybe Alex was right and the receipts and notes were a waste of time, but the fact that he'd claimed to meet the same person three times suggested that Benson had been working on something.

Among the notes were Benson's address and phone number, although Alex had left the cryptic message – 'Unobtainable – disconnected?'

I don't suppose bills were a priority when you needed a drink.

I decided to spend the rest of the day with Jenny. There were so many bits and pieces of information floating around inside my head that I needed time to absorb and grade them. Then I would decide the next move, though I had it in mind to reconnect with Eileen Sheldon pretty quickly.

Before we'd left the penthouse she'd said an application for bail would be made on Monday; if successful I would ask for an interview with Stephanie early in the week.

There were lots of leads to chase, but the same could be said of a bowl of spaghetti.

I put everything back into the grip bag and stowed it behind the sofa.

Jenny still hadn't stirred, so I made coffee and

woke her. She smiled as she opened hers eyes, and reached up for my neck.

'Kiss me,' she said.

I kissed her and felt myself become aroused again.

'Come back to bed,' she whispered.

Early afternoon we drove out to Bedfords Park and watched the red deer in their enclosure. This time of year the stags were devoid of antlers, but they were still impressive beasts.

I always felt it was wrong to confine them.

From time to time we got called to road accidents involving deer, but they were usually the smaller fallow deer that ran wild in the area. We'd also had one or two calls to fallow deer stuck between railings; a consequence of the local yobs chasing them with dogs.

The thought that wild deer roamed the hills and woods overlooking Romford was satisfying, the product of being brought up in the city, where trees were sparse and grey and the wildlife consisted of cats and dogs and the occasional policeman's horse.

I must have been more lost in reverie than I realised, for out of the corner of my eye I caught Jenny grinning at me.

She squeezed my arm. 'Happy?'

'I like it here,' I said simply.

'This is Wanstead for you. Isn't it?'

'Sort of.'

'Want to try and catch sticklebacks?'

'Wrong time of year.'

'Oh. Caterpillars, then?'

'Same.'

We walked through the park with the earlier sunshine threatened by dark clouds rolling in from the east. After a while a thin drizzle fell, pearling our coats and making the grass slippery.

Neither of us complained.

The park was deserted, the final visitors driven away by the wind that had picked up and turned the drizzle to rain.

'It's going to get worse,' I said.

'Drink, then?' said Jenny.

I nodded. 'How about the Morris Man at South Weald?'

Her eyes sparkled. 'That was the first place you ever took me.'

'Was it?'

Chapter Thirteen

Monday, 20 April, 7.45 a.m.

'Are you awake?'

I opened my eyes to see Jenny leaning over me.

She was dressed in a charcoal-grey business suit and for a moment I was puzzled, then remembered that she'd mentioned a job interview the previous day.

'I'm going now.' She reached out and brushed a lank lock of hair from my forehead.

'Wish me luck,' she said.

'You won't need luck.'

She kissed me.

The Sunday had stripped three years from our relationship. After the pub, we had called in on John and Sarah Blane. John was surprised, but delighted to see us. Sarah, always the earth mother, hugged us both and smiled so much it was embarrassing.

She dragged Jenny into the kitchen at the first opportunity.

Left alone, John and I talked about everything except the job. A few times I found him searching my face, perhaps looking for the fatigue and stress he had seen there only a few days before; whatever it was he saw now, he seemed reassured.

After a while Jenny and Sarah joined us and over Sunday afternoon tea and cake we immersed ourselves in the warmth of the Blane household.

Jenny was aglow and I felt brand new.

We'd stayed for an hour and left them on the doorstep, beaming like approving parents. Then we drove back to the flat and made love again.

'Where's the interview?'

'Brentwood. Are you out tonight?'

I shook my head.

She smiled. 'Good.'

With Jenny gone, I closed my eyes and dozed until half-eight.

I spent breakfast going over the case file and drawing up a list of priorities. There was plenty to do, but just in case I missed it Alex had laid it on the line when I left him Saturday night. 'If your life wasn't complicated enough, Stevie, you now have two goals. First you have to find out who started the warehouse fire, and second you have to prove Stephanie Sheldon innocent of the murder of her father. Take care you don't screw yourself.'

Despite his warning we both knew Eileen Sheldon's offer was remarkable and too tempting to refuse. None of which stopped me from feeling like a donkey entered for the Grand National.

So top of the list was a rematch with Eileen Sheldon, and with luck, if Stephanie Sheldon made bail, she was next. I needed to speak to them separately, but I had a feeling that this would prove difficult. Eileen Sheldon was fiercely protective.

In the meantime there was plenty to keep me occupied.

I searched the Yellow Pages and found the Amery Lodge. The ad described it as being in South Woodford, comfortably furnished with a well-appointed location and good road links. If that was the best they could come up with, then it wasn't at the luxury end of the market. I jotted down the address.

Finally, around ten, I left the flat and went in search of a fast photo shop. I found one in South Street, ordered three sets of enlarged prints and was told that they'd be available late afternoon.

Then I drove to East Ham.

Roley Benson had a big, red-brick 1930s house at the back of Central Park, an area in South Newham that was once considered smart. Estate agents would have you believe it was still the cat's drawers, but like the rest of the borough it was on the slide. The Byzantine local politics ensured that.

I found it easily enough, but Roley wasn't home. Either that or he wasn't answering the door. I poked a note through the letterbox explaining who I was and asking him to give me a bell. I mentioned that there was a drink in it for him.

Next on my list was bear-baiting.

Stephanie Sheldon's bail hearing was to be at Stratford, some time after lunch. Even if Eileen

Sheldon hadn't told me I would have known; every newspaper carried the story.

Stratford should have been only twenty minutes from Central Park, but the traffic was snarled from Green Street onwards and eventually I arrived at the court a little after twelve.

On asking, I was told that the hearing was due in Court One at two-fifteen. With an hour and a half to kill, I decided that Alex owed me lunch and found a steakhouse just off the Broadway.

Over a chunk of rare porterhouse and a low-alcohol beer I asked myself a few questions and admitted that although the main reason for attending the bail hearing was Stephanie Sheldon, my deeper need was to see Kris Mayle. Preferably without him seeing me, for the moment at least.

The last time I'd set eyes on him had been at a shop launch, shortly before Jenny had left me. There had been a look in his eye that night, a look that had haunted me throughout Jenny's absence.

It was as she had approached him to discuss the handing over of the shop. He smiled on seeing her and then realised she wasn't alone. He'd glanced over her shoulder and our eyes met. His smile was naked contempt, and he didn't care that I saw it. It was then that the penny had finally dropped.

In that moment, I felt the weakness of the betrayed and knew that he could see it in my face. It was as though something was falling from me, accelerating away, leaving me hollowed out and empty.

Jenny caught his look and glanced back at me. Her attempted smile of reassurance made me feel a fool.

Afterwards, I told myself that I was wrong, that I had no proof. There's no greater shame than lying to yourself, but my need of her was so strong that I stayed in denial until she disappeared.

So I needed to see him, to choose my moment to look into his eyes and be sure that that look was no longer there.

After lunch I headed back for the court and was still a hundred yards out when I glanced up and saw the hackfest.

I had expected some kind of press presence, but nothing like the mob that had descended. The court-house entrance was seething. There must have been fifty or more of them.

I shouldn't have been surprised. Nowadays hard news belonged to the brothers and sisters of cable and satellite, and they were leaving everyone else dead in their wake. Under that kind of handicap, to your average hack, a case like the Sheldons' was a godsend. On offer were class, tainted money and an oven-ready carcass to pick over.

It was Christmas and Hallowe'en all rolled into one.

The paparazzi were in their element, snapping at anything that vaguely approached the court; hoping for that sweet shot that was going to tie the whole story down to a haunted look and a grainy image.

I would have to tread carefully; the last thing I

needed was my face on the fringes of a front-page spread.

Intent on avoiding them, I walked past and crossed the road a hundred yards down, but I wasn't the only one with the idea and in my haste nearly walked straight into trouble.

A white Mercedes pulled up ten yards short of me, and out of the driver's side jumped the smooth-looking young guy from the warehouse. At the same time the passenger door opened and out climbed the shaven-headed pug.

I stood still. Neither so much as looked at me.

The pug jumped behind the wheel and drove off and the young guy ran towards the court entrance, pulling his jacket over his head at the last moment. A volley of flashes greeted him and, seizing my chance, I walked nonchalantly in behind him, virtually unnoticed.

Inside, the spectators' gallery was full, and the usher was doing her best to control the mixed crowd of press and public.

Grateful that their antics allowed me to remain unobserved, I tried to see where Eileen Sheldon was seated and I cranked my head through a hundred and eighty degrees, but all I could see was three empty chairs behind the defence desk.

The noise was building by the minute, and the usher recruited two policemen to help control it. Overcome by the drama of the moment, a paparazzo ignored the signs all around the room and flashed a shot.

The policemen tore into the pack and ejected the idiot photographer before he could disappear into the crowd.

I wouldn't have wanted them on my back, but they were definitely entertainment.

Over the far side of the court a door opened and in walked a large, florid-faced barrister flanked by a female clerk holding a cache of books and files, and a round-faced guy in pin-stripes with a briefcase.

Behind these came Eileen Sheldon, dressed in a tailored full-length black coat with a black pillbox hat and veil. At her throat was a bone-white silk scarf.

Next came the young guy from the warehouse.

Seeing him and Eileen together for the first time I wondered why I hadn't hooked them up sooner. The hair was a different colour, but the shape of the face was distinctive.

Like his mother, Michael Sheldon was dressed in black. He wore a smart, well-cut suit and a black tie with a thin red diagonal stripe. The bored arrogance I had seen in his face at the warehouse was missing, replaced by stark hostility.

There was something else as well. Something that kept drawing my eye back to him . . . them. I looked from the mother to the son, uneasy and unable to name the feeling. Whatever it was had disturbed me, it would neither flesh nor flee.

The chair next to Eileen Sheldon was empty. I guessed it was for Mayle, but he still hadn't shown.

Suddenly there was a violent surge from my left and I saw the policemen's expressions change.

Guessing that Stephanie Sheldon must have entered the courtroom, I leaned forward for a better view, but a scuffle broke out at the back and by the time the gallery had settled down Stephanie Sheldon was in the dock and out of my view.

There followed several minutes of jostling, with the police growing more and more impatient. The usher looked like she was losing it, and threatened to clear the court unless order was restored. I took the opportunity to squeeze nearer to the front.

Finally I saw Stephanie, or at least glimpsed her, between the bobbing heads of the gallery.

She stood in the dock flanked by two female prison staff with an additional escort of two policemen at the back.

She was dressed in a similar black coat and veiled pillbox hat to her mother, her shoulder-length hair the same blond as her brother's. Like her mother she was small, barely over five feet, but something came off her; an aura would have been putting it too strongly, but a presence certainly.

It wasn't lost on the packed gallery; they were rapt.

It crossed my mind that if witch-burning was off the statute books then not everyone had heard.

Michael Sheldon stared intently at his sister throughout, and from the angle of her head she seemed to be staring right back at him. Minutes passed, and their locked gaze became so obvious it drew everybody's attention.

Whatever it was that they communicated to each other, it gradually affected the court until the murmurs fell away, leaving the entire room silent, watching.

That was the moment that Kris Mayle chose to appear.

The adrenaline shot through me like an electric current, turning my mouth dry and making my hands ball into fists.

So strong was my reaction that several people near me edged away. Had it been anywhere but a court, I would have dragged him into the street. I wanted him so bad I could taste it.

He hadn't changed a bit. From the dark, angular features, slicked-back hair and an expensively tailored suit, it was easy to see why Jenny had taken the bait. He looked dangerous; handsome and ugly at the same time. A glittering shark with sleek lines and dead eyes.

Well, the wheel had spun and now it was my turn.

He slid down the side of room and sat down next to Eileen Sheldon. She turned and greeted him with an anxious smile and he kissed her on the cheek. Next he gave a small wave to Stephanie and placed the same hand on Michael Sheldon's shoulder.

Sheldon turned, saw him and, without reacting, turned back to face Stephanie.

The clerk of the court got to his feet. For the

moment the circus had gone, and all that was left was a young woman facing a charge of murder.

'All stand!'

The three magistrates filed in and took their seats.

There were a few moments as the clerk discussed something with the magistrates, followed by the announcement of the reason for the hearing, then we were straight into the Crown's opposition to the bail application.

'The Crown strongly opposes bail in this case. The serious nature of the charges, these being arson, murder and violently resisting arrest, are such that we ask for a remand in prison until the case is heard in full.'

At the mention of violently resisting arrest, the gallery erupted, and the clerk called for order.

'Further,' continued the Crown barrister, 'it is felt that the defendant, Stephanie Sheldon, may try and flee should she be given bail.'

The lead magistrate, a dark, thickset woman in her fifties, consulted with her two colleagues, wrote something down and asked the defence to make its statement.

The defence barrister turned back to Eileen Sheldon and there was a brief exchange, then he stood up.

'My client, Miss Sheldon, will strenuously deny the charges brought before her. Prior to her arrest, she was of good character and has never been brought before a court before. I would point out that she is in a state of extreme shock and grief caused by the horrific death of her father . . .'

The magistrates listened impassively, but the gallery grew noisy again and the clerk called for silence. The defence barrister waited until he was given the nod to continue.

'It is traumatic enough for my client to deal with these feelings without the extra imposition of being incarcerated. My client is prepared to meet any conditions the court would impose and her mother, Mrs Eileen Sheldon, is prepared to stand surety to whatever amount the court sees fit.'

The magistrates discussed the points made and then the dark-haired woman spoke to the defence barrister.

'We are concerned about the charge of violently resisting arrest. If your client is applying for bail she must see that such actions cannot reflect favourably on her case.'

The barrister nodded. 'I'm obliged, ma'am. This charge . . .' He turned and looked impassively at the Crown barrister. '. . . this accusation has to be seen in context. From the moment of the fire and subsequent death of her father, Miss Sheldon, and indeed her entire family, have been subjected to enormous pressure from the media.'

Then he turned slowly and looked at the gallery. 'At the time of her arrest she had just run the gauntlet of a pack – I put it that strongly – of photographers, television and newspaper reporters. She literally had to fight her way to the front entrance of her mother's residence, arriving bruised and with her clothes torn.'

All three magistrates stared across at the gallery.

The barrister pressed home his advantage. 'I cannot stress enough that when the police arrived shortly after this my client was in considerable distress and, given these circumstances, the arrest could have been handled with perhaps a little more sensitivity than was shown.'

Eileen Sheldon gave a single emphatic nod.

'I would ask the Bench to recognise that what was interpreted as violent resistance to arrest was in fact hysteria, brought on by grief, shock and the unruly and unsympathetic actions of the media.' He let the sentence hang in the air and then sat.

There followed a recess while the magistrates withdrew and made their decision. When they returned, the female magistrate read out their ruling.

'We have decided to allow bail in this case, However, we shall impose conditions that require the accused, Stephanie Sheldon, to report to the police every day and to surrender her passport to this court. Further, the court will impose a surety of ten thousand pounds.'

On hearing the decision, Stephanie Sheldon turned towards the gallery and lifted her veil and I saw her face for the first time.

A shiver went through me; it might have been the face at the window.

Chapter Fourteen

Released from the dock, Stephanie Sheldon walked across the court into her mother's arms. The gallery took their cue and stampeded for the court entrance, in order to meet the Sheldons with a blizzard of photoflash.

Then Eileen, Michael and Stephanie locked in a three-way hug, but Mayle stood to one side, excluded. He didn't seem fazed by it, but wouldn't have missed the fact that he was made to wait.

The barrister reached across and shook his hand, but other than that there was no mistaking his second-citizen status.

Intrigued by the afterpiece, I stood back and watched.

It was Eileen Sheldon who first acknowledged Mayle. She turned, placed a hand on his arm and pressed her cheek against his, like you might to a grieving relative that you don't especially like. I enjoyed that and made a mental note to remind him of it, when the time was right.

Then Stephanie detached herself and approached him.

Quickly, he stepped between her and the others

and kissed her. She reacted almost as if she'd just awoken to his being there. Her arms went around his neck and they kissed again. He held her tight, seemingly reluctant to release her.

Eileen managed a patient smile, but Michael looked away.

The second that Mayle let Stephanie go, Eileen Sheldon slipped her arm around her waist and led her back to the barrister, and once again Mayle stood alone; irrelevant.

With the courtroom virtually clear, the usher hovered, trying to catch the barrister's eye.

It was time to go.

Outside, it was raining hard on the media pack, which if anything had grown in size.

I saw a well-known face doing a 'piece to camera', and looking around it seemed that most of the national press had sent their finest. One character I knew for sure; a local reporter called Joe Cardy, a vinegary man in his fifties with a smoking habit so lethal it might well have originated the term 'hack'.

He worked for a newspaper that stretched its coverage across the greater part of East London, including my fire ground. If he recognised me he didn't show it.

Like the rest of them, he was primed for one set of faces and automatically filtered out the fry.

It would have been interesting to hang around and see how the Sheldons and Mayle reacted, but instead I turned my collar up against the weather and walked back to the multistorey carpark above the shopping mall.

Despite the driving rain I walked slowly, absorbed in my thoughts.

Detached from the drama of seeing Stephanie Sheldon for the first time, reason had reasserted itself, arguing that she couldn't have been the face at the window. The woman I had seen had been enveloped in flame.

Life isn't a movie. Get near a fire and it will melt your skin like wax; stay around long enough and it will consume you, fat, muscle and bone. It doesn't compromise or make exceptions. The woman at the window would have been horrifically scarred, and Stephanie Sheldon was whole.

Yet the likeness . . .

The same eerie feeling I'd had in the warehouse draped itself across me. Before, I'd put it down to tiredness, but I wasn't tired now. At least, not that I was aware of it.

By the time I reached the carpark I was soaked through. I took my barn jacket off, shook out the excess water, and threw it on the back seat, then climbed behind the wheel.

I had intended to head back to Romford, the direct route to which was through Ilford, and that thought decided me. If I couldn't shake the nagging uneasiness, then I was going to embrace it.

Something in me needed to look up at that window; to think and to feel.

On the way the sky darkened and the rain fell harder, while beneath it the traffic oozed grudgingly. I'd given up counting the days since the 'wet season' had begun, and instead had taken to counting the weeks. By the time I reached Ilford the wipers were barely clearing it from the windscreen.

The nearest I could park was in a side road off the top of Ley Street; a good two hundred yards from the shop. I retrieved a torch from the boot of the car and set off at a run, ducking in and out of shop doorways, trying to avoid the worst of the rain.

When I reached the shopfront I stopped at the spot where I'd stood the night of the fire. The whole of the ground floor was blocked off by wooden hoarding. I looked up at the boarded window of Robin Sheldon's flat. It looked stark and lifeless; there was nothing to see and nothing to feel.

A passer-by grinned at me. I must have looked stupid; everyone around was rushing, head down, trying to get out of the rain, and there I was, looking up at a deserted building without knowing quite why.

I was on the point of returning to the car, but decided instead to make my way around the back of the shop via the service road.

At the rear I stopped by the entrance. The staircase was a communal one, serving other shops and flats; its surrounding brickwork was scorched and the paint was blistering from the door timbers.

In the grey, wet light it was very different. The fire

seemed a lifetime ago, but as I pushed through the doors and stepped across the threshold that detachment was pushed aside by the stale reek of smoke.

I switched the torch on and looked up into the fire-scarred structure; residual soot clung to the edges and corners of the stairwell and everywhere dirty water had marbled the plasterwork. It was a dead place; the fire seemed to have sucked all life from the building.

As I started up the stairs a flash of blue-white lightning pierced the stairwell windows and a single loud crash of thunder shook the building. The rain hissed as it swept across the damaged windowpanes, the sounds merging and echoing around the boxlike structure.

I don't suffer from claustrophobia, but the building definitely felt like it was closing in on me, and I was happier when I emerged on to the balcony access to Robin Sheldon's second-floor flat.

My legs were suddenly heavy; the tiredness had caught up with me again. I turned my face into the rain and let it soak me, attempting to shock the fatigue from my body.

A gusting wind pulled at my jacket as I stood watching the storm rolling around the sky; the heavy, swollen cloud lit for milliseconds as the inevitable crashes of thunder moved it slowly westward, across the wan urban landscape.

I found the entrance to Sheldon's flat at the very end of the balcony access. The door was intact.

I stood for a moment, thinking back to when Mike

Scott and Wayne Bennett had helped me search for the seat of fire. I remembered that the door from the first-floor workroom had held most of the fire back from the flat, and how Robin Sheldon had tried to escape by fleeing into the flat, his clothes alight, until he plunged through the window.

Was it instinct that had taken him that way? Had he got to the balcony he would still have had to go down the staircase, and that would have been impossible.

I leaned my shoulder against the door and pushed. It was solid. There was a plain double lock plate, which took a Yale-type key, about halfway up.

I looked about then leaned back and drove the heel of my foot hard against the lock. The was a loud crack and the woodwork split from the door jamb. I pushed against the door, but it still held.

Quickly, I kicked the lock again, and then slammed my shoulder hard against the door. It flew open and I fell inside.

Closing the door behind me, I switched on the torch and swept the beam around the small hallway. It was untouched – the fire hadn't reached this part of the flat. I went through to the lounge, where Sheldon had thrown himself through the window.

Standing in the centre of the pitch-black room, I could hear the traffic in the high street and the rain drumming against the plywood boarding across the picture window. It seemed different from what I remembered, but I'd been shattered then, cold and wet from fighting the fire and with a dozen different tasks vying for my attention.

The torch beam fell on the remains of heavy curtains either side of the window. The main fire had been kept back by the smoke stop door connecting with the workshop on the first floor, so the damage here was slight. That much I'd remembered, but now I realised that it was perfectly possible for someone to have been in the room with Robin Sheldon and not have been touched by the fire.

True, there would have been smoke and flame, but the fire that I'd seen from the street two floors below could only have been from the curtains; there was insufficient damage in the rest of the room to account for it.

That begged the question, how did they get out of the building?

The stairwell had been completely smoke-logged, so going out of the door on to the balcony was only to walk into trouble. Also, it would have meant being seen by the fire crews at the back.

With a final sweep around the lounge, I went through to the bedroom.

Apart from a strong smell of smoke, the room was completely untouched. Diagonally opposite, in one corner of the room and partially hidden by a heavy curtain, was another door.

I realised then what had been nagging at me. The flat had originally been separate from the shop. Robin Sheldon must have bought it and then had a staircase put in to connect it to the workshop below.

I examined the door. It was locked by a spring-loaded bolt that could only be operated from inside the room. I pulled the bolt back and the door swung outward, as I suspected it might.

I went through the door and found myself in a small roof garden overlooking the high street to the front and the carpark at the rear. On the wall that made up the fourth side of the garden was an iron Jacob's ladder leading up to the roof.

The spring-bolted door was an old-fashioned fire escape.

I climbed the Jacob's ladder and saw the raised walkway laid across the roofs. It occurred to me to follow the walkway and see where it came out, but I was conscious that I had been on the premises for some time and had been making a little too much noise. I decided to leave.

As I reached the foot of the Jacob's ladder I heard a sound behind me.

'Stop where you are!'

I turned and saw two men in blue security uniforms standing in the fire escape doorway. They looked ready for trouble. The bigger of the two came towards me, his body language all business. I stood back and held up my arms.

'It's all right, I'm . . .'

'Quiet.'

The smaller of them, a thin guy about my height,

had a smirk on his face. He looked at the bigger man, who grabbed me by the arms and pushed me until my back was against the Jacob's ladder.

'Search him,' said the bigger guard.

The smaller man took my torch from me and ran his hands through my pockets.

'Hold it right there . . . you've got no powers to search me,' I said angrily.

'What d'you know . . . an indignant burglar. I seen it all now,' said the smaller guard.

'I'm no burglar, you prat.'

The big guard tightened his grip. 'Watch your mouth.'

The smaller guard reached into my inside pocket and pulled out my wallet. He shuffled through the contents of the card flap and pulled out my Fire Brigade ID card.

'He's a fireman . . .'

The bigger guard glanced down at the card. 'Write down the details.' He turned back to me. 'Okay, so you're a fireman. What the hell are you doing here?'

His grip on my arms slackened. I pulled myself free and took back my wallet.

'I'm working for the loss adjusters who . . .'

They stopped, looked at each other, then both burst out laughing. The bigger of the two shook his head from side to side.

'Where do you people come from? . . . I mean, is there a home up the road specialising in nutters or something?'

I looked from one to the other. 'I work for the loss adjusters, who are employed by Carter and Woodley Associates, and my boss is . . .'

'Alex McGregor,' finished the smaller guard.

My jaw must have dropped a little because they were grinning fiercely.

'Look sir . . .' began the bigger guard.

The 'sir' was emphasised in a way that I recognised only too well. I tended to use it the same way myself when in uniform and dealing with the less-than-sharp of this world.

The bigger guard continued, 'You're the second inquiry agent we've had here tonight . . . in fact, when we saw you on the camera we thought it was him again.'

'Look, Alex McGregor really is my boss . . .' I took out my mobile phone. 'I can call him on this and he'll verify it if you want.'

'I don't want. Now if it's all the same to you, I'm getting very wet and you're pushing your luck. I'll make a report of this. Inquiry agent or not, you've no business breaking and entering these premises, so consider yourself lucky and go home before I change my mind. And I shall want McGregor to contact us tomorrow to confirm what you said.'

'My ID card?'

The bigger guard nodded and the smaller one handed the card back. Then they each took an arm and gently but firmly took me back through the flat and down to ground level.

When we exited the stairwell they let go of me. I'd started to walk away when I heard the smaller guard say, 'Well, at least he didn't claim to be an ex-copper.'

I stopped. 'What did you say?'

'Goodnight, sir!'

'No, I'm serious . . . did you say ex-copper?'

'That's what he said . . . and he was pissed as a handcart.'

'You dealt with a drunken ex-copper who said he worked for Alex McGregor?'

'Got it in one. Mate of yours, is he?'

'When was this?'

They said nothing, but stood with their arms folded and hard expressions on their faces. The conversation was at an end.

I walked back to the car slowly, trying to wrap my head around the knowledge that Roley Benson was still on the case.

As Alex had said he had been paid off, that left two possibilities. Either Benson was under the illusion that he was still working for Andrew and Alex, or he was now working for someone else and passing himself off as Alex's man.

I stopped in a shop doorway and rang Alex.

'Hello, McGregor Loss Adjusters.'

'Alex, Steve.'

'Stevie boy, where are you?'

'I'm standing in Ilford Broadway getting wet and trying to work out why Roley Benson is snooping around the scene of the fire here.'

'What?'

'There's nothing you want to tell me, then?'

'Eh? Christ, no, Stevie! I wouldn't do that to you.'

'Only I've just been thrown out of the building by two security guards who told me that I was their second inquiry agent of the day and that the other one was drunk and claimed to be an ex-copper. What d'you make of it?'

'I genuinely have no idea. Can we meet?'

'Not tonight, Alex. I'm going home for a hot bath and a stiff drink. It's been a fun-filled day.'

'Did you go to the court?'

'Oh yes. Stephanie Sheldon got bail and Mayle showed up.'

'He didn't see you?'

'No, but I saw him, and as far as the Sheldons are concerned, his arse is colder than a penguin's.'

'That's useful to know. D'you want me to try and get hold of Roley Benson?'

'No, leave it to me. The thought occurs, though, that someone might be using him to throw us off the trail.'

'I hope you're wrong. Anyway, go have your bath and ring me tomorrow. Early!'

'Will do. Oh, and Alex, you're going to have to contact the security firm at Ilford and sort this little lot out with them. If this sort of thing is going to keep on happening I'm going to need some kind of proper ID; something simple, no photograph.'

Chapter Fifteen

I arrived back at the flat around five and found Jenny in the kitchen cooking; a sure sign that her day had gone well. When she saw me she released a smile you'd walk over broken glass to receive.

'Hi, where have you been all day?'

'Running errands for Alex and getting soaked in the process.'

'Errands?'

'Some odd jobs he wanted doing. Have I got time to have a quick bath?'

She looked back over her shoulder. 'Plenty. Paying you, is he?'

'As it happens, he is. What're we eating?'

'Soup followed by red snapper with a spicy salad . . . a sort of celebration. There's a bottle of white in the fridge.'

'You've got a job?'

She laughed. 'Don't sound so surprised.'

'This is the one that you went after this morning?'

'Not exactly.'

'What, then?'

She turned back to the cooking. 'Later. After we've eaten. Go have your bath.'

As I stripped off in the bedroom, I felt a shiver pass through me.

The wet, cold and tiredness had taken their toll, but what I felt was more than that. If it was stress, and I was nearer the edge than I knew, then I was going to have to cut myself some slack; allow for mistakes. Just pace myself a little.

I filled the bath with the hottest water I could bear and lowered myself gingerly into it. The heat nigh on scalded me. At first, I just lay there, lobster red, my face sweating and steam fogging the mirror, but gradually, as my body got used to it, I closed my eyes and surrendered to the heat; letting the worry seep from my bones.

It was Jenny calling that roused me. I must have drifted off.

'Steve! How long will you be?'

The water was tepid. 'Give me five minutes.'

I climbed from the bath and sat down on the side. I felt a little woozy, but better than when I came through the door. When I was dressed, I came through to the kitchen. Jenny tilted her head to one side when she saw me.

'You okay?'

I grinned. 'Fell asleep in the bath.'

'I'm just going to warm the soup through.'

I looked at the wall clock. It was two minutes to six.

'Have I got time to catch the headlines?'

'Just.'

The news was topped by a wrangle in Europe over the single currency. That was followed by the death of a Russian general in a helicopter crash over Chechnya.

The Sheldon case was way down the bill, but it attracted a full treatment.

Chuckling grimly, I watched 'Team Sheldon' reprise their three-way hug outside the court. It crossed my mind that the sight of Stephanie receiving benediction from her mother wouldn't harm her chances with any future jurors who might be watching.

Mayle, on the other hand, was nowhere to be seen.

The round-faced solicitor in pin-stripes read out a prepared statement to the effect that Stephanie Sheldon denied any involvement in the Ilford fire and that, like the rest of her family, she was in deep shock following the horrific death of her father.

He went on to say that Stephanie was closely supported by her family and was co-operating with the police in their efforts to find and bring to justice her father's killer.

Seeing the Sheldons lined up behind their solicitor, their arms linked and faces wearing a mixture of defiance and joy, you just knew they were going for the big audience.

The correspondent I'd seen outside the court summarised the bail hearing and described the Sheldons as being '. . . a charismatic family caught up in a tragic cycle of events'.

This was followed by some amateur footage of the Ilford fire taken with a hand-held camcorder.

The film was jerky, but caught the scenes of bedlam so well that I tingled as I watched. I caught sight of myself, back to the camcorder, with my hands cupped around my mouth, shouting instructions to someone out of shot.

Then the camcorder zoomed in to a tight knot of people hunched over Robin Sheldon. You couldn't see much, but the voice-over left you in no doubt as to what you were watching.

The coverage finished with the correspondent outside the court again, stating that this was only the opening round of the case, and that for the Sheldons the ordeal had just begun.

You couldn't call the coverage lopsided, but there was no mistaking the way the television people had decided to play it, if only for the moment. Others, tabloid body-snatchers in the main, would be working the other end of the story; burrowing like maggots into the host.

By playing the celebrity card, the Sheldons were screwing with the Devil.

'What are you watching?' Jenny was standing in the lounge doorway.

'It's about the fire we had at Ilford the other night . . . bit of home-grown video.'

'See yourself?'

'Among others.'

'You've not spoken much about it . . . was it bad?'

I nodded. 'Was for the guy that jumped to his death. He was alight at the time.'

'Are you okay?'

My smile must have been forced, because concern flickered across her face and she came over to where I was sitting.

'Bit tired, that's all, Jen. We had two bad nights back to back and it's just taking longer than normal to recover.'

She looked unsure. 'Not the fire, then?'

'Don't think so . . . maybe . . . just a little. Nothing to worry about.'

'Are you ready to eat?'

'Mmm.'

As we ate, Jenny steered the conversation around to the work I had been doing for Alex. There were no direct questions, but her curiosity had been aroused. Without lying, I said that it was connected to the Ilford fire and left it at that.

The soup and fish were excellent. Jenny studied my face to make sure.

'What's for dessert?'

She became serious. 'Me.' She stood up, came around the table and sat on my lap. 'We have to talk.'

'Oh.'

'You know we do.'

'Here, like this?'

She nodded.

'Okay.'

She took a deep breath. 'I'm sorry.'

'For what?'

'Leaving you.'

'That's . . .'

'Please, Steve, just hear me out.'

'Okay.'

She looked directly at me. 'I love you. I've always loved you, even when . . . when I was with Kris.' There was a curious emphasis on his name, as though she dreaded speaking it.

'I made a mistake . . . and I know it hurt you. I won't lie, I was infatuated with him.'

'Sexually infatuated with him.'

'Yes,' she said quietly.

'Is all this honesty supposed to make me feel better?' I just about managed to keep the bitterness from my voice.

'It's supposed to draw a line under what happened, to let us be together again.' She took a deep breath and kissed my forehead. 'I never loved him, it was more a want. I physically needed to have him inside me.'

Her eyes were shut fast as the words tumbled out. 'He's in the past now and part of me . . . most of me regrets having slept with him.'

'Because?'

Her head went forward. 'Because it hurt you so very much.'

I felt winded, not able to find the words to reply to her. I had wanted her so much to say she was sorry, but hearing her describe her need of him was like having the skin flayed from my back.

I took her chin in my hand and made her look at me. 'And now?'

'Now?'

'Do you still want him . . . need him?'

She shook her head.

'Say it.'

She almost made it. She tried and I could see she was trying, but it fell short.

'I . . . I will not sleep with him again. I . . .'

'That's not what I asked. Do you still want him . . . physically?'

Her mouth opened, but nothing came out. Then, very quietly, she said, 'I don't want to.'

'But?'

Her eyes pleaded. 'Steve . . . I'm trying to make this right between us.'

'If he were here now . . . and he wanted you. What would you say?'

'That's not fair.' Tears welled up in her eyes.

'Not fair? How can it be right between us if you are lying next to me and thinking of him.'

'It's not like that. It's kept separate in my mind. When I'm with you I think of you . . . I'll never sleep with him again, Steve; I promise you.'

We sat in silence, my arms loosely around her waist as she hugged my head to her chest. Hurt as I was, I couldn't push her away.

Eventually I said, 'Is there any more?'

She nodded. 'Yes, but you must hear me out.'

I could feel the panic rising. 'Go on.'

'I didn't get that job this morning. In the past two weeks I've gone to five interviews and got nowhere. I must have phoned a dozen places. It's hard even getting the interviews.'

'So?'

'So, today was the final straw. The people who interviewed me were just going through the motions.' She paused. 'I came across some of the bills last week . . . and a letter from the bank. I didn't realise how bad things had got, how bad they'd been for you.' She took a deep breath. 'When I left the interview . . . I phoned Kris.'

'You did what!'

'You promised to hear me out, Steve . . . please.'

I shook my head in disbelief.

'I asked him for a job . . . he owes us, Steve . . . he took my business away from me, I can see that now. He has to give something back.'

'You're serious, aren't you? You all but tell me that you still feel for him and then in the same breath tell me that you went to see him about a job . . . for us!'

'I don't feel for him . . . it's just that . . .'

'What? That part of you wants to fuck him still? Have I got it right?'

'Don't, please.'

'Jesus, Jenny, you should hear yourself. You want to work for him and you want me to . . . to . . .'

'I want you to realise why I'm doing this. He owes us.'

'Wrong! He owes you. Me he owes nothing. It was me that remortgaged, me that dug the hole I fell into. My choices . . . my mistakes.'

She was crying now, the tears falling as her head tilted forward. 'For me . . . you did it for me . . . oh, Steve, I'm so sorry.'

She got up and ran towards the bedroom. I was about to follow her when the mobile phone rang inside the grip bag. I remember thinking, not now, Alex . . . for Christ's sake not now.

I was wrong. It was Eileen Sheldon.

It took over an hour to reach Virginia Quay, fighting the traffic the whole way. That was plenty of time for Jenny's words to ricochet around my skull until I didn't know whether to feel guilt or anger.

There are times to stay and talk and times to run. The smart move would have been to stay, no matter what had been said.

I knew what Jenny needed from me. She had said sorry and now to seal it, to put it behind us, I had to say that she was forgiven. The problem with that was it would have sounded like an endorsement of her approach to Mayle.

Perhaps I knew Jenny better than she knew herself. By asking him for help she had made herself vulnerable to him, and Mayle, being the arsehole he was, would be only too willing to use her. He might have chosen Stephanie Sheldon, but a little sex on the side was very much his style.

I had no doubt that she believed it when she told me that she wouldn't sleep with him again, but there are no more plausible lies than the ones we tell ourselves.

By the time I reached Virginia Quay the solution had become obvious; tell her to ring Mayle and say that she had found a job and no longer needed his help. Then for me to make it clear to her that if she planned to stay, I needed her to stop looking over her shoulder at what had once been.

There were lots of other things I might have said as well; like I loved and needed her and would always forgive her, but to do that would have been to let my guard down totally and instinct was screaming at me not to.

So the phone ringing was an excuse to back off and lick my wounds. It was also a reminder that mine wasn't the only life going through a meat-grinder. Eileen Sheldon had sounded desperate. Stephanie was missing.

Suzanne met me in the lift lobby and showed me up to the penthouse.

Eileen Sheldon was sitting hunched on the long white sofa, her arms wrapped around her legs and a cigarette burning between her fingers. The ashtray was full.

'Thank you for coming, Mr Jay.'

'No news, then?'

'Nothing.'

'Have you rung the police?'

'She's just been granted bail . . .' She studied me to make sure I caught all the implications. 'Besides, I believe that somebody has been leaking information to the media, and the last thing Stephanie needs is to be the focus of a hue and cry.'

'You think the police have been leaking information?'

She shook her head. 'Someone is. I don't know what to think any more.' She glanced at Suzanne and then back at me. 'Would you like a drink, Mr Jay?'

'No.' I paused. 'On second thoughts I'd love one.'

'Scotch?'

'Fine.'

'I'll have one too, Suzanne.' She stubbed the cigarette out and immediately lit another; she was wrapped tight and hiding it badly.

Suzanne fetched us our drinks and then, at a nod from Eileen, backed out the door.

'What time did Stephanie disappear?'

'Three hours ago. Please sit down, Mr Jay.'

'It's Steve.'

Considering the major dramas that had fallen out of the sky on to her, the use of my first name seemed genuinely to take her by surprise. She gave an odd little laugh, like I had made the social gaffe of the week and she couldn't wait to tell the neighbours.

'We got back from the court and . . .'

'Who's we?'

'Stephanie, my son Michael and myself. After Stephanie was granted bail this afternoon we all came back here. Michael left virtually straight away. I was on the telephone to our solicitor when she must have slipped out.'

'She's not with Michael?'

'No. That was the first place I checked.'

'Why would she go?'

'I don't . . .' She didn't finish the sentence. Suddenly she turned away from me and covered her face with her hands.

Chapter Sixteen

I helped her back to the sofa, intending to get her a drink, but she pulled me down with her and turned, drawing her legs up. Without thought, my arms went around her.

That did it. A sobbing shudder rippled through her body and she clung to me. The pressure had been building for days and the ultra-cool fashion diva had finally lost control; able only to watch as her life was ripped apart.

I held her because she wanted it, but I felt awkward, embarrassed; the last time I'd seen someone this vulnerable was in a mirror.

The awkwardness had another root; for in the state of mind I was in it was hard not to react to her. I think she sensed my ambivalence, but didn't pull away.

Then out of nowhere she kissed me.

It wasn't passionate, and I didn't read it as sex, but it was warm, open. It felt like the act of a woman beaten to the ground and with nothing left to offer except herself. Perhaps she felt the pain within me and could allow her guard to slip. But it was a dangerous act, because she really was a beautiful woman and I was totally unarmed.

Gradually, I felt her regain control.

The sobbing stopped and the fierceness of her embrace melted into simply holding. There were no apologies, no explanations; she just stood up and straightened her dress, then raked her fingers through her hair.

'Would you like some coffee, Steve?'

'Please.'

She started towards the door, but then stopped and walked back to me. Reaching out, she cupped my cheek in her palm of her hand.

'Thank you,' she whispered.

She was gone a while and I used the time to dampen the emotional jet-lag that I'd arrived with. My needs had nothing whatsoever to do with Eileen Sheldon or hers with me. A little professional detachment was in order.

When she returned she was carrying a tray with a rectangular white china coffee pot and two large square cups.

'Suzanne has gone out,' she explained, pouring the coffee.

'Would Stephanie have told Suzanne where she was going?'

She hesitated, absorbed in pouring the coffee. 'No.'

'You're sure of that?'

She didn't look at me, but gave a single nod of the head.

Maybe it was something about the body language

or just the suggestion of evasion in the non-verbal reply; either way, I suddenly became aware that the obvious had once again been stalking me for a good twenty minutes before I'd managed to bump into it.

'You know where Stephanie is, don't you, Eileen?'

The hand holding the coffee cup stopped halfway between us. It was as good as a yes.

'Why am I here?' I took the cup from her, still unable to get her to look me in the face.

'I'm scared.' She said it flat.

I took a sip of coffee. 'Tell me.'

'It's complex.'

'So tell me.'

She put her coffee down and lit a cigarette, blowing the smoke away from me. It crossed my mind that I'd been summoned to hear a fiction; prepared for the planting of a lie.

I stared at her, deciding that she was playing it straight.

'You asked me last time about James Chasteau . . . and Ladyfair.'

'Go on.'

'It threw me at first. I was surprised to hear the name; it's not one I usually associate with Kris.'

'But in the file James Chasteau is given as the owner of Ladyfair and as your business partner.'

'It's a convenient hat for Kris to wear.'

'You'll have to explain that one.'

If there was a moment for her to back off, that was it. Equally, if she was innocent and as much in need of help as she said, then it was also the time to open up. In the event she did neither, deciding instead to pick at the edge of her story, while testing my motives and reading me as hard.

'Jimmy Chasteau was a charming old-school high-street fashion merchant. He started out with nothing and became one of the biggest. His real name was Paul Greenbaum . . .' She gave a small, affectionate laugh. 'He thought the name Chasteau would imply a connection with the French fashion scene . . . it was the kind of naivety that you could get away with in the late fifties.'

I smiled and she waved her hand dismissively.

'Yes, well, I suppose it's not that different now, is it? Anyway, his customers in the main were working-class women aspiring to something better, and Jimmy was shrewd enough to know that and cared enough to let them think they were special.'

'You liked him.'

'Everybody loved old Jimmy, and he lived for the business. He had the most loyal customers you could want. It was all 'off the peg', but the cutting was sharp and the materials the best that could be had for the price. When we started out we wanted to build on the ideas that he'd started . . . bring the fashion scene to the high street.'

'Class for brass,' I said.

She smiled and nodded. 'You have done your research, haven't you. Jimmy had ruled the East End, but the sixties changed all that. Fashion became linked with music; Carnaby Street and the King's Road turned the high street on its head. People like Jimmy struggled to keep up, but when we started out in the early seventies he was still the biggest.'

'How does this all fit in with Mayle?'

'Jimmy's business shrank over the years, but up to a few years ago he still owned half a dozen shops. He lost his wife to cancer at about the time the recession hit. His business ran into serious cash flow problems and Kris Mayle bought him out . . . along with the firm's name and customer base, such as it was.'

'You say that like you weren't happy to see it happen.'

She shrugged. 'Jimmy needed the money, the business was on the slide . . . if Kris hadn't done it then the whole lot would have gone into receivership.'

'But you were unhappy still?'

'Yes. It was the way it was done . . . Kris pared the offer to the bone . . . Jimmy was too tired, too grief-stricken, to argue.'

'Nevertheless you went into business with him?'

'Not me, my husband . . . and Michael.'

'Tell me again how that happened.'

She drew on the cigarette and then stubbed it out, half-used, in the ashtray.

'My husband was persuaded by Michael to expand the business. We already owned a good-size chain of shops selling our own label, but running shops isn't cheap. Michael came up with the idea of franchising. That way we'd keep our overheads low while expanding our customer base.'

'What did your husband think of that?'

'We all thought it was a brilliant idea. The problem was that franchising meant a large volume of stock and that in turn meant warehousing space. We were going to be stretched pretty fine by all the increased production costs, so Michael hunted for a potential partner . . . one with ownership of a warehouse that was under capacity.'

'And he found Mayle.'

'Well, in a way Kris found him.'

'Oh?'

'There was nothing unusual about it . . . we'd put the word out about our interest and Kris was one of several people who got in touch. His was the best deal.'

'And what was that deal?'

'That Kris rented us as much or as little space as we needed, according to turnover, and in return we let him act as a franchising wholesaler.'

'You let him sell your label?'

'Supply other people to sell our label.'

'What about his own shops, the ones he'd bought from James Chasteau?'

She paused and took a sip of coffee. 'He sold them once the partnership with us was under way . . . he said he needed the capital to gain full benefit from the deal. It looked a wise move. In a way his motives were the same as ours – reduce overheads and sell more goods.'

'And Stephanie? How did they meet?'

The answers took a little longer to come as the questions got closer to home. We both knew her credibility depended on her letting me in, but she was determined to lead me slowly.

'Because of the business she would have met him one way or the other, but it was Michael that really got them together . . . not that he'd ever admit it now. He hates Kris.'

'Why?'

'Not long into the partnership we suffered a devastating blow. In one month we lost two major outlets for our goods, both big high-street retail chains. My husband decided that we had to sell off shops or we'd be in serious trouble with cash flow . . . Kris bought two shops from us and offered to sell only our label. On paper it looked good. We'd get the money for the shops that we needed and we'd still have the outlets.'

'First Jimmy Chasteau, then you.' I was also thinking – Jenny. What did surprise me was that Mayle was able to operate on such a scale; where had he found the wedge?

'There's more. Kris said that although he'd buy the two shops he didn't have enough money straight away and asked for a month to raise it.'

'What happened then?'

'The bank threatened to cut off our overdraft . . . it was the only way we'd managed to pay the staff through the tight period we'd had. We intended to pay it back immediately the sale of the two shops went through.'

'So in effect, by delaying the money for the shops, he made you even more vulnerable.'

She nodded. 'As the weeks passed Michael became increasingly worried by what was happening. He suspected Kris of deliberately delaying payment. The bite wasn't long in coming. Kris waited until the last possible moment to pay the money and then told Michael that he wanted to renegotiate the deal.'

'Why doesn't that surprise me? What did he want?'

'Fifteen thousand off the price of the shops and a bigger percentage of the franchising.'

I shook my head. 'And you all came up for that?'

'There was a hell of a row between my husband and Michael . . . Stephanie and I tried to keep clear of it, but by then Stephanie and Kris were an item, and she took his side. Although I don't believe for one moment that she understood just how devious he could be.'

'What was the outcome?'

'There was no room left for manoeuvre. The bank gave us a week to put things in order. We had to accept Kris's offer. A month later we had the fire at Stratford.'

There was no mistaking the inference. 'You're saying that it was Mayle that started the fire?'

'Michael believes he did.'

'And you? What do you believe?'

She shrugged. 'Without stock we couldn't supply either our shops or the franchise side of the business. If he didn't start the fire he certainly made it work to his advantage.'

'He made an offer to buy you out?'

She gave a bitter laugh. 'Kris would never be so obvious, though by then it was clear that's what he had in mind.'

'Just go over that again for me, will you? You're suggesting that Mayle had the warehouse burnt to kill off your financial muscle so that he could then buy out your entire business?' She didn't answer immediately. 'Eileen?'

'Sorry.' She sighed. 'Where was I?'

'Kris Mayle taking bites out of your life.'

Again that bitter laugh. 'I don't think he had the money to buy us out, at least not in one go. We were the host . . . being kept alive for him to feed on. Michael said he planned to consume us piece by piece.'

'What did your husband say?'

'To me, nothing. By then we were communicating through Michael.'

The energy, the pain, coming off her was intense, and part of me wanted to hold her again, but she was haemorrhaging priceless information, and although it was hurting her I might not get a second chance at going so deep.

'Is this what you brought me over to hear tonight?'

'No.' She whispered.

'What, then?'

She brought her legs up to her chest and wrapped her arms around them in the same posture I'd found her in when I'd arrived. If she was acting then it fooled me. Her eyes darted backwards and forwards, as though searching, looking for the confirmation that I could be trusted.

When she spoke again her voice was so soft, so tiny, that I had to lean forward to hear what she was saying.

'I think Stephanie's with Kris.'

'Kris? Why does that frighten you, Eileen?'

Her face had become pale and intense. She was sitting very still, but her words arrived like a building collapse.

'Kris was with Stephanie at Ilford.'

I forced myself not to react. 'Do the police know this?'

She looked down and shook her head. 'Stephanie won't tell anyone.'

'Then how do you know?'

'I know.'

'When you say you know . . .'

'I know because she won't discuss it with me. He was there, Steve, I feel it.'

She had just given me what I wanted most in the world; a solid, non-negotiable way to remove Kris Mayle from my . . . from our life. I should've been glad, relieved even, but I was wary.

'Eileen, the police say that Stephanie was caught

on CCTV arriving at the building some time before the fire was reported. As far as I'm aware Kris Mayle wasn't on the tape.'

She had the answer. 'The cameras only cover the rear exit in the service road, not the shop door entrance in the Broadway.'

'Have you spoken to her solicitor about this?'

'No.'

'Eileen, Stephanie is in the frame for murder . . .'

'No!'

'No?'

She took a moment, weighing me yet again. Then she uncoiled herself slowly and reached across to take my hand between hers; the vivid blue eyes locked on to mine.

'She's the only one who can place him there . . . do you realise what that means? I am so scared . . .' Her words fell away. 'I thought if you could get proof that he was at the shop after Stephanie then she could tell the police and your evidence would corroborate her story.'

'And they would arrest him?'

'Yes.'

It made perfect sense. 'This was why you hired me, wasn't it?'

She lit another cigarette and drew slowly on it, taking comfort from the coarse, nicotine-infused smoke.

'Yes.'

A thought nagged. 'If she's so frightened of him,

Eileen, why slip out to meet him? That's what you said earlier on . . . that she just slipped out.'

'I don't know.'

'After what you've told me, if she doesn't reappear soon then you're going to have to go to the police yourself.'

At this she fell silent.

There was an obvious question for me to ask, but it was going to take me into a place I didn't want to go. I waited, hoping she was going to suggest something, but she'd clearly pinned all her hopes on me. It had suddenly all grown too serious to walk away from, but the potential cost kept me dumb and rooted.

The longer the silence went on, the more it became necessary to ask.

'Where does Kris Mayle live, Eileen?'

'I don't know . . . but Michael does.'

'Ring him.'

She dialled the number.

'Hello, Michael . . . yes. Stephanie still hasn't made contact and I'm getting very concerned. What? I don't know. Look, I think she might be with Kris . . . yes, Kris . . . don't, Michael, please . . . please! I want to go and pick her up only I don't know exactly . . . what? I've got someone with me, an inquiry agent. He works for Alex McGregor. Pardon? Okay, if you think that's best. Ten minutes.' She put the phone down. 'Michael wants to come.'

'I'm sorry, I couldn't help overhearing . . . he sounded angry.'

Her hands started shaking. 'He's furious . . . look, Steve, I don't think I could drive. Could you drop me at Michael's place?'

'Sure. Where is he?'

'Limehouse.'

Chapter Seventeen

Limehouse seemed to be able to reinvent itself periodically. Although it would always be linked to dockland and the Chinese migrant communities of a hundred years ago, it had changed from underclass to oversold in less than a generation.

In its recent past, the neighbourhood had become associated with the kind of media celebrities that saw themselves as the nouveau cognoscenti and whom everybody else saw as second-rate talking heads.

Michael Sheldon's place was a nineteenth-century three-storey terraced house with arched windows and wrought-iron railings overlooking a garden square. Part of the square had been reallocated to parking, and I thought I recognised his white Mercedes Sports among the other cars.

We parked opposite the house, thirty yards down from the Mercedes. Eileen took out her mobile phone and rang the number three times.

'Wait here, Steve. I want a word with him before we go. I want to try and calm him down.'

'No problem.'

She climbed from the car and started to cross the road. At that moment Michael Sheldon came down the steps and waited for her on the pavement. He was wearing a full-length dark coat with a scarf wrapped around the lower half of his face, which he pulled away from his mouth as they spoke.

It quickly became apparent that they were arguing, and Eileen turned and looked back in my direction. He stared across the road to where I was. I doubted that he could recognise me from the warehouse incident, it was too dark, but either way he shook his head and turned his back to me.

Eileen seemed to be pleading and grabbed him by the arms. Although I could hear their raised voices, I was too far away to pick up what was being said. Then he turned away from her and walked towards his car, pulling up his scarf again.

Eileen called after him, but then came back towards me. I wound down the window.

'I'm sorry, Steve, there's a change of plan. There's no need for you to come now.'

'If that's what you want . . . is everything okay?'

'No. Michael is so angry . . .'

'You should call the police, Eileen, and tell them what you told me.'

She glanced back towards Michael. 'If we don't find her at Kris Mayle's I promise I will.'

'Ring me either way.'

She placed a hand on my arm. 'I can't thank you enough for tonight, Steve. I would've preferred you to come, but Michael thinks that it's best if you don't.'

'It's not a problem.'

'I know what you said about paying you only by results, but you must let me reimburse you for this evening.'

I turned the ignition. 'We can discuss it tomorrow. Take care.'

She leaned through the window and kissed my cheek. 'Thank you again.'

I watched her walk back towards his car. She was barely twelve feet from me when a soft explosion from the front of the Mercedes sent a fireball upwards and outwards, enveloping the vehicle and throwing vivid yellow and black streaks across the square's brickwork.

'Michael!' she screamed.

I was out of the car and retrieving a powder extinguisher from the boot without consciously thinking. I glanced at her as I ran past; she was shocked, but not injured.

'Stay there! Don't move!' I shouted.

The front of the car was an inferno. Heavy black smoke rolled over the roof. I approached in a crouch from the rear, using the bodywork as a shield and the extinguisher to drive the flames from the driver's door.

The dry powder rapidly knocked the flames down, but the source was under the bonnet, and as soon as I stopped they reared up again.

The fierce heat was searing my face, so I turned my back and pulled open the door. Thick carbon-laden smoke had penetrated the passenger compartment, and it was impossible to see Sheldon. As I groped for him I took a lungful of the smoke and began coughing violently, blanking my mind off from the panic that always threatens with smoke inhalation.

My eyes were watering, and I was reduced to touch to locate him and body sensation to judge the heat. I knew that without protective clothing or breathing apparatus I had seconds to get him out.

Reaching in farther, I felt his head, ran my hands down to his coat and pulled hard, but he was slumped away from me with the seat belt holding him fast.

I could feel myself going dizzy and forced the concentration, dealing with only one action at a time. I turned and gulped for cleaner air, then followed the seat belt back to the buckle. His weight was jamming the lock mechanism. With one hand I pulled him towards me and with the other pressed frantically on the release button.

It came free on the third attempt and I pulled him clear.

We fell in a heap on to the concrete just feet from the flames, my head spinning and my lungs threatening to explode. Sheldon was motionless.

Trying to keep the open door between the fire and us, I dragged him backward along the length of the car at virtually the same time that the flames entered the passenger compartment and burned away the front seating.

At a safe distance I stood up and pulled him by his coat collar until we were a good ten yards clear of the car.

The front of his hair, eyelids and forehead were all scorched, but the burns were a lot lighter than I expected. The thick coat and scarf had helped to protect him.

I ripped the scarf away from his mouth and saw he wasn't breathing, so I turned him over and hit him hard between the shoulder blades. He gave an involuntary shudder, but there was no telltale gasp of air.

Pulling back his head, I pinched off his nose and enclosed his mouth with mine, inflating his lungs twice, then placed two fingers on his carotid artery and felt for a pulse. It was weak, but there.

I restarted mouth-to-mouth resuscitation and almost immediately felt him start to vomit. I turned him and hit him again between the shoulder blades. The vomit splashed out on to the ground, and I placed a finger inside his mouth to clear away the excess, before inflating his lungs again.

I kept it up for several minutes, monitoring the rise and fall of his chest, until he gasped and started to breathe on his own, then I turned him on his side and beckoned Eileen towards me.

'Stay with him, Eileen. Make sure he keeps his head to the side.'

I returned to the car and emptied the remainder of the extinguisher on it. It was a hand-held car type and lasted only for a few more seconds. The flames quickly reasserted themselves and I backed from the rising heat.

The noise and flames had brought people from their doorways and towards the fire. They gathered in a loose semicircle around Eileen and Michael Sheldon.

'Stay back!' I shouted. 'The petrol tank hasn't gone yet.'

Michael was coughing and retching by then, with black-streaked mucus running from his nose and mouth, so I helped Eileen wipe away the mess.

'Will he be all right, Steve?'

'He's taken a lot of smoke and needs to go to hospital.'

As if on cue, Michael Sheldon doubled up and gave way to a fit of deep, violent coughing that made his body spasm. He'd been shit lucky, and for that matter so had I.

I pulled out my mobile and rang for the Brigade, the police and an ambulance, giving the name of the square and the next street as a cross-reference. Then all I could do was sit back and watch the fire spread rapidly from car to car.

The crowd, some of them obviously owners, edged nearer and looked about helplessly as their vehicles were consumed by the fire.

'Keep back!' I shouted again.

This time, because of the heat radiating outwards, they shuffled back.

Shadwell fire station was only minutes away in Cable Street, but I wasn't sure how long the ambulance would take. The London Hospital wasn't that far, under a mile away in the Whitechapel Road, but there was no telling how busy they were.

When Shadwell's Pump Ladder arrived, they quickly got a jet to work and knocked the flames down; three cars were burning well by then and several others had just caught.

I scanned the crew's faces to see if I knew any of them. There was one that was half familiar, but I couldn't put a name to him.

He came running with a Laerdal resuscitator and fixed it over Michael Sheldon's face. He shot a quick look at me, but said nothing.

With the oxygen, Sheldon started to come around, and I left the fireman to his task and pulled the Sub Officer to one side.

'Sub, have you got a minute?'

He cast an eye over me to see if I was one of the usual cranks that always seemed to gather at fires. I pulled my Brigade ID from my pocket and showed him. He didn't react.

'Look, I don't want to get in your way, but there was an explosion from the Mercedes . . . it wasn't your run-of-the-mill-type car fire.'

He looked over to where his crew were damping down the cars.

'Explosion?'

'A soft one . . . like a lot of petrol going up at once.'

He nodded. 'Thanks . . . who are you again?'

'I'm a guv'nor at Wells Lane.'

He waited until the fire was out and steam was rising from the distorted metal, then walked with me towards the Mercedes and told one of his men to open the bonnet. It was twisted and buckled and they had to use a crowbar. As they prised it open and pulled it back, one of the firemen swore softly.

There, strapped to the engine, was a ruptured metal petrol can. In the neck of the opening, one of the spark plugs had been fixed; primed to blow as soon as the ignition was turned.

When the ambulance arrived, the paramedics took over from the fireman dealing with Michael Sheldon. They gave me the once-over as well, but apart from singed hair and a slight wheezing from the smoke, I was more or less intact.

Before the ambulance left, Eileen Sheldon pressed a key into my hand.

'Wait at the penthouse for me. I want someone there in case Stephanie returns.'

'What about Mayle?'

She paused. 'Give it an hour . . . no, two. If she hasn't appeared by then ring the police and tell them what you know.'

I glanced over to where two patrol cars were parked. 'Why not just tell them yourself now?'

'Please, Steve . . . just do this for me.'

She gave me a worried smile, and although I

agreed I had the nagging feeling that I was being pulled farther and farther into the Sheldon camp, as Alex had predicted.

'One hour, Eileen, then I'll call them.'

'Thank you,' she mouthed.

As I watched the ambulance depart for the London Hospital with the Sheldons in the back, I felt a tug on my arm.

'Can we have a word, sir?'

I turned to face two men.

'You are?'

'I'm Detective Sergeant Menzies and this is Detective Constable Coleman. I understand you saw the explosion which started the fire?'

Menzies was a ginger-haired Scotsman in his thirties with grey-green eyes that I immediately distrusted. Coleman was dark haired, hard looking and in his mid to late twenties; they couldn't have been anything else but Plod.

'Yes.'

'Who are you exactly, sir?' asked Coleman.

'My name's Steven Jay.'

'Someone said that you're a fireman.'

'Yes.'

They waited; so did I.

'What were you doing here this evening?'

'Driving Mrs Sheldon.'

At the mention of the name they exchanged a glance that could only be interpreted one way. Coleman walked away a few paces and spoke into his radio, looking at the rear number plate of Michael Sheldon's Mercedes.

Menzies placed himself in line between Coleman and myself and started pumping questions at me.

'Is she a friend of yours?'

'No.'

'Then what is your relationship with her?'

Coleman was back alongside Menzies and looking directly into my face in a way that was bordering on hostile. I had no reason to lie, but their negativity made me want to make them work for it.

'I met her for the first time the other day.'

'Business? Pleasure?'

There was the suggestion of a smirk on the word 'pleasure', and I smirked back and shrugged.

Menzies asked the same question again and Coleman edged nearer in a way I imagine he thought was intimidating. Had I done something wrong it might well have been, but as I hadn't I found it laughable.

'Well?'

'Business,' I said.

'What kind of business?' asked Coleman.

'Loss adjustment.'

'Oh?'

At that moment Coleman's radio started calling him, and he walked some distance away to answer it. Menzies just smiled at me and waited for Coleman to return. When he did, he took Menzies off to one side and they talked at length, stealing the occasional glance at me. Eventually they came back and the questions started again.

Menzies said, 'You said something about loss adjustment?'

I told them about Alex and said that I was a freelance inquiry agent retained by him. I kept the details to the minimum and said nothing about Stephanie Sheldon going missing. I went on to say that I had interviewed Eileen about the Stratford fire and had agreed to drop her off at Michael's house after the interview.

'So why say you're a fireman?' asked Menzies.

'That's my full-time job.'

'A London fireman?'

'Yes.' I didn't like the way the conversation was going, but there was little I could do about it.

'Have you any ID?'

I pulled out my Fire Brigade ID card and Menzies studied it.

'Where are you stationed?'

'Wells Lane.'

They asked a lot of questions about the explosion and I simply told them what I'd seen and what I'd done.

'You pulled him from the car?'

'Yes.'

'That was brave of you.'

'You'd have preferred it if I hadn't?'

Menzies didn't like that, but then again I didn't like his tone. I watched countless situations like this on the fire ground and I wasn't a fan either watching or taking part. The pair of them were experts in needling people. Coleman was reading my reactions about right and called me a hero in a way that conveyed a zero.

I wasn't sure whether it was tactics or sport, and I doubted they could separate it for themselves. By the time they'd finished with me I was well and truly hacked off.

'Well, Station Officer Jay, it seems you were the right man in the right place tonight. I'm sure Mrs Sheldon will want to show her thanks . . . you can go, but we'll be in touch.'

Chapter Eighteen

I drove back to Virginia Quay, more conscious of the wheezing in my lungs once I was free of the aural irritation.

Menzies and Coleman's promise to 'keep in touch' suggested that they might turn up at the station, and the ramifications of that didn't bear thinking about.

The Brigade wasn't too enthusiastic about revealing confidential information, and firemen have many powers that the police would envy, particularly with regard to right of entry into premises.

Part-time work as an inquiry agent threw up a million possibilities for embarrassing the Brigade and for the abuse of statutory powers. I would be unlikely to gain permission.

There was nothing I could do about it except register for part-time employment at the first opportunity; under a suitably misleading title.

I yawned and tried to shrug the lurking cramp from my shoulders.

Monday stretched back behind me like a dark tunnel; from my redundant visit to Roley Benson's house, the court, the débâcle with Jenny through to Eileen's revelations and the attempted murder of

Michael Sheldon, it had been the perfect way to overload a stressed-out system. Yet the weird thing was that at that moment I wasn't feeling stressed.

Logically, if anything should have thrown me it was the car explosion, but I'd dealt with that. I had reacted exactly as you'd expect a fireman to react; adrenalised, touched by healthy fear, but thinking on my feet.

Perhaps it was because I'd been doing something physical, as opposed to standing back, directing and controlling. Whatever it was, the only noticeable symptom resulting from the day was tiredness; heavy-limbed, gritty-eyed tiredness.

I'd promised Eileen one hour before contacting the police and I intended to stick to that. Then I would call it a day, drive back to the flat and try to sort the situation with Jenny.

From this distance I could admit that my earlier reaction to her visit to Mayle had been based on fear, which was a sound basis for jack shit. Forget Mayle – the biggest threat to our 'born again' relationship was me. I was going to have to toughen up.

Yet if what Eileen had said about Ilford was true, then I had very authentic reasons for stopping her having anything to do with him, though how I was going to sell that to her without telling her everything or appearing to be insecure and manipulative was beyond me.

It seemed that I'd been driving for barely minutes before I was pulling up at the underground carpark barrier. The guard peered out of his kiosk and came out to me.

'On your own, sir?'

I explained that there had been an accident and that Eileen had gone with Michael to the hospital. I told him that I was to wait and tell Stephanie when she returned. I showed him the key.

'Miss Sheldon came back about three-quarters of an hour ago, sir. Shall I buzz the penthouse and let her know you're coming?'

'No. No, I'd prefer it if you didn't. I noticed some press were still hanging around by the main entrance?'

'They didn't notice Miss Sheldon return, if that's what you're asking, sir.'

'Thank you. Was Miss Sheldon on her own when she returned?'

'Yes.'

'Which is her car?'

'It's the red BMW down the far end.'

On the way up in the lift I tried to think of how to introduce myself. It's not every day that a stranger opens the front door of your home unannounced. I wasn't sure if Eileen had mentioned my involvement, and if she hadn't then the opportunity of having Stephanie on her own would be lost.

I knocked on the door and waited. Nothing.

After knocking several more times and waiting again for something like five minutes, I decided to let myself in.

The living room was barely lit. One table lamp, next to the sofa, had been left on. Other than that the room was exactly as we'd left it.

I called out, 'Hello?'

No one came. I took off my barn jacket, threw it over the back of the sofa and settled myself down with as much noise as I could. Still no one appeared.

Gradually, in the warmth of the room, my eyes grew heavy and I closed them for what I intended to be a few minutes. In the event I must have fallen fast asleep, because I was jerked awake by a shrill voice.

'Who the hell are you?'

I opened my eyes to see Stephanie Sheldon standing on the other side of the room by the shoji door, looking angry and very frightened. Clasped between her hands was a mobile phone, held in front, like a pistol.

'You've got seconds to explain what you are doing here before I call the police.'

She was dressed in a pale blue bathrobe with a towel wrapped around her head like a turban.

Seeing her close up for the first time, I was struck by how beautiful she was. Although she looked like Eileen, I could see then there were difference, nuances of facial shape that suggested her father.

I stood and held up my hands to show they were empty. 'I'm an inquiry agent working on behalf of your mother.'

At that I thought I saw a glimmer of recognition, but there was no relaxation of the wariness.

'What's your name?'

'Steve.'

'Just Steve?'

'Hasn't your mother mentioned me?'

'Alex McGregor was the name I was given.' She looked like she was going to run at any second, so I worked at keeping the conversation going.

'Alex is my boss . . . I'm the foot-soldier.' I smiled.

'What are you doing here now?' She was looking around the room as she spoke.

'I'm on my own,' I reassured her. 'Eileen gave me the key to let myself in and wait for you.'

She frowned. 'Where is she?'

'You'd better sit down . . .'

'I'm fine where I am. Where's Eileen?'

I took a few steps towards her, but she backed and shook her head, then motioned me to sit down again.

'She's at the London Hospital,' I said.

'What's wrong with her?'

'It's not her. It's your brother Michael . . . there has been an explosion . . . his car.'

Her face became pale and she stared at me as though not understanding what I'd said. 'Explosion? That's not . . .'

'A petrol bomb . . . he's not in any danger, Stephanie, I saw him myself, just some light burns and smoke inhalation. They'll probably keep him in overnight.'

'You're lying . . .'

I could see the panic in her face and I kept my voice

soft to calm her. 'I was there, Stephanie . . . I drove your mother over to Michael's place. When he started his car there was . . .'

She wasn't listening.

The shock had hit. Vacant-eyed, she stood still for a moment, then suddenly slumped back against the door, the mobile phone falling from her hands. I ran to her as she slid towards the floor.

As I caught and held her she said his name over and over and shook her head from side to side as though unable or unwilling to accept what she'd heard. I positioned her with her back to the door and knelt down, supporting her head.

'Stephanie . . . Stephanie, he's all right. Really he is. A bit shaken up . . . nothing that won't mend.'

She looked straight through me, but didn't resist as I helped her over to the sofa. Sitting her down, I said nothing, just waited for her to snap out of it and ask questions, but she was in too deep a shock. Several times her mouth moved, but no words came out.

I leaned forward. 'Stephanie? Stephanie . . . who would do this to your brother?'

She turned her head to look at the shoji door, then back at me. Still she said nothing – just a blank expression and the wide, staring eyes. Some shock was understandable, but the reaction I saw was extreme.

There was no getting through. It was as though she were in another place, with a private conversation going on inside her head. Maybe the explosion was the final blow. First her father, then the stress of the court appearance, and now the attempt on Michael's life. When viewed that way, the reaction wasn't so bizarre, but it was still unnerving.

Disturbing, George Harris had called her, and I could see why.

Suddenly she let out a high-pitched scream and broke out in a hysterical wailing that was neither crying nor laughter. She tried to get to her feet, struggling fiercely, but I pushed her down into the sofa. She twisted hard and tried to bite my right hand, but I pulled the hand away and then leaned heavily on her shoulders to keep her from rising.

'Let her go!'

I spun around and saw Suzanne standing in the shoji doorway.

'I said let her go!'

Suzanne ran over to the sofa and I backed right off. I wasn't sure how long she'd been standing there, but it couldn't have looked good. I started to explain.

'All I was doing was stopping her from harming herself.'

Suzanne shot me a look and then turned back to Stephanie.

'Stay still, Stephanie . . . stay still,' she whispered.

Immediately, Stephanie went limp and lay back on the sofa, her eyes fixed on Suzanne, who continued to soothe her by brushing her forehead.

'Stay with her . . . and don't touch her!'

Suzanne went out through the shoji door and returned a couple of minutes later with some tablets and a glass of water. She wrapped one arm around Stephanie's shoulders and pushed the tablets into her mouth with the other hand.

'Pass me that glass, would you?'

I handed her the glass from where she had laid it down on the coffee table as she encouraged Stephanie to wash down the tablets,

Suzanne handed the glass back to me, and then rocked Stephanie in her arms as you would a small child, talking softly to her.

I found it creepy and wanted to leave, but I felt explanations were due and the thought of the story that might be told, if I just left, kept me rooted.

'Help me up with her and I'll put her to bed.'

Between us we lifted Stephanie. Suzanne wrapped one arm around her waist and walked her back over to the shoji door. I sat down again, determined to hang around till Eileen returned, whether I was tired or not.

Suzanne came back about ten minutes later. She was obviously unhappy to see me still there. I held up the key Eileen had given me and explained what had happened.

At the mention of Michael and the explosion, she lost some of the starch from her body language.

'Well, Stephanie's in bed and I'm here to look after her, so there's really no need for you to stay.'

Her eyes kept straying towards the telephone, and I could feel she was just itching to ring and check my story out.

'Eileen's at the hospital . . . she's got her mobile with her.'

'That won't be necessary.'

'Are you sure? I might "attack" you next.'

My sarcasm was a reaction to being hassled earlier by Menzies and Coleman, though that was hardly an excuse. I started again. 'Look, Miss . . . ?'

'Munroe,' she replied.

'Miss Munroe . . . Suzanne. Eileen has retained me to help Stephanie. It must have looked bad just then, but all I was doing was trying to stop her hurting herself . . . truly.'

'Yes, well, she's not been well since Robin was killed.'

'You seemed to handle her pretty efficiently.'

She declined the bait and just looked at me.

'You've had to do that before?'

She gave me a cool sweep of her eyes. 'I have no intention of telling you anything, Mr Jay.'

I nodded. 'Fair enough, but as I said, Eileen has retained me to help Stephanie . . .'

'And Alex McGregor? What has he retained you for?'

'Pardon?'

'McGregor's Loss Adjusters . . . you do work for them?'

'Yes.'

'So how can you help Stephanie by working against her family?'

I'd underestimated her, or maybe someone had primed her.

'Eileen's briefed you?'

'That's what a PA's for.'

'You're Eileen's PA?'

She shook her head. 'Robin's.'

'Robin's?'

She explained that Eileen was using her to assist with the storm of phone calls, faxes and e-mails that had erupted in the wake of Robin Sheldon's death.

'Were you close to him?'

'I . . .' She faltered.

'It must have hit you hard . . . Robin dying like that?'

Her face tightened. 'It was murder.'

'So who had reason to kill him? Ruth Heller?'

She looked as if she'd been struck in the face. 'Why . . . why d'you say . . .'

'Did she?'

There was a pause, and she looked at the door as though frightened someone would come through it. I decided to press with more questions before she could organise her answers, but ruined it by going straight for the kill.

'Just what was Robin Sheldon's relationship with Ruth Heller?'

Her expression changed from worry to wariness in one sweep.

'Don't . . . you were just guessing . . . you don't know anything, do you?'

'Then tell me, Suzanne.'

She shook her head. 'Go!'

'I'll find out . . .'

'Not from me. You people have been hounding Robin for months . . . well, now he's dead, I hope you're satisfied. Get out!'

Chapter Nineteen

I arrived back at the flat shortly after midnight to find Jenny asleep in the bedroom. I showered the smell of smoke from my body, dumped my clothes in a plastic bin-liner and shoved them into the grip bag in the living room.

It briefly crossed my mind to sleep on the sofa, but I talked myself out of it and slid in next to her, though I was careful not to touch or wake her.

She was naked.

Around five I woke to find her pressed against me. It wasn't reassuring. It just emphasised the limbo to which being with her confined me; somewhere between safety and shipwreck.

After a while I heard her breathing change and realised that she'd woken as well. I kept still with my eyes closed, but I could feel her watching me.

Finally I drifted off again and slept for another two hours. Then, as the dull morning light gave gradual shape to the room, I opened my eyes and took stock.

Lying with my hands behind my head, I rehearsed my 'him or me' speech over and over, until it actually dawned on me that it was my bed she was in and that possession is nine-tenths of a relationship.

That was when she woke.

'You're back,' she whispered.

'Around midnight . . . I didn't want to wake you.'

'Where did you go?'

'Alex,' I lied.

She thought about that. 'I rung him after you left.'

'Alex?'

'Kris.'

'And?'

She turned on to her front and raised herself on her elbows. 'I told him I had another job . . . that I didn't need his help any more.'

'What did he say?'

'Very little. I don't think he was on his own. If I were to guess I'd say that there was a woman with him.'

'That couldn't have been pleasant for you.'

Again, she took her time replying, 'Is any of this pleasant for you?'

'No.'

She looked directly at me. 'So what now?'

'I'd say that depends on you.'

I thought for a moment that she was going to accuse me of sidestepping the question; instead she sat up, kneeling before me. She looked beautiful, effortlessly erotic, and it was hard not to react to her; perhaps that was the point.

'I'll starting looking for a job again . . . today. It may take some time.'

'Okay.'

'And I'll not contact him again . . . for any reason. But in return you must make a promise.'

'I'm listening.'

'If we are going to be together again then the past must be the past . . . forget Kris Mayle. Don't talk about him or ask me about him. Or how I feel . . . particularly that. Because the truth is, Steve, I don't want to think about him. I made a huge mistake and, as you made me realise last night, I'm still paying for it . . . in all sorts of ways.'

And there it was; the conditions for the truce. She was asking for privacy for her pain and in return giving herself.

'You're sure about this?'

'Yes.'

I reached out and pulled her to me.

We should have made love then, but neither of us would make the first move. I sensed that she just wanted me to hold her and deep down that was all I wanted. That and Kris Mayle banged up.

Over breakfast we had a curiously detached conversation. We discussed everything, but it was as though we were talking about two other people. Negative as that sounds, at least it wasn't lunging and hoping. I believe she meant it when she said that Mayle was out of her life.

We left the flat together around half-ten; Jenny to search for work and me to pick up the photographs taken at the warehouse.

Considering the circumstances under which they were taken, the photos had come out surprisingly sharp. Looking at them raised the question of whether there was a continuous link from Stratford through to the Limehouse car bomb.

George Harris's theory about a professional arsonist was looking more probable, in that the spark-plug petrol bomb was unusual and to my eyes, at least, looked too subtle for a lucky novice. I'd certainly never come across anything like it before, and made a note to ask George if he had.

I'd said to Alex that I thought Eileen was scared; then it was just a gut feeling, now I knew why. She'd thought Stephanie was next on the killer's list, but it had been Michael.

In retrospect Monday had been pivotal. I now had a motive for Mayle starting the warehouse fire, plus Eileen's strong suspicion that he was at Ilford.

Ilford was the key.

Whatever was going on had exploded that Thursday night. Eileen had aimed me at Kris Mayle and everything she told me about him rang true, but I had to watch myself around her; she had a tendency to draw you on to her side.

I tucked the photos into a pocket and rang the penthouse.

Suzanne answered the phone. Eileen wasn't in and Suzanne refused to confirm whether or not she was at the hospital. I asked for Eileen's mobile number, an oversight by me the previous night, and she just stonewalled me.

'I'd like to come over and wait, perhaps talk some more about Ruth Heller.'

The line went dead.

Touching base with Alex at some stage was a must. He needed to be brought up to speed, and he might have something for me from other sources. Then I remembered that I was supposed to be going to his gym that night. I rang him to cry off, but all I got was his answerphone.

I left an abusive message.

Feeling that the day was slipping away from me, I drove over to Roley Benson's place. There was no reply, although a neighbour said he could sometimes be found at his local, the Rifleman, a dingy boozer in the Barking Road.

I gave it a try, but the landlord said he hadn't been in for days. He wondered if Roley was all right. I shrugged and left my mobile number, in case Roley surfaced.

That decided me.

I went back to the flat, changed into my running gear and drove to the start of Orange Tree Hill.

Being my second run didn't make it any easier; the effects of the smoke from the previous evening had turned my lungs into net curtains. I pushed on out of bloody-mindedness, only to be rewarded by the skies opening.

I crested the hill wet from sweat and rain and swore with relief as I ran the loop of Broxhill and dropped down to Lower Bedfords Road. Giddy with exertion, I felt the high that comes from the rush of endorphins in the system, only to throw up hard the minute I came to a halt by the car.

As I was hunched over, the mobile rang; it was Alex.

'Stevie, I hear you played the hero last night.'

'It was an experience . . . who told you?'

'The widow Sheldon . . . she talks highly of you, Stevie, highly.'

'I've been trying to get her all day, but that Suzanne, who believe it or not was Robin Sheldon's PA, just gives me a hard time. I'd like to know what her problem is.'

'You sound out of breath.'

'Spot on . . . I've got this nutter for a pal with a mission to turn me into a contender.'

'How many runs?'

'Two . . . and it isn't getting any easier.'

'You'll thank me.'

'Don't count on it.'

'We need to meet . . . are you still on for tonight?'

'I was going to back out, to tell the truth, but if we have to meet then perhaps we can combine the two.'

'Great. Pick me up at seven and bring those photographs.'

'Why is it me that always drives?'

'You like to be in control.' He laughed and rang off.

The gym was on an industrial estate just off the A13 in Dagenham. It was in a shabby, run-down building with iron-sheeted doors and bars on the windows. As we walked in, I heard the steady slap-slap-slap of leather skipping ropes beating the floor, and caught the aroma of sweat and horse oils.

Adrenaline flowed through me, and I wasn't sure I enjoyed the sensation.

Along one wall hung a line of heavy bags, maize and floor-to-ceiling balls; each busily employed. Along the opposite wall was a line of full-length mirrors with a ragged string of men shadow-boxing in front of them; their bodies loose, curving and dancing, and their faces gaunt.

There weren't many young men; most seemed to be early thirties plus, with signs of past battles shaping cheek bones and noses.

Just for the craic, Alex had said; the bastard had brought me to a wolf pack.

The two in the ring were something special. One was a coloured guy, about six foot and built as solid as it gets; he moved like liquid, never forcing, missing nothing. When he jabbed I almost didn't see; it was that fast.

The other was an older guy possessing a fast-talking, weather-featured face sitting atop a body so lithe and whiplash hard it denied his fifty-plus years.

'That's Paddy Ryan,' whispered Alex. 'Brilliant boxer in his day and now a physio with the golden touch.'

I watched him as he moved at fifty miles an hour around the ring; head, trunk and legs in constant motion and the punches flowing like bursts of gunfire.

He never stopped talking.

Each exchange, each incident, was met with a comment or a curse. He smiled, sang and laughed; nodding in appreciation when the coloured guy tagged him and whooping when he returned the compliment. I'd never seen anything like it; it was total entertainment.

Even the boxers outside the ring weren't spared his wit; streams of acidic barbs shot across the room at some infringement of technique or timing.

Alex's face shone like he'd seen the love of his life.

On catching sight of Alex, Paddy Ryan stopped sparring and climbed through the ropes.

'Alex! Did you see me? I was beating his black arse!'

The face of the coloured guy in the ring split into a huge grin, and he shook his head from side to side. I was to learn later that he was Tommy Grant, a Barbados-born light-heavyweight who had fought most of his pro career in the States and had been a sparring partner for just about every title contender at one time or another.

I knew the name, but would never have recognised him.

There was more skill in the little things, the things he didn't do, than in most fighters' entire fighting vocabulary.

'This is your boy, then, Alex?' said Paddy, extending his hand.

'Aye, he's feeling a touch shy.'

I shook Paddy's hand. 'Frightened is the word he's searching for,' I said.

'Nothing wrong with fear . . . it's the glue that keeps our arse attached to our bodies.'

'Is it all right if Stevie trains tonight, Paddy?'

He nodded. 'Get changed and warm up with some shadow and skipping, then you can move around with Tommy.'

'I wasn't intending to spar.. . .' I stared hard at Alex, who was grinning like mad. 'Maybe I could just do some bag work,' I suggested.

Paddy cocked his head on one side. 'If I see you shadow-box I can tell fifty per cent of your strengths and weaknesses, and if you spar I can see the other fifty per cent.'

'I'm very rusty . . .'

'Good! The natural prejudices will come out.'

Trapped, I walked slowly to the changing room, wondering if there was a fire exit.

When I came back Alex was showing the photographs to Paddy, who was shaking his head.

I warmed up and stretched, trying to squeeze some of the tightness from my legs; a legacy of the afternoon run. After three rounds shadow and two of skipping, I was gloved up and virtually manhandled into the ring by Alex.

Tommy grinned and shook gloves with me. Paddy stayed inside the ring, 'for safety', as Alex put it. It didn't help my confidence when Paddy reminded Tommy to 'go easy on the power'.

I watched the hand of the gym clock as it came up slowly to signal the start of the round and desperately told myself to stay relaxed.

At the second the buzzer rang a left jab instantly squashed my nose followed by a jackhammer right that thankfully Tommy 'controlled'.

'Adjust your distance,' advised Paddy. 'Distance is determined as much by speed as reach . . . adjust!'

I moved back six inches and this time got hit by a double jab that drove my head back violently. Out of fear and survival, I threw an overhand right as the next jab came in and almost caught him on the cheek. Tommy grinned and nodded his approval before unleashing a rapid combination, which finished with a tight uppercut to my ribs.

Every bit of air was forced out of my lungs and I fell back against the ropes.

'You all right, man?' asked Tommy, with a surprisingly soft voice.

I nodded and a halt was called while I got my breath back, then it was on with the show.

I fought back harder. Trying to keep it fast and simple.

'Switch!' Paddy's voice stung me through the haze of sweat and punches. 'Straight and round, body and head . . . switch!'

Jabs, crosses, hooks and uppercuts came in clusters; mercifully Tommy held back. I had no doubt that he could have broken every rib I had, and taken out my jaw as well, with just half an inch more penetration. He was a gentleman, and I was truly grateful to him.

My pulse pounded in my ears as I slipped a blistering right hand and whipped in left hooks to his liver and jaw.

'That's it,' screamed Paddy, 'stay on his case . . . make him react to you so that he's always one move behind.'

And so it went on. We sparred three rounds, but it felt like more, a lot more. Towards the end my only agenda was to breathe and not to get hit. When a halt was finally called I was totally wasted.

Paddy was beaming and called over his shoulder to Alex. 'Not bad . . . nice double hook combination and the overhand right would have been a bitch if it had landed, but Mr Jay is unfit!'

'Tell me about it,' I said as I slumped against the ropes.

Tommy came up and put an arm around my shoulders. 'How long since you last sparred, man?'

I thought hard. 'Four years and then only light. It's much longer since I've done any serious stuff.'

He grinned. 'Well, you fooled me.'

I climbed out of the ring and Alex took my gloves off.

'What did I tell you, Stevie . . . that was interesting to watch.'

'Interesting in the Chinese sense,' I snarled.

I got showered and towelled myself dry. It was only as I came out of the changing rooms that I saw a cartoon pinned up above the door. It was a brilliant caricature of Paddy sitting cross-legged with his hands held in front of him as though in prayer; underneath was written 'The Sandpaper Buddha'.

It was signed Thomas B. Grant.

In the gym the ring had been reoccupied by two serious-looking characters who were going at it like cats in a sack. Paddy was standing with Alex and calling out what I could only term 'technical abuse'.

'That's it, drop your hands, yer fuckin' idiot! That way you'll get knocked out and we can all go home early! Never, ever, take your hands away from what you're trying to protect!'

Alex beamed.

I joined him and Paddy and all three of us watched the sparring.

The Irishman didn't miss a thing. Praise and criticism were reinforced by a deadly accurate wit that had the two boxers curling their toes and the rest of us crying with laughter. I could see where the sandpaper bit came in, but I had to wait till the sparring stopped before I witnessed the Buddha.

As Paddy climbed into the ring the boxers closed in on him.

'You're both trying to win too much . . . forget the other man . . . he's merely the reflection of your errors . . . control yourself . . . stay detached, but see what there is to see, not the shadows, not your fears. Relax and let your body do what it knows.'

They fought one more round and the effect of his words on them was fascinating to see. They fought just as hard, but the tension was gone, replaced by a freedom of movement and action that lifted their technique until the two of them were seamless. Punch and counter-punch flowed and defence and attack became impossible to separate.

Paddy stood, his eyes still and calmness moulding his features; perhaps in the purest sense enlightened.

I knew the deeper reason for Alex wanting me to come was to heal not box, but it wasn't until that moment that I knew how. Paddy was to be the balance, the shifting weight that would adjust my preoccupations.

The gruffness of Alex's voice retrieved me. 'Paddy thinks he recognises one of the faces in the photos.'

Paddy nodded. 'This one here, the big fella. Can't put a name to him, though.'

He pointed to the thug who had first challenged me at the warehouse.

'I think one of the others called him "Len", if that's any help,' I said.

Paddy took another look and then gave a small nod. 'Maybe . . . Tommy!'

Tommy Grant came over and looked at the photograph. It was the last one I had taken, and the big thug's face filled the frame.

'His name's Len,' said Paddy. 'He's put weight on, but I think it could be Lenny Gibson.'

Tommy looked at Paddy, then peered at the picture. He took his time and then smiled. 'You're right . . . man, he has put weight on!'

'Lenny Gibson?' I asked.

'He was pro fighter, a light-heavyweight with genuine class . . . could have made British champion,' explained Paddy.

'Could have? What happened?'

'He blew it. Beat a man half to death in a pub brawl . . . left him paralysed down one side.'

'And?'

'He got ten years,' said Tommy with a shake of the head.

'Served six and reapplied for his licence . . . the Boxing Board of Control laughed him out the room,' Paddy added.

'D'you know what happened to him?'

Paddy's mouth turned down at the edges. 'He was doing the unlicensed circuit . . . a mug's game. He was banging them over too quick and he ran out of opponents, except the occasional gypsy boy . . . they'll fight anyone. Last I heard he was into debt collection.'

Tommy looked at the photo again and then at me. 'Have you got trouble with this dude?'

'I had a run-in with him . . . and a couple of others.'

'Don't screw with him, man. He's as mean as they come and he hits very hard . . . his best punch was a left hook,' he added.

'You fought him?'

'Not in a contest, but I got to spar with him once . . . must be all of ten, maybe twelve years ago now.'

'And he's good?'

He nodded his head slowly. 'The hook's heavy and he cuts the angle, like a bolo.' He demonstrated a swinging punch and shortened the arc of delivery by bending his elbow at the last moment. 'Makes it hard to read. He's got faults, mind . . . drops his right hand when he throws it.'

I smiled. 'Thanks for the info, Tommy.'

'No problem. I hope you don't have to use it.'

I drove Alex back and we used the time to discuss the case. I told him that although I thought I was making headway, the suspicion was beginning to lurk that much of the truth was locked up inside Stephanie Sheldon's head, and on the last showing she wouldn't make the world's most reliable witness.

I still hadn't mentioned to him that I was convinced that the face I'd seen at the window was hers.

'Mayle was at Stratford and Ilford, you say?'

I nodded. 'According to Eileen . . . logic dictates that he must be in the frame for the car bomb as well.'

'But why try to kill Michael Sheldon?'

'Stephanie and he are close and she's the one who can finger Mayle . . . what better way to pressure someone?'

Alex frowned. 'Just suppose for a moment Mayle was in it with the Sheldons and you can place Mayle at the Ilford fire. We could start court action to reclaim the insurance money.'

'You've lost me there . . . all of this is pointing at Mayle right now and from what Eileen's told me about the stunts he pulled with the business I can't see them all in this together.'

'Not a falling out of thieves?'

I shook my head. 'Not that I can see. Eileen is frightened of him, Alex, and she was right to be frightened. Mayle's fingerprints are all over this.'

'Don't overlook Robin Sheldon, Stevie. He was up to something and the others must know what.'

He was starting to put doubt in my mind and I had to admit nothing could be ruled out. I had to find another way of coming at the situation. Ruth Heller?

'What's your plan from here?'

'Believe it or not, try to talk to Roley Benson,' I said.

He pulled a face. 'That's a waste of time, Stevie.'

'Maybe, but I'm intrigued to find out what he was up to at Ilford.'

'Well, it's your party, but try not to waste too

much time on peripherals. Remember, Stratford's the reason you're involved here.'

When we reached Alex's house I declined his offer of a nightcap and went home. Between the running and the gym I was wrecked and needed a good night's sleep; I was back on day work the following day.

Chapter Twenty

Wednesday, 22 April

I got to work around eight-fifteen and relieved an out-duty Sub Officer who had been standing by while my opposite number was off sick.

There was a mountain of paperwork outstanding from the last shift, and I hoped to make inroads into it before fire calls, appliance exchanges and the sudden gearshifts of activity that peppered tours of duty derailed the day. John had the same idea and booked on duty ten minutes after me.

We met up in the station office and had a brief discussion about how we were going to schedule the day. John reminded me that I'd said we would run a drill session on cylinder fires with Sandy Richards, so that he could log it in his task book as a fire ground simulation; part of his promotion process.

John looked at the list. 'We've run out of time and we haven't even started.'

The nine o'clock roll-call saw the entire watch, all thirteen of us, on duty together for the first time in months. With so many present the place was buzzing.

Two of them, Rod Brody – the fourth angler – and Doug 'Tick-tock' Russell, so named because of his tendency to 'watch' while others were working, had missed the Ilford job and were quizzing the others.

'We're one over the top, someone's going to have to go out-duty,' said Dave Chase, looking pointedly at Doug.

'Must be 'Tick-tock', said Harry Wildsmith.

Doug looked from Dave Chase to Harry and nodded. 'That's what I've missed.'

'What?' said Dave.

'The telepathy of the damned.'

John let them carry on for a few minutes then brought them to attention and called the roll. At the end of the parade he read out a flood warning for parts of the Thames and its tributaries, including the River Rom.

The Rom was a small, suspect-coloured river that used to flood regularly until it was confined by concrete walls and a series of tunnels. Even with all the rain we'd been having it was unlikely to break its banks in the town, but it might cause a problem to the north-east where the concrete ran out and it flowed past housing estates that bordered fields.

'I'll go out first thing this morning and take a look, John,' I said.

After the checking BA sets, radios and the attendance paperwork, the watch gathered in the Mess for the morning cup of tea. The first day on shift was invariably noisy, and with everyone present it was hard to hear yourself think.

I looked around the table at each of them; from Jimmy McClane, a tall, thin man who was quiet and watchful, and his cousin Martin, very much in the same mould, to Tom Reed, the oldest on the watch at fifty-three and with only one more year to go, and all the others – Wayne, Rod, Dave, Harry, Mike Scott, Doug Russell, Simon Jones, John and Sandy; they were the best watch I'd had.

John called them a bunch of pirates and it suited them.

Image was the one area that he was sensitive about. He hated to see anything detrimental about the job and often observed that fire-fighters were portrayed in black-and-white terms by the media – either heroes at a fire or militants about to strike.

'They're neither,' he would say with a shake of the head, 'just ordinary people doing an extraordinary job.'

When the phone rang I could hardly hear it above the din.

Tom Reed, the dutyman for the day, answered it.

'Guv, its ADO Grant.'

John caught my eye and called for quiet; on the third time of asking he got it.

'Morning, Steve, good four days off?' said Bob.

'Almost.'

'What have you got on today?'

'We're buried alive.' I ran a list of jobs by him.

'It'll have to keep,' he said. 'The police investigating the Ilford fire want to speak to all the crews on the initial attendance.'

'Today?'

'This afternoon. A teleprinter message is being sent out by Staff to all affected stations to cancel their outside duties and be at your station at 1430 hours. The police are interested in anything that might've been seen on arrival.'

'Who's attending from Area?'

He sighed. 'Charnley.'

'What about yourself?'

'Wouldn't miss it for the world, Steve.'

I let Bob go and told the watch.

'If Charnley's coming I want us in good order, so we'll start by having the appliances cleaned inside and out,' I said.

'What's El Niño coming for?' said Dave Chase.

'El Niño?' queried Sandy.

Dave turned towards him. 'Charnley . . . he's a bleedin' disaster!'

'It means the Christ-child,' sniffed Harry.

'What?'

'Christ-child, Dave . . . it means the Christ-child,' Harry repeated.

Dave's mouth opened, but for once he was speechless. Harry let out a low chuckle, and everywhere Dave looked he was met with silent grins.

At half-nine the watch started to blitz the appliances and the station in preparation for the afternoon. John, Sandy and I got stuck into the paper-work and Doug was sent out-duty to Dagenham.

At half-eleven, after tea break, I took the pump ladder down to the bridge at the lower end of Water-loo Road, close to our station border, to inspect the Rom.

Normally it was a six-inch-deep dirty ribbon of water running in a wide gully at the bottom of a larger concrete conduit some eight feet wide and five feet deep. That morning the river was in full spate, filling the larger conduit to within two feet of the top in a swirling black flood littered with floating debris.

Harry joined me and stared down at the water.

'Never seen it that high before, guv.' He glanced up at the sky. 'And I'd say it's going to get worse.'

I agreed. 'I'll send a 'printer message when we get back. It'll need watching.'

We drove north and checked out the river where it ran by the housing estates. Again the water was high and had in some places spilt over into the surround-ing fields, but not to the point where it was an immediate threat.

Back at the station I sent a message via the Eastern Staff office to make all local stations aware. Then it was back to the paperwork. Sandy pulled me as soon as I entered the office.

'We're not going to have time to fit in the cylinder drill, are we, guv?'

'First thing tomorrow, Sandy.'

He nodded. 'Have you done one of these police briefings before, guv?'

John looked up.

'No, Sandy, I haven't, and I've never heard of it happening to anyone else.'

'Does it go in my task book?'

'Yes, I think it should. Enter it under advice and assistance to outside agencies.'

After lunch, around two, machines descended on us from all over the Eastern Command. With each new arrival the upstairs lecture room became more crowded, until the last crews had to stand at the back.

Jack Grocott and George Harris arrived last with Bob Grant, and sat propped on the window ledge at the back. Bob seated himself in one of the reserved chairs at the front. I waited downstairs for Charnley and the police.

Ten minutes later two cars swung into the yard, One driven by Charnley and the other by Menzies.

Chapter Twenty-One

A Detective Inspector Graham, a fleshy man of about forty with dark curly hair, accompanied Menzies across the yard. Charnley caught them up and then led them to where I waited at the back of the appliance room.

When he introduced them, neither policeman gave any hint of recognition, but as Charnley showed the way up the stairs Menzies hung back and caught my eye.

His look wasn't hostile, but it was cold; neutral. Perhaps it was just professional detachment, but the impression given out was of someone who enjoyed his status as inquisitor.

I'd disliked him before and saw nothing then to make me change my mind.

Bob Grant stood up as all four of us entered the lecture room and motioned everybody to do the same. There was a slow, erratic response, as station culture dictated, but they all got there in the end.

Charnley effected a tight smile. 'Please sit!'

The response was, if anything, slower and, although not personal, appeared to irritate him.

'For those of you who don't know me, I'm your

new Group Divisional Officer, Maurice Charnley
. . . I arranged a briefing this afternoon in order to
assist the police with their murder investigation . . . it
is also my intention afterwards to conduct an infor-
mal debrief of last Thursday.'

A debrief so quickly was unusual.

'Why, guv?' That was Dave Chase.

Charnley smiled. 'We need to look at what happened the other night . . . examine the mistakes made
in order to learn from them.'

That grabbed everybody's attention for all the
wrong reasons.

Oblivious, he ploughed on. 'Because of the Performance Review of Command debrief will cover all
aspects of Command and Control, I don't propose to
go into the actions of those people who at various
times were Incident Commander, but to concentrate
on the actions of the crews themselves.'

There was complete silence. By any yardstick it
had been a desperately fierce and complex fire that
had stretched everybody to the limit. Common sense
called for a few words of congratulations for the
efforts made and an appreciation of just how hard it
had been for the first crews on scene.

Barely minutes had passed and the man had alien-
ated the room.

'Let me start by introducing Detective Inspector
Graham and Detective Sergeant Menzies.'

Menzies nodded to the room and Graham stepped
forward. If Charnley had blundered, then Graham

was as sure-footed as they come. Reading the room right, he started by thanking everyone for attending and asked them to bear with him if he asked naive questions.

'An uncle of mine was a fireman, but I'm only a copper!' he said with a grin, and as quickly as the room had frozen it thawed.

'I want to start by asking you to think carefully about the fire at Ilford last Thursday night.' There was a pause and he placed his hands in his trouser pockets. 'Crimes and crime scenes are composed of bits of information,' he continued. 'Each one may be a one-off or it may be linked to something more significant.'

His voice was soft, soft enough for you to hear, but also soft enough to make you listen carefully. He looked to see that he had everybody's attention and moved on.

'I know that your job is to save lives and put out fires . . . and just one look at that fire and I know you had your hands full, so if today reveals nothing then so be it, but . . . but sometimes the small things build into a mosaic. So I want you to go back to that night . . . what did you see? Was there anything unusual that caught your attention, even if you have since dismissed it?'

He turned towards a white marker board behind him on the wall and then looked at Charnley.

'By all means,' said Charnley.

Graham picked up a marker pen and drew a rough

sketch plan of the Ilford fire scene, including the roads off to the sides and the traffic lights.

'We're particularly interested in what you saw when you first arrived. I wonder if I could ask the drivers of the various machines to come up to the board and mark in where you parked and the direction of your approach.'

One by one the drivers trooped up to the board and drew in the required information. When they had all sat down again, Graham drew some circles on the board.

'Here . . .' He indicated the back service road. '. . . is a system of security cameras that monitor the back of the buildings and the carpark that serves them. The problem is that although these cameras sweep across the whole area, they don't cover the entire area at any one time. So it's possible for people and vehicles to come and go without being detected.'

To a man, the room was leaning forward. Our involvement with the police was generally peripheral. This type of briefing was not only unusual, it was intriguing.

'Did you see anything out of the ordinary?'

At first there was silence. Graham tried again.

'It doesn't have to relate to the fire. Perhaps you noticed someone in the crowd . . . a car parked unusually . . .'

Again there was a silence that stretched on, broken only by a cough or someone moving in his seat. After a couple of minutes Charnley got to his feet, and from somewhere there was a low groan. It didn't stop him.

'The police have come here specifically to request our help . . .'

'We can't help if we didn't see anything, guv,' came a flat, anonymous voice from the back of the room.

Graham and Menzies exchanged glances and Menzies took out a pack of cigarettes and offered one to Charnley, who shook his head. Immediately the smokers in the room took their cue and lit up. George Harris swung open a window behind him before taking his pipe and filling it. Blue-grey smoke curled in the breeze from the open window.

Menzies waited, drawing on his cigarette, looking around the room. The embarrassment factor was now kicking in and there were a few smiles and the odd comment, but nothing else. It seemed that the briefing would be a dud and would be called to a close, but Charnley was determined to be of use.

'I believe Station Officer Jay saw something a bit strange,' he said.

I played it straight. 'Guv?'

'Well, you directed a BA crew to the second floor . . . in fact your brief to them was to specifically search for a woman. Am I right?'

All eyes in the room swung on to me as I thought back to what exactly I'd seen. The image was clearer than it had ever been, and it was Stephanie Sheldon.

The room fidgeted, and out of the corner of my eye I saw George studying the contents of his pipe a touch too closely. I felt hot, uncomfortable, and I thought I was going to have to go outside and get some air.

'Station Officer?'

'Pardon?'

'Did you see something, Station Officer?' Menzies asked.

'I think so.'

Graham stepped forward. 'Tell me what you saw, please . . . what's your first name?'

'Steve.'

There were a few grins at this attempt at informality.

'My name's Dave,' said Dave Chase, and the room rippled with laughter.

Graham grinned and nodded. 'Okay, just take us through what it was that you saw.'

I was trapped now. Whatever I'd seen had made me direct a BA crew, so either here or at the Performance Review of Command debrief I would have to explain my thinking.

'I saw very little,' I began. 'A face . . . a woman's face . . . on the second floor a fraction after the jumper hit the deck in front of me.'

'A woman . . . how old would you say?' That was Menzies.

'I can't be sure. In fact I can't be sure of anything. A search was carried out and no body was found. Also there were no casualties that fitted.'

'So what did you see?' Menzies asked.

'I saw . . . something.' I shrugged.

Charnley looked sideways at Graham as if to apologise for me. I felt the anger rise and saw the expression of Harry Wildsmith and some of the others change.

'So you directed a BA crew into the building without knowing for certain what they were looking for?' said Charnley.

'I made a judgment, guv . . . perhaps I was wrong.'

He folded his arms and stood looking at me. I wouldn't have minded so much normally – mistakes occur and all I'd done was err on the side of safety – but to see Charnley adopt an air of superiority when his own operational experience was so limited galled me.

There was silence, and if I read the room right it wouldn't have taken much to turn it into a slagging match with Charnley the target.

'I saw something too.'

All heads turned.

'What's your name?' asked Graham.

'Richards. Leading Fire-fighter Sandy Richards.'

Sandy stood up, nervous now as all eyes were focused on him.

'Just what was it that you saw, Sandy?' said Graham.

Sandy swallowed and his eyes darted towards me. 'It was like the guv'nor said . . . it was hard to make out. It looked like a woman.'

Graham nodded. 'Where were you when this happened, Sandy?'

'By the "jumper" . . . I . . . er . . . looked up at the window where he'd jumped from and saw it.'

'The woman?'

Sandy shook his head. 'Like the guv'nor said . . . you couldn't be sure.'

Menzies and Graham looked pensive.

'Did anyone else see this . . . woman?'

There were murmurs, but no one else spoke up. Charnley looked at Graham and shrugged.

'Okay, everyone, I think that's all, but if anything else occurs to you please let one of your officers know and we'll come back to speak to you. Mr Charnley, I wonder if it would be possible for Station Officer Jay and the Leading Fire-fighter to make a statement?'

Sandy's faced coloured as I stared at him.

Charnley nodded. 'If that's what you'd like. ADO Grant will sit in if you've no objection.'

Graham agreed.

'Bob, I'll run quickly through the debrief if you accompany Station Officer Jay and Leading Fire-fighter Richards downstairs.' He turned to Graham. 'You can take the statements in the Station Officer's office.'

At the top of the stairs, Bob pulled me to one side.

'Careful what you say, Steve. If you're confident, speak up; if not, say so clearly.'

'Advice received, Bob.'

Downstairs in my office, DI Graham was sat down

behind my desk by Bob and Menzies was given a chair next to him. Sandy was sent for a couple of chairs from the Mess for Bob and me. When we were all seated, Graham and Menzies took my statement down. It was so generalised it must have been worthless. Not once did Menzies mention the fire and explosion in Michael Sheldon's car. Maybe he was trying to keep something over me, though why exactly escaped me.

I explained just how hectic the first few minutes of the Ilford fire were and stated that although I had seen something I couldn't be sure what. I agreed that I had thought it was a woman at the time and had directed the BA crew to search for her.

The statement was then read back to me and I signed it.

I stood outside while Sandy gave his statement. He was in the office for quite some time, and when eventually they all emerged Bob Grant took me to one side.

'That Leading Fire-fighter of yours is a little too loyal for his own good. They think that he only said he saw something because Charnley was on your back.'

'What? How have the police taken it?'

'Considering it's a murder investigation . . . very well. I think you should have a word with him and explain the difference between loyalty and stupidity.'

'Does Charnley have to know this?'

'I won't say anything . . . and if I weight that DI

Graham right, neither will he. I don't think either of them took to Charnley, for all his trying.'

When the policemen emerged from the office, Graham had a word with Bob and Menzies came over to me.

'You certainly get around, don't you, Mr Jay? First the car bomb . . . then you turn up at Robin Sheldon's Ilford flat . . . oh yes, we know about that . . . now you say you saw a woman at the very window Robin Sheldon jumps to his death from.'

I said nothing.

'Was that face at the window Stephanie Sheldon?'

'It could have been anybody,' I said.

He nodded slowly. 'I'll spare you the lecture on withholding information from the police, but you must see that working part time for a loss adjuster and being in the thick of it, so to speak, makes you of interest to us.'

'You've got my statement.'

'Yes,' he said, 'let's just hope it doesn't come back to haunt you.'

With that he rejoined his boss and Bob Grant, who showed them off the station. Sandy and I hung around, waiting for the debrief to finish, and I took the opportunity to pull him about the statement.

'I'm told that you made up that business about seeing the woman.'

He looked down. 'I told them what I saw, guv . . . if they don't believe me . . .'

'Sandy, I appreciate the thought, but this isn't a

question of backing your mates up. They're investigating the most serious crime there is, and wasting police time is an offence. Between you and me . . . did you see something?'

He straightened up and looked me in the eye. 'Yes, guv.'

'Let's just hope you never have to say that in a court of law. There's a stack of work in the office – you'd better bury yourself in it till six o'clock.'

I watched him walk away. He'd make a lousy witness, and I doubted the police would ever call him.

Shortly after, the door upstairs opened and the crews came out of the lecture room. As they tumbled down the stairs, you could tell by their faces that the debriefing hadn't gone well. Charnley was the last to come down the stairs, and by then Bob Grant had rejoined me.

'Walk with me to my car, please, Bob.' As an afterthought he turned towards me. 'I'll see you at the PRC next week, Station Officer,' he said.

I watched them cross the yard with Charnley talking and Bob listening. Bob had a way of switching off when people annoyed him, and even from a distance you could see he was suffering.

At that moment Dave Chase and Harry Wildsmith appeared. They saw me watching Charnley, and perhaps my face reflected my thoughts.

'I'd ignore him, guv,' said Dave. 'The man's a cretin! If he upset the Mafia he'd wake up with a horse's arse on his pillow!'

I smiled. 'I take it the debrief didn't go down too well?'

'He's been sitting and thinking since last Thursday and what he came up with was total bollocks!' said Dave.

Harry gave a thin smile. 'Hmm, when it comes to fire-fighting our friend Mr Charnley does seem to have a number of hideosyncrasies.'

Chapter Twenty-Two

When the police and Charnley departed, I was told by John that George Harris had hung back.

'He wanted a private word, guv, and asked me to keep Jack away until he had. Is there something I should know?'

I shook my head and John gave me a long look. 'Where's George now?'

'He's waiting in the station commander's office.'

'Thanks, John.'

I went upstairs and along the top corridor to the commander's office. We'd been without a station commander for two weeks and were waiting for the new man to arrive. Rumours were thick with possible names, including one or two prominent bogeymen whose shadow was always invoked whenever watch paranoia reared its head, but no one knew for sure.

Bob Grant had been filling in, but it would have been wishing for Christmas to suppose that we would get him permanently. Ultimately it really didn't matter who we got, provided he was fair and independent.

As I walked into the office I could see that George was hacked off.

'Is there a problem, George?'

For the second time in as many minutes I got a long stare.

'We had a phone call this morning . . . from that DS Menzies.'

'Oh?'

'He wanted to know if you were acting in any kind of official capacity at a car bomb incident the other night.'

'And what did you tell him?'

His face was set, angry. 'I told him I didn't have the faintest idea what he was talking about . . . what else should I have said?'

'I'm sorry, George. I didn't know that was going to happen.'

He wasn't impressed. 'When yer asked me to help I made it plain that I couldn't afford to become exposed. I said I'd help with the database and that's it. I don't know what you're involved in, guv, but obviously the police have taken an interest . . . you've even got your Leading Fire-fighter sticking his neck out for all the world to see.'

'I didn't know that was going to happen either,' I said lamely.

He jammed his pipe into the corner of his mouth. 'Guv, we've never quarrelled and if helping yer is going to lead to hassle between us I'd just as soon leave it.'

I shook my head. 'I'd rather you helped me . . . I need your help, George.'

He stared at the floor with his arms folded. 'Well, I'll be straight with yer. People are starting to point guv.'

'I . . .'

'Look, if you're ill . . . or somethin's bothering yer . . . whatever, then take some time off. At the moment you've got idiots of the stature of Charnley riding yer. People are very protective towards yer, guv, but at the moment the buzz is you're not coping too well.'

I swallowed. 'I'm not ill, George. I've had a few problems, but I'm okay. And I'm genuinely sorry that you found yourself in the position you did.'

He grunted and leaned back against a filing cabinet, apparently calmer after getting it off his chest.

'Is that what you wanted to say?'

He glanced up and shook his head. 'I think I've got something for yer.'

'Oh?'

'But if there're any more enquiries from the bill or senior officers, I'll walk.'

'I hear you, George. Has Charnley said anything?'

'No, thank Christ! That idiot should be shipped back to Fire Safety or whichever hole he crawled out from. How do people like that get promoted?'

'They volunteer, George.'

He smiled grimly. 'We really do it to ourselves, don't we. This must be the only job in the world where the main requirement for advancement is ego.'

'And a little ruthlessness . . . the desire to cut down others so that you're the tallest tree in the wood.'

He sighed. 'I shall be glad to go, really I will.'

George was forever playing the pessimist, but I'd heard that particular sentiment from so many people over the last few years that it was attaining the status of a creed.

'So, what is it that you've got for me?'

'A discrepancy.'

'Go on.'

'After I left you the other night I went back and reread everything on the Stratford fire. I came across Brian Worthington's notes in a file on my laptop and something struck me as very odd. Worthington's original notes have long since been destroyed, but I'd made a copy of them, and as I read through I realised that the last two people on the premises made conflicting statements to Worthington.'

'This is Stephanie Sheldon and Kris Mayle?'

'So you know it wasn't this geezer called Chasteau?'

'I found out the other day.'

'But do you know that both Sheldon and Mayle claimed to be the last person on the premises?'

'What's the significance, George?'

'Think about it, guv. If a crime has been committed and you were guilty, you'd hardly admit to being the last person there.'

'I take your point. Could one be covering up for the other?'

'I wouldn't know, but I do know that if I'd torched a warehouse I wouldn't want to own up to being the last person there . . . it would be asking for trouble.'

'Didn't Worthington tell the police all this?'

'Christ knows. He was technically in charge and I was only the Sub Officer so I did what I was told . . . Worthington was a nice bloke, but he never really got to grips with fire investigation.'

'Anything else, George?'

'Yes. I've run through a list of all fires in fashion shops and warehouses, and even been on the Internet. As far as I can see there are no other fires that could be even remotely linked to either Stratford or Ilford.'

'I see.'

I sat down in an easy chair by the window and George relaxed for the first time and sat in the commander's seat. 'I appreciate your efforts, George, particularly after that phone call from the bill.'

He puffed at his pipe and nodded.

'I've got something that might interest you,' I said.

'Oh?'

'That car bomb the other night . . . the one the police rang you about. It would take too long to go into detail . . .'

'The less I know the better, guv.'

'I'll keep it brief. Michael Sheldon, Robin Sheldon's son, was driving the car. So it's a pound to a penny that it's connected to Ilford and Stratford.'

'I'm listening.'

'I managed to get a look at the remains of the bomb and I've never seen anything like it before, and I remembered what you said about a professional torch being responsible for Stratford.'

George was listening hard, his body still and the pipe frozen in midair.

'It was clever . . . like Stratford was clever . . . a spark plug from the ignition system had been taped into the mouth of a petrol can . . . when Michael Sheldon turned over the ignition . . . bang!'

'That is clever. Simple, but subtle. Is he dead?'

'No. He received minor burns to the face and suffered bad smoke inhalation.'

His mouth turned down. 'Lucky . . . dead lucky.'

'Does this ring any bells for you?'

'Not off hand. Could you draw it for me, guv?'

I got up and went over to the commander's desk. Taking a notepad from the top drawer, I sketched what I'd seen. Then I drew a rough plan of the square and marked in the carpark and Michael Sheldon's Mercedes.

'I've not seen the like of this before, guv. In fact . . . if I were a copper, I'd say the very method might well help pin down a suspect.'

He studied the drawing for a few moments and asked where I was standing when the bomb went off. He shook his head. 'It's amazing it never killed him. How fast did the fire spread to the rest of the car?'

'Very fast, George. I don't think he could have got himself out of there.'

'Lucky you were there, then.'

'I think so.'

He fell silent and studied the sketch again. Then sniffed.

'I might be gettin' fanciful 'ere, but if you were clever, yer could measure out the petrol to give someone a nasty fright, but not kill them.'

'It's a thought.'

'Otherwise, if you're clever enough to think up a bomb like this, how come you get the amount of petrol wrong . . . if yer were trying to top someone?'

'Unless it wasn't professional . . . just a lucky amateur,' I said.

'Possible, but for what it's worth I think your first guess, a pro, was right.' He picked up the sketch and folded it before placing it in his pocket. 'I'll go through the database and phone all the other Fire Investigation Teams. With luck our man may have been too clever this time.'

After George had left I went downstairs and sat in my office, thinking things through. Sandy's misplaced loyalty shamed me; more so for being transparent to everyone. What did it say about me that the youngest member of the watch thought I needed rescuing?

I was sinking slowly into a dark pit of self-criticism when John stuck his head around the door.

'You okay, guv?'

'Come in, John.'

He stood there, looking awkward and waiting for me to ask him.

'Go on, then.' I smiled. 'Tell me that they all think I'm losing it and you've come to give the "we are all very concerned" speech.'

'We are concerned, guv.'

I sighed. 'Sorry, John, that was flippant of me. I appreciate the sentiment, but I'm fine. Really.'

He played it light. 'So you don't fancy a pint after work, then?'

'Providing it is a pint and not a communal hug.'

He smiled. 'No, no . . . I don't think that was mentioned.'

'Where?'

'Dave Chase thought the Astronaut.' He grinned.

'Says it all doesn't it. Okay, count me in.'

When he had left I leaned back in my swivel chair, cupped my hands behind my head and went back to basting myself in embarrassment. The question that wouldn't go away was whether I was suffering from stress or not, and from that flowed bigger questions – did I tough it out or seek help?

I didn't want to buckle or for that matter appear to buckle, just because a few problems had backed up in my life, but when people are looking at you out of the corner of their eye it's usually because they don't want to look you in the face.

It didn't help that I started to feel hot, claustrophobic, when Charnley mentioned the face at the window.

Was that it? Was the problem that I'd been traumatised by Robin Sheldon hitting the ground in front of me? Had that taken me to the edge? And was pride keeping me from admitting it, laying it all off to tiredness?

I picked up the phone and dialled the Welfare, the Brigade counselling service. A female voice at the other end said hello and I froze, the phone pressed against my ear.

I could hear the professional concern in her voice, the 'speak-to-me-I'll-understand' tone. They were good people in Welfare. I knew because I'd known fire-fighters who had gone to them and been supported, helped, but I hadn't reached the stage where I needed or wanted to go to others with what was in my head. I needed sleep and a short period when no further pressures were added to the woodpile.

I took the phone away from my ear and stared at it for a minute, then gently put it down.

If the symptoms continued or got worse I would ring Welfare, but I still trusted myself enough to carry on unaided. I would see the investigation through, make the money that I so desperately needed, and then deal with whatever it was that was spooking me.

My thoughts were interrupted by the shouts and laughter of the watch as they played volleyball in the appliance bay. They sounded as if they hadn't a care in the world, and it heightened my sense of isolation and vulnerability.

Suddenly the door burst open. It was Harry Wild-smith.

'Come on, guv, we're losing, and Chasey's trapping off something rotten.'

An hour later, after five games of furious intensity and acid sarcasm that punctuated every point won, I re-entered my office feeling a whole lot better about my situation and grateful that I hadn't rung Welfare.

I stripped off and was just about to take a shower when the mobile phone rang in my grip bag

'Hello, Steve Jay.'

'Steve? It's Eileen.'

'Eileen. What's wrong?'

'I think now would be a good time to talk to Michael and Stephanie. I've brought Michael back to the penthouse. The security is better here.'

'How is Michael?'

'Alive, thanks to you . . . Look, can you come over tonight . . . say around eightish?'

'I'll have to make some phone calls . . . but it shouldn't be a problem.'

My mind was racing. I looked at the office clock. It was a quarter past five. I was due off at six, providing we didn't get any calls.

'I'll be there at eight sharp, Eileen.'

Chapter Twenty-Three

The Astronaut pub was a five-minute drive from Wells Lane, and a scan of the carpark revealed that everybody on the watch had made the effort.

I intended to have only the one beer, but as soon as the conversation came around to the Ilford fire debrief and Charnley's observations, I got dragged in. Everybody was less than happy, and Dave Chase, in particular, was close to anger.

'He was bang out of order, guv . . . I wouldn't have minded so much, but all he knows comes out of a book. I ran my bollocks off in the first half-hour and so did everybody else. There was no way that we could have done more.'

I played devil's advocate. 'I don't like him either, Dave, but part of his job is to monitor our performance.'

Tom Reed, not known for his outspokenness, made his point eloquently.

'It was a horrible fire, guv . . . I was frightened. We did well to come out of it without anyone injured.'

The honesty of Tom's words seemed to take the edge off everybody's anger, and there was a moment of awkwardness before Harry restored the right balance.

'The trouble with Charnley is, he suffers from post-traumatic intelligence . . .'

'Eh?'

'He's wise after the event.'

There was a round of applause for that, and Harry raised his glass in acknowledgment.

'Sharper than Zorro, "H",' added Dave Chase.

With that the mood was broken.

In all I only spent an hour in the pub, but it was a golden hour. Harry and Dave were on top form, and I laughed more than I had done in months. At one point Sandy started to approach me with a serious look on his face and I saw John shake his head. Wise and kind – I never had a better sub officer.

Around twenty past seven, I left them to it and drove over to Virginia Quay.

It occurred to me on the way over that once again Eileen was deciding where and when. Maybe I was being over-sensitive, but where manipulation was concerned my antennae had been calibrated by Jenny, a master of the art.

I decided then not to fight any manipulation that surfaced. It would be better to let it run. The reasons why people need to manipulate are as important as the end to which they are trying to bend you. Going with the flow might reveal latent motives.

In Eileen's case I had no doubt that part of it was habit. She was a businesswoman and it was her trade, but her desire to protect Stephanie was also an influencing factor.

So, antennae up and paranoia honed, I was ready.

It was Eileen who let me in, saying that Stephanie was out with Suzanne and that they would be back soon. Michael was waiting, and peered at me curiously as I came into the room.

His forehead and cheeks were vivid red and down one side of his face he had a gauze dressing held in place by zinc tape. On the same side his hair was down to the scalp where the fire had singed him. On his left hand he had a plastic protective burns glove, and I could see blistering beneath it.

Lucky, George had called him. From where I stood lucky didn't apply.

I searched his face for the arrogant young man who had nearly got me beaten to pulp, but he wasn't there; just a grateful penitent with a soft handshake and apologies written in every line of his body.

He stood up as we approached him and glanced at Eileen then back to me. When he spoke there was a rasp in his voice, a legacy of the smoke.

'My mother tells me I owe my life to you.'

'Probably.'

He paused, then nodded. 'Saying thank you seems so inadequate, Mr Jay . . . particularly in view of my behaviour at the warehouse.'

'Yes, I think you owe Steve an explanation, Michael,' said Eileen.

He gave a racking cough. 'Please,' he said, 'sit down.'

I sat down opposite him and Eileen sat next to me. She looked tense and anxious to put things right. Her hand drifted over and grasped my forearm.

'I'm listening.'

He hunched forward. 'I had you run off the warehouse when I saw the camera. I assumed you were another press photographer . . . they've made our life hell since my father was killed.'

'Go on.'

'That's it, really. When you asked for James Chasteau I realised you meant Kris Mayle and for obvious reasons that angered me. I'm truly sorry.'

He extended his hand. I let it hang there.

'Beating up the press is acceptable, is it?'

He looked at Eileen. 'No, it isn't, but perhaps it's understandable given the tremendous pressure we're under at the moment . . . it's like living in the proverbial goldfish bowl. They don't care what they do to get their story . . . even if it means trampling all over somebody else's grief. You should have seen them at the court . . . they were animals.'

'And those three thugs . . . you keep them around just in case, do you?'

'They're not our people, Steve,' said Eileen quickly. 'Kris employs them.'

Michael nodded. 'They were very suspicious when you started asking after James Chasteau. I believe my mother has explained this business of the name change to you. When I arrived and thought you were the press I sent them after you to get the film back . . .

nothing else. But it seems they had their own ideas on what should happen. I am truly sorry.'

I said nothing and watched his face.

'It was never my intention that you should be beaten up, Mr Jay. Please take my hand.'

Eileen was watching me anxiously. On balance there was no reason to disbelieve him and the regret seemed genuine. All the same, I wasn't totally convinced, but as he offered his hand again I shook it and he smiled.

'Thank you . . . naturally I'll pay for the damage to your car . . .'

'And we'll compensate you for any injuries you received,' cut in Eileen.

The wound to my face had healed, leaving only a pink semicircle where the glass had entered. I was surprised that Eileen knew about the warehouse incident and said so.

'The night of the car bomb . . .'

'Monday,' I prompted.

'Yes, Monday. When you dropped me off at Michael's he recognised you and we had an argument about it,' she said.

'I still thought you were press,' Michael put in.

Eileen looked at him. 'Yes. Anyway, I persuaded him that you were working to help clear Stephanie . . . I don't think he was convinced . . . but then of course after the bomb . . .'

Michael sighed. 'I'm sorry. I don't trust many people at the moment, but now that I understand

. . . well, I think you know what I'm trying to say.'

'Eileen has told me that you believe Mayle is behind both Ilford and Stratford . . . is that so?'

He leaned back into the sofa. 'I believe my sister, Mr Jay.'

Out of the corner of my eye I saw Eileen light a cigarette.

'Yet your sister stated at the time of the Stratford fire that she was the last person to leave the building.'

'She was last at the warehouse on the Friday night, around eight-thirty I believe. The fire occurred in the early hours of Saturday morning.'

'Still,' I persisted, 'she was, by her own admission, the last person on the premises.'

'Yes . . . although we, my mother and I, believe that wasn't true, and that she was covering for Mayle.'

'Why would she do that?'

Eileen leaned forward. 'Infatuation, Steve. When she first met Mayle he turned her head.'

'That doesn't explain why she would say that, Eileen. After all, the fire went down as an accidental . . . the insurers have paid out . . . now you all claim that Mayle was probably responsible?'

She shook her head. 'Yes, but proving it is next to impossible, especially as the Fire Brigade and police stated that it was an electrical fault.'

She had me there. I changed tack.

'Michael, tell me all you know about those three thugs . . . starting with their names,' I said.

He shook his head. 'Mayle employs them. I know a couple of their first names . . . the bald one is Len, I think, and the other big guy is a Frank. That's all I know, I'm afraid. Why?'

'Just trying to find out where everybody fits.'

'Look, I know what you're thinking . . .' he began.

'What am I thinking?'

'That we were mugs to get involved with Kris Mayle, but you'd have to know him to understand. He starts off by being friendly and gradually takes you over. Half the time you think the ideas are your own, and then you find you're outmanoeuvred and being shafted.'

I had no trouble believing that.

'And your father, was he taken in as well?'

Michael looked uncomfortable. 'My father was a clever businessman and he warned me off Mayle, but I thought I knew better . . .' He was shaking his head from side to side. 'I thought we could all make some money and rescue our business.'

'Rescue?'

'Prior to becoming involved with him we were on the slide. My father was reluctant to admit to the extent of it, but we were going down farther every month. I came up with the idea to franchise shops, cut back on our premises and increase our turnover.'

'And your father didn't agree?'

'He was in full agreement. It was Mayle that he disliked. He thought we should find somebody else . . . but we were losing a lot of money and . . . and I didn't listen to him!' Tears ran down his face and he turned away.

Eileen got up and put her arms around his shoulders.

'It's not your fault that your father is dead, Michael,' she soothed. 'That bastard Mayle has us so twisted we're feeling guilty for things he's done. Look, Steve, I think Michael has been through enough in the past forty-eight hours and he needs rest.'

I was about to agree when Michael shook her off.

'Look, I don't care what anyone else thinks, but I know Mayle burned the Stratford warehouse and killed my father.'

'How do you know?'

'Because the day after the fire he threatened me, like he threatened my father. He told me that if I didn't keep my mouth shout I would be next.'

'Were there any witnesses to this?'

'Of course not . . . he's not a fool!'

'Doesn't count for much, then, does it?'

The redness of the burns on his face deepened with his anger, and the racking cough started up again. I noticed also that he cradled his damaged left hand in his lap, but if I wanted to get to the truth I had to ignore that.

'He killed my father, Mr Jay. He cold-bloodedly burned him to death, and he booby-trapped my car and nearly killed me. You were a witness to that yourself.'

Eileen started waving her hands, as if to say enough. I ignored her.

'Did you have access to all the warehouse, Michael?'

'Yes. Why . . .'

'The layout of the warehouse is different from what it was at the time of the fire, isn't it?'

He looked at Eileen. 'I don't really see where this is going . . .'

'Well, there's an area shuttered off from the rest of the warehouse . . . that shutter wasn't there before the fire, was it?'

'I don't know,' he said slowly.

'Only there's a new padlock on it. A big, shiny securi-fast padlock. Yet at the moment the rest of the warehouse seems disused.'

'You'd have to speak to Kris Mayle about that,' he said dismissively.

'I will.'

Eileen put a hand on my shoulder.

'I think we have to leave it there for the moment, Steve.' She turned back to Michael. 'The doctor said you must rest. Getting upset isn't going to help anything.'

She took his good arm and helped him from the sofa, but as she got him to the shoji door he turned.

'I want you to get him, Mr Jay . . . I want you to see to it that Kris Mayle goes down for killing my father.'

As Eileen pulled the shoji closed behind her I sat

back and weighed everything Michael had said. It all rang true. As a personality sketch of Mayle it was so close to my own experience I just wished Jenny had been there to hear it with me.

The problem was that suspicion and uncorroborated evidence were worthless. I was back to trying to pin Mayle down to Ilford. If I could do that then Stephanie could tell the police and Mayle would feel a door slam shut behind him for fifteen to twenty years, but as I knew to my own cost he was slippery and only hard evidence would see him nailed.

Chapter Twenty-Four

When Eileen returned she came straight over and kissed me.

'Oh, Steve . . . you know what I want to say, but there are no words that can describe it.' She squeezed me hard and buried her face in my chest. 'Michael would be dead if it wasn't for you.'

She looked exhausted and her pain was genuine, but she was developing a habit of clinging to me, like a form of ownership, and it had a way of confusing things. I held her by the shoulders and gently eased her back. I didn't want to be owned.

When she was near she had the same effect as Jenny. A week before I would have taken some persuasion that that was possible, which proves how little I knew about myself.

But how much did I know about Eileen?

From another angle, what I read as need could just as easily have been manipulation, but there was no denying that she was on the rack. Was it so surprising that she needed a shoulder to lean on?

She closed her eyes.

'Hold me, Steve . . . please. Just for a moment, put your arms around me.'

I did as I was asked and was immediately aware of her pressing her body into me.

'I'm so frightened, Steve.'

'It's time to talk to the police, Eileen. You have to tell them what you know.'

She pressed into me harder. 'Not yet. If we all stay here we're safe . . . and Stephanie's out on bail so that buys us a little time.'

'Time?'

She pulled away and looked at me.

'For you to find proof that Kris was at Ilford.'

'Eileen, I may not be able to find proof. What then? The longer you leave it the more suspect it's going to look. They'll think you're just pointing the finger to get Stephanie off the hook, and at the moment she's the only one definitely placed at Ilford.'

She shook her head. 'You'll find the evidence, Steve . . . I'll double my previous offer.'

'It's not a question of money. It's finding hard evidence . . . witnesses, something that positively places Mayle at the scene after Stephanie.'

'Please, Steve.'

'I'll try, Eileen, but the police have better men and resources than me, and so far they are concentrating on Stephanie.'

She thought about that. 'Perhaps you should confront Kris?'

'No.'

'Why?'

My voiced reasoning was sound.

'Because all that would do is alert him to the fact that someone is digging. Better to find the proof and then confront him, preferably with the police present.'

'If you think that's best.'

'It's the only way to do it, Eileen.'

She accepted the point, but the whole exchange had taken me another step towards an encounter with Mayle.

I'd hoped from the start that it could be done at one remove, with me finding the evidence, handing it over to the police and then stepping back to watch from the sidelines.

Since then I'd been drafted into the role of rescuer and, if I wasn't mistaken, nascent bodyguard.

At least I looked like winning. If Mayle was guilty of Robin Sheldon's death I would get my ten grand from Eileen, and if Stephanie was guilty I would get my percentage of the reclaimed insurance money, not to mention Alex's pay and expenses.

Eileen offered me a drink and I asked for a small Scotch. She fetched it and continued to talk to me as she did.

'I gather that you and Stephanie met the other night.'

'I think she thought I was an intruder.'

'Yes, she told me. You really frightened her.'

'We scared the hell out of each other . . . does she understand now that I'm trying to help?'

'Mmm.' She turned and gave a half-smile. 'It's

strange, I have more confidence in you than in the police.'

'Have you spoken to them much?'

'Constantly. Ever since the warehouse fire they have taken to turning up at our shops, here, Michael's place . . . you name it. There's one in particular, a Detective Sergeant Menzies, who gives me the creeps.' She took a sip of her drink. 'He has spiteful eyes.'

She handed me my drink and sat next to me again. I told myself that she was the one breaking down the barriers, so that gave me *carte blanche* to ask anything I wanted.

'Can we talk about Robin?'

She went still.

'Eileen, I understand that for all sorts of reasons this is difficult, but if I'm to help Stephanie . . .'

'What do you want to know?' she said tightly.

'Last time we talked, you mentioned that when you entered into the warehouse deal with Kris Mayle, you and Robin were talking through Michael.'

'Yes.'

'Why? What had happened that made that necessary?'

'You know that, Steve . . . we were going through with the divorce.'

'Correct me – the fire was last November and logically the warehouse deal must have been some months prior to that . . .'

'September.'

'So when did your marriage come off the rails?'

'Is this really necessary, Steve?'

'I think so.'

I thought for a moment she was going to refuse to answer, but then she gave a long sigh.

'All right. It's no secret . . . my marriage to Robin had been disintegrating for years. There had been several rough patches, and although I wanted the marriage to continue he wanted a divorce.'

'So how long had it been before the warehouse deal since you had stopped talking?'

'A couple of weeks . . . maybe three.'

'Did he ever talk to you about Kris Mayle?'

'Yes.'

'And?'

'He despised him. My husband had always liked Jimmy Chasteau and took it badly when Mayle bought him out so cheaply.'

'But you still went into business with him . . .'

'We've already been here, Steve,' she said flatly. 'Michael pushed the deal with Mayle. My husband didn't like it, but accepted we were going under and there were few alternatives.'

'Never once in our conversations have you called him Robin . . . why?'

The air just seemed to go out of her and she turned her face away. I wanted to ask her then who Ruth Heller was, but it would have been leaping blind. Maybe Roley Benson had found out something of value, but I had no idea what that might be or its significance.

'Eileen?'

I reached out and touched her shoulder; she turned back. When she spoke her voice was broken.

'Have you ever loved someone, Steve, and seen them walk away from you? Have you ever given yourself to someone body and soul and had to take it as they rejected you . . . time after time, so that you no longer have any pride . . . any shame?'

I shrugged.

She was staring at me. 'Pathetic, isn't it, Steve. Eileen Sheldon, the woman who had it all, begging her husband to stay . . . well, I can't help the way I am. I don't speak his name because I can't speak it . . . I loved him and now because of Kris Mayle I'll never have another chance to make it good.'

'Could you have turned it around?'

She paused before answering. 'Yes. He loved me . . . but wasn't in love with me . . . those were his words.' Her voice was soft. 'And it hurt, Steve, it really hurt.'

She turned away again and my first instinct was to put my arms around her, but again that little voice cried 'manipulation' so I stayed where I was.

After a couple of minutes she dried her eyes and apologised.

'Everyone leans on me, Steve . . . I'm not allowed to be weak, but I seem to lean on you . . . and you're virtually a stranger.'

'Perhaps it's easier because of that,' I said.

'Tell me about yourself, Steve. Tell me who you

are . . . who you love . . . what you want from this life.'

'I . . .'

She touched my arm again. 'Please.'

'What I want from this life? That's easy. I want a period of calm . . . a moment of complete serenity unobscured by people and events.'

'Yes, I can identify with that.' She gave a bitter little smile. 'And who do you love?'

'Difficult.'

She turned her head to one side, studying me. Then touched my cheek softly.

'You love someone who doesn't love you . . . no . . . no . . . you love someone who loves somebody else . . .'

I said nothing.

'Oh, Steve . . . Oh, Steve, I'm so sorry . . . I didn't mean to . . .'

'Forget it.'

She moved closer and took my hands.

'That was wrong of me . . .'

The door opening interrupted her.

Suzanne Munroe and Stephanie came into the room, and I moved back as Eileen got up to greet them. Suzanne looked from Eileen to me, and her expression said that she seen something she wasn't happy with.

'Where's Michael?' asked Stephanie.

Eileen explained that he wasn't feeling too good and asked both of them if they'd like a drink.

Suzanne suggested making some coffee for everyone. As she went out to make it, Eileen brought Stephanie over to the sofa and sat her down next to me.

'You can trust him, Stephanie. Steve works for us and he's the best hope we have of proving you innocent.'

Stephanie nodded. 'I'm sorry about the other night . . . it was a shock . . .'

'It's my fault,' I interrupted. 'I should have let the security guard in the carpark phone up.'

She smiled, and I saw her father's face in her. She seemed much calmer than she had the other night. A little edgy, but under the circumstances that was to be expected.

'Steve wants to ask you some questions, Stephanie.'

'I'm tired . . . and I've done nothing but answer questions lately. Can we keep it brief?'

Eileen threw an arm around her shoulders. 'Five minutes . . . is that all right, Steve?'

'That's plenty. Stephanie, I want you to think back to the warehouse fire. Apparently there was some confusion over who was the last person on the premises?'

'It was Kris . . . I know I said it was me, but that was because the police were being horrible to him. I thought that if I said it was me they would leave him alone.'

'So what happened . . . I mean, what was the sequence of you both leaving?'

She took a moment. 'We both came out together. We had just got into Kris's car and I noticed I'd left my scarf behind . . . it was strange because I thought it was in my coat pocket. Anyway, Kris said he'd get it for me and he went back inside.'

'How long was he gone?'

She frowned. 'Quite a long time. I told him it was probably in the office.'

'What would you call a long time?'

'Fifteen, twenty minutes.'

'Did he find the scarf?'

'No.'

'Okay, now I want to jump forward to the other night . . . at Ilford.'

Eileen nodded and edged in beside Stephanie. 'Go ahead, Steve.'

'Was Kris Mayle with you at Ilford the other night?'

'Not with me as such . . . I went to speak to my father about some designs I'd been working on.'

'What time was that?'

'Quite late. About ten o'clock.'

'Why so late?'

She looked at Eileen out of the corner of her eye.

'It's all right, Stephanie . . . Steve knows about the divorce.'

'Daddy had a flat above the workroom. He'd been staying there for a few weeks . . . I arrived about ten-fifteen.'

'And Kris Mayle? What time did he arrive?'

'Ten-thirty.'

'You seem very sure.'

'Daddy and I heard the front entrance door close. Daddy looked at his watch.'

'Was he expecting Mayle?'

'I don't think so. Daddy went downstairs and I heard shouting. I tried to intervene, but Kris wouldn't stop.'

'He was angry?'

'Very.'

'What happened next?'

'Daddy refused to argue with him and said that they should call a meeting of everyone to discuss the problem.'

'And what was the problem?'

'Money. The same as it always was when they argued.'

'They'd argued before?'

'All week. I've never seen Kris so furious. Daddy said I should go.'

'And did you?'

She looked at Eileen. 'No, but my presence seemed to be making things worse, so I went upstairs to Daddy's flat and waited.'

'You left Kris Mayle alone with your father?'

'Yes.'

'What happened then?'

Her voice became tiny, childlike. 'There was a noise. I didn't know what it was at first . . . then about five minutes later there was a scream . . . a

ghastly scream. I went to the top of the stairs and
Daddy came through the door from the workroom
. . . he was on fire . . . came up the stairs and I ran
back into the lounge . . . he was alight . . . dying . . .
he ran past me and jumped through the window . . .'

'How did you escape, Stephanie?'

'Across the roof . . . I used the old fire escape.'

Chapter Twenty-Five

Before I left the penthouse I qualified Stephanie into the ground; questioning and cross-questioning her, until eventually Eileen stopped me.

Had I just met her for the first time I would have thought that Stephanie was beautiful and fairly normal, the latter of which was a hundred and eighty degrees different from my previous opinion. Her story rang true to everything known.

There was just one incident that jarred. It was when I asked her where she was on the Monday night, when Michael's car was booby-trapped. She giggled; a small laugh so completely out of keeping with the situation that I shook my head in disbelief.

Eileen immediately intervened and asked me if I wanted another drink, taking the opportunity to shoot Stephanie a look. After that Stephanie kept her answers brief and helpful.

She denied that she was with Kris Mayle that night and said that she went out for a drive to clear her head. The experience in court had been overwhelming and she needed be alone for a while.

Eileen, at that point standing behind her, mouthed 'no' to me.

It was interesting watching Eileen throughout the evening. Alone, she was fragile and angst-ridden; around Michael and Stephanie she grew into the archetypal protective matriarch.

At the door she'd said goodbye and then called me back in order to plant a kiss on my cheek and whisper 'thank you'. I smiled wryly. Possessed on arrival and scent-marked on leaving; I'd been drafted on to Team Sheldon.

I was constantly aware of just how beautiful she was. Complex and beautiful, because her back may have been to the wall, but she was capable of bending into any shape that the game required.

Going down in the lift, I felt some satisfaction that I was at last making headway. The time had come to talk to Alex and decide the best way forward. With Stephanie's information, the aims had narrowed.

I thought of ringing Jenny and telling her to wait up, but the night hadn't finished with me yet. As the lift reached the ground floor and the door opened, I found myself looking directly at Kris Mayle.

'Well, well, well . . . if it isn't the sad bastard fireman.'

He jammed his foot against the lift door and blocked my exit by putting his arm across the gap. He eyed me, uncertain as to why I was there, then gave a thin smile.

'Neighbourhood's a bit out of your league, I'd have thought,' he said.

'Visiting friends . . . the view's lovely from up there.'

As he thought about that the smile vanished from his face and a range of possibilities auditioned themselves.

'I don't know what you're playing at, but I'd crawl back to that shithole you call a flat if I were you . . . there's a lady waiting . . . bit used, but if I remember rightly you never were that fussy.'

I think that if I'd hit him then I wouldn't have stopped. Instead I somehow forced a smile.

'How's the rag trade, Kris? I hear if conditions are right you can make a killing . . . My own line of work? Funny you should ask, I've never been busier.'

His face went pale.

'Listen very closely to me, dickhead . . . go back to your squalid little life and stay away from the big boys.'

'That sounds like a threat . . . I'll take it seriously.'

'Do that.'

'I think you're getting your role models mixed, Kris. You were always a hyena, never a lion. You're at your best going behind people's backs. Confrontation's a little too straightforward for you.'

I looked at the arm that was blocking my way. He withdrew it, stepped back and gave me a hard stare.

Pushing past him, I walked towards the staircase that led to the underground carpark. As I reached it he called after me, his voicing echoing.

'Tell Jenny to give me a ring . . . I might have a job

for her. Pal of mine's opening a place . . . discreet services, you know the sort of thing. Better still, I'll ring her myself.'

In the carpark I pulled out my mobile and rang Eileen. I told her he was on his way up and not to let him in.

'And if he doesn't take the hint, ring the police, Eileen.'

'Will do, Steve . . . leave your mobile switched on. I call you if there's a problem.'

I drove back to Romford with my mind on anything but the road and got flashed by a speed camera just past Canning Town Bridge.

I'd fronted off Mayle, but Jenny was so obviously my Achilles' heel that I had to be ultra-careful. He had the option to lure or threaten her. Seeing him taken out of circulation had replaced money at the top of my wish list.

The task that had priority was how to find evidence that would corroborate Stephanie's version of events. Everything needed to be considered, no matter how slim or left-field.

At that point I was on the A13, approaching the flyover at East Ham and barely a five-minute drive from Roley Benson's house.

Within ten minutes I was slamming his doorknocker hard enough to wake a drunk, but as before there was no reply. I gave it two more hefty whacks, and the neighbour's front-room light came on. The curtains moved a fraction, and I smiled as the face appeared around the side of them. The curtains moved back into place and the light went out.

I hovered, debating whether to drive to the Rifleman or to the flat and Jenny. It had started raining again, and I'd just decided on the flat when I looked down the road to see the figure of a man walking unsteadily. His left arm was in a sling.

Alex had described Roley Benson as a big man with a battered face and shrewd eyes that had seen a little too much of life.

'He's a good man gone to the drink, Stevie, and what one of us hasn't been stalked by that monster at some time or another?'

I waited, watching his erratic progress down the road towards me. It was a sad, pathetic sight; a hero reduced to a caricature. It struck me that Alex had been right – I was wasting my time. I debated just getting in the car and going when Benson looked up and saw me.

He blinked, trying to recognise me.

He held up a hand in greeting and then let it flop by his side as he peered again and shook his head. He was six feet from me when he stopped.

'Do I know you?'

'My name's Steve Jay. Alex McGregor sent me.'

Suspicion entered his eyes and he shook his head again. 'What d'you want?'

'A word . . . about the fire at Ilford.'

For a moment he stood straight. 'I'm a drunk . . .
didn't anyone tell you? I can't be trusted.'

'Well, I can see you've had a skinful tonight, but
other than that I prefer to make my own mind up.
Shall we go in?'

'ID?'

I shook my head. 'Ring Alex and ask him.'

He swayed and fished for a key in his coat pocket.
He found it and tugged at the pocket, trying to free
his hand. I stepped forward to help him.

'Leave me alone!' There was dulled anger in his
eyes.

He finally pulled the key clear and I stepped back
as he made his way towards the front door. On the
third attempt he managed to get the door open and
he walked in, leaving the key in the lock. I removed
the key and followed him in.

Inside, I was surprised to find the house spotless,
and there was the smell of fresh polish in the hallway.
I couldn't remember if Alex had said he was married
or not.

In the lounge Benson slumped into an armchair
and closed his eyes.

'Can I make you a coffee?' I asked.

The eyes opened and he shook his head.

'Rum . . . in the cabinet . . . pour yourself one.'

He pointed to a drinks cabinet, just out of reach of
the armchair. I poured him a large rum and handed it
to him.

'Don't you drink?'

'I've been on the Scotch already tonight . . . probably over the limit as it is,' I replied.

He gulped at the rum and gave that telltale shake of the head again. He stared at me, as though trying to work out what I was doing in his house.

'Steve Jay, you said your name was . . . doesn't ring a bell.'

I sat down opposite him. 'I'm not an ex-copper.'

His head tilted over to one side and the eyes did what they could to get a fix on me.

'No . . . no . . . I can see that. So if you weren't in the job what were you?'

'Fireman.'

He nodded. 'Makes sense. Sure you won't have a drink? . . . there's some Scotch there.'

'I'm fine. I'd like to ask you some questions . . . about the investigation you did for Alex and Andrew.'

The eyes became shrewd. 'I gave McGregor everything.'

'I know, but I've been through it and some questions occur.'

He gave a half-smile. 'Why should I?'

'There'd be a drink in it for you.'

'You taking the piss?'

'What would you like, then?'

He gulped at the rum again and leaned back in the chair.

'An exchange.'

'Pardon?'

He chuckled. 'An exchange of information. You tell me what you know and I'll tell you what I know.'

'Have you got a client?'

He shook his head. 'Personal satisfaction.'

'I don't believe you.'

Anger swept across his face. 'You know nothing about me . . . nothing.'

'That's true, Roley, but personal satisfaction doesn't ring true.'

'For a drunken ex-copper . . . go on . . . say it.'

'All right . . . for a drunken ex-copper.'

'That's the end of the conversation, then . . . pull the door to as you leave.'

He closed his eyes again. If he fell asleep I'd never wake him up. Christ knows how much he'd put away during the evening.

'All right. An exchange of information.'

The eyes opened and he gave a slow nod. 'Go on, then, ask.'

'What were you doing at Ilford Monday night?'

'Investigating a murder. Next question.'

'Alex paid you off. Why are you still involved?'

'Someone tried to kill me by running me off the road. I take exception to that. My turn.'

'Go ahead.'

'Did Robin Sheldon have the Stratford warehouse burned?'

'Don't know, but at the moment the finger is pointing elsewhere.'

'Does it point to Kris Mayle?'

I sat up. Drunk or not, Benson was no idiot.

'It's a distinct possibility.'

'Ha!'

'What does that mean?'

He reached over for the rum bottle and poured a healthy measure into his glass.

'It means whatever you want it to. You can ask another question.'

'You must know that the police have got Stephanie Sheldon in the frame for the murder. Why snoop around at Ilford?'

'Good question, Steve . . . you did say it was Steve, didn't you . . . but it's not the right question.'

'Sorry?'

He seemed to be having a private joke at my expense. 'You should ask whether I think she's guilty or not.'

'Okay. Is she guilty?'

'I don't think so . . . leastways not on her own.'

'Why?'

He shook his head. 'My turn.'

'Okay.'

'Eileen Sheldon . . .'

'What about her?' I said.

'How much will she earn from her husband's death?'

'You think she murdered him for the insurance money?'

'You're supposed to answer my question.'

'I don't know how much she'll make . . . man like that, I'd guess it would be substantial.'

'Nothing.'

'Sorry?'

'Nothing. She'd make absolutely nothing. He'd altered his policy.'

'In whose favour?'

'Don't know.'

'You said someone tried to murder you . . . this was when you were run off the road?'

'Yes.'

'Why didn't the police believe you?'

He held his hands up. 'I was drunk. Three times over the limit.'

'Fair, but according to what I've been told you're a hero. There must be people in the job who'd listen to you.'

He went quiet and his face clouded.

'Roley?'

'There's no one in the job that'll listen to me . . . no one!' he said bitterly.

'You saved a colleague's life . . . that must count for something.'

He shook his head and glanced down at the floor. At first I thought he was laughing, but when he looked up his face was wet from crying.

'I'm a drunk, see!'

'I can see that, but you're not the first in your job to go under to drink . . . and you hold a commendation for bravery . . .'

'Ha! Now that really is the sickest joke.'

'Tell me.'

'Tell you what? How I saved Peter Carver only to watch him die three weeks later? How I nicked a dangerous drug dealer and was awarded a commendation before being pensioned off? That's what you've been told, isn't it? That's what it says about me in the fucking reference that McGregor got from the job, isn't it?'

'So?'

'Well, it's a crock of shit! A lie . . . a fairy story that protects certain people.'

'Go on.'

'I'm not a drunk because Peter Carver died . . . he died because I was drunk!'

'I don't understand.'

'We went to arrest a drug dealer . . . a nasty bastard, Mickey Jameson, and I'd been on the drink . . . like I'm always on the drink . . . good old Roley, the pisshead. Only this time I was too far gone.'

'Drunk before you went on duty?'

He nodded. 'Peter covered for me. Didn't say a word, and when we trapped Jameson in his flat he pulled a knife and stabbed Peter.' Benson was shaking with anger. 'He stuck that knife in him again and again . . . until I thought no more blood could come out of him. And me, the hero, what did I do? I froze. I was so fucking scared I literally shit myself . . . now d'you understand?'

'I see.'

'Do you? Roley Benson, the brave copper who tried to save a mate . . . only I didn't save him.' The rum glass fell from his hand and he covered his face. 'At the funeral Carol Carver threw her arms around me and kissed me! Thanked me for what I'd done . . . and those bastards gave me a commendation because if they hadn't the truth might have got out and brought the Met into disrepute. That's what's so bloody awful.'

Chapter Twenty-Six

It was an awkward five minutes. I sat there trying to imagine the torment he was carrying inside him. No wonder he kept climbing inside a bottle.

'Roley . . . Roley?'

He looked up slowly.

'Who arrested Jameson?'

He blinked, trying to focus on what I was saying.

'I did. After Pete fell to the floor I snapped out of it . . . went berserk . . . drew my baton and clubbed Jameson unconscious. I hit that bastard so hard I cracked his skull in two places . . . wasn't till afterwards that I realised I'd been stabbed as well.'

'Badly?'

'Bad enough.' He pulled back his coat and lifted up his shirt. There was an untidy scar running down his left-hand side. 'He got me in the side, but the knife bounced off my ribs and came out the back . . . messy, but nothing to what he did to Pete.'

'What happened then?'

'I radioed for help and by . . . by the time it arrived I was covered . . .' He stopped, tears flooding his eyes as he choked on the words. '. . . in Pete's blood . . . the whole . . . room was covered.'

'I'm sorry.'

He looked at me fiercely. 'Not as sorry as I am. I live with it every day. See this house . . . fucking spotless it is. Carol comes round three times a week . . . does the place top to bottom. She even cooks and leaves a meal for me . . . me!'

'She has no idea?'

'That's the worst of it . . . I think she does, or at least suspects. She's a Christian, you see. An old-fashioned Christian . . . she's forgiven me. Well, I don't have to forgive me, do I? I'm no fucking Christian.'

He fell silent again, his eyes glazing as the rum took effect. I thought he was going to fall asleep so I tried to keep him talking.

'Roley . . . Roley?'

He stared at me.

'You started to tell me about being run off the road . . . you took exception to it, you said?'

He closed his eyes again, his words slurring. 'I wasn't drunk the night I was run off the road. I'd had a drink . . . wasn't drunk.'

'Okay, you weren't drunk. Tell me what happened.'

He suddenly lurched sideways and reached for the rum bottle again, but I leaned forward and stopped his hand.

'I need to know, Roley. There are still lives at risk here.'

He nodded, drowsy, finding it hard to keep awake. I shook him by the shoulders.

'Don't go to sleep on me, Roley. This is important.'

His head slumped. 'Was about three weeks ago. I'd been out to the warehouse . . . to interview Mayle. I was suspicious of . . . statements . . . on the way back . . . saw someone following me . . . looked again it was gone.'

'What was? Roley? What was gone?'

'Big . . . white van . . . blue flash down one side . . . ran me off the road.'

'Okay. I want to change the subject, Roley . . . Roley? Who is Ruth Heller?'

He frowned. 'Have you found her?'

'No! Listen, Roley . . . who is she?'

He looked at me bleary-eyed. 'Sheldon's lover . . .'

His voice trailed away and he slid into an alcohol-soaked sleep. I got up quietly, turned out the light and left him to his nightmares.

Thursday, 23 April

I left the flat late and just made it to work in time for roll-call.

Jenny and I had talked into the night when I got back from Roley Benson's. We discussed the need to find a new place to live and start over. I felt more than ever that we had a good chance to bury the past and move on.

We slept in each other's arms and woke late, not hearing the alarm.

At work an appliance had come off the run after failing to start on a fire call just before nine. I asked John to get the guys to strip it and arrange with Eastern Staff to sort us out a spare.

He came back to me ten minutes later.

'There's a spare at workshops, guv. I'll send Doug Russell and Mike Scott to pick it up.'

'Cheers, John.'

With the watch involved in the vehicle swap, I crashed through the morning routines, eager to get them over and phone Alex to give him a summary of the night's events. I caught up with him on the second attempt.

He listened without interrupting, but as soon as I'd finished he pitched in.

'And you believed Benson?'

'Yes, Alex, I did.'

He sounded irritated. 'Why?'

'Because when I was at Stratford last week I saw a white Luton van, with a blue flash, parked near the warehouse, and coincidences of that kind just don't happen.'

'So what now?'

I could tell that he wasn't convinced.

'He knows more, Alex, I'm certain of it.'

'Like what?'

'Don't know, but he's a haunted man, and I think he's looking for absolution.'

'Solve the crime and buy back some self-respect, eh?'

'That's my guess . . . could be me, couldn't it?'

'No, Stevie. Benson's a drunk and, cruel as it may seem to say it, he's living a hell of his own devising. He gets no sympathy from me.'

'You're a hard man, Alex McGregor.'

'Aye, maybe, but not unfair, I think. I get the feeling Benson might start muddying the waters.'

'Deliberately?'

'Depends who he's working for, doesn't it.'

'Jesus, Alex, you're like a dog with a bone.'

'Got to be, Stevie. I'm paid for it . . . so are you now.'

'Well, you're right there. I'm not sure you're reading Benson the right way, though. If ever I saw a man determined to do the right thing, it's him.'

He went quiet. 'Try not to have any more run-ins with Mayle. Stick to gathering what evidence you can and just bring it to me.'

'My thoughts exactly.'

'Meet me for a drink tonight?'

'No can do. We're going to see a film.'

There was the suggestion of a pause. 'She's staying, then?'

'Looks that way.'

'Enjoy yourself. Stay in touch.'

After the morning tea break we ran a cylinder drill as a simulation for Sandy's task book, after which I ran a short Q and A session with him. He got every question right, and the depth of his knowledge spoke of the hours he spent studying.

What he lacked in experience Sandy was always willing to make up in hard graft. John took time out to mentor him and had high hopes for his long-term promotion prospects.

When the training period was over, John and I discussed his progress.

'The only reservation I have, guv, is that sometimes he's impulsive. There are times when he could take another ten seconds to think things through.'

'I agree, but you can't put an old head on young shoulders, John, and sometimes you have to make mistakes . . .'

'. . . in order to learn. I know. Am I being a bit of a nanny?' He grinned.

'Probably.' I watched the crew make up the equipment used in the drill. 'How do the blokes rate him, John?'

'Doing well . . . plenty to learn. Harry told him that he was chief officer material.'

I laughed. 'How did Sandy react?'

'His face held all the wariness that Harry intended.'

In the early part of the afternoon Bob Grant rang and said that the Performance Review of Command debrief on the Ilford fire would be at Stratford, Friday week.

'Do you think Charnley intends to ride me again?'

'Possibly. He's determined to be seen as the man of the moment. Just don't give him the chance.'

'Suffer in silence, you mean?'

'Most people know the score, Steve.'

I spent the rest of the day catching up on paperwork and writing up my assessments of Sandy's task book entries. It was an involved process, and I didn't want to rush it. I lost track of time, and only became aware of it when the bells crashed down.

Jimmy McClane's voice came over the Tannoy. 'Four-pump fire . . . persons reported . . . Robe Fashions, Heathway, Dagenham. Multiple calls being received.'

He handed me the call slip as the watch came from every direction towards the appliance bay. The time on the slip was 1725 hours.

I caught John's eye as he passed me on the way to the front of the pump and he called out to me.

'Let's hope it's not another Ilford.'

The fire was just off our ground, and Dagenham's pair had been the first attendance. I estimated it would take between ten and fifteen minutes 'on the bell' to get there. Without needing to be told, Harry put his foot to the floor and we screamed out of the station with the wailers going.

We had barely got to the lights at the junction of Wells Lane and Chadwell Heath High Road when the first informative message came over the radio.

'From Station Officer Weissman, at the Heathway, Dagenham . . . Shop and dwellings of four floors, fifteen by ten metres, I repeat, one five by one zero metres, fifty per cent of ground and first floors alight. Further traffic, over.'

The female control room operator's voice came back at them. 'Go ahead with further traffic, over.'

'One male and one female rescued from second floor via 135 ladder.'

'Sounds like a goer, guv,' said Wayne Bennett from the rear cab.

I turned as I pulled my tunic jacket on. 'I wonder if four's going to be enough.'

'Do you want us to rig in BA, guv?' asked Sandy.

'No. Let's see what they want when we get there.'

I turned back to the front and watched as Harry steered a frantic slalom between the rush-hour traffic and the street furniture. Vehicles pulled into the side of the road to let us pass, some misjudging it, causing Harry to veer sharply and brake hard.

He shot me a cynical grin. 'They don't pay me enough, guv, I swear they don't.'

Half a mile farther on, another message came over the radio. The words were spoken clearly, but the control was forced, tension seeping between the words.

'From Station Officer Weissman at the Heathway, Dagenham. Make pumps eight, over.'

Minutes later we turned into the Heathway and Harry went for broke, the engine roaring as we hammered along the road at breakneck speed, swerving around a battered minicab and causing it to break hard.

The hump of the Heathway Underground station loomed up from the road in front of us, and beyond it a tongue of orange-red flame flared against the sky.

'Shit, shit, shit,' chanted Wayne. 'That's overtime if ever I saw it!'

A hundred yards out and closing fast, we couldn't see much because of the rise in the road, but the ragged column of flame and smoke seemed to be growing with each passing second.

As we breasted the hump there was a surge of flame and a ball of fire curled out of the shopfront and rolled upward, searing the face of the building. Frantically, Dagenham's two branch crews pulled their hose-lines back and to the side of the building to protect themselves from the radiated heat.

Harry hit the brakes twenty yards short of the nearest branch crew, and in the wing mirror I saw the pump pull in right behind us. Dagenham's station officer, Solly Weissman, ran a wide loop around the gouting flames and headed towards us.

'What do you want, Solly?' I shouted.

'I need two of your blokes to find us another hydrant, Steve, the one we're using is fucked! And I need you or John to take the back – it's going like a train around there.'

'Will do, Solly. What about those dwellings above the shop?'

He shook his head. 'It's all clear . . . we pulled an old couple out just after we arrived.'

I scanned the row of continuous shopfronts and turned to John. 'We going to have to gain access through one of the side premises . . . stay there for the minute, I'll take a look. Sandy! With me now, please.'

The shops immediately either side of Robe Fashions were shrouded in thick smoke, so I missed out those and headed for a baker's two doors away. A policeman stopped me.

'Excuse me, guv, what would you like done?'

'For starters you can clear all these people back . . . we're going to have to come through here with hose. See him?' I pointed at Solly standing on the other side of the street directing his men. 'He's in charge . . . I'm sure he's got a wish list.'

Chapter Twenty-Seven

I pushed at the baker's door, but it was locked. A small, agitated man appeared alongside me.

'It's my shop . . . do you want to get in?'

I nodded. 'Can we get to the back of Robe Fashions from the rear of your shop?'

He looked uncertain. 'There's a high wall between us. Six or seven feet, it is, and then another wall, just as high, to get over into the rear of Robes . . . I . . .'

'Show me.'

He fumbled with his keys, smiling nervously. Finally the door swung open and he motioned for us to follow as he ran ahead through the shop section and out into the bakery at the back.

At the rear of the bakery was a fire exit, and beyond that a small cobbled yard. The walls were so high and the yard so narrow I couldn't see a thing.

'Leg up, Sandy.'

He braced his back against the wall and cupped his hands. I stood in his grip and seized the top of the wall, hauling myself up until I could see the rear of the Sheldons' shop.

Smoke spiralled up above the roof from the other side of the building, and sparks swirled and fell silently down on to the yards, settling as black-grey ash on the dank cobbles.

The dry, sharp smell of burning was everywhere, and from the top of the yard wall I could see the heavily smoke-stained windows on the first floor. I slid down the wall and spoke into my radio.

'Wells Lane Station Officer to Wells Lane Sub Officer, over.'

'Go ahead, guv, I can hear you.'

'We're at the rear of the baker's, John, two doorways to the right of the Robe shop as you look at it . . . we can get to where we want, but we're going to need a short extension ladder, breaking-in gear, BA, and a jet with seventy-mill hose.'

'I hear you, guv . . . Dagenham are having all sorts of trouble getting in at the front . . . it's probably down to us.'

'Right.'

Sandy tugged at my arm. 'Guv?'

'Yes, Sandy.'

'BA crew?'

I shook my head. 'John'll lead it.'

My first instinct was reluctance to put Sandy into such a fierce job, but then I reminded myself that he was a trainee crew commander, not a recruit.

He smiled and voiced my thoughts. 'Got to let me off the lead some time, guv.'

I hesitated. 'Okay, but watch yourself. Get Wayne to rig as well.'

He sprinted away and I turned my attention back

to the problem of access. I looked around and my eye fell on the door at the rear of the baker's yard. It was secured by a panic bolt.

I turned to the bakery owner. 'Where does this lead to?'

'There's an alleyway along the back. All the fire exits from the shops lead to it.'

'Where does it come out?'

'Tilney Road.'

'Could I get my machines nearer to the rear of the shops from Tilney Road?'

He shook his head. 'You're probably as near as you're going to be.'

I pushed the panic bolt and went out into the alleyway. It was barely four feet wide; we'd struggle to get ladders through it, let alone bring the appliances up. I ran to where the fire exit from the Sheldons' shop met the alleyway. It was wide open.

I stepped inside. The yard was empty and silent, in contrast to the chaos at the front of the building. I walked towards the rear entrance of the shop and noticed that a hasp-and-staple door fitting was swinging loose. A cut padlock lay on the ground at the base of the door.

There was a noise behind me and the baker appeared by the alleyway door. He stood still, looking on anxiously.

'Best stay there,' I advised.

A thin trickle of heavy smoke was percolating around the edges of the rear entrance to the shop, and heat was peeling the paint from the timber. It suggested very high temperatures inside the building. Somehow the fire at the front hadn't reached the back of the building, but it was cooking through, superheating everything.

The sound of my radio interrupted my thoughts.

'Wells Lane Station Officer from Dagenham's Station Officer. Are you receiving me, Steve?'

'Go ahead, Solly.'

'We're in danger of losing this one, Steve. I need you to get me a jet crew in there fast.'

'Understood, Solly. It's not going to be easy, though . . . it's cramped and awkward for access at the back and it looks like the fire's going to burst through any minute.'

'If you're going to do it for me it's got to be in the next few minutes, Steve . . . it's looking that tight.'

'My best efforts, Solly . . . my best efforts.'

I called John up on the radio. 'Where are you, John?'

I could hear him breathing heavily as he ran. 'We're entering the baker's now . . . Sandy says that you want him to lead the BA crew in?'

'Yes.'

He hesitated, then said, 'Right you are, guv.'

I started back. 'I'm coming to meet you now . . . stay in the baker's yard with all the gear and I'll lead you through.'

Just as I reached the baker's yard, John and the others came through the rear door. Sandy and

Wayne wore BA sets, Dave Chase carried a BA control board and a sledgehammer, and Mike Scott and Rod Brody carried a short extension ladder and the bolt croppers.

I looked at John. 'Hose?'

'On its way, guv . . . Doug and Martin are bringing it through.'

'Right. Follow me.'

I led them back to the rear of the Sheldons' shop via the alleyway.

'Dave, I want the entry point to be the door from the alley to the yard . . . John, I want another two BA wearers as safety crew . . . who have we got?'

'Mike and Rod.'

The two firemen looked at me. 'Right. Get sets on and get back here as quick as you can.'

They ran off, back through the alleyway, towards the machines at the front of the building. Because of the access problems it was taking time to organise, and all the while I was conscious that the fire was eating its way through the building.

John inspected the rear door. 'Paint's peeling off the door, guv.'

'I've seen it . . . now let's get this organised as quick as we can. I want the jet laid out and charged before we do anything. Then I want the safety crew standing by . . . then and only then do we force entry followed by Sandy and Wayne going in. Right, let's do it.'

'Guv . . . guv . . . where are you?'

It was Doug Russell and Martin McClane. They had reached the baker's yard with the hose and were calling for us.

I nodded at John. 'Right, let's all give 'em a hand bringing it round.'

Doug and Martin were sweating hard, their faces red from exertion. We took the hose from them and ran it through the alleyway, each man spacing himself six or seven feet from the next man, feeding around the corners and through the doorways, to the rear of the Robe shop.

When sufficient hose had been brought up, Dave Chase snapped a branch into the end of the hose and laid it down, facing the door. Doug and Martin bent over, sobbing for breath.

'Which machine is the hose plugged into, Doug?'

He held his hand up, signalling he needed to get his breath first. '. . . Pump Ladder, guv . . . Harry's waiting for the word.'

I spoke into the radio. 'Water on, Harry!'

It took about a minute for the water to arrive. First there was a hiss and then came a sudden pressure that convulsed the hose, till it kicked and straightened like a maddened serpent.

I spoke into the radio again. 'Harry? Harry . . . the pressure's too high . . . drop it down a couple of bars.'

He yelled into the radio, above the noise that surrounded him. 'I'm not cranking up the pressure,

guv . . . it's coming straight off the hydrant like that
. . . pressure's unbelievable.'

John went forward and reinspected the door, then
stepped back and looked up at the blackened windows on the first floor. I saw him shake his head.

'Are you going to vent it first, guv?'

I nodded.

'First-floor windows?' he asked.

I shook my head. 'We'll open it up here and let it
breathe John. If we vent it on the first floor from
outside there's no telling what effect it might have.'

He looked up grimly at the first-floor windows
again. I knew what was going through his mind. He
thought that there might be a back-draught, an
explosive flash fire, caused when an oxygen-starved
fire is suddenly ventilated by someone entering a
room, but I was also worried about the effect that
uncontrolled venting at the front and back of the
building might have – a through draught would turn
the fire into a blowtorch.

The sound of running feet carried across the yards
and Mike and Rod appeared with BA sets on their
backs. Now I had the safety crew I could commit
Sandy and Wayne.

John looped the hose so that it was touching the
yard wall, in order to absorb the jet reaction when
Sandy and Wayne opened the branch up. He was
fretting, wishing it were him and not Sandy leading
the crew.

'Right, Sandy, it's very hot in there. We're going to

open up the door to ensure that the fire hasn't been smouldering without air . . . do not move forward until I give you the okay.'

He held a thumb up.

John used a hand axe to hook the edge of the door. Turning his head away, he eased the door open and a thick swirl of dense smoke rushed through the opening, but there was no bursting into flame as John and I suspected might happen. Sandy watched me, eager to go in, but I waited, giving the air time to enter and circulate. I wanted no surprises.

Finally I gave them the nod and they started their sets up, giving the tallies to Dave Chase, who slotted them into the BA control board. Dave switched his radio to the BA channel and ran a radio check on Sandy's 'comms' set.

The 'comms' allowed us to talk to the crew via a BA set specially adapted with a microphone and earpiece fitted into the face-mask. It allowed me to gain hard information from the crew inside as to the conditions and the way the fire was behaving.

Dave swore. There was a problem with the 'comms', Dave could hear Sandy, but Sandy couldn't hear Dave.

'What do you want to do, guv?' shouted Sandy through his face-mask.

'There's no time to replace it . . . keep feeding us back info as you go.'

Sandy and Wayne picked up the hose and crouched to let the heat go over their heads as the door was pulled back. They moved forward, keeping low. Three feet inside the doorway, the smoke swallowed them up. Mike and Rod knelt by the doorway and continued to feed the hose in slowly.

My radio crackled into life again. It was Solly.

'Steve . . . are your blokes in there yet?'

'Just this second, Solly . . . it took us a while to get it organised. Listen . . . it's very hot in there . . . we had to vent it before we let the crew go in.'

There was a pause; he'd picked up on the concern in my voice.

'If you have to pull them out, Steve, do so . . . we're doing little that's effective here. I intend to send the additional crews round to you as soon as they get here. Keep me posted.'

John paced the yard, looking up at the first-floor windows and then returning to stand alongside Dave, in case a message came through. I had never seen him so ill at ease.

He was visibly relieved when two minutes later Sandy sent his first message. It was difficult to decipher. The sound of his breathing and the popping of his exhaling valve distorted the words, but there was no mistaking the tone; they were struggling.

'. . . so hot . . . keeping the jet . . . moving . . . to drop temperature . . .'

Dave tried to reply, but it was obvious Sandy couldn't hear him as they spoke over each over. I signalled to Dave not to try any more.

Two minutes later another message came through.

'Tell . . . guv . . . smoke . . . gettin' thicker . . . very hot.'

As the message stopped, John turned his head to one side, listening intently. He held his hand up for silence and we stopped talking to watch him. He knelt down by the door and continued to turn his head from side to side.

'What is it, John?' I asked.

He frowned. 'Not certain . . . thought I heard a faint whistling.'

'BA set whistle?'

'No!'

I had just bent down next to him when suddenly there was a rumble deep within the building. At that moment the windows on the first floor blew out and flames erupted across the rear of the building.

From Dave Chase's radio came a horrific scream.

Chapter Twenty-Eight

Panic flooded my brain.

For an instant I was unable to think or move. It was as if the air had been sucked out of my lungs. Nausea washed through me and I turned away, on the verge of being physically sick.

The realisation that it was down to me to do something, to get them out of there, hit me like a second wave, and forced me to focus on what needed to be done. I looked around at the others. They stood in stunned silence, their faces drained.

'Back-draught,' I said. 'We've got to get them out.'

The words seemed to break the spell. Mike and Rod started up their BA sets and Dave Chase shouted in the radio, trying to raise Sandy.

'John . . . Mike and Rod will need water . . . a hose-reel . . . another jet . . .' His eyes held mine. 'Now, John . . . they need it now!'

Nodding, he ran out of the yard, making for the front of the building. I called Solly Weissman up on the radio.

'Solly . . . Solly . . . it's Steve. Send a priority message . . . ambulance required.'

'What's happened, Steve?'

'Back-draught, Solly . . . I've got two men in there, but no water . . . John is coming out to you . . . we need a hose-reel . . . something . . .'

'Will do, Steve . . . we'll bring one of the jets from the front . . . doing it now . . . just hold on.'

'And sets, Solly . . . we'll need another BA crew.'

Mike Scott and Rod Brody started forward and I blocked their way.

'We're going in, guv,' said Mike.

'No! You'll fry . . . wait for the water.'

I forced my voice to stay calm, but then came a sound that tore away logic and training; Sandy's voice screaming from Dave's radio.

'Help me . . . for God's sake, help me . . . I'm burning!'

Mike and Rod looked at me.

'They're dying, guv . . . we can't wait for the water,' Mike shouted.

I was about to say no again, but instead stood to one side.

'Follow the hose, Mike . . . get in, grab them and get out.'

'I intend to,' he said grimly.

They went past me, pulled open the door and got down on their bellies to crawl in beneath the heat band. Inside the doorway I could see the glow from the interior of the building and could hear the hollow roaring of the flames. Like Sandy and Wayne before them, they were quickly swallowed up by heavy smoke.

I tried to stay cool and think only about what needed to be done and not of the horror Sandy and Wayne were going through, but I now had four men in there, two in trouble and two without water.

Every instinct made me want to crawl in with them, to find and pull Sandy and Wayne to safety, but without a BA set I wouldn't last seconds. So I stood in limbo and used every ounce of self-discipline to gain some detachment and run through the options.

After that last harrowing cry for help there had been no further messages. Dave had been visibly shaken by the screaming and was unable to stay still. He kept stepping back into the alley, looking for John returning with help.

'Mike and Rod will get them,' I said softly.

I looked up at the first-floor windows. Flames reached up to the next floor, and the sounds of the building disintegrating could clearly be heard. The conditions inside could only be imagined.

Mike and Rod were good firemen, but without water they would soon be in trouble unless they somehow managed to recover Sandy and Wayne's jet and use that to keep the fire off, but they couldn't do that and rescue them.

Their best hope was grab and go, and that was no plan at all.

I could hear in my head the words of accusation that would be thrown at me. Where was my risk assessment? What was my plan of action should

Mike and Rod get into trouble? Why commit a safety crew without water?

I didn't need other people to accuse me. The silence from Dave's radio was condemnation enough. I knew I was gambling, but the alternative was to stand back and leave Sandy and Wayne to their fate, and all the accusation in the world wasn't a balance to that.

Just then I heard voices from the baker's yard, followed by John bursting through the rear entrance to the shop yard.

'I've got four BA men, two "comms" sets and there's three extra blokes dragging the jet through now, guv . . . where're Mike and Rod?'

'Snatch rescue.'

If he doubted the wisdom of what I'd done he didn't show it. He gave all his attention to organising the new crews.

'Right. D'you want one crew of four or two in and two safety, guv?'

'Two in and two safety . . . we're extended enough as it is,' I replied.

The crew designated to go in started up their sets and gave their tallies to Dave Chase, who slotted them into the control board and wrote 'emergency crew' in the remarks column.

A minute later the charged length of hose was manhandled through the yard door by three of Dagenham's men and quickly brought into position. I briefed the emergency crew just before they went in.

'You're to give protection to the snatch rescue crew and assist them in any way necessary to get my men out . . . follow the hose and move carefully . . . it's dangerous in there.'

The crew leader was an experienced Leading Firefighter from Dagenham, Roy 'Chico' Marx. He gave me a single nod, took up the hose and, with the other BA man backing him up, crawled into the building.

We didn't have to wait long for their first message. Everyone outside was grouped around Dave Chase's radio.

'Tell the guv'nor we're at the foot of the staircase . . . and it's red hot! The hose is going up the staircase and we're about to follow it . . . not sure we can get right to the top.'

'Dave, tell them to let us know the minute they make contact with either of the other two crews,' I said.

He nodded and spoke quickly into the radio.

Less than a minute later 'Chico' Marx sent another message.

'Guv . . . guv . . . I think we've found them . . . hold on . . . Jesus! The fire's really got a hold in here . . . we're taking punishment. If this isn't them . . . may have to come out.'

The radio fell silent again and we clustered even closer to it. More fire-fighters were coming into the yard by the minute, some with BA sets and others carrying a whole range of equipment, including first-aid kits; with them was Stuart Docherty from Ilford.

'The ambulance has been ordered, Steve, and Charnley's just turned up and taken over,' he said.

'They think they've found them,' I replied.

As if on cue, Chico's voice came on the radio again.

'Guv . . . we've made contact with Mike and Rod . . . they've got Wayne Bennett . . . I repeat, Wayne Bennett, over.'

Dave said it for me. 'Where's Sandy, Chico? Have they got Sandy Richards with them?'

'No. Mike and Rod are bringing Wayne out . . . we'll keep searching for Sandy, over.'

Stuart Docherty leaned forward. 'He'll find him, Steve . . . Chico's a good hand.'

For what seemed an eternity we waited. There was a crowd in the yard now but there was no talking, no movement; we just stood still, listening to the radio. A few minutes later I saw Bob Grant slip into the back of the yard and I went across and briefed him.

He listened in silence. If he disagreed with what I'd done, like John, he didn't show it. Equally he didn't say well done. The gravity of what had happened and the uncertainty of the outcome stunted sentiment, and there would be time enough for analysis and criticism.

There was a sudden flurry of movement around the rear door and two BA-wearers dragging a third emerged into the yard. Bob and I pushed our way to the front.

At a glance I could see the one being dragged was badly burnt. His flash hood was burnt away and there were terrible burns to his face. One glove was missing and his right hand was seared to the bone.

John and two firemen immediately got to work applying burns dressings while the two BA men who'd dragged him out were helped to their feet. They looked all in.

The first to remove his face-mask was Mike Scott. He rubbed his face with both his hands, then he saw me and shook his head at my unasked question.

'We found Wayne at the top of the stairs . . . couldn't find Sandy,' he said. Then he saw Bob Grant standing behind me and, although he continued to speak to me, he looked directly at Bob Grant. 'If you hadn't let us go in when you did, guv, Wayne would be dead.'

Rod Brody had now taken off his face-mask and stood behind Mike. He had only one thought and spoke it.

'Any news from Chico?'

I shook my head. 'Not yet, Rod. Are either of you injured?'

They both said no, but appeared on the verge of collapse. Someone produced some rehydration fluid and they were sat down to drink it. I squatted by Mike and spoke quietly to him.

'Could Sandy be alive in there?'

He looked gaunt and close to tears. 'It's possible.'

'Possible?'

'I can't tell you how bad it was in there, guv. We were very lucky to find Wayne.'

'Well done, the pair of you ... we'll talk more later,' I said, and patted them both on the back.

The yard was buzzing after the rescue of Wayne, and Bob Grant called for silence.

'There're still people in there,' he said firmly.

The pockets of activity around Wayne, Mike and Rod apart, the talking ceased, and again people congregated around Dave Chase. Two paramedics arrived, and they got to work on Wayne before taking him away. I asked one on them to which hospital they were taking him.

'Oldchurch, guv, but I'm certain he'll be transferred to Broomfield Burns Unit,' he replied.

Several of the fire-fighters standing around helped to lift Wayne and carry him to the waiting ambulance. As soon as he was gone, another two paramedics arrived. While Mike and Rod were checked out, I suggested that they might want to go to hospital, but they both declined and said they would wait for Sandy.

Time dragged on and I started to believe Sandy's chance was gone. An air of desperation descended on the yard, and I found I couldn't look people in the eye. I saw John standing alone in the corner, his eyes closed. I didn't think he was religious, but I had no doubt he was praying.

Then came a message.

'Guv! Guv!' Dave Chase called. 'Chico's found him!'

Dave called up Chico and the reply, distorted by Chico's heavy breathing, came through.

'Tell the guv'nor . . . we've got him . . . he's breathing!'

The message gave no clue as to Sandy's condition, but there were tight smiles of relief. The main thing was he was alive.

Bob Grant and John stood with me by the rear entrance to the shop. The minutes dragged by with no further messages. Charnley came from nowhere and joined us. There were silent nods of greeting at his arrival, but that was all.

Seconds later Chico's BA crew emerged into the yard.

Everyone moved back to give the paramedics some space to work in. Bob and I stood as close as we could without getting in their way. Sandy looked dead. The burns were horrific, but then he groaned and my stomach rolled over.

Chapter Twenty-Nine

The paramedics took Sandy away.

Harry Wildsmith and the others of the watch had been alerted to the drama at the rear of the fire by the increasingly frantic efforts to get water and BA men for the rescues. As we emerged from the baker's into the Heathway, they approached us for explanations, but caught the glazed, traumatised expressions and fell silent.

For once, Charnley excelled himself and made a sensible and humane decision. He ordered all Wells Lane personnel withdrawn from fire-fighting and brought together by the control unit.

There he took a few minutes to speak to us and say how deeply sorry he was for what had happened to Sandy and Wayne. Then backed off and allowed us some space.

We formed a circle, shutting out the fire, the other fire-fighters, everything, turning in on ourselves in a collective state of shock. Dave Chase was probably the most resilient character among us, but even he was staring at the ground, unable to speak.

After a while Bob Grant beckoned me and we walked out of earshot of the circle.

'I know what you're going to say, Bob . . . before I go off duty I've got to make an entry in the accident book and send off an area commander's message.'

He gave a glum smile. 'I'm sorry. I've just heard that a Senior Accident Investigator has been appointed. I know this is difficult, but I think you'll have to talk to him tonight . . . if you're up to it.'

'Of course.'

'And the police are here . . . one of your blokes said the padlock on the rear entrance had been cut . . .'

'Yes.'

'Well, they'll doubtless want a statement.' He sighed. 'I'm really sorry about this, Steve. The main thing is you got them out. The rest is beyond our control . . . let's just hope . . .'

'Did you see them, Bob?' I blurted out. 'Did you see the state they were in? Who's going to tell Sandy's parents . . . and Wayne's wife?'

'I'll do it,' he said quickly. 'Perhaps it might be best if you don't . . . they'll want to ask questions.'

I shook my head. 'I don't want to tell them . . . isn't that shocking . . . it should be me, but I don't think I could face them.'

He folded his arms and lowered his voice. 'It's best that you don't . . . it's a serious accident and it's probably good advice not to . . . legally speaking.'

It took a moment for his words to sink in. 'What? What are you saying . . . that there was negligence?'

'No! No, but there's bound to be an inquiry of

some sort. Maybe even a compensation hearing . . . look, you know what I mean.'

But his words got me thinking. Had I made a mistake in putting Sandy and Wayne into the building, or for that matter Mike and Rod? My mind was in turmoil. Did people think I'd blundered?

I must have staggered, because the next thing I knew Bob was holding me by the arm.

'You okay, Steve?'

I looked at him and then at my men grouped by the control unit. They were staring. John and Harry started to come over, but Bob motioned them away.

I felt foolish. There was Sandy and Wayne badly hurt and Mike and Rod exhausted by their efforts and my contribution was to have an attack of the vapours. It was pathetic.

I got angry with myself and pushed the giddiness aside. I had to be there for them, not wrapped up in my own weakness. What was the point of being in charge if you folded when the shit was coming down?

'I'm okay, Bob . . . I'm okay,' I said a little too sharply.

Bob shrugged. 'I've been there, Steve . . . where you are now . . . I've been there and I'm not judging.'

When my head had cleared, we walked back over to the control unit and Bob thanked everyone for their efforts.

'You couldn't have done more . . . and you got them out. Now collect your nominal roll boards from the control unit and go home.'

As we drove from the fire ground I looked back at the building. The fire was raging on all floors and the fire-fighting was confined to preventing spread to adjoining premises.

An aerial ladder platform was being brought up, a sure sign that the building was lost.

As we drove into the station yard the oncoming watch came out to us. They'd heard the messages on the listening post in the watchroom. As if rehearsed, they stopped by the rear doors of the appliance bay and the Green Watch Station Officer, Mark Kinch, came around to my cab door.

'There's a cup of tea in the pot,' he said simply. 'Leave the gear, we'll deal with everything. There's been quite a few phone calls, Steve. Your guys can use the phone in the commander's room. My dutyman's got the list of wives that have rung.'

I rang Jenny immediately from my office and explained to her what had happened and why I would be late home.

'Are you all right?' she said softly.

'Better than Sandy and Wayne.'

'How's everyone else . . . John and the others?'

'We're all sick to the stomach . . . I may go down the hospital after I've sorted out the paperwork here . . . I can't say when exactly I'll be back.'

'It's not a problem. I can grab a cab to the station and drive you if you want.'

'No. No thanks . . . I need some space.'

By the time I'd showered the Senior Accident Investigator had phoned and agreed to interview me on our second night duty. Over a cup of tea I gave the details of the accident to Mark Kinch and he formulated an ACO's message and sent it. Then he made an accident book entry as I dictated it.

I thanked him for his help.

'Would you like me to phone the hospital and find out how Sandy and Wayne are?'

'No thanks, Mark. I'll go straight there.'

I pulled out of the station just after eight and was halfway to Oldchurch Hospital when my mobile rang. It was Eileen.

'Steve, we've had another fire.'

'Where does Kris Mayle live, Eileen?'

'Did you hear what I said, Steve? There's been another fire.'

'I heard. Have you got Mayle's address?'

'River Mews . . . it's not far from Michael's.'

'Give me the exact address.'

'Wait a moment.'

I pulled into the side of the road and waited for her to fetch it. When she returned she gave me the full address and asked me to come over.

'Not possible. I'll speak to you later.'

'Steve . . . Steve . . .'

I switched the mobile off.

Heavy rain made the drive to the hospital slow, and I arrived to find John and most of the watch

there. They were congregated around a drinks machine in the main corridor.

'They've moved Wayne to Broomfield, guv,' said
John.

'Sandy?'

'Too ill. They're trying to stabilise him before
attempting the transfer.'

'Any sign of the relatives?'

'The Brigade's arranging transport for them.'

I told John about the advice that Bob Grant had
given me.

'He's right, you know, guv. It wasn't your fault,
but until the whole thing has been investigated, you'd
be wise to keep your own counsel. Go. I'll give you a
ring if anything happens.'

I gave him my mobile number, exchanged a few
words with the blokes and left. Walking out of that
hospital was the hardest thing I'd ever had to do – it
felt like desertion.

River Mews was the best part of an hour's drive
and during the journey the concern I felt for Sandy
and Wayne deteriorated to something darker.

I found the place fairly easily. It was a modern
town house of quality, with a clean, pristine, seriously expensive look. I parked the car and crossed
the rainswept mews.

There was a speakerphone next to the door and I
buzzed it. There was no reply. I gave it several more
tries before deciding he wasn't in, then went back to
the car and waited.

Over the next hour, I sank into a black mood the like of which I'd not known since Jenny had walked out on me. Slowly, one by one, I reprised my reasons for paying Kris Mayle a visit, but the thing that had eventually brought me to his door wasn't on the list. The history just added weight.

His car pulled up around half-ten and I waited to see if he was alone. He was.

When he climbed from the black Lexus I timed it so that I could slide out and reach the front door a fraction behind him. He wasn't even aware of me until I barged through the closing door.

'What the . . . ?'

My first punch was a left hook into his short ribs. I followed up with a knee to the groin and then slammed his head against the wall. As he groaned, I turned him and dug two right hooks into his kidneys and, as he fell, dropped with my knees on to the small of his back.

Then I turned him over and straddled his chest.

Helpless, he tried to cover his face, but I ripped his arms away and put both my hands around his throat.

'There are two young firemen in hospital tonight because of you . . . you'd better pray that they both make it . . . because if they don't I'm coming back for you.'

He was white faced and panting, but he didn't say a word. I climbed off him and turned to go, but then spun on my heel and kicked him hard in the ribs.

'You won't forget, will you?'

I turned the hallway light off and slammed the door shut behind me. As I walked back to the car, the adrenaline rushed through me, making my limbs tremble and my stomach writhe.

Only then did I cry.

The drama of the day, the heartache of the past six months and the worry for Sandy and Wayne all combined to overwhelm me. I sat in my car and sobbed like a child. I knew that to hang around was tempting fate, so with my eyes still streaming I drove off back the way I'd come.

The first set of traffic lights I came to I switched the mobile back on and scanned to see if there were any messages. There was one from Alex. It said simply, 'Heard about the fire. Ring me.'

He would have to wait. Eileen would have to wait. The whole bloody world would have to wait, because I was going back to Oldchurch, advice or no advice.

Chapter Thirty

I arrived at the hospital to find Bob Grant and Sandy's parents there. Apparently Sandy had regained consciousness at one point and had spoken to his parents.

I went straight up to them and said how devastated we all were. They were both near to tears, but the first thing they did was to ask about Wayne. I told them what little news I had and gave them my home telephone number.

'Ring it at any time, day or night. If I'm not in, leave a message and I'll get right back to you,' I said.

Bob raised his eyes, as if to say 'thoughtful, but stupid'. I didn't care. These people were suffering and I was their son's guv'nor. Legal caution is one thing, cowardice another.

'Okay, Steve,' he said firmly, 'you've done what you needed to do. Now, for everybody's sake, just go home. I'll ring you if there's any change.'

'Is that an order, Bob?'

'No, it's the recommendation of a friend.'

Reluctantly I took his advice.

Jenny was waiting up. She said that the fire had

been on the news and it had been mentioned that two firemen had been injured, one critically.

'Is Sandy going to make it?'

'God knows, Jen.'

'How are you feeling . . . really?'

'Really? I'm gutted. Two of my people have been seriously injured and here am I without a scratch on me.'

'It's not your job to go in any more. What could you have done that they weren't able to do?'

'Something, anything. John picked it up. He heard something just before the back-draught.'

'You can't be everywhere . . . see everything. That's why you have other officers, like John. You're not God, Steve. You can only do your best.'

'And I did, but I can't help feeling that somehow it was avoidable.'

'Has John said anything?'

'No. He wouldn't, but there was a look in his eye, Jen.'

'That meant what, exactly?'

'Doubt,' I said quietly.

After a meal eaten in virtual silence we went to bed. I fell asleep instantly, but woke one hour later. The rest of the night I spent going over in my mind all that had happened, particularly the choices I'd made on the fire ground.

John's idea to vent the first-floor windows would have dealt with the situation there, but not on the ground floor, where the greatest danger had lain for the crew as they entered. In theory I could have vented both, but that would have been to put air in at two levels, creating a through-draught with the chance of turning the entire building into an inferno.

My choice had been to give them a safe entry and brief them well about the dangers within. It hadn't been enough.

Charlie Bimpson, my first guv'nor, once said that there were no perfect choices on the fire ground, just better options. He was a wise old bird, who prided himself on dealing honestly with people and regarded fairness as the true test of authority. He would have detested the sleight-of-hand merchants who currently ran the shop.

Frustrated at being unable to sleep, I got up at six and sat drinking coffee in the living room. Jenny found me there an hour later.

'Can't sleep?'

'Barely an hour. I dozed from time to time.'

She came and sat on my lap, her arms around my neck. 'Want to talk some more about it?'

'Not at the moment. After breakfast I'm going to drive up to Chelmsford – the Broomfield Hospital.'

'Do you want me with you?'

'No.'

Around nine I rang Oldchurch and was told Sandy remained critical. Then I drove up the A12 to Chelmsford. I spent the journey trying to dissect the Heathway fire, but I couldn't think straight.

Wayne's wife Sally was there with the family. The

latest news on Wayne wasn't good. They had amputated his right hand and he needed extensive skin grafts. The positive news was that he was out of danger.

'I don't care about his injuries,' Sally cried. 'He's alive and that's all that matters.'

I couldn't look her in the face.

Wayne wasn't allowed visitors except immediate family, so I hung around in the waiting room, drinking coffee and talking in turns to Wayne's father and brothers. Like Sandy's people, there was no recrimination, no anger, just relief and gratitude for the rescue.

The amputation was sickening news, and although I tried to remain positive for his family's sake I felt like crawling into a hole and pulling a rock after me.

At midday Alex McGregor showed up. He took in the atmosphere immediately and suggested we get a breath of fresh air.

'Pretty heavy in there, eh?'

'They're brave people, Alex. Christ knows what they feel in their hearts. I take it you spoke to Jenny?'

'She sounded concerned. Just how bad is your lad?'

I told him about the amputation and from that flowed a discussion about the fire. He didn't interrupt, just listened with an experienced ear. When I'd finished he weighed what I'd said before passing comment.

'It sounds a tough one to call, Stevie. People will know that.'

I sighed. 'The Brigade's changed, Alex. There aren't that many senior officers with real operational experience. Most don't hang around at station level . . . too many opportunities to get a blemish on your record. Make an impression, make the right allies, move on and don't look back.'

'Is it really that bad?'

I shrugged. 'Feels like it sometimes.'

'Perhaps it's time for you to move on. You've done your share and are still young enough to make senior rank. Take your experience where it'll count.'

I laughed. 'Wouldn't be welcome . . . too independent . . . no longer malleable.'

His face was impassive. 'Can't complain *and* opt out, Stevie.'

'Yes, I know, but it's hard to commit to something you're losing faith in.'

The wind was gusting, sending litter scudding across the ground. I buttoned my jacket and we turned our backs to it. Alex lit a cigar in the cover of his coat lapel and puffed the smoke away from me.

'Can we talk business?' he asked.

I nodded.

'I've spoken to Eileen Sheldon this morning. She's coming apart.'

I anticipated his next question. 'It's Mayle, Alex. From beginning to end the trail leads to him.'

'I've spoken to that DS Menzies this morning,' he said. 'His charm's a bit thin. He wouldn't talk about the latest fire, but obviously it takes a little of the heat off Stephanie Sheldon.'

I smiled. 'Does it? How?'

'I was hoping you'd tell me.'

I sighed. 'I don't know what I believe at the moment, Alex. My head feels like a sandbag and . . .' I looked at my watch. 'I'm back on duty in less than six hours.'

'Time to be heading back, then?'

I nodded.

When we reached the carpark he stopped and caught my arm.

'This fire ground business . . .'

'Yes.'

'You're facing a hard test at the moment,' he said gently. 'There may be no right and no wrong. Friends may hesitate and enemies may seize the moment. It calls for guts, Stevie. Now there's an old-fashioned word for you. Not the hell-for-leather, wailers screaming, kick-arse sort of guts. No, the quiet, no one to help you, dig deep and pray kind of guts . . . and it's the hardest test on God's earth.'

'You're a sane man, Alex, and there're precious few of those around. Thank you.'

He dug into his coat pocket and pulled out a heavily taped envelope.

'This arrived at the office for you this morning. Were you expecting it?'

'No.'

I ran my car keys down the side of the envelope

and tore away the parcel tape. Inside was a key taped to a postcard. On the postcard was written '7 Melrose Court, Toomey Close, Hornchurch'.

Hornchurch was only a short way off my route back to Romford. I stopped off at a service station on the A12 and topped up the petrol tank, stuffing an extra pair of polythene gloves from the drum dispenser in my pocket.

I found Toomey Close easily enough; it was in the Nemles Way area of Hornchurch, a neighbourhood so rich it could boast several almost famous celebrities among its occupiers. Come June, when the school fête season started, the place was practically a ghost town.

Melrose Court was a tidy two-storey block of flats at the bottom of the close. An ornate wrought-iron fence surrounded the block and the gates were locked. A speakerphone was mounted on a brick pier to one side of the gates.

I pressed the button and said I had a delivery for number seven. A buzzer sounded and the gates swung open.

Up until that point I hadn't thought much about what I was going to do. Clearly someone had sent me the key in order to enter number seven, but was I being set up or helped? I decided to knock first and see what happened.

Number seven was on the first floor. The door was solid oak with brass fittings and a spyhole just above

the knocker. Like the wrought-iron fence, Melrose
Court's front doors were built with security hidden
as decoration. I knocked twice and waited. Nothing.
I knocked again.

After a long wait I felt for the key in my pocket and
tried it. The lock opened smoothly. Still I waited,
expecting any moment to be screamed at by the
alarmed owner. Quietly I stepped inside and closed
the door behind me.

The flat was silent.

I slipped on the polythene gloves and advanced
slowly. There were four doors off the expensively
furnished hallway. I tried the one to my right and
found myself in a large kitchen equipped with a state-
of-the-art array of cooking utensils and hand-painted
tiling worked by someone with real artistry.

In fact everything spoke of style and taste.

I hunted around for clues to the owner, but the
room was bare of personal effects.

Next I tried the lounge. Again the matching of
colour and fabric impressed me. I knew nothing
about interior decoration, but I was sure that
whoever owned the flat was more than a gifted
amateur.

There were no letters, no bills, no junk mail;
nothing that could tie a name or a face to the
property. I went back out to the hallway to check
for an answering machine. There wasn't one.

I couldn't relax. Every sense was alive to the sound
of footsteps, a voice, anything. I decided to do a

quick sweep of the flat and go. The longer I stayed, the more I ran the risk of being caught.

A thin film of dust on the telephone table made me lean towards the belief that no one had been here for several days, but that didn't mean they wouldn't show up in the next ten minutes.

Finally I tried the bedrooms.

The master bedroom was something special, with a huge bed and an ivory carpet so deep I hesitated to walk on it. Leading off it was an en-suite bathroom complete with a Jacuzzi.

A thorough search of the drawers and wardrobes revealed nothing, not even a bathrobe, and that was when the blurred shape of an idea started to form.

I tried the last bedroom.

I found the photographs in a bureau.

All of the same woman, album after album of deeply erotic images; a nude, shot from different angles, capturing different shapes, never revealing the full figure, the owner's identity, the playing of light and shade rendering some almost abstract.

There was one that stood out, even among the other beautifully lit studies.

Half a woman; a figure dissected from head to toe. The arm drawn back behind the head, lifting the breast; the leg out to the side, deliberately ambiguous, neither invitation nor form.

The theme of the image was the theme of the series; of giving and withholding; of never having the complete woman. I studied the half-face; its monochrome features yielding nothing, adopting a style of no-emotion, a pose of watching, of waiting.

I slipped the photograph from its mounting and placed it carefully in my inside pocket. Suddenly, as I was putting back the albums, my mobile rang, sending a bolt of panic through me.

I listened hard, but there were no other sounds. As I was about to answer, it stopped. I pressed ring-back and got a mobile number I didn't recognise. I was debating whether to press redial when it rang again.

'Steve! Where have you been . . . I . . . trying . . . times . . .'

'Eileen? Sorry, Eileen, I've been up to . . . Eileen? Eileen . . . are you there? Listen, my battery's going . . . ring off and I'll ring straight back.'

I went through to the hallway and dialled the mobile number.

'Eileen? Sorry for not getting back to you, but . . .'

'Steve, we've had a terrible fire . . . in the Heathway, Dagenham.'

'I know . . . Alex briefed me and I've been watching it on the news.'

'Why haven't you been in touch? I've been going frantic.'

I tried to calm her down. 'Are you all okay?'

'Yes, yes. Stephanie and Michael were with me when the fire happened. Why are you speaking so quietly, Steve?'

I took a deep breath. 'I'm in an office with some

people just outside . . . look, it's not a good time to speak at the moment. Can I ring you later?'

'Yes, of course, but tonight, please?'

'Nine . . . half past?'

'Fine.'

I rang off and replaced the phone.

The call had scared me witless. I decided to get out of the flat quickly. I had a quick look around to make sure I hadn't left any trace of my visit. With luck the missing photograph might not be discovered for weeks.

I saw no one as I left the flats and walked back to my car, but I don't think my heart stopped beating till I got back to Romford.

Chapter Thirty-One

I was conscious of being watched from the moment I entered the station yard.

As I walked through the appliance bay I got a few muted hellos from the day watch, but that was all. At changeover there was none of the usual laughter; no wisecracks, no shouts of 'have a quiet one'. The off-going watch just walked quietly to their cars.

Roll-call was tense. After John had read out the riders' board I told the watch that I'd been up to the Broomfield Hospital. The news of the amputation of Wayne's right hand was received in absolute silence.

'Get your checks done as soon as you can,' I added. 'I want to speak to everybody in the Mess at a quarter past six.'

As the watch dispersed, I took John into my office and closed the door.

'There's something I need to ask you, John.'

'Guv?'

'Do you think I made a mistake at the Heathway? Were Sandy and Wayne injured because I wouldn't listen to you?'

'What?' He looked genuinely surprised.

'Loyalty aside, did I screw up?'

He stared at me. 'No, guv.'

'Honestly, John.'

He swayed from foot to foot, not knowing at first how to answer. His hands came up in a pacifying gesture.

'Guv, my concerns were that Sandy and Wayne shouldn't get caught in a back-draught on entry . . . and you dealt with that. What you did was by the book . . . it wasn't wrong.'

'And later . . . just before the back-draught, when you heard the whistling?'

'I wasn't sure that I heard whistling.'

'But you were uneasy all the same.'

He stood still, and the hesitancy went from his voice. 'I watched you, guv . . . we were both uneasy . . . and for the same reasons. The only difference between us was that you had to make the decision. In your place I wouldn't have done any different.'

I sat down on the edge of my desk. 'And when you thought I'd lost the plot the other day, when we were talking to George Harris and Jack Grocott . . . and you did, John, I saw it in your face . . . are you saying that that didn't affect your judgement of me on the fire ground?'

He walked over and looked me straight in the eye.

'You were tired the other day . . . anyone with half a brain could see that.'

I persisted. 'So the verdict, then, is everything's fine?'

He laid a hand on my shoulder. 'Steve, I haven't

heard one of the blokes criticise your actions. There's general agreement in fact that you faced a bloody awful decision with the emergency crew and you called it right. No one, but no one, thinks you got it wrong.'

His use of my first name removed any lingering doubts that I may have had about him being diplomatic. I was grateful for his strength of character. A weaker man might have fallen short of endorsement.

'Shall I get everybody in the Mess, guv?'

'Please, John.'

He closed the door behind him and I breathed a sigh of relief. Reassured, I felt able to face the watch. I still felt partially responsible, but at least I hadn't lost the support of my people.

Suddenly the phone rang. It was John in the Mess.

'Guv, I think you should know that Charnley and another DO have just pulled into the yard.'

I straightened my tie in the mirror, put my cap on and went out to greet them.

The other Divisional Officer with Charnley I recognised as Cyril Williams, a tall, thin-faced man who looked more like an accountant than a Fire Brigade officer. He had a reputation for a 'by the book' approach to issues.

I saluted them, and Charnley asked me if my Sub Officer was on duty.

'Yes, sir.'

'And how many men are you riding?'

'Eleven, sir.'

'Right. Take yourself off the run, put your undress jacket on and wait outside the Station Commander's room,' he said directly.

'Can I ask what for, sir?'

'Just do it, please, Station Officer.'

I went to the Mess, called John into my office and told him.

'What's going on, guv?'

'I've no idea, but I've a feeling I'm about to find out.'

I went to my room and donned my jacket. As I went up to the first floor I got a feeling that the shit was about to fly over the Heathway fire, and I prepared myself for the worst.

A few minutes later I was called into the commander's office. Charnley was behind the desk and Cyril Williams sat at right angles to it. Charnley's tone was brisk and businesslike.

'Come in, Station Officer. Sit down, please. You may remove your hat.'

In front of him, on the desk, he had a file, and from it he took a single piece of paper.

'This,' he began, 'is a complaint received today from a member of the public. It alleges that you have abused your authority to gain access to a warehouse in Stratford by falsely stating that you were on London Fire Brigade business. It also alleges that you have been working as an inquiry agent and passing on confidential information to people not authorised to receive it.'

Mayle!

'Station Officer . . . is this true?'

'I did visit the warehouse, sir, but I did not state that I was on official Brigade business.'

'Are you now working or did you at any time work on behalf of an insurance agency?'

To lie would be fatal. A falsehood alone, under the right circumstances, could get me dismissed from the Brigade, and I had no idea what hard evidence they had. I would have to buy time.

'I cannot answer that question, sir.'

His face was stone. 'In the light of the seriousness of these accusations, I would remind you that you are obliged to answer my questions and a failure to do so might be interpreted as an admission.'

'Sir, the allegations are serious and I would respectfully ask permission to seek legal advice before replying to your questions.'

He shook his head. 'You are being interviewed under the Brigade disciplinary regulations and are not entitled to legal advice. You must answer my questions. Should you say anything that may incriminate you, I will stop the interview and caution you. Then and only then may you appoint a member of the Brigade to act as an accused's friend to assist your defence.'

'I have nothing to add, sir.'

Charnley wrote something on a notepad and then looked up.

'Station Officer Jay, I am handing you a Regulation

Seven letter and suspending you from duty forthwith. Divisional Officer Williams will go with you to your locker and you may take any personal items from there that you need. You will then be escorted off the station. You are forbidden to enter any Brigade premises while under suspension. Do you understand what I have said?'

'Yes, sir.'

The faces of the watch as I drove out of the station said it all.

Speculation would be rife and they would guess wrongly that it was something to do with the Heathway fire. Then the rumour mill would start, and before you could say 'fuck-up' it would be all round the Brigade that I'd been suspended for getting two firemen badly hurt. Once those sorts of rumours started they couldn't be recalled.

Charnley would tell the watch nothing; discipline policy didn't allow him. Job done, he would depart into the night, leaving the watch in confusion.

I drove a few hundred yards from the station, pulled off the road and rang Alex. How and why were his first questions. I told him what I'd done to Mayle the previous night and he exploded.

'You stupid bastard.'

I was unrepentant. 'Wayne is minus a hand because of him and Sandy is in a very bad way. He's lucky I didn't break his neck.'

'Aye, maybe, but what you've done plays right into

his hands. You could be out of a job! Your pension, everything, is under threat now. Jesus fucking Christ, Stevie, I told you to keep away from him . . . you agreed!'

'I know.'

He swore again and I could feel his agitation down the phone.

'It's an unmitigated disaster, Stevie. There's no way you can carry on working for us now, you know that, don't you? And what if he's made a complaint to the police?'

'He won't go to the police, Alex, he's red hot, and he knows it. The last place he wants to be is inside a police station answering awkward questions. I'm sorry about the investigation.'

'Aye, so am I. Couldn't you have waited until the proof was in your hands? It makes us look like we're deliberately placing him under duress. Your vendetta has just about scuppered any chance we had. How could you be so daft, Stevie?'

'You asked me to do this because of the vendetta.'

'Aye, to give you a chance to nail him properly and gain revenge the shrewd way. Beating the shit out of him is a luxury neither of us can afford. He might get off the hook now . . . have you thought of that?'

'What will you do?'

'What will I do? For me it's just further embarrassment; for you, Stevie, it could be goodbye to everything.'

'You could give it back to Roley Benson.'

'Oh yes . . . now that would be shrewd.' He paused and then said, 'How much do I owe you?'

'Under the circumstances . . .'

His voice rose again. 'You can't afford to be proud now, laddie! Work out a figure and let me know. Then, if you want my advice, get hold of a good accused's friend from the union. Chris Adamou used to be the best. You've really done it this time, Stevie . . . there may be no way back.'

Up until then my anger had kept logic at bay, but Alex was determined to drag me back into the real world. The enormity of my indulgence loomed.

'I'm sorry, Alex . . . really I am. My timing was wrong.'

He grunted. 'Well . . . what's done is done. You'd better think up something to tell Jenny, and I have to break the news to Andrew. I'll speak to you tomorrow.'

And with that he rang off.

I sat there for a moment, staring at the phone.

He was right – my career as an inquiry agent was finished before it had barely begun. Under suspension, I wasn't allowed to work part time, and any further complaints would crush any chance of holding on to the Fire Brigade, which was where my energies would now have to go.

I started the car and drove slowly, trying to think of what to say to Jenny. The most convenient lie was that I'd been suspended due to the Heathway fire, but sooner or later the truth would out.

Jenny was shocked, but she accepted what I said. 'That's not fair, Steve.'

'It's almost routine under the circumstances, Jen.'

'Will you get paid?'

'Yes.'

'What's the worst that can happen?'

I shrugged. 'The sack.'

'They can't sack you! Even if they find you guilty, it was a genuine mistake.'

She was right there, but they could easily sack me for the reasons Charnley quoted. We talked for an hour or more and it was hard not to add to the lie in order to support it. Eventually I said I didn't want to talk about it any more and that I would contact the union in the morning.

I could see that Jenny was far from happy, but she let it drop. We went to bed early, and despite everything that was on my mind I fell asleep quickly.

The shrill ring of the phone tore me from deep sleep. I lay there for a moment, gathering my wits. It continued to ring and, as I reached for it, I peered through slits at the alarm clock; it was half-twelve.

'Yes!' I said irritably.

'Guv?'

'John? What . . . ?'

There was a pause, and I could hear voices in the background.

'Guv . . . guv, Sandy is dead.'

'Oh, Christ!'

'He died twenty minutes ago.'

I dressed and drove to the station through driving rain. The gutters were overflowing and long sheets of water cut the road in places, so that I aquaplaned and nearly lost control a couple of times.

I willed myself to slow down, but my foot kept the accelerator pushed to the floor.

I was fifty yards from the station when I first saw them. They were standing motionless on the fore-court, waiting, knowing that I was forbidden to enter the station.

Silent and white with grief, they stared at me as I climbed from the car. John spoke first.

'His father rang us . . . they're badly cut up . . .' He shook his head. 'I can't take this in.'

'Come in out of the wet, guv,' said Harry Wild-smith.

I shook my head. 'Not wise, Harry.'

'Screw 'em. We're not going to tell anybody, are we?' he said.

John nodded. 'Come inside, guv . . . please.'

We went through to the Mess and someone made cups of coffee for us all.

In low, hesitant voices, we all expressed our grief. John buried his face in his hands and Dave Chase put a hand on his shoulder.

'It's murder . . . that padlock was cut,' said Mike Scott.

'I hope he rots in hell,' said Tom Reed, 'a lad like that with all his life before him.'

'They'll get him,' I said, 'the police will hunt him.'

Once the talking started it didn't stop. Anger, pain and shock all came out, but most powerful were John's comments.

'I feel like I've lost family.'

After fifteen minutes I said that I would have to go to Oldchurch, to see Sandy's parents.

They followed me out to the forecourt, ignoring the heavy rain. The powerful emotions running through me wouldn't allow me to look back. I drove out of Wells Lane not knowing if I'd ever return.

The hospital was ten minutes away, but the driving conditions were getting worse by the minute. At the Oldchurch end of Waterloo Road, I noticed something driving right up against my rear bumper and I shook my head at the stupidity.

Suddenly there was a flash of white on my right-hand side and a large van swung across my front, causing me to turn left instead of going around the roundabout. I hit the horn and steered away from the vehicle as we flashed by Bridge Close, just short of the River Rom.

Again the van veered across my front and I changed down to third to accelerate away, but there was a violent bang and the sound of tearing metal. I was forced off the road and hit the metal railings of the bridge. The car leaped into the air and then lurched sideways as the windscreen shattered and raked my face with glass fragments.

The car arced through the air and I saw the concrete ramp below the bridge and the silver-black water of the river rushing beneath. I braced myself for the impact, but when it came the force was sickening, jarring every bone and joint. Violent pain shot through my arms and legs and the seat belt dug deep into my chest.

Harsh edges of concrete bit into the car's bodywork, slicing through the doorpost behind my seat, crushing the floor pan and leaving the car suspended just above the water. It hung there for a split second, on the lip of the ramp, and then fell into the fast-flowing river.

Filthy, ice-cold water poured in through the broken windows, making me gasp. I felt for the seat belt buckle with my left hand, but the car was already half filled with water and turning over slowly in the current. My weight shifted to the left, and just before the car slid beneath the water I caught a fleeting glimpse of a figure running down the ramp.

The car continued its roll, forcing out the last of the air, leaving me upside down and trapped by the twisted seat belt. The release catch was above and behind me and I clutched frantically for it.

There was a scraping noise as the car moved against the bottom of the river, then settled uncertainly on its roof. A thin trail of silver bubbles escaped the corner of my mouth as I threshed around, trying to locate the release catch.

My chest tightened as I wrenched from side to side,

twisting and turning in panic, desperate for air. A white light sliced through my head as it hit the car roof and I nearly lost consciousness. I pushed and pulled, my right arm on fire with pain, but the need to breathe was overriding everything.

In a last effort of will I forced myself to stop fighting the belt and use slow, exact movements. The car lurched again in the current, and I used the momentum to roll and release the tension on the belt. Reaching behind me, I located the catch and pressed it. The belt came free and I pulled down the door lever and kicked through the gap.

With a rush I broke the surface, gulped for air and clutched at the edge of the ramp.

Immediately something exploded against my face. Slowly, vaguely, I turned and saw the boot swing again.

Instinct made me twist away and take the kick on my shoulder. My hair was seized and a hard metallic surface struck my cheek. I flailed at the air, trying to ward off the frenzy of blows, but metal again smashed into my jaw and the debris of my teeth, lubricated by blood, filled my mouth.

I was half in and half out of the water and instinct made me drag myself on to the ramp. It was a poor choice.

I got to my knees with my head tucked down and blocked a leg that swung in a long, impossibly slow arc. My body was screaming, but it needed air more than it wanted the pain to stop. Then a savage blow to my stomach merged the two needs in one agonising instant.

Hands grabbed me and pulled me upright and I saw Gibson, white faced and crazed, lashing at my head with a steel pipe. Against my will, my broken right arm came up to ward it off, and I heard myself cry out as the pipe crushed the bone.

I was sobbing, yelling, screaming at them, but the anger was dying with each new spasm of pain. Fear was growing into a monster that consumed air and sacrificed all in the need to live.

The blows rained down, and as I tried to stand again a boot slammed into my groin and I jackknifed. The steel pipe smashed into my arm once more; they had found the weak spot and were going berserk in their attempts to down me again.

Fists, boots and the pipe struck me from all angles and I lurched left and right, confused and in agony, wanting only for it to stop.

Then Gibson swung the pipe in a wide arc, smashing into my shoulder, and I fell backwards off the ramp, into the racing water.

Chapter Thirty-Two

It was Dave Chase that found me.

Wells Lane Pump and Pump Ladder were called to a road traffic accident and on arrival saw the rear wheels of the car just above the water. A lowering line was placed around Dave's waist and he reached the car by jumping in upriver and letting the current carry him to the vehicle.

When he dived inside and saw that the driver was gone he came out and swam downstream, under the bridge, to where my unconscious body had wedged itself against a dam of river debris.

He hadn't known me. My face had swollen and the blood, filth and bruises made me unrecognisable, but the car boot, buffeted by the river, had risen enough for John to see the rear number plate.

The entrance to Oldchurch Hospital was a hundred yards from the bridge, and it was probably that which saved my life.

I remained unconscious for several hours in the intensive care unit, and when I opened the one eye that wasn't completely closed I couldn't focus. The world had become distorted. The ward lights were too bright, voices sounded far off, and faces were pale circles without form or substance.

I was aware of my right arm feeling like it was made of lead, and as I explored my mouth with my tongue it produced exquisite sensations of ragged pain.

Over the next few days they pumped drugs into me, so that sleep merged with periods of semi-sleep. People came and went, each as unknown as the next. Once someone took my hand. I assumed it was Jenny, but the one good eye refused its function and my hearing was intermittent.

I was adrift on a sea of blurred pain with only the shattered teeth providing reality.

But if reality was elusive, then the nightmares were all too vivid. They took the one simple recurring form – being chased and beaten – and they ended by my falling, a feather touching my cheek, as I lay helpless.

On the fourth morning I awoke to find I could see reasonably clearly, albeit that the left eye was a slit with a peculiar pillbox view of the world.

My first discovery was that I was alone in a side ward, with my jaw wired.

The next thing that came to my attention was my grotesquely swollen right arm, suspended to the side, away from me. Wrapped in plaster, the fingers that protruded were thick and discoloured and a drain tube hung from the plaster and disappeared over the side of the bed. When I tried to see where it led, the pain hit me everywhere.

I cried out, but managed only a distorted gargling.

In a sweat, I lay there waiting for my breathing to steady. After a while I trusted myself to turn my head slowly and look around the room.

A buzzer on a wire ran by the pillow. I pressed it and waited. Several minutes went by and I pressed it again; eventually a nurse appeared.

Through a wire-restricted mouth I managed to say, 'Drink . . . water.'

She fetched me some water and a straw and supported me as I drew the liquid into my mouth. The water hit the damaged teeth and I stiffened with the pain.

'Slowly,' she said.

I glared at her. I hadn't drunk fast, but caution made me sip the water more carefully, and I managed to down some without splashing it all over the damaged teeth.

I nodded an acknowledgment of her advice and she smiled.

'Enough?' she asked.

I nodded again.

'A doctor will be in to see you soon, Mr Jay. Use the buzzer if you need anything.'

Alone, I pondered the consequences of losing my temper with Mayle.

There was no getting away from the fact that between the suspension and the beating he'd double-shafted me. It seemed whenever I encountered him he outmanoeuvred me and left me floundering like a man with a sack over his head.

The bottom line was as harsh as it was inescapable; I hadn't a single shred of proof that he had been involved in anything. I was made for him. It was a wonder he didn't ring me up and shout *Ole!* down the phone.

Well, now I'd have to learn patience, if only because I hadn't a choice.

An hour came and went and then another and another. I fell asleep again and was eventually woken by the nurse.

'Mr Hussein will be in shortly.'

'Mirror?' I asked.

A professional face replaced the smiling one and she said it was better to wait until I'd spoken to the consultant. Ten minutes later the consultant, together with two junior doctors, appeared.

Mr Hussein had deep brown eyes and a thin, sensitive face. His voice was soft, and as he examined my injuries he impressed me with his gentleness.

'Mr Jay, you have had a very bad car accident. Your right arm has been broken in two places and we have had to use plates and screws to repair it, but the breaks were clean and should mend well.'

'Other injuries?' I asked, sounding like a failed ventriloquist.

'You were concussed when brought in and I'm afraid it may have alarmed you to find your hearing and sight were not functioning quite as normal. You had also swallowed a considerable amount of water and were resuscitated at the scene of the accident. In many respects you are lucky to be alive,' he said.

'Left eye?'

He smiled. 'It's very swollen.' He took out an ophthalmoscope. 'Keep still, please.'

He examined each eye in turn and invited the two junior doctors to do the same.

'Bad?'

'No, Mr Jay. Nothing that won't repair.'

'What else?'

'A depressed fracture of the right cheekbone, a fractured jaw and several teeth . . .' He looked at the notes. '. . . four in all, are broken; again on the right-hand side. We'll have a dental surgeon look at those for you. Also you have very extensive bruising all over your body, as well as cuts to your face and hands.'

'Back hurting,' I grunted.

He nodded. 'Yes, we think you may have sustained a torn latissimus dorsi . . . that should also heal given time.'

'How long . . . here?'

He smiled again. 'That depends on how quickly you heal. Many of the injuries are superficial, although they may cause you quite a lot a pain, but your arm and cheek will need to mend properly.'

'Guess?'

'A week, maybe two. We won't keep you any longer than we need to. Beds are precious commodities nowadays. Try not to be too impatient and don't talk unless it is absolutely necessary.'

He turned and in a low voice discussed things with

the junior doctors. When he'd finished I asked if could have a mirror.

He shrugged. 'It won't look very pleasant, Mr Jay, but you should realise that many of these cuts and bruises will disappear over the next two to three weeks.'

As soon as he left the nurse brought me a shaving mirror.

Gibson and his pals had done a thorough job. The right-hand side of my face was distorted from the broken jaw and the left-hand side enjoyed the benefits of a huge blackened and swollen eye. The windscreen glass had sliced my face in a dozen different places and the bruises ranged from nasty purple through to mottled yellow and brown.

I felt defeated. I had started the investigation hoping that something good would come out of it, but I had miscalculated on just about every level, and the proof was in the mirror.

I sank back into the pillow and closed my eyes, shutting out everything. Eventually I drifted off.

Late afternoon, I received visitors: Alex and Menzies. If I expected them to bring good news I was quickly disappointed. Menzies started with the only positive thing they had.

'A witness saw the white van drive off, although he didn't manage to get a registration number, Mr Jay.'

Alex bent over me. 'Was it an accident, Stevie?'

'No!'

'What happened?' asked Menzies.

'Run off road . . . beaten . . . three or four of them . . . nearly drowned . . .'

'Pardon?' Menzies cranked his head forward.

'Drowned!'

'Oh, drowned . . . go on.'

'Gibson . . . saw Gibson.'

Alex explained about the warehouse incident at Stratford and said that I had a photograph of Gibson.

'So you think Kris Mayle is behind it?' Menzies asked.

I nodded. He said that they would question him, but unless they could tie him to the attack there was little chance of charges being brought.

'Wasn't there . . . it was Gibson!' I snarled through the wire.

Menzies seemed unimpressed. 'We have no one who saw the crash or the beating, only the van leaving the scene.'

'I . . . saw . . . Gibson!'

Menzies wore the same expression I'd seen the night of the bombing of Michael Sheldon's car; somewhere between disbelief and disinterest. He was seriously pissing me off. It didn't help that his logic was faultless.

'Proof, Mr Jay . . . you can't drag people into a court of law without proof. At the moment you can't place Mayle at the scene, and climbing from the wreck of a car crash . . . apparently concussed . . . your evidence on Gibson would be suspect.'

'Concussion . . . because . . . Gibson,' I managed, 'not . . . crash.'

'Whatever.' He shrugged. 'The problem you've got is that you'd make an unreliable witness.'

I thought the bastard was winding me up deliberately and I shot a glance at Alex, expecting support, but he was shaking his head.

'He's right, Stevie . . . knowing is one thing, proving it another.'

Menzies made some notes and then said he had to go.

'Tomorrow I'll come down and take a proper statement from you. In the meantime I'll try to find Mayle and question him, but don't get your hopes up.'

When Menzies left, Alex pulled up a chair and took out a cheque book.

'I'm making out a cheque for two thousand four hundred.'

'Good . . . why?'

'Twelve days' pay at two hundred a day.'

Twelve days since the Ilford fire – it didn't seem possible.

'Give . . . to Jen . . . bank.'

He glanced at the floor.

'What's wrong?'

He shook his head and changed the subject. 'I hate to say it, Stevie, but you should never have beaten him up. You were getting near. A little more patience might have got the job done.'

'I'm sorry, Alex . . .'

'Aye, well . . . perhaps it was my fault too. I've spoken to John, your Sub . . . he seems to feel that you've not been yourself lately. I should have noticed that.'

'Tiredness.'

He smiled. 'Plenty of time for bed rest now, Stevie. Just lie back and take your time about getting better. Is there anything you want done?'

'Have you spoken to Jen?'

'No.'

'Not at all?'

He looked vaguely uneasy. 'I've tried ringing a few times.'

'She was here yesterday,' I said.

His face brightened. 'Oh . . . well.'

'I expected her . . . here . . . today . . . ring her for me. Tonight.'

'Aye. Aye, I'll go around to the flat.'

'Please.'

He went silent and crossed his arms.

'What?'

'Benson . . . looks like he was telling the truth after all, doesn't it?' he said wistfully.

'See . . . you got there . . . slow, but got there.'

'Not much good now, though. I'm going to re-commend to Andrew that we pull out.'

'Sorry again!'

'No, no, I wasn't having a go at you, Stevie. I'm just as much to blame. Time to cut our losses and run.'

He got up to go, but stopped and turned back. 'Let the police handle it now, Stevie . . . they'll put Mayle away . . . just concentrate on getting better.'

'Not much choice . . . have I?'

Chapter Thirty-Three

Around half-ten that evening I was woken from a half-sleep by a commotion outside the ward. I switched on a bedside lamp and wriggled painfully into a propped position. The door of the ward opened slightly and a nurse peered in. She looked annoyed.

'Mr Jay . . . are you awake, Mr Jay?' she said quietly.

I grunted a yes.

'There's a man outside with his arm in a sling who insists on seeing you. I've explained that visitors are not permitted at this time of night . . . but he's drunk and won't listen to me. One minute he says he's a policeman and the next that he's an ex-policeman!'

I smiled. There was a kind of irony in Roley showing up, but the last thing I wanted was a self-righteous drunk breathing 'I told you so' all over me. I was about to say 'Tell him I'm asleep', but then hesitated and, without quite knowing why, said that I'd see him.

She looked unhappy. 'I'm not supposed to let him in.'

'Please.'

Another nurse appeared and behind her loomed the unsteady bulk of Roley. He held up a hand as he saw me and pushed past the nurses. I asked them to leave us.

'Five minutes, Mr Jay,' said the first nurse firmly, and she gave Roley a look of warning.

Roley grinned and brought a chair up to the side of the bed. He smelled of drink and he had a slight slur, but he was in a much better condition than when I'd last seen him.

'Come to mock?'

He shrugged. 'Not exactly.'

'What, then?'

He studied me, as though just realising how badly I'd been injured. As a policeman, he must have seen dozens of cases where people had been beaten up, and the fact that he seemed genuinely shocked was instructive.

'How are you?' he asked.

'Sore . . . and intrigued. Why're you here?'

He fished a two-day-old copy of the local paper from his coat pocket and flattened it out.

'Says here that you were run off the road by a white van. Same thing happened to a drunken old copper I know and no one believed him.'

I took the creased paper from him with my left hand and read the story. It was reported as a road traffic accident with the van failing to stop. There were a couple of pictures of the bent bridge railings and the car upside down in the river. Somehow they had got hold of my name and the fact that I was a Station Officer at Wells Lane. The hook for the story was that my own men had rescued me.

There was no mention of the suspension.

As I continued to read down the page, I glanced sideways at Roley. He smiled and indicated that I should read it all. When I had finished I handed it back to him without comment. He tilted his head to one side, but I wouldn't be drawn.

'It says you're a fireman. That's how come you know McGregor.'

'Right.'

He nodded, as though working his way through a puzzle, then leaned back in the chair with his arms folded. In the muted light of the table lamp his drink-flushed face looked ghastly.

'What have you found out?' he asked.

'Nothing.'

'Must have,' he said confidently.

'Why?'

'Why else would they try to take you out?'

'Personal.'

'Oh? Tell me.'

I felt tired suddenly. 'No.'

The grin disappeared.

On impulse I said, 'Did you send me a letter with a key in it?'

He shook his head. 'Why?'

'Doesn't matter,' I said.

Irritated, he stood up. 'I've come here to help you,'

he said, 'but if you're going to play silly buggers, I'm off. I thought that seeing as we'd both been "had over" you'd want to join forces.'

'Not involved any more.'

He pushed. 'Why?'

'Take too long,' I sighed. 'Go to . . . police.'

'No point.'

'Don't they listen to drunks?' I said unkindly.

His mouth turned down at the edges and he thrust his hands deep into his pockets.

'If you're so fucking clever, how come you're lying there?'

I deserved his anger, but I wanted him to go. I wanted him to take his guilt elsewhere and leave me to mine. I reached for the buzzer, but stopped. He was a loser, but he'd done me no harm.

'Listen . . . hurts to talk . . . jaw broken . . . hear you out . . . that's all.'

'That's big of you,' he said.

'Going to tell me or what?'

He sat down again

'You're like McGregor . . . an amateur. I might be a drunk, but I was always a good copper. I'll tell you what all your running around has got you – nothing.'

'So you're a genius . . . pissed, but a genius,' I replied.

He grinned savagely. 'You've got Mayle in the frame, but can't nail him. You're suspicious of everyone because they're all a touch artificial . . . how am I doing?'

'Passable.'

He shifted in the chair and raised his eyes upward in thought.

'I'll ask you some questions,' he said. 'Don't hesitate, just tell me your gut feeling.'

'Okay.'

'Who's in the frame for Stratford?'

'Mayle . . . possibly Robin Sheldon.'

'Why?'

'Last one in building.'

He shook his head. 'That you know of. Who's in the frame for Ilford?'

'Mayle.'

'Why?'

'Don't know.'

He shook his head. 'Must have a reason, if only a wrong one.'

I was trapped now. If I really was out of the investigation, what did it matter what I told him; but I was reluctant to give him it all.

'Rumours,' I said.

'Well, I've got better than rumours,' he said quietly.

'Oh?'

He reached into his inside pocket and took out an envelope. From it he took a handful of photographs. He selected one and handed it to me.

'I took these the night of the Ilford fire,' he said. 'I'd been following Mayle for weeks.'

When I looked at it I nearly jumped out of bed. It

was a picture of Mayle entering the front entrance of the Ilford shop. The quality was good, which I took to be down to the camera rather than Roley's prowess.

He selected another and passed it over. This time it was of Mayle coming out of the entrance. Two more shots showed him looking left and right as he crossed Ilford High Road.

'When taken?'

'Between ten and eleven.'

I closed my eyes. 'When? . . . just after ten? . . . a while after? . . . nearer eleven? When, Roley?'

He sniffed. 'Can't say for sure . . .'

'Why?'

He looked unfazed. 'I'd had a drink.'

'Fuck you!'

'Fuck me?'

I took a deep breath and let it out slowly. 'They're no good . . . must prove Mayle there after Stephanie arrived.'

His face grew crafty and he handed me another photograph. 'This person will know when.'

I took it from him.

The photograph was perhaps the best of all. According to Roley, it was taken from a shop doorway with a telephoto lens. It showed Mayle climbing into his Lexus. In the passenger seat, face caught perfectly by the camera, sat Jenny

I spent the night going quietly mad.

Around five in the morning I reached the seventh

level of stupidity and decided that if all I had was a broken arm and a busted jaw, then I should be able to grit my teeth and walk out of the hospital.

The nurse found me half an hour later, slumped on the floor with my arm still suspended above me.

She summoned help, and I was put back in bed while a doctor was called.

That was my first escape attempt. There were several others during the morning, until a thoroughly pissed-off sister turned up and told me where I was going wrong in life.

'If you're really determined to leave, Mr Jay, then I can't stop you,' she said coldly, 'but you're in no condition to leave here on your own. Is there someone we can ring?'

'No one.'

She frowned. 'No one?'

'No one. Please call me a taxi.'

She was more compassionate than I deserved, and she sent the other nurses out and sat down on the edge of my bed.

'I don't know what's going through your head, Mr Jay . . .'

'Steve . . .'

'Steve . . . you're not well enough to cope on your own and the chances are that if you go home you'll have an accident and be back here in a worse condition within a matter of hours.'

'I'll stay in bed,' I said sagely.

She sighed and took her glasses off.

'What's wrong, Mr Jay? Is it a domestic problem?'

'Was.'

'Oh.'

'Oh doesn't cover it. Please call me a taxi,' I repeated.

Mr Hussein showed up a short while later and I went through a similar routine with him. Finally, having convinced them that I was determined to go, a taxi was called and I was helped into tracksuit borrowed from one of the porters.

Mr Hussein made sure I was given enough pain-killers for a few days and wrote me a prescription for more. They also found an elbow crutch for me. Stroppy and deaf to reason, I didn't deserve their kindness.

Just as I was set to leave, the sister came back, looking happier.

'Some friends of yours have arrived.' She smiled.

Her unspoken words were 'thank Christ there's someone to steer the idiot home safely', but what suited them didn't suit me. I didn't want anyone to see me in the state I was in. I didn't want questions or advice.

So when she showed in Dave Chase and Harry Wildsmith I breathed more easily; with them I could be as blunt as they would be with me.

'You look awful, guv.'

'Thanks, Dave.'

'I mean it. You need hospital care.'

'He's right, guv,' added Harry. 'It's barely four days since we fished you out of the Rom.'

'I'm going to the flat . . . you can either help me or not.'

There followed a few minutes of sterile debate, but when they saw I wasn't about to change my mind they said that they would drive me home. The sister and one of the nurses tried one more time to dissuade me, and then stood at the end of the corridor watching as Dave and Harry helped me past a series of startled personalities hanging around the hospital entrance. All I needed to complete my embarrassment was a cap and bells.

In the carpark I threw up, and only determined argument stopped them taking me straight back. It didn't help that in my determination to flee the hospital it had slipped my mind that I didn't have any keys.

'I've a spare at work . . . can I ask one of you to get it for me?'

'I will, guv,' said Dave.

They helped me into Harry's car, and then Dave went to retrieve my keys. Harry drove me back slowly; he had to stop at one point for me to throw up again.

'I'm sorry, Harry.'

'It's not a problem, guv, but I do wish you'd reconsider.'

I shook my head.

'What does Jenny say about all this?'

'If I knew where she was, Harry, I'd ask her.'

'Sorry.'

We parked at the back of the Ford and Firkin and waited for Dave to show up with the keys. While we were sitting there Harry filled me in on the details of Dave's rescue of me. He said that so much water came out when they tried resuscitation that they thought I was going to croak.

'What really happened to you, guv? It looked more than an RTA to us.'

'Long story, Harry. Will you do me a favour?'

'Of course.'

'Contact Chris Adamou for me. I'm going to need an accused's friend.'

When Dave arrived back with the keys, they hauled me upstairs. At one point I thought I would pass out, but being so near I fought it off. I told them to leave me at the front door. Dave asked where Jenny was, but I ignored the question and Harry gave him a look.

'Let's just help you in, guv?' pressed Dave.

'No . . . please!'

Reluctantly they left me, but said they would phone.

When they were gone, I opened the door and listened. The flat was quiet and smelled vaguely stale. Sweating fiercely, I struggled as fast as I could, up the hallway, past the lounge and into the bedroom.

As I pushed open the door, I saw my grip bag on the bed with the file notes scattered beside it. With a final effort I pulled open the wardrobe door and then collapsed in a heap on the floor. Jenny's clothes were gone.

Chapter Thirty-Four

I dragged myself into bed and stayed there until late into the following day.

When I eventually struggled up, I found moving around was intensely painful and tiring, so I located myself in front of the television with my mobile phone on my lap.

The practicalities of my decision to leave the hospital demanded some attention. There was little in the flat by way of food, so I ordered groceries by phone and then sorted the mail. Two letters referred to the imminent removal of my overdraft facility.

I rang the bank manager and said I was about to deposit a cheque for over two thousand pounds within the next few days. He was sceptical, but gave me till the coming Monday to make good.

Alex rang as soon as he heard that I had discharged myself. I told him Jenny was gone and that I needed to be on my own to get my head straight. He understood, but said he would send Paddy Ryan around.

'You're going to need some help.'

I agreed.

'Is there anything you want, Stevie?'

'Apart from a job, my health and future . . . not a thing.'

'You know where I am if you need me, Stevie. I'll ring every day.'

'Do that, Alex.'

What I didn't say was that I was back on the case.

I wanted the truth, every last bit of it, otherwise I wouldn't have any peace. The photograph had seen to that, and if I had no choice but to rest then I would use it to revise and plan; turn a vice into a virtue.

I spent the remainder of the afternoon going through the Sheldon files and thinking through everything I'd learned.

Paddy arrived around seven in the evening and shook his head when he saw me.

'You caught up with Lenny Gibson, then?'

'Caught up with me.' I grunted.

He inspected my face carefully. 'Was it the crash that broke your jaw or a left hook?'

'Short length . . . scaffold pole.'

'Ah . . . On his own, was he?'

'Just a few close friends . . .'

He gave a tight smile. 'He always liked winning, did Lenny.'

'Not over yet, Paddy . . . not yet.'

His eyes shone with amusement. 'If it's a party you're planning you'd best take a friend, especially if it's going to be as lively as the last one.'

'Maybe.'

'Well, you'd be the best man to judge, eh? Now, let's take a look at those bruises,' he said.

He moved each limb gently and rhythmically; to pump out the blood and the toxins, he said, that had settled in the muscles from the beating. Despite myself I cried out.

He stopped immediately. 'You should have stayed in hospital, Steve.'

I shook my head.

'Alex said you were bloody-minded.'

'Necessary,' I replied.

He opened a small bag he'd brought and painted the bruises with tincture of arnica. Then gave me some sachets of a herbal tea that tasted like mud and smelled of lavender. The homoeopathic brew was to be taken four times a day.

'As long as you're determined to go it alone, Steve, you're going to have to be disciplined. It'll be days yet before you can walk properly. Learn some patience.'

'Thanks for . . . help, Paddy . . . I'm listening.'

When he'd finished he put me back to bed and told me to stay there.

'Sleep's the big healer, Steve . . . let it do its work. I'll be back tomorrow.'

Friday, 1 May

I slept well and was woken just before nine by the mobile phone ringing. It was George Harris.

'Guv . . . 'ow are yer?'

'Not good, George, but mending . . . you've heard I'm suspended?'

'All round the Brigade, guv, speculation is rife. I 'eard one disturbing rumour, though.'

'Go on.'

'That your suspension was connected with you passing on confidential information.'

'Where are you, George?'

'A phone box just outside the station. Tell me, am I in trouble too?'

'No, not as far as I know. Complaint was personal . . . haven't told a soul about you.'

'Will you lose your job, guv?'

'Doesn't look good, George.'

'Are you sure I'm in the clear?' He sounded anxious, as I would have done in his position.

'Pretty certain, yes.'

'In that case I have some information for you. Nothin' to do with the Fire Brigade as such . . . it comes from the copper I know.'

'Met's Fire Investigation Unit?'

'That's the one. It's about the fire bomb in the Mercedes,' he said.

'Oh?'

'D'you remember me saying that our "torch" might have been a bit too clever this time? Well, that method of booby-trapping a car has been used before. My contact tells me that a similar car bomb were used in a turf war between two families of villains a few years back.'

'Go on.'

'The name I was given was Ronnie Gibson . . . he was described to be a small thin geezer with a nasty attitude. He's got a brother with a serious cocaine habit and form for violence. Guv, guv . . . Did you 'ear me?'

I closed my eyes and smiled. 'Loud and clear, George. How good is this "torch"?'

'I was told that he's the best, but no one's ever been able to pin 'im down . . . lots of shadows, no substance.'

'Could have done Stratford, then?'

'Yeah. Why? What's the connection, guv?'

'That's what I intend to find out.'

'Listen, guv . . . I don't 'onestly think I can 'elp yer any more. It's risky.'

'No problem. Done more than enough, George . . . thanks.'

George's information was the first solid evidence that had come my way. It linked the attack on Michael to Stratford and by implication to the warehouse fire. It was the boost I needed.

When Menzies and Coleman turned up around twelve I gave a full statement about the car crash and beating. Menzies listened as Coleman wrote it down and then got me to sign it. That should have been the cue for their exit, but Menzies just couldn't resist needling me.

'I was speaking to your boss this morning,' he said.

'Boss?'

'Maurice Charnley. He tells me you've been suspended.'

'Does that involve you?'

'Probably not, but you do seem to attract trouble. My boss, Mr Graham, seems to feel that you've interfered in our murder investigation. Still, I don't suppose that it'll happen again. I told him I thought you'd learned your lesson.'

'There's a door at the end of the passage . . . use it,' I said.

I followed them out and slammed the door shut behind them. Two minutes later there was another knock. I thought it was them returning. I lurched back to the front door and pulled it open.

It was Paddy and Tommy Grant.

The effort of getting up twice in a short while made me dizzy, and they caught hold of me as I swayed like a drunk on the dance-floor. They grabbed an arm each and took me back into the living room.

'Have you got trouble with those guys who just left?' asked Tommy.

I nodded. 'Yes, but they're police.'

'Can we help?' asked Paddy.

'No.'

'I've been telling Tommy that you ran into Lenny Gibson,' said Paddy.

'He ran into me . . . with a van.'

They sat down and I gave them an abridged version of what had happened, leaving out any reference to the Sheldons or Mayle. I said it was personal.

'How many of them were there?' asked Tommy.

'Not sure . . . three, maybe four . . . and they were tooled up.'

Paddy frowned. 'You're lucky to be alive, boy.'

'Is it over?' asked Tommy.

'No.'

He shook his head and whistled low. 'If things get rough . . . I mean rougher . . . call me. I'll bring a couple of the guys from the gym to even up the odds.'

'I'll do that.'

After Paddy had treated me they stayed and talked for a bit, Tommy letting it slip that Alex had suggested he keep an eye on me.

'He's worried about you, man, and it's easy to see why.'

Tommy gave me his mobile number and I promised to ring it in an emergency. I was grateful and slightly embarrassed. I'd never been so vulnerable and my instincts were to depend on no one, but there was little choice.

Over the next few days Paddy came and went, and so did Alex. So much for letting me have some space. I received at least a dozen phone calls, from various members of the watch, wanting to come around, but I pleaded rest and thanked them for their concern.

So when the phone rang Monday night I expected it to be one of them. I was as wrong as you can get.

'Jay?'

I froze in the chair. It was Kris Mayle.

'What do you want?'

'I've just spent several hours being grilled by a bastard named Menzies . . . it's time we dealt with this . . .'

'How?'

'Face to face . . . here, at my place. You know the way.'

'Just like that?'

'You're safe . . . bring a friend if you need to.'

'Thanks . . . I will.'

I rang Tommy Grant and he came straight over. Then I rang Alex and left a message on his answerphone. Lastly I dug a cold chisel out of my toolbox and slipped it into my pocket. It was tempting to let the paranoia surf, but I reined it back in by telling myself that not even Mayle would be so stupid as to set up a meeting and then have me done.

Paddy's physiotherapy had got me walking, and whatever was in the herbal teas had taken away a lot of the stiffness. Nevertheless I was in no condition to do anything but sit and talk. The cold chisel was more for confidence than anything else.

Tommy brought with him one of the boxers I'd seen sparring at the gym; a sawn-off brute of a man called Danny Carpenter. If there was to be trouble I couldn't have been in better company.

As we drove over to Mayle's place Tommy suggested that he go inside with me and check out that I wasn't walking into something nasty. Danny Carpenter would stay outside and watch the street.

Just as we reached Mayle's house I caught a

glimpse of something metallic inside Danny Carpenter's coat.

'No one's going to use anything, Steve. It's just insurance,' said Tommy.

'Are you carrying as well?' I said in disbelief.

Tommy shook his head. 'Alex told me some of the background, Steve. Danny won't use it unless things get very serious.'

I shook my head in wonder.

'One look at you and I feel safer for carrying this,' said Danny. 'Tom's right. I won't use it unless it's desperate.'

Less than relieved, I climbed from the car and, with Tommy, made my way slowly towards Mayle's house.

Chapter Thirty-Five

Tommy stood in front of me as Mayle answered the door. I stayed on the pavement with Danny as Tommy searched the house and then came out to give me the all-clear.

'Satisfied?' asked Mayle.

'Tommy stays outside the room we talk in,' I said.

His eyes went past Tommy to Danny, who was sitting in the car.

'And him?'

I nodded. 'Stays where he is.'

Mayle led the way as we went through to an open-plan lounge. Tommy positioned himself directly outside, but before he went he loomed over Mayle.

'If this isn't on the level I'll see to it that you don't smile for a long time. D'you hear me, man?'

Mayle tried to keep his cool, but Tommy was a big, fit man and intimidating without trying. Mayle gave a slow nod.

Tommy's last act before leaving the room was to help me sit down. Mayle's eyes were on me, assessing the damage. Although I was moving more easily, my face and arm gave clear testimony to the severity of the beating.

'You look like you've been through a bit,' he said as he sat down opposite.

'Must be gratifying to see your handiwork,' I replied evenly.

His face set. 'I'll tell you what I told Menzies . . . that was nothing to do with me.'

'Bollocks!'

He hunched forward and brought his hands together. 'I mean it.'

'You'll have to work hard to make me believe that.'

He looked pale. 'You think that tough-guy act you pulled the other night was the trigger?' He shook his head. 'You overrate yourself.'

Had I not known what he was like, I'd have believed him there and then. His tone was so dismissive it set doubt in my mind.

'You're denying it?'

'Totally. Look, I know why you took it out on me, but it wasn't all my idea . . . Jenny wanted me as much as I wanted her.'

'Don't push your luck,' I said angrily.

'Pride. That's why you steamed into me. Admit it.'

My voice was a whisper. 'I think you'll find it was something more important than that. One of my firemen has been murdered.'

He leaned back and shook his head. 'You think I'm someway connected to the fires the Sheldons have been having. Well, I'm not guilty of that either.'

'Not Stratford?'

He hesitated and looked down. 'Not in the way you think.'

'Not Ilford?'

'Not Ilford . . . and especially not the Heath-way.'

I threw him some bait. 'Where were you on the night of the Ilford fire?'

'Why?'

'Why d'you think?'

His eyes hardened, but he didn't answer.

'It's a straightforward enough question . . . where were you?' I pushed.

He swallowed. 'Here.'

'All night?'

'Yes.'

I shook my head. 'You're a liar.'

He studied me, unsure. 'All right, I was at Ilford, but I left before the fire.'

'How long before the fire?'

'I'm not sure exactly. Talk to Stephanie Sheldon.'

'I have.'

'And?'

'She says you're the man.'

The effect of my words seemed to mould his face slowly into astonishment, and the self-assurance went quickly from his voice.

'She's lying!'

'What, your fiancée? Hardly romantic, is it?'

'I left before her!'

'Now that I do believe. She also says that you were

the last person inside the warehouse before the Stratford fire.'

A thin film of sweat glazed his forehead. 'How did you ever get involved in all this?'

'I'm doing a favour for an old friend,' I replied.

'McGregor?'

'That's him.'

'Well, you two might think it funny to try to stitch me up for this, but it won't work.'

I shifted my weight. Sitting still for any length of time hurt my back where the muscle had torn. It was a niggling pain that had denied me proper sleep since I left the hospital.

'So tell me, then. I'm listening, because there's little else I can do after your man Lenny Gibson finished with me.'

'Gibson's not my man. He's paid by Michael Sheldon.'

'Tell me about Ronnie Gibson,' I said quietly.

He looked wary. 'So you do know something about what happened.'

'You tell me.'

'If I do, it doesn't go outside these walls.'

'What?'

'I mean it. If I tell you what I know, even if it implicates me, you don't repeat it.'

I shook my head. 'Two people have been killed and one maimed. Punishment is coming your way; it's just a question of how hard and when.'

Keeping my tone neutral was hard. I had spent

days thinking about Sandy and Wayne and several times, late at night, I had burst into tears. I told myself that it was genuine grief and guilt, but deep down I knew that the stress had finally caught up with me.

'Hear me out before you condemn me.' Mayle's voice was reedy and he coughed to clear it. 'I'm no murderer.'

Again, his body language and expression rang true.

'I want you to say it, Jay.'

'What?'

'Say that it doesn't go outside this room.'

'Can't do that. I have proof . . . photographs . . . that place you at Ilford just before the fire was detected.'

'Photographs?'

'Of you and Jenny . . . and Stephanie Sheldon's testimony that you were at Ilford . . . arguing with her father.'

Fear drained his face and his hands came up to his mouth. I won't deny that I enjoyed seeing him spin in the wind.

'I swear to you I didn't kill Robin Sheldon!'

'What do I care?'

He looked incredulous. 'You don't mean that!'

'Don't I?'

'Just because I screwed Jenny you'd let me go down for murder?'

I nodded. 'That and the murder of my Leading

Fireman. There's also the malicious complaint to the Brigade that looks like costing me my job. It's a case of reaping what you've sown, Mayle.'

With the full weight of the accusation before him, he just sat with his head in his hands. Then suddenly he looked up, puzzled.

'I never made a malicious complaint to anyone.'

'You did, directly after I hit you,' I said softly.

'But I didn't do it! You have to hear me out.'

I kept my voice cold. 'As far as I know the police aren't aware of either the photographs or Stephanie Sheldon's testimony. If what you say convinces me I'll hold off for a while . . . till you can get a solicitor. I'll trade you that for the truth . . . that's all.'

'You have reason to hate me, but you have to believe me when I say that I'm not guilty.'

'Of what precisely?'

'Of any of it!'

'You'd better tell me what you know, then.'

The sly look and the sloping body language that always seemed part of him were missing, but I reminded myself that this man had mugged me off before.

'What exactly do you want?' he said finally.

'Everything . . . and if you give me a load of crap it'll swing straight back at you.' I glanced towards the door. 'You get one try at this, Mayle, so it had better be good.'

He got to his feet. 'I need a drink . . . d'you want one?'

'No.'

He went over to a drinks cabinet and poured himself a large brandy. He downed half of it and refilled the glass. When he sat down again his face was flushed.

'Where do you want me to start?'

'At the beginning . . . the Sheldons.'

He leaned forward, cupping the brandy glass between his hands.

'I first met Robin Sheldon through a man called Jimmy Chasteau. When the Sheldons ran into trouble with their business, Robin and Michael came to see me. They wanted to reduce the number of shops they had and sell their stuff through franchising. For that they needed warehouse space and I had what they wanted.'

'You met Robin Sheldon first, not Michael?'

'Yes.'

'Go on.'

'They couldn't afford the price I wanted . . . or so they said. Then Michael came to me with the idea of accepting two of their shops in place of payment. I didn't want that. The market was depressed and shops cost money to run. I delayed, hoping that they'd somehow raise the money. Eventually Michael came back to me with a revised offer.'

'What was that?'

'That if I took the two shops they would drop the valuation. Reluctantly I accepted . . . as a long-term option. I figured that when the property market reinflated I'd make a profit.'

'You're sure about that . . . they forced the shops on to you?'

'More or less. I won't deny that I could see they were vulnerable, and like any other businessman I sat still and let them think about it.'

'What happened then?'

'They ran into bigger problems. They lost the franchise on two department store chains. They were sinking fast. That's when Michael approached me again.'

'What for?'

'The Sheldons had a sale-or-return option on the franchised goods . . . that was the only way they could get the big contracts.'

'Sorry, you'll have to explain that to me.'

'Basically it meant that if the shops did not sell their goods within a given time they could hand them back at no cost.'

'So?'

'So when the two department store chains closed the contracts, the Sheldons got back an incredible amount of goods . . . they were financially ruined.'

'Ruined?'

'The clothes were worthless . . . it was well into the winter season and they were up to their necks in winter goods and no way to sell them. I believe they had raised money to fund their winter lines, banking on moving them. As I said, they were ruined.'

I was slow getting there. 'But the clothes still had an insurance value?'

He gave a slow nod. 'Yes. That was why Michael approached me with the insurance scam.'

'You're saying that Michael wanted you to help torch the warehouse?'

'Yes. Oh, he was subtle. He didn't spell it out, but there was no mistaking his meaning.'

'What did you say?'

'I said no. They were the ones in trouble, not me.'

'So?'

'So when I refused they set me up.'

'How?'

'By having Stephanie get me to re-enter the warehouse on the Friday night. I was the last one on the premises and naturally a prime candidate for suspicion. Plus the fact that Michael made it clear that they would point the finger at me.'

'But you got off the hook when the fire went down as accidental?'

'Yes. They were clever enough to go for two options, one an accident and two with me as the villain. Either way they were in the clear.'

'You're saying that you weren't involved in any way with Stratford?'

He hesitated. 'I . . . made a mistake . . . afterwards.'

'Mistake?'

He swirled the remainder of the brandy in the glass and downed it.

'I let them buy my silence . . . with a chunk of the insurance money. That, I swear, was my only involvement. I still have the money untouched. I'm prepared to return it with certain guarantees.'

'Such as?'

'No prosecution.'

'You mention Michael all the time . . . not Robin Sheldon?'

'Robin Sheldon wasn't involved in the fire . . . it was Michael. Robin was behind selling the shops to me. He was a sharp businessman, was Robin. No, it was Michael behind the fire, I'm convinced.'

'With a little help from Stephanie?'

He sighed. 'I wasn't sure till tonight. If she said I was at Ilford when the fire started then she's involved as well. She'll do anything Michael tells her to do.'

I believed him. When I pushed my hate and anger to one side and reviewed what he said, it all slotted into place, but why had I been ambushed? Who had made the complaint to the Brigade? Michael? Why?

'The warehouse . . . why is a part of it sectioned off with a padlocked shutter?'

He gave a thin smile, knowing I was accepting the possibility that he wasn't guilty.

'I don't know.'

'It's your warehouse . . .'

'Not since the fire. They bought it off me. Cheap. I wanted to sever my dealings with them and when they made the offer I jumped at it.'

'They used the insurance money? That was how they covered the pay-off to you?'

'You're getting there, Jay.'

'So what's your guess about the shutter?'

He peered down into the empty brandy glass. 'Fire-damaged stock.'

'Explain.'

'The remains of the warehouse fire. I think Michael planned to have other fires and fill the premises with ruined stock.'

'To collect twice on the insurance money?'

'Yes.'

'Proof?'

He shook his head. 'I don't have any . . . makes sense, though, doesn't it?'

I thought back to the night after the car bomb when I'd pressed Michael about the shutter. That's why I was ambushed. Between the visit to the warehouse and the questions I'd got too close and he'd taken me out the game.

I'd been bone stupid. I'd let my emotions rule my head and missed it completely.

Chapter Thirty-Six

I'd wanted so much for Mayle to be guilty, to see him suffer, that I'd hobbled myself before the chase had even begun. My rank stupidity had seen me nearly killed and my job in jeopardy. If the first rule of holes is 'When you're in one, stop digging', then the second rule must surely be 'Climb out and look around'.

Mayle was watching me, and it must have been apparent that I'd finally woken up. Our eyes met and I knew I had to begin again.

'Okay, tell me exactly what happened the night of the Ilford fire,' I said.

He held his glass towards me. 'Sure you don't want a drink now?'

'Certain.'

He refilled his glass, then walked around the room. He halted in front of the window and spoke at the glass.

'I got a phone call . . . about nine. It was Stephanie. Robin was threatening to go to the police. She said she didn't know what it was about, but he had indicated that I was in trouble.' He turned and looked over his shoulder at me. 'You're not going to like the next part . . .'

'Go on.'

'Jenny had rung earlier and had asked to come over . . . you were on night shift.'

I could feel the anger rising, but kept my face impassive. If I wanted the truth I had to have the courage to hear it.

'We talked and shared a bottle of wine . . . when Stephanie rang I was well over the limit and I asked Jenny to drive me.'

'What happened at Ilford?'

'Stephanie was already there with Robin. He was furious. Someone had told him that an ex-policeman had been snooping around asking all sorts of questions about Stratford. He was terrified that the insurance money would be reclaimed. I told him that it was nothing to do with me, but he didn't believe me.'

'Robin Sheldon thought that you'd spoken to this ex-copper?'

'Yes.'

'And had you?'

'Yes.'

He stared into the brandy glass. At one point I thought he was deliberately keeping his back towards me, but there was an authenticity to his words.

'What did you tell this ex-copper?' I asked.

'What I told you . . . but not the part about being bought off with the insurance money.'

'Did you tell Robin Sheldon this?'

'Of course not! I said the man had questioned me

and that I'd said I knew nothing other than that the fire was electrical.'

I suddenly felt giddy and asked Mayle if I could have some water. He left the room. Tommy came in, looking concerned.

'You all right, Steve?'

'I feel a bit sick . . . probably the travelling. I'll be okay in a minute.'

Mayle came back in with a glass of water and I sipped it slowly. After a minute or so my head cleared and I asked Tommy to leave us again. Mayle sat down and I forced myself to concentrate and ask questions again.

'Do you think that Robin Sheldon was in any way responsible for Stratford?'

He took his time answering. 'I honestly don't know. I did, but when he was killed . . .'

'Why would Michael kill his father?'

'I'm not sure, but there was never any love lost between them. Hate wouldn't be putting it too strong.' He took a sip of brandy. 'There was a lot of trouble between them over money.'

'And Stephanie? Why would she have helped Michael.'

He shrugged, then said, 'She's strange . . . there were times when I didn't have a clue what was behind those eyes. When she was younger she started a series of fires . . . a protest about something involving Robin, I believe.'

'What do you know about Ruth Heller?'

'Who?'

'Ruth Heller.'

He frowned. 'Never heard of her.'

'You're sure?'

'Certain. Should I know her?'

'Never heard her name . . . a passing reference?'

'No.'

My next question was direct, and I wasn't sure that I even wanted the answer.

'On that Thursday night, did you and Jenny make love?'

'What?'

I thought for a moment he was going to smile.

'You heard . . . did you screw Jenny?'

He shook his head. 'No.'

'Have you been in contact with her all the time?'

'Sort of.'

'Meaning?'

He studied me, delaying his answer. I'd always felt that he held me in contempt, but there was none of it in his face, just baffled amusement.

'She asked me for a job . . . she said I owed her . . . actually she said I owed the pair of you. Shortly after she said she no longer needed the job.'

'How did you manage to juggle Jenny and Stephanie at the same time?'

'Jenny was never possessive.'

'Come again?'

'She knew all about Stephanie . . . it didn't bother her.'

'What was the strength of you and Stephanie?'

He laughed. 'According to her we were engaged.'

'And you weren't?'

'She attached herself to me. Michael introduced us and within a few weeks she was referring to me as her fiancé . . . it's pretty obvious now that I was being set up.'

'Why did Jenny leave you?'

He looked down at the floor, studying his feet. I'd hit a nerve.

'Because of you.'

'You'll have to take me through that one slowly.'

His hands came up. 'Oh no! That's for you and her to sort out.'

'Where's Jenny now?'

'She's sitting in my car, just around the corner . . . waiting for you,' he said softly.

Tommy walked with me to the end of the mews. The Lexus was parked about fifty yards from the corner. I told Tommy to wait with Danny.

As I limped towards the car, Jenny got out. I'm not sure how pathetic I looked, but her hand came up to her mouth. She started towards me, but I shook my head and she stopped.

The anger I'd felt when I saw the photographs dissolved on first sight of her. I was right back to where I was nine months ago; my want of her fighting my need to protect myself.

She opened the passenger side for me and then

went around and sat behind the wheel. At first I didn't say anything. I wanted to give her a chance, but true to form I was made to ask, made to feel it was me who had to make the effort to understand her rather than she explain her actions.

'Tell me I'm not going mad, Jen,' I began. 'You left me. I didn't like it, but I'd finally started dealing with it. Then you show up without explaining anything . . .'

'I . . .'

'Not why you'd come back or even if you were staying. You tell me you love me and that you want a fresh start, draw a line under everything. Then, just when I really did need you . . . when I nearly died . . . you disappear again and turn up at his place.'

She looked away from me. When she turned back there were tears running down her cheeks.

'I wanted us to work, Steve. I thought we agreed to let the past be the past, but you were never going to let that happen. You were never going to trust me . . . not deep down. Oh, you say that you wanted me back, but in your heart what you really wanted was me to say sorry . . . admit I was wrong to leave you.'

'That's not true . . .' My words fell away. There was truth in what she said. Not the whole truth, but enough to make me pause.

'When I discovered the files I couldn't believe what you were doing . . . just revenge . . . sterile, pointless revenge, Steve.' Her hands were clenched, white.

'You'd won! I was back. I . . . loved you. Wasn't that enough?'

'I'm human.'

She turned back to face me and started to talk, but instead her hand came up and touched my face gently. Over the past few days the bruises had lost tone but spread, making me look even worse. The wired jaw and distorted cheek finished off the effect.

She shook her head. When she spoke her voice was barely above a whisper.

'All the while you were telling me that you could let go of the past, Steve, and instead you were aiming to get Kris.'

'And what about you? While I was on night work you were meeting him!'

She sighed. 'Yes! Yes! Yes! To tell him that I'd made my decision. That he and I were over for good . . . that whether you accepted me back or not I wouldn't be going back to him.'

'So why didn't you tell me . . . why did I have to find out from somebody else?'

She took my hand and squeezed it. 'Because I was afraid . . . and wasn't I right to be afraid? Why couldn't you let the past go?'

I closed my eyes. 'Why do you need to see him? And you do, Jen . . . you give reasons for it, but you're drawn back to him on the slightest pretext . . . to say goodbye, to ask for a job . . . and then to say you don't want the job. Who's being honest with themselves now?'

She swallowed and nodded. 'Yes . . . that's true. Sometimes I'm weak too!'

'And I'm expected to stand by while you weaken, is that it?'

'No! You know me so well, but do you know yourself? When I look at you I see that same little boy deserted by his parents, desperate to own. You can't own people, Steve . . . they either want to be with you or they don't.'

'Ah, I was wondering when we'd get around to it all being my fault. You were the one that left . . . not me.'

'And I was wrong! There, I've said it. I had a fling with Kris and it was my fault, not yours . . . but I came back, because I love you.'

I had no more words. I knew that she meant what she said. The equation was simple; if I loved her I would forgive her, allow for her weaknesses.

I opened the door and edged my way out.

She started to follow me out of the car, but I shook my head. She mouthed 'please' through the windscreen, but I turned and limped painfully back to the mews.

Chapter Thirty-Seven

I had wanted Mayle to be guilty.

Even now I wanted it to be him, but so much of what he'd said made sense that I was forced to admit it had confirmed lingering doubts about Michael Sheldon.

Sheldon had said that the Gibsons were Mayle's men, yet I'd seen him being driven to court by Lenny Gibson, and on the night of the car bomb there was no way he could have recognised me from Stratford across that darkened street. That begged the question, if the Gibsons were in Sheldon's pay, then who was behind the car bomb?

The answer, when it came to me, was so simple I got angry with myself.

He had the bomb planted.

He'd arranged for Ronnie Gibson to fake an attack on his life, so that he could push the suspicion straight in Mayle's direction, but Gibson had used too much petrol and Sheldon had nearly been incinerated.

Then there was Stephanie.

If Mayle hadn't killed Robin Sheldon, then she was

in it with Michael. Mayle had gone to Stratford Court unaware that he was being set up for all of it, and wasn't it the king of ironies that I'd saved Michael Sheldon's life only to have him try to take mine when I got too near the truth.

Proving all of this was going to be difficult. Why would a court accept Mayle's version over Michael and Stephanie's? And Mayle was never going to stand up in a court of law and give evidence without assurances. He was too vulnerable for that.

My own evidence was important. I could place Stephanie at Ilford during the fire, but it looked certain that in court she would tell the same story that she told me, and no doubt claim that it was fear of Mayle that made her withhold her story. My evidence, that she was at the flat at the time of the fire, and of her escape route, would only corroborate her version of events.

Around seven o'clock I ran out of ideas and patience.

I decided that I needed a breath of fresh air. I wasn't sure that I was up to going for a walk, but the flat was closing in on me, and even if I only hobbled to the end of the road it would be something.

I fixed myself some strong coffee with honey, hoping that the caffeine and sugar would boost my energy levels for the walk. As I sipped the coffee, I settled down to watch the tail-end of the news.

There was little to hold my interest, and I was about to switch off when the local news came on.

The first item immediately caught my attention. It was a piece on the joyrider who had died the night of the Ilford fire. The presenter related the details of the incident and said that the police had released a computerised image of what the person may have looked like.

A grid-lined head shape appeared on the screen and turned slowly through a hundred and eighty degrees. I sat very still, totally focused as the computer rebuilt the face, layer upon layer, retexturing the skull, muscle and skin, until the process of incineration had been reversed and the face of the dead woman was complete.

A number appeared on the screen and the presenter asked anyone with information on the woman's identity to phone the confidential line.

I abandoned the idea of a walk.

For the next hour I channel-hopped, trying unsuccessfully to get more information. When finally eight o'clock came, I switched on the video and waited.

The joyrider incident had been pushed down the list, but they showed the same clip of the computerised head. I played it back a dozen times and freeze-framed it.

Stress had warped my perceptions and my judgment to the extent that I no longer completely trusted myself, but the more I saw the forensic reconstruction the more sure I became that I was watching the face of the model in the photograph. The one I had taken from Melrose Court.

Ten minutes later I got a text message on my mobile.

'Must see you urgently – at the penthouse – Suzanne Munroe.'

The journey to the penthouse took barely forty minutes, as the cabby pulled every stunt in his repertoire to earn a twenty-quid bonus for getting me there in under three-quarters of an hour.

When we reached the building I paid him and told him to wait. I made my way up to the top floor, expecting Suzanne to be waiting, but when the lift doors opened there was no one there. The heavy glass door to the spiral iron staircase was open.

I climbed the staircase, stopping halfway up to wipe the sweat from my eyes and lean on my elbow crutch. I felt a wreck; my back ached from the journey and my legs threatened to buckle.

Like the glass security door, the penthouse door was pulled to, but not locked. I was about to call out, but checked myself. Slowly, I pushed the door open.

Inside, the dimly lit lounge was empty, and a strong draught was making the heavy drapes buckle and sway. The shoji door was slid half open; the air current seemed to be coming from there.

An armchair and a coffee table had been knocked over and an ornate table lamp lay smashed alongside the telephone. There was a dark smear on one of the lamp fragments.

Suddenly, the front door slammed shut behind me and I froze, every nerve on edge.

Nothing. Reluctantly, I accepted that the draught was responsible, but became increasingly uneasy as I started to absorb the details of the room. There were two wineglasses on the floor, not far from the up-turned armchair, and the contents of an ashtray were spread across the carpet.

I knelt to examine the area around the upturned furniture, touching nothing. I was about to back·off and ring the police when I heard a sound. It was a faint, muffled sound that seemed to be coming from beyond the shoji door. I listened, but the draught was snatching it away.

I pulled myself up on the elbow crutch and went over to the shoji door.

On the other side was a long, narrow room, and directly opposite were patio doors that led out on to a roof terrace. The patio doors were open, and wind was driving the rain into the building.

I walked out on to the terrace and looked around.

Fifteen floors up, the wind was stronger than at ground level, and I could feel it push me off balance. I was about to go back inside when I heard the sound again.

The penthouse had a second level set back from the terrace. The windows were dark, but the sound seemed to be coming from up there. I went back to the long room and through the door at its far end; immediately the noise grew louder.

Off to my left was an open-plan staircase surrounded by a well-lit gallery. I could hear the noise plainly now – a dull hammering coming from a door at the far end.

I climbed the stairs as fast as I could and made my way along to the door. Immediately I heard Suzanne call out.

'Who's there?'

'Suzanne? Suzanne, it's Steve Jay.'

'Help me . . . let me out . . .'

'Stay back from the door,' I shouted.

I grasped the gallery rail with my good hand, raised my foot and kicked the door lock. The door didn't move and my body hurt everywhere from the impact. I took a deep breath and drove my heel at the lock again. This time it burst open and I slumped to the floor.

Suzanne stood at the back of the room. There was blood down the side of her face and she was pale. When she saw me on the floor she came towards me.

'Are . . . are you all right . . . what's happened to you?'

'I could ask the same question,' I panted.

'Eileen . . . attacked me . . .'

'Why?'

She looked to be in shock; shivering and close to tears.

'Because she was scared of what I . . . what I might tell you.'

'Slow down . . .' I helped her over to the bed and sat her down. 'Start at the beginning.'

'The beginning?'

I sat down on the bed next to her and inspected the head wound. There was a deep cut just above her right eye with heavy bruising down the side of her face.

'Tell me everything you know.'

She took a moment to gain control of herself, but when she started her hands were still trembling. She looked towards the door, anxiously.

'It goes back a long way . . . years . . .'

I nodded. 'Take your time.'

There was an air of confession about her, though I couldn't understand why.

'A number of years ago Robin had an affair and the girl got pregnant.'

'When was this?'

'Twenty-one years ago . . . the girl was under-age; fourteen years old.'

'Fourteen?'

'Yes . . . If it had got out, Robin would have gone to prison.' Her voice was choked with emotion. 'But it wasn't in anybody's interests. The business was taking off . . . he was needed. Eileen paid for the girl to go into a private clinic and forced her to give the children up for adoption . . . to herself.'

'Michael and Stephanie?'

Suzanne's mouth turned down at the edges. 'Yes.'

'How did they manage that?'

She gave a shake of the head, as though finding her own story hard to accept.

'The girl was Eileen's younger sister, Ruth.'

'Go on.'

'Eileen was furious, but she had Robin where she wanted him . . . if he stepped out of line, or left her, he'd go to prison.' She gave a bitter laugh. 'She likes to control people.'

'Forgive me . . . if you knew all this, how come you worked for him?'

She looked at me, knowing her reasons were weak.

'Robin made a mistake . . . many people make mistakes. That doesn't make them bad.'

I raised my eyebrows. 'A fourteen-year-old girl?'

'He knew it was wrong.' Her eyes dropped.

I stared at her. There was something else, something she wasn't volunteering. I sighed, knowing the answer before she gave it.

'Did you ever have any involvement with him?'

She paused. 'Yes . . . we had a brief affair.'

'And?'

'It came to nothing. I loved him, but he didn't want me . . . not permanently. He cared for me, but was in love with Ruth.'

'Sorry . . . Ruth was still his lover?'

'Always was. They carried on the affair in secret. At first Ruth was made to move in with them . . . it was a means to control her. Later, when she was seventeen, Eileen set her up in a flat. And from that point, she was forbidden to see the children.'

'Robin told you all this?'

She nodded. 'When we were in bed, when I held him, like a child, giving him what that bitch Eileen always denied him.'

'And?'

'Ruth started to kick. She wanted to see her children . . . it took her a while, but then she got smart and threatened to go to the police.'

'What did Eileen do?'

'She tried to buy her off. Ruth got a job with the business, as a manageress in one of the shops . . . and hush money, but no private access to Stephanie and Michael.'

My head spun. 'Ruth was the manageress of the shop where Stephanie started the fire, wasn't she?'

'Yes. Robin had had enough. He wanted to leave Eileen once and for all and he planned to take Ruth with him. Shortly after, Stephanie overheard Robin and Ruth talking . . . Stephanie and Michael were brought up to be fiercely loyal to Eileen and to hate their father. When she discovered that her father and Ruth were having an affair she started a series of fires . . . but what sent her over the edge was overhearing that Ruth was her real mother. That's when she lit the big one . . .'

I smiled. 'And Eileen took control and forced them all into therapy?'

'It was either that or prison for Robin.'

'You're certain of all this, Suzanne?'

'As certain as I can be.'

I believed her – she was too shaken to concoct such an elaborate lie.

'Do you know what happened at Ilford?'

She gave a bitter laugh. 'Robin never stopped looking for a way to escape . . . the fire at Stratford meant he finally had the means to leave . . . the insurance money . . . he was going to leave that grasping bitch behind, but there was no way she was going to let him go . . .'

'You're saying that Eileen had Robin killed?'

Her voice was breaking. 'Yes . . . I'm saying that . . . but there's more. Ruth has been missing for nearly three weeks. This evening her face appeared on the television as the victim of a car accident that happened the same night that Robin was killed . . . Eileen had them both murdered.'

Chapter Thirty-Eight

'It was you that sent me the key to Melrose Court, wasn't it?' I said.

'Yes . . . it was Robin and Ruth's hiding place . . . they never lived there, just used it to meet.'

'Did you ever go there?'

She closed her eyes again and in a whisper said, 'Yes.'

'When?'

'Eight . . . nine months ago. Robin and Ruth had argued . . . she had given him an ultimatum . . . leave Eileen or she would find somebody else.'

'And he used you for comfort?'

'No! It was me that started it. He was lonely . . . Eileen was an absolute bitch to him. I wanted him . . . but I couldn't replace Ruth.'

'Did Eileen know about Melrose Court?'

'Yes . . . though I didn't know that till this evening. I sent you the key because I'd begun to grow suspicious when Ruth didn't show up after Robin's death . . . tonight I found out why.'

'Is that why you sent the text message to me?'

She frowned. 'What text message?'

I went cold. 'Suzanne . . . we've got to get out of here . . .'

'What . . . why?'

'Don't argue . . . just come.'

I grabbed her by the hand and got to my feet, leading her out on to the gallery and down the stairs. Immediately I smelled the petrol. I put the back of my hand against the door handle. It was cold.

'Bend down!'

'What?' She looked bemused.

'Do it!'

I knelt and opened the door carefully. The first wisps of smoke were curling through the shoji door. I closed the patio doors, denying the fire the oxygen it needed; the oxygen that someone had wanted it to have.

'Stay there,' I said.

I peered around the edge of the shoji door. The lounge was well alight and the sweet, metallic smell of petrol was everywhere. Black smoke was starting to curl from the ceiling and vivid red flames flickered like snakes' tongues, consuming everything.

The temperature was already high and climbing by the second; with an accelerant to fuel it, the fire would reach between five and eight hundred degrees rapidly.

Only a fire-stop door would give any chance of holding the fire back, and nothing I'd seen so far would hold it for more than twenty minutes.

I pulled Suzanne back behind the door at the base of the stairs and shut it.

'Get some sheets . . . towels, curtains . . . anything . . . and wet them . . . now, Suzanne, or we're going to die!'

I pulled out my mobile and rang 999. I gave the operator the details and told them that there were two of us in the upper part of the penthouse.

Smoke was starting to percolate through the edges of the door and I could hear the crashing and banging as the long room started to disintegrate. Then I heard a sound that made my blood run cold. The patio doors shattering.

Now the air would be sucked in and the fire would become a blowtorch. Our lives were being measured in minutes. Think!

Suzanne came down the stairs with the wet sheets.

'Stuff them into the cracks around the door.'

Between us we rammed home the sheets as best we could, and then retreated up to the far bedroom where I'd found her.

'What's out that window?'

She had started to panic, and I fought to keep my voice level.

'Suzanne . . . the window . . . where does it lead?'

She shook her head, her eyes wide with fear.

I went over to the window and opened it. There was a sheer drop, fifteen floors to the street.

Off to one side was the terrace, about twenty feet away. Flames were roaring out of the patio door, scorching the terrace and climbing upward. To go that way was impossible.

To the other side, a steep sloping roof went down to a box gutter with a one-foot-high parapet. It was too far away to reach and would take us nowhere.

Suzanne was frantic. 'We're trapped . . .'

I racked my brains. 'The other bedrooms . . . there must be a way out.'

I stumbled from bedroom to bedroom, but every window led to sheer drops or roofs so steep we wouldn't have stood a chance of getting to safety.

We went out on to the gallery again. Smoke was seeping around the edges of the door and a central panel was discoloured where the fire was starting to eat its way through. I'd hoped for twenty minutes and it would last barely ten.

Suzanne had started to moan. Hysteria was taking her over and I felt myself start to shake. Think!

I dragged her back into one of the bedrooms that had an en-suite bathroom. I slammed the door and fetched some towels from the bathroom, wet them and stuffed them into the cracks around the door.

Suzanne watched me, frozen in fear.

'The bathroom . . . come on!' I dragged her into the bathroom and again shut the door and packed the cracks with wet towels. If I couldn't escape I would buy time. There were no alternatives. If my gamble didn't work then we were dead.

I rang 999 again.

The calm, modulated tones of the operator reminded me to keep calm and speak as clearly as I could.

'Hello . . . Fire Brigade, please.'

I waited while she switched me to Computer Mobilising Control at Fire Brigade Headquarters in Lambeth. The voice of the control room officer asked me where the incident was.

'Please listen very carefully to me . . . My name is Steve Jay. I am a station officer in the London Fire Brigade . . . I have already informed you of the fire . . . and the address.' I repeated it to her. 'We are trapped by the fire in the upper storey of the penthouse. I have closed and packed two doors between us and the fire . . . I estimate we have about twenty to twenty-five minutes at the most before the fire gets to us . . . have you got a senior officer en route to this incident?'

'Yes, ADO Newbury – F23 has just booked in attendance. F23's Pump Ladder and F22's pair are already in attendance.'

I didn't know Newbury.

'Right. I want you to give me his Vodaphone number. Then, I want him to give his Vodaphone to the BA Entry Control Officer and for the Entry Control Officer to pass my instructions via comms to the BA crew searching for us . . . I'll guide them via the quickest route to where we are . . . it's the only way they will find us in time. If they carry out a normal search pattern we're dead . . . do you understand?'

'Yes . . . please hold.'

The light failed.

'Short circuit . . . fire's hit the electrics.'

In the dark Suzanne grasped my arm tightly.

'It's okay,' I whispered.

I was thinking about how difficult it would be for the BA crews searching for us. Because of high rise building procedure, they would have to set up BA entry control one floor below us. Then they would have to find the glass door leading on to the spiral staircase and then negotiate their way through the penthouse to the bedroom.

'Hello, Station Officer Jay?'

'Yes . . . yes, go ahead.'

'I have informed ADO Newbury and he has agreed to your plan. Give me your phone number and I will pass it to him. He intends to be located next to the Entry Control Officer. Ring off and wait.'

I gave the number and seconds later it rang.

'Steve Jay?'

'Yes.'

'This is Dave Newbury . . . I'm on my way up to the fourteenth floor in the fire lift. Stay calm . . . we're going to get you out. Now give me as much information as you can.'

I talked him through the situation, trying not to confuse him with too many details.

'Am I making sense, guv?'

'Yes, Steve . . . we're going for a snatch rescue. How bad do you estimate the conditions in the penthouse are?'

'Not good, guv. Someone has poured a lot of petrol in there . . . it's red hot.'

'Understood.'

The next five minutes seemed a lifetime. Dave Newbury spoke to me from time to time . . . telling me that they were just setting up on the fourteenth floor with all their equipment and then that two BA crews were donning and starting their sets, prior to entry.

'Has the fire reached the bedroom door yet, Steve?'

'I think so, guv . . . have the BA crews gone in yet?'

'This very second. They have two spare sets with them . . . when they reach you they'll get you rigged and lead you out.'

'Understood, guv. When they reach the fifteenth floor, tell them to search for a glass door . . . it'll be to their right as they enter from the staircase. Tell me when they're there.'

There was nothing to do but wait.

'Will they reach us in time?' pleaded Suzanne.

'Yes,' I said too quickly.

I could hear the fire now. It was penetrating the bedroom door. I told Dave Newbury.

'Okay, Steve . . . Steve, they've found the glass door and the spiral staircase. There's a lot of flame, Steve, it might . . .'

'It's got to be faster, guv . . . we don't have that much time.'

'Got you . . . where do they go from the top of the spiral staircase?'

'Left, guv . . . then stay on the left-hand wall till they find the sliding door . . . then . . .'

'Not too fast, Steve . . . let them reach the sliding door . . . okay?'

'No choice, is there?'

The fire was in the bedroom now. I could hear a low roaring as the air from the patio was entrained into it. I tried to stay positive, but the noise was eerie. In the dark Suzanne pushed against me. If the bathroom door was the same as the others, we had ten minutes maximum. I pressed the light button on my watch and noted the time.

'Steve . . . Steve, they're at the sliding door . . .'

'Tell them to turn left and then keep to the left. At the end of the room there's a door that leads to a staircase . . . it's on the left once they're through the far door.'

'So it's left . . . keep to the left . . . through the door and left on to the staircase?'

'Yes! Guv . . . it's getting hairy . . .'

'Hang in there, Steve.'

I smelled the first wisps of smoke as the fire attacked the other side of the door. I pulled Suzanne over to the window and opened it. Our final position would have to be here, our heads out the window with the fire at our backs. It might buy us another minute, two at the most. After the smoke would come the flame.

I started to get light-headed. Suzanne was coughing, so I pushed her head out of the window and told her to stay there.

'Steve . . . Steve . . . they've found the staircase . . . where now, Steve?'

The smoke was gagging me and I leaned out the window, next to Suzanne, trying to breathe.

'Up the stairs and it's . . .' My lungs went tight as I sucked in more smoke and went into a fit of coughing. I could hear Dave Newbury asking for more directions, but the smoke was getting thicker by the second and I couldn't speak.

I hauled myself up until I was half out the window and looking down fifteen floors. It bought me just enough air to get another message out.

'Guv . . . third bedroom along . . . repeat, third bedroom along . . .'

I slipped forward and nearly fell. I had to release the mobile to grab the window frame and pull myself back. I fell back into the bathroom and spun around. I held my breath long enough to see the first small orange-red flames creep around the edges of the door.

I was aware of Suzanne slumping forward and felt myself start to lose consciousness. I didn't want to die in a panic, but there was nothing more I could do, and fear was suggesting that I jump from the window; anything to get away.

I tried to stand up and get my head out the window again, but I couldn't make it. In a last act of self-protection I rolled into a ball and turned my back to the door.

Suddenly there of a tremendous noise behind me and I was being grabbed by the shoulders and turned. I heard the sucking sound of their exhaling valves and a voice saying, 'We've got them . . . I repeat, we've got them.'

Chapter Thirty-Nine

Wednesday, 6 May, 12.40 a.m.

I was sitting in the London City Hospital waiting room when Menzies found me.

An examination had shown that I'd taken down some smoke, but was otherwise unhurt if you discounted the injuries inflicted by the Gibsons. Suzanne wasn't so good. She'd been unconscious when the BA crew had reached us, and although we'd both been given oxygen she was still groggy on arrival at the hospital.

Menzies looked irritated and his partner, Coleman, had the look of someone needing to insert his spite into the nearest target.

'Where's Eileen Sheldon, Jay?'

'I'm fine, thank you for asking,' I replied.

'Where is she?'

'I don't know.'

Menzies sat down next to me and Coleman moved in close.

'Why were you at the penthouse tonight?'

I didn't reply straight away and the irritation showed in his face.

'Amazing, isn't it?' he said tightly. 'Every time

something happens to the Sheldons, you're there. Why is that?'

I glanced at Coleman, who was giving me a hard stare. I nodded to Menzies.

'Your pal's in need of a good laxative.'

'I'm waiting.'

I sighed. 'I received a text message.'

'Go on.'

It was then or never, so I began at the beginning and led him through what had happened from the moment Alex asked me to become involved. I gave him almost everything. He didn't need to know about Jenny and Mayle.

Menzies and Coleman exchanged looks throughout but they didn't interrupt me. Coleman was making notes, so I turned away from him and spoke quickly to wind him up. When I got to the end, Menzies was actually smiling.

'I've met some prats in my time, but you're up there with the best of them. What did you think you were playing at?'

It was a fair question.

A look passed between them and Menzies said, 'We've arrested Michael Sheldon and the Gibsons.'

'Oh?'

'Eileen Sheldon was caught on the CCTV cameras in the lobby of the building, leaving shortly before you got your call. We're pretty sure she contacted Michael on his mobile and he got hold of the Gibsons. They torched the penthouse.'

'How do you know all that?'

He gave a cold smile. 'They were careful to take out the security cameras in the carpark and lobby of the building, but there's a discreet one on the approach to the penthouse. We've got the Gibsons on film torching it.'

'But you don't know where Eileen is?'

'No. You must have got to know her quite well. Where would she go?'

'Michael Sheldon's place?'

'She not there.'

'Then I've no idea.'

'Think!'

I took a moment and an idea started to form, but I had no intention of telling Menzies. I wanted the answers for myself, then I'd tell him.

They were both glaring at me again, but I just shrugged.

Menzies breathed out slowly. 'Don't piss-ball me about. I could nick you for obstructing our investigation.'

'I don't know where she is . . . all right?'

He stood up. 'If I find out that you do know, I'll take it personally . . . d'you understand? I want a statement tomorrow and I want all the little bits you've left out tonight. I'll have a car pick you up tomorrow morning. Be at home.'

I gave them half an hour and then caught a black cab back to Romford. I kept looking out of the back window, but couldn't see anything suspicious.

'You all right, mate?' said the cabby.

'Just a couple of dickheads I've upset. Wasn't sure if they decided to follow me from the hospital.'

'Have they?'

'No. I don't think so.'

'Whereabouts in Romford do you want?'

'The high street. I need to pick something up, then we're going on.'

'Where?'

'Melrose Court, Toomey Close, Hornchurch.'

I picked the key up from my flat and we drove on to Melrose Court. I made the cabby stop at the end of the close; the noise of the diesel engine would have carried at that time of night.

The wrought-iron gates were closed, but not locked. I made my way up to the first floor, conscious of how loud my shuffling gait sounded in the stair-well.

I unlocked the door and pushed it gently. The flat was quiet, but there was light showing around the edge of the lounge door. I swung it open.

'Hello, Steve.'

Eileen was sitting on the floor, surrounded by the photographs of Ruth. In one hand she had a cigarette and in the other one of the photos. She held it up to me. It was a facial shot taken at an angle with a spotlight accentuating the lines of the head and neck.

'My sister . . . my kid sister. Pretty, wasn't she?'

Her eyes were bright, bitter, and I fought an impulse of pity.

'I've seen them, Eileen, but of course you know that.'

Her eyes fell. 'It wasn't personal, Steve.'

I shook my head. 'Murder's about as personal as it gets, Eileen. It was you that had me run off the road, wasn't it? Why? Because I was getting too close? Just like Roley Benson got too close.'

'Something like that.'

'When my mobile battery went flat and I used the hallway phone out there, you used the recall number service and realised I was in this flat. You thought I'd made the connection with Ruth, didn't you?'

'Yes.'

'I was so stupid. You saw me as a means to an end, feeding me bits of the puzzle that sent me straight towards Mayle.'

'His hands weren't so clean,' she snapped. 'He tried to take over my business. He almost bled us dry.'

'He was a clever businessman. Snide, I'll grant you, but that's not a crime. Michael tried to turn him over in return, as I'm sure you know. All the rest is self-justification, Eileen. I'm not buying it any more.'

She stared down at the photographs scattered on the floor around her and switched her logic to firmer ground.

'And infidelity isn't a crime either, is it?'

'Revenge, Eileen? All this was because of hurt pride?'

Her head went back and her eyes hardened. 'Do you know how I first found out about the two of them, Steve? It was two days before our wedding anniversary.' She drew on the cigarette and inhaled the smoke. 'I was going through his briefcase. I needed his diary to make some appointments for him and I found . . . photographs.'

I nodded.

She shook her head. 'Not like these.' She snatched up a handful from the floor and pushed them towards me. 'More . . . graphic!'

'I see.'

'Do you? She was fourteen years of age, Steve. He took pornographic pictures of my kid sister and carried them around in his briefcase. That filthy, disgusting man seduced my sister and took pictures of her!' she hissed.

'You could have gone to the police.'

She looked away. 'I loved him. God help me, I loved him.'

'So why kill him now?'

Her voice was breaking and she started to sob. 'He was leaving me. I stood by him all these years and he was walking out on me . . . with her. They knew that their affair was destroying me, eating into me like a cancer, but they didn't care.'

'And Suzanne? Why try to kill her?'

'She slept with him as well!'

I shook my head. 'You can't kill people for that. What about me? Twice you tried to kill me.'

'As I said, it wasn't personal, Steve.'

'You bitch.'

A bitter, self-regarding smile crossed her face. 'Never mind, Steve, I'm getting my just rewards.'

'What?'

She gave a weak laugh, as though surprised at her own cleverness. 'Paracetamol – I've taken fifty or sixty.'

I pulled out my mobile phone and started to dial for an ambulance.

She shook her head. 'There's no point, Steve. I took them hours ago. The damage is irreversible.' She shifted her legs and tucked them under her. 'I heard it on the news, you see – "two people rescued from penthouse blaze". It had to be you and Suzanne.' She took a final draw on the cigarette and then stubbed it out. 'I panicked when I saw that computerised image of Ruth. I tried to wipe away the evidence, you and Suzanne together, but you're a hard man to kill, Steve.'

'So you came here?'

'Where else? This was their place, where they betrayed me.'

'How did you find out about it?'

'I overheard them talking.'

'Overheard?'

She looked me in the eye. 'I picked up the phone at the same time as he did.'

'Of course you did. And?'

'I searched for his key and had a copy made. I came

here once and trashed it. Cut his suits into bits and threw bleach over all her clothes, the furniture, everything. He never breathed a word to me about it. It was like nothing I did mattered.'

'Oh, it matters, Eileen,' I said softly. 'It matters a lot.'

She closed her eyes and breathed deeply. 'What are you going to do now, Steve?'

'I'm going to ring for an ambulance, Eileen. If you really took the pills it won't alter anything, but if you're lying and there's a chance of seeing you get life, then I want that chance. I owe it to some people, good people, that you've never met.'

Chapter Forty

Friday, 8 May

Alex picked me up around ten o'clock and we drove out to Corbets Tey cemetery on the Ockendon Road.

The day was overcast and a raw wind blew the slanting rain into the uniformed ranks of fire-fighters lining the route from the cemetery gates up to the crematorium.

Alex parked the car and, with heads down, we made our way slowly towards the building, together with a large group of mourners. Several people caught my eye, some shocked at my injuries and others yielding embarrassed smiles, aware that I was suspended.

By the entrance to the crematorium a knot of tense senior officers awaited the cortège. Beside them, the pall-bearers, made up of the watch, with John at their head, were being given a final briefing by Bob Grant.

They looked gaunt, still in a state of shock, and it felt horrible not to be standing with them.

Alex and I joined the crowd sheltering along the edge of the building. Harry Wildsmith looked up and saw me, and then the whole watch turned in our direction. Bob Grant inclined his head.

For what seemed an age the eyes of the senior officers and other ranks, were settled on the silent conversation between the watch and myself.

'Steady, Stevie boy,' whispered Alex.

Suddenly all heads turned towards the gates. A lone uniformed fireman was holding an arm aloft, indicating that the cortège was in sight.

At three minutes to eleven, a line of black cars, led by the hearse, drove slowly through the gates up to the crematorium. The coffin was disembarked and the pall-bearers took up the load and waited.

Sandy's parents, Bill and Maisy Richards, were assisted from the car by Sandy's brother and sister. Maisy looked near to collapse, and Bill hung on tightly to her arm. It was a pathetic, harrowing sight, and the entire crowd was moved by it.

The chapel couldn't contain all the mourners, and many had to stand outside in the rain. Estimates of numbers later ranged from two hundred and fifty to three hundred. The deputy chief represented the chief officer, who was abroad, and in total there must have been a hundred and fifty fire-fighters.

The Brigade Missionary led the service, and as the flag was taken from the coffin and the curtains closed, there was a gasp from Sandy's family.

In that final stark act, the last remains of control went and a noise that chilled my blood erupted from Maisy. Half-cry and half-wail, it lifted up and took the hearts of the room with it.

Everyone wept.

When it was all over, and the crowd were standing in line to offer their condolences and glimpse the flowers, Alex went with me up to Sandy's family. No words were exchanged; Bill shook my hand and Maisy hugged me. God knows how they found the strength to stand there and greet mourner after mourner.

I saw Sandy clearly in the faces of his brother and sister and I tried to say something, anything, but just shook my head and moved on.

'Are you all right?'

'Jesus, Alex, what a question. No is the answer. I feel dreadful.'

We walked away from the main group and gradually I regained some form of composure. To distract me, Alex brought up the subject of the case.

'I heard from Menzies just before I left.'

'Oh?'

'Eileen Sheldon died just after seven this morning.' I nodded.

'It seems the Gibsons are talking,' he continued, 'but only about the penthouse.'

'That's all?'

'According to Menzies, once they heard that Michael Sheldon denied being involved in his own car bomb they realised that they were going down for attempted murder, so they offered their hands up for arson with intent to endanger life for the penthouse.'

'And Michael and Stephanie Sheldon?'

'Denying everything. They're saying that the fact

that the Gibsons torched the penthouse proves they were the victims.'

I shook my head slowly. 'Clever.'

'They've a good brief.'

'The Gibsons did what Michael told them . . . but it was Eileen who gave instructions for Robin Sheldon and Ruth Heller to be murdered. It was revenge; pure bloody-minded vindictiveness.'

'You sound very bitter.'

I stopped walking and closed my eyes. 'She made a fool of me, Alex. No . . . that's not true . . . I made a fool of myself. I always felt she was holding out on me, but figured it was to protect Michael and Stephanie. She read me like a book . . . even to the point of the text message to get me in the penthouse.'

'You had no choice, Stevie . . . and in the event you saved Suzanne Munroe's life. You've done well, and your percentage of the insurance money will be worth having . . .'

I turned back towards the main group of mourners and caught sight of John talking to Bill and Maisy Richards.

'Yes . . . there's always the money.'

GREG ILES

24 HOURS

*The perfect family
On the perfect night
About to be trapped in the perfect crime.*

Will and Karen Jennings and their adored five-year-old daughter have every reason to celebrate. From modest beginnings they have worked hard to build the life of their dreams.

But now they have been targeted by an evil madman who has found the key to one of the oldest crimes in the world. Kidnapping. Joe Hickey has turned the crime inside out, creating an unbreakable knot of technology and terror. Five times he has executed his plan – and not once has he been caught.

This time however he has reckoned on every factor but one: Will, Karen and Abby share a bond that only the closest families know. That link will prove vital in the fierce battle for survival played out over the next 24 hours.

HODDER AND STOUGHTON PAPERBACKS

A selection of bestsellers from Hodder & Stoughton

Greg Iles	24 Hours	0 340 77006 6	£6.99	☐
Jess Walker	Over Tumbled Graves	0 340 81991 1	£6.99	☐
Peter May	The Killing Room	0 340 76865 7	£5.99	☐
Frederick Lindsay	Darkness in My Hand	0 340 76573 9	£6.99	☐
Victor Headley	Off Duty	0 340 77022 8	£6.99	☐

All Hodder & Stoughton books are available at your local bookshop or newsagent, or can be ordered direct from the publisher. Just tick the titles you want and fill in the form below. Prices and availability subject to change without notice.

Hodder & Stoughton Books, Cash Sales Department, Bookpoint, 39 Milton Park, Abingdon, Oxon, OX14 4TD, UK. E-mail address: orders@bookpoint. co.uk. If you have a credit card you may order by telephone – (01235) 400414.

Please enclose a cheque or postal order made payable to Bookpoint Ltd to the value of the cover price and allow the following for postage and packing:
UK & BFPO: £1.00 for the first book, 50p for the second book and 30p for each additional book ordered up to a maximum charge of £3.00.
OVERSEAS & EIRE: £2.00 for the first book, £1.00 for the second book and 50p for each additional book.

Name ....

Address ....

....

....

If you would prefer to pay by credit card, please complete:
Please debit my Visa / Access / Diner's Club / American Express (delete as applicable) card no:

Signature ....

Expiry Date ....

If you would NOT like to receive further information on our products please tick the box. ☐